DRIVING
THE
AUBURN

PETER SULLIVAN

NFB
Buffalo, New York

Copyright © 2023 Peter Sullivan

Printed in the United States of America

Drving the Auburn/ Sullivan 1st Edition

ISBN: 978-1-953610-53-9

  1. Fiction>Literary
  2. Fiction>Family
  3. American Literature
  4. Family Life Fiction
  5. Fiction> Irish Heritage
  6. Fiction> Suspense
  7. Historical Fiction

NFB
NFB Publishing/Amelia Press
119 Dorchester Road
Buffalo, New York 14213

For more information visit Nfbpublishing.com

To my sister Janie, and brothers Jerry and Tim

Acknowledgments

I want to thank Linda Jenkins of *Red Pen Services* for her thoughtful evaluation of the novel. Linda suggested the section titled Author's Note for those who might like to delve more deeply into some of the historical information that is embedded in this work of fiction.

Thanks as well to Casey Sullivan for his resourcefulness, technical skills, and reassuring approach to problem-solving when I would periodically encounter fire-breathing dragons threatening to walk across the keyboard and screen in the world of word processing.

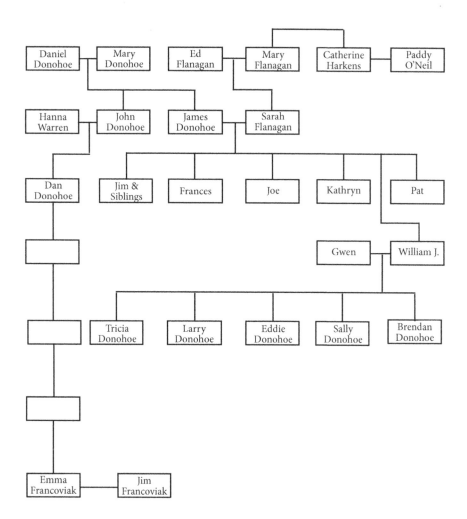

Contents

Chapter 1 Can Anyone Here Speak Canadian?   11

Chapter 2 The Unforgiving Restraint   12

Chapter 3 A Muddle of Murmurs   23

Chapter 4 To Pique or Not to Pique   27

Chapter 5 Onward Salesmen Soldiers, Christian or Not   38

Chapter 6 The Weavers   47

Chapter 7 One Good Meal Deserves Another   52

Chapter 8 Your Common Cow Diseases   57

Chapter 9 Row Row Row The Boat, Gently Down The Dream   62

Chapter 10 Das Boat   67

Chapter 11 Armed Chair   72

Chapter 12 Not a Hoe   77

Chapter 13 Gavel to Gravel   83

Chapter 14 Rattling Windowpanes   95

Chapter 15 Crossing the Bar   101

Chapter 16 What a Difference a Letter Makes   105

Chapter 17 The Fenians are Coming, The British are Staying   108

Chapter 18 Journal Volume 18   112

Chapter 19 A Proclamation   116

Chapter 20 Paddy Aboard the W. T. Robb   124

Chapter 21 After Binghampton   128

Chapter 22 A Miniature Salute   136

Chapter 23 St. Albany   139

Chapter 24 Into the Spirits   151

Chapter 25 Moonlight in Vermont, So Was Paddy   155

Chapter 26 It's History, It's Important, Stay Awake   159

Chapter 27 Your Branch of the Family   171

Chapter 28 Some Call It Hogwash   178

Chapter 29 The Kicker   183

Chapter 30 Just A Few Feet of Land   189

Chapter 31 Recording More Than Sales   197

Chapter 32 Let's Blame Parnell   207

Chapter 33 Let's Blame Parnell Part Two   213

Chapter 34 The Fire Maiden   223

Chapter 35 The Nina, the Pinta and the Santa Maria   235

Chapter 36 And Then It All Gets Buried   240

Chapter 37 Out of the Shadows   245

Chapter 38 A Canadian Fenian   250

Chapter 39 Hiding in Plain Sight   254

Chapter 40 Late For Class   259

Chapter 41 The Known before the Unknown   264

Chapter 42 Missing the Boat   272

Chapter 43 Making The Call   277

Chapter 44 Exorcism   279

Chapter 45 Thank you Nokia   286

Chapter 46 See if?   295

Chapter 47 A Wake   307

Chapter 48 Stan Musial at the Last Supper   320

Chapter 49 The Photo Albums   326

Chapter 50 The 'F' Word   334

Chapter 51 A Memory for Dates   337

Chapter 52 The Lap and Thicket   342

Chapter 53 That Ocean is Too Big   351

Epilogue All He Has to Do   354

Historical Sources   357

Author's Note   359

CHAPTER 1

CAN ANYONE HERE SPEAK CANADIAN?
Friday, November 24, 1865

It was difficult at first to hear what was being said, then finally, shouted. The winds had picked up at precisely the wrong time for such an adventure, or misadventure as some were beginning to fear.

A certain voice rises above the rest, "Can anyone here speak Canadian?"

"What?"

"Don't be using Irish. I don't know if he can understand it."

"Oh, sir, he remembers it."

"Has anybody seen him?"

More wind, howling, as those aboard struggle with the small boat, anticipating a landing in the dark, and wouldn't you know that this is when the rain starts, not a thinly veiled mist, but a pounding down hard flood of water, falling at will from the dark heavens, a rainfall that would wash them back out to sea if it had its own way.

The wind relaxes momentarily just enough for someone to ask, "Who?"

The boat bumps up against something, tall bits of vegetation reach up over the edge near the oar lock, as if grabbing at the men who mean to push farther in toward the shoreline, fronds that are cold and wet, a welcoming grip or slapping rebuke.

"Who?" the same voice calls out again, louder and slower this time, a voice that rises in pitch, followed by the wind.

CHAPTER 2

The Unforgiving Restraint
Friday, August 31, 2001

"T HE LOST HAVE BEEN found," Eddie pronounces with some satisfaction, sitting back in his seat.

Brendan, Eddie's brother, looks across the table at the diner. As he leans forward he says, "The found is getting us lost."

The two brothers, both now retired, are finishing breakfast at the South Wedge Diner in Rochester. This is one of their favorite places to gather, an unassuming place situated in one of the city's older neighborhoods, a place that might be up and coming but is far removed from any hint, yet, of gentrification.

Brendan, happily married with adult children living in the South and West, is younger by a small handful of years. He has observed how his brother Eddie, happily divorced with one daughter in San Diego, moves more slowly now, being careful to watch his step. Both will groan audibly in a short time when they rise from the table, the best meal of the day. If nothing else, they agree about this.

For Brendan it is has been his usual order of two pancakes, two eggs scrambled, two pieces of bacon, and hash browns, along with one too many refills of coffee from the underpaid yet efficiently busy waitress. The menu always insists that this selection is a "morning special," hinting that it is a good deal for your money.

"The mysteriously missing journals," Brendan summarizes to no one in particular. His own editorial comment.

"Missing no longer," Eddie interjects.

Brendan looks at his brother, "No, of course not, we were the ones to find them after all," he says, as if he thinks Eddie needs this reminder.

"Actually," Eddie clarifies, "it was the very lovely Emma nee Donohoe, our much younger second or third or whatever cousin who had them and told us about them."

Brendan's voice drops slightly, "I can never remember those degrees of family connection."

"Separation."

Brendan looks at his brother, squinching his eyebrows together, "Ok," he challenges, "can you explain, for example, second cousin once removed?"

Eddie hesitates, and in a rather somber tone answers, "That would be when an individual in your family tree failed to pay the rent and had to vacate his or her branch."

Brendan looks at his brother, "We do come from people who were probably evicted." He stabs at the last bite of the pancake on his syrup smothered plate, adding "violently."

After a moment Eddie says, "Well, they were still controlled by the British over there, for all intents and purposes. I doubt an eviction was accompanied by tea and crumpets."

Brendan leans back in the diner's bench seat. It reminds him, just then, of a church pew. "What are crumpets, anyway?"

The waitress has spotted the two older men and appears to be heading over. The diner has taken on a thick-ceramic-cup-and-saucer restlessness, silverware has landed in the kitchen's metal sink with a hint of agitation. The door has opened several times in the past couple of minutes. The sweet spot between breakfast and lunch has ended.

"Is everything alright over here?"

Eddie looks up and says, "Couldn't be better."

The ambitious waitress smiles and leaves the bill strategically between the two of them. Tables are filling up fast and she slips away, moving out with the tide.

Brendan says, "Wow, that's pretty optimistic."

Eddie answers, "Younger brother, life is short."

"And it's getting shorter all the time."

Eddie nods his head toward the recently departed waitress, says, "Cute as a button."

THEY had carpooled from Brendan's house. They've settled in the front seat of Brendan's car and Eddie, for years now a man of considerable girth, is having a little trouble finding the seat belt.

"They're going to stop making her," Brendan says.

Eddie interrupts his struggle with the belt to turn suddenly and ask "Who?" his voice rising with the question.

"This little beauty," Brendan says while tapping the steering wheel of his one-year-old Ford Escort. "Next year is her final year."

Eddie turns back to his struggle, there is a decided click followed by a sigh of relief. "Okay," he says, "I'm belted in. It's safe to proceed." When he looks over at his brother, it appears they may not be leaving any time soon.

Brendan is staring out the front windshield, but Eddie doubts that he sees the delivery van parked in front of them.

Finally Brendan says, "You know I was over there again not too long ago."

Eddie waits to see what Brendan might say next. He takes an experienced guess, "Well I know it wasn't Ireland. You're talking Dunnville?"

"Dunnville, Ontario, Canada." Spoken with an air of conceit, noble heritage.

A hesitation, Eddie says, "Oh that Dunnville. And?"

Brendan seems to brighten, "You know this was a place of so many stories."

"Was?" Eddie asks.

Brendan turns to look at his brother, "Thanks, yes. Is a place of so many stories." Brendan resumes his gaze through the windshield, the gauze of dust and haze of light, filtered, speckled. "Eddie," he announces, and then remains silent.

"Yes?"

"Most of them are forgotten."

Eddie is good at practicing patience. Sometimes. Finally he says, "Most of what are forgotten?"

"The stories."

Eddie wants to be helpful. He also wants his brother to start the car for god's sake. He asks, "What stories?"

Brendan looks in his direction again, "The ones we don't know."

Eddie pauses. "Okay, dear brother, if we don't know them, how can we miss them?"

"Think about it."

"Trust me, I am."

"May they all rest in peace, those colorful aunts and uncles, Joe, Frances, the whole gang of them. And didn't they have stories to tell? They were the first generation. It was their parents who had come from Ireland…"

"You're talking ancient history."

"Not so ancient. The famine, 1849, leaving the old country and settling in Canada. Can you imagine?"

Eddie takes a deep breath, "Actually, no."

"Get out," Brendan exclaims.

"I can't, I had a hard-enough time buckling the seatbelt."

"What did our grandparents say to them, those uncles and aunts?"

Eddie gives in. "Well, and dad too, of course," Eddie adds, "he was one of the younger siblings."

"Yes!" Brendan says. "What stories did dad hear from his parents?"

Eddie sighs, shifts in his seat, puts a hand around the part of the seat belt that is pressing against his chest. In a subdued voice he says, "And what stories did dad share with us about whatever he may have heard?" He waits and says "I can answer that. Virtually none."

Brendan looks at his brother, shakes his head in agreement. "Dear dad, he of the 1932 Auburn motor car, traveling the highways, William J. "Bill" Donohoe, salesman extraordinaire."

And now Eddie takes on that faraway look. "When we were kids, the get togethers of dad and his siblings were something else. Endless games of Euchre, the arguments and pranks."

"The drinking."

"May they rest in peace."

It had been as if Eddie and Brendan's generation had awakened one day in their late middle years with questions, only to realize that those who might have answers were gone. They wondered why so few stories had been shared, and the drive to understand their past seemed to grow. Someone suggested the word 'quest.' That fit. And then they became lucky, though some of them would prefer to call it 'blessed.'

There were times when Spirits seemed to lead the way. When they arranged a visit to the ancestral farm in Dunnville, the farm's owner wondered if they might be interested in having an old round top trunk he had discovered. They knew at once what this was, the name their dad had always called it: 'Paddy O'Neil's Trunk.' And it wasn't long afterwards that they met Emma.

There had been so much excitement when the journals were discovered. John Donohoe was their grandfather's older brother. He was a self-taught reader who began to write not long before stepping aboard what would later be called a Coffin Ship. He joined his family in the emigration from Ireland, 1849, escaping the famine, hoping against hope to survive and start a new life in Canada.

"We have the journals now," Brendan says.

"Indeed we do," his brother answers. "A firsthand historical account."

A moment passes, Brendan asks, "Do you think they knew about the journals?"

Eddie looks at his brother, "Did they know about the journals, you're talking dad and his siblings?" He's not sure he wants to get into this topic just now. "Great Uncle John Donohoe's journals," he says, buying some time.

"They were interesting at first." Brendan says. "I mean his description of their ship, the crossing, the first days in the New World. Good stuff. But then, oh my god, how many pages can you read about the wonder of dry goods, herding cows."

"Hog futures," Eddies adds.

"And then he seems to get kind of lost, abstract."

Eddie considers this, "I spoke with Emma who has read all the volumes, and she says some of it gets into politics."

"I need to get back into them," Brendan says.

Eddie hesitates, "Don't get too excited, she said a lot of his later comments are extremely vague, meandering."

"Oh great."

"Well, she has some suspicions that his writing was unclear for specific reasons."

"Such as?"

Eddie looks at his brother, "To keep things under wraps, need to know basis, that kind of thing."

Brendan hesitates, "Just what we need. More mystery." He opens and closes his fingers around the steering wheel. "I don't think Uncle John needed to worry about that."

"Worry about what?"

"Need to know basis, being clandestine."

"How so?"

"You saw his handwriting. Cursive, in pencil. Gave me a headache."

Eddie nods his head without enthusiasm. Brendan's complaints about the absence of old family history could get old itself. "Emma says that his handwriting, and language for that matter, improve in later volumes. And he switches over to writing in ink, somewhere along the line."

Brendan feels the delayed fullness of his large breakfast settling in, likely to be an unwelcome resident for the next few hours. He tastes the acidity of warmed-over coffee. He asks, "How far did you get in the journals?"

Eddie really wants Brendan to start the car. He says, "I read the first two right away." He adds, "Interesting as you say. And poorly written, in my view."

Brendan nods his head. "Hey we should give him a break."

"We should?" Eddie asks.

"I mean he was only a kid when he started writing, a teenager. Product of the lack of Irish education."

"Right, with bodies falling down left and right due to the famine. Sort of impinges on the learning process," Eddie says.

Such an image gives them both pause, sitting in the car, stomachs expanding, seatbelts restraining.

"So," Brendan says, "the question, did Dad know about Uncle John's journals. Answer, of course he did. It was Emma's relative who had them, after all. After all these years. But why didn't we know about them?"

"Dan Donohoe."

"What?" Brendan asks.

"The lovely young Emma Donohoe Francoviak, Dan was her great great something grandfather."

"Yes?"

"The oldest of our Great Uncle John Donohoes's boys."

"Yes."

"Dan Donohoe was Dad's cousin. He was the one who kept the journals. He inherited them when his father died."

"Dan's father," Brendan clarifies, "is our Great Uncle John, the author of the journals."

"*Tres bien*" Eddie says in poorly accented French.

Brendan nods his head, summarizing, "So Dad knew about Uncle John's journals. But he never told us about them. As well as any other stories he may have heard."

Eddie says, "We did hear a few stories."

"I'm talking about the ones we didn't hear," Brendan says.

Eddie nods his head, "Well that's a bit tricky, you said that before, about the stories we didn't hear. But overall I guess you're right, for whatever reasons, Dad chose not to tell us things that he'd heard." He looks at his brother, "So can we go now?"

"Just one thing," Brendan says.

"Oh god," voice sloping downward toward a moan.

"Why all the secrets?"

"I knew it."

"What?"

"I knew you were going to say that," Eddie says.

"Well?"

"Let me ask you this."

"Okay."

"Why do you call them secrets? Isn't that a judgement call on your part?"

"Judgement call?"

Eddie pauses for a moment, "Maybe they were protecting us. You might call it, in your words, a loving omission of the narrative."

"Oh for Pete's sake."

Brendan finally puts the key in the ignition and starts the car. He looks into his side view mirror, ready to pull out.

"Brendan," Eddie says suddenly, surprisingly, "Hold on."

Brendan looks over at his brother, sees a certain urgency in his brother's eyes, enough that while leaving the engine running, he shifts back into park.

"Think about this," Eddie says. "Our grandfather James, his older brother John, that whole family, they were first person witnesses who could have become first person victims of the terrible scenes they saw all around them. Suffering and death."

"So we surmise," Brendan adds.

"And who in their right mind would want to dwell on such stories? Especially after you'd left them behind over there."

Brendan doesn't take long to consider his response. "I think they're learning now that to be in your right mind, you have to revisit such stories.

At least until they start to lose some of their power. You know. Memory. Trauma."

Eddie doesn't respond at first, and Brendan takes this as a sign to shift back into Drive. As he pulls away from the curb, he hears Eddie say, "How very modern of you."

CHAPTER 3

A Muddle of Murmurs
Friday, August 31, 2001

"**J**ESUS!"

"Don't take the name of the Lord in vain."

"I'm not," Brendan says. He reads again:

> *The renegade sampling was made into a kind of juicy sauce,*
> *so to speak. Never was there seen such a bungling camaraderie,*
> *just ripe for the picking.*

"I think he's mixed his metaphors there," Eddie says.

"He's certainly mixed something."

The brothers had decided at the last minute to come over to Emma's after they had finished breakfast and left the restaurant. It was one of those spur of the moment things. They hadn't notified her that they were coming, not realizing that she might not be home. She wasn't. Husband Jim Francoviak let them in, and then let them alone. They had spotted the volume of Uncle John's journal on the coffee table.

Brendan continues to read:

> *The Canadians fought valiantly, even if for the Queen. What a*
> *sorry lot from Buffalo. Of course they had history on their side.*
> *Even with the odd slaughter, the tide was clearly going to turn as*
> *indeed it did in such short order.*

"He's not talking about the Bills is he?" Eddie asks.

"What bills?"

"Buffalo Bills," Eddie says.

"Oh, give me a break. This is the 19th century."

"So?"

"The Bills weren't playing then."

"That must have been a relief to the citizenry."

Brendan looks up from the page. He knows he gets very emotional about family history. He secretly envies how Eddie seems more detached about it all. He takes a measured breath, asks Eddie, "You told me you had read two of the volumes?"

Eddie hesitates, looks at Brendan. It had become uncomfortable to stand and try to look over Brendan's shoulder as Brendan was reading aloud, which is why he took the seat opposite, on the couch. Also, this couch in Cousin Emma's house always looks so inviting.

Eddie is astonished whenever he walks into much-younger-cousin Emma's home. Elegant, tasteful, and dare he say it, expensive looking. He is impressed by how tidy it looks every time he is there. She usually dismisses his compliments with a little laugh and a wave of her slender arm. It leaves him feeling depressed, how organized she keeps everything. He attempts to reassure himself that the lived-in look of his home makes visitors relax. Books and magazines overflowing any available flat space.

Emma is very kind, very nice. She would never say anything that wasn't complimentary, or maybe forgiving, to the older folks of Eddie's generation. Eddie is in that group of her relatives who are approaching a fragile state of endearment. He hopes.

"Yes," Eddie answers finally. "I did read two of the volumes, I think it was the first two. Initially. Remember 'On the banks of the Savior Larynx'?"

"Which we later understood meant 'Saint Lawrence'," Brendan says, still looking at the journal page. "Our family, the pioneers. They were just coming down the river into North America, old Country left behind."

"Up the river," Eddie says.

"What?"

"If they were going down the river, they might be headed back to Ireland," Eddie says.

Brendan looks up as Eddie leans forward in the couch.

Eddie raises his eyebrows and says, "Just like Paddy O'Neil did some years later."

"Wait a minute!"

"Yes?" Eddie says, smiling now.

"I thought you only read the first two volumes."

"Well, maybe I went a little further."

"Farther," Brendan corrects.

"No, further, like I think you are reading from volume eight."

Brendan watches as his brother settles back into the all-embracing sofa, its soft texture overflowing with neatly arranged and colorful pillows. Brendan carefully closes the leather cover of the journal, then turns to the first page, sees what is written in pencil and pronounces "Volume 7."

"Ah," Eddie intones, "I guess I was getting ahead of myself."

"Oh my god," Brendan says. "What else don't I know?"

Eddie adjusts himself in the couch again, "Quite a bit, I would imagine."

"Where is the part about Paddy?"

"Where isn't the part about Paddy?" Eddie teases, and notices that Brendan looks quite agitated. "Okay, relax, I jumped around a lot. Skimmed. Not a careful reader like yourself. I could only read so much about grain futures and the farm life."

Brendan doesn't look terribly comforted. Eddie adds, "You do a much more comprehensive reading."

"It isn't easy," Brendan says. "I'm not always sure what Uncle John is referring to."

"Join the club."

Brendan looks at his brother who appears for the moment to be sympathetic. "I have a confession to make."

"Go ahead my son," Eddie intones like a priest out of central casting.

"This is as far as I've ever gotten."

"In regard to what?" Eddie asks.

Brendan wonders if he should have kept his mouth shut. "These journals."

"Ah."

"I absolutely know more about grain futures than I ever wanted to know."

"Yes," Eddie says, as if consolingly, "but don't let that stop you. It gets better. For a while."

They hear the sound of a car coming in the driveway. The two brothers remain seated and quiet until they hear the door open in the adjoining kitchen, at which point they start to stand. Emma comes into the room so quickly and with such grace, that Eddie is still in the process of reaching the edge of the couch with a plan to stand up.

"Oh," Emma says, looking in a rapid-fire glance that is surprised-irritated-relieved. Her smile is both attractive and effective, icing over any vestige of awkwardness that otherwise might have appeared.

Emma takes after her descendent Dan Donohoe who was said to be taller than other family members. She is in her early 30's, slender, toned and exquisitely fit looking, a former college athlete, now a trainer at a trendy gym.

"The two of you went out to breakfast again?" she asks.

Brendan wonders how Emma would know this, Eddie hadn't called on his brand new Nokia phone. They were lucky that Emma's husband Jim had let them in the door, Jim, sheepishly disheveled. They had unintentionally awakened him, not realizing that he was on a night shift rotation this week. With their exuberant apologies and encouragement, he had agreed to go back to bed.

"I wondered," Emma said, "I didn't recognize the car in the driveway." And then as if just remembering, she said "You saw Jim?"

"Yes, yes," the brothers intone in unison, a chant imploring her kindly forgiveness that they know will be forthcoming.

"Sit, sit," Emma says to Brendan who, though standing, is shorter than she. To Eddie, who appears about to stand, she says, "Please don't get up."

She takes a moment to put her keys and purse on the table nearby. When she turns around, she says, "Brendan, always nice to see you," which leaves Brendan feeling that she may be leaving his older brother out of such a welcoming, and then she says, "Eddie, I see you have picked your usual spot on the couch. What can I get you both?"

Brendan would like to say 'answers.' He is feeling rattled and wishes he felt differently. He hears Eddie say, "I love this couch."

"I know," she says, with a tone of quiet confidence.

Brendan can't quite recall the last time that he had been here. As if reading his mind, Emma addresses him directly, "Been a bit of a while for you, cousin?" Almost, but not quite a question, probably rhetorical, if anything at all, and before he can respond Eddie says, "the usual, my dear."

"Sugar, no cream," she answers. Then she looks at Brendan, who has by now seated himself.

Brendan almost says "What?" but luckily remembers her question and he answers, "Oh, no, nothing for myself, thanks."

"No?" she says, sounding genuinely disappointed, and maybe surprised.

"No, I can't stay long, I've got a few errands to run."

Eddie registers a look of alarm, says, "You drove me here. From the restaurant. Remember?"

There is a momentary pause before Emma asks, "South Wedge Diner?"

"*Exactement*," Eddie says in the poor accent that can annoy his brother at times.

Emma goes into the kitchen to pour a cup of coffee for Eddie and decides to pour one for herself as well. When she returns, she brings the two cups and a bowl of sugar on a tray and puts them within easy reach on the coffee table.

"Are you sure I can't get you something?" she asks Brendan, who is now re-considering his earlier refusal. She notices and says, "I'll be right back, cream and sugar?"

"Thanks," Brendan says. "Black."

"Ah," she nearly purrs, "cafe unadulterated for you, eh?"

It is that simple term, 'eh', that none of them consciously recognize in the moment, but that nonetheless becomes a soothingly short lullaby of days and a land gone by.

When she returns from the kitchen she says, "You picked a really good time, I had a few clients cancel and something told me to swing by home. Some folks want to get out of town, last week of summer and all that, and the holiday coming up. I can't blame them."

Her cousins look slightly confused, she ventures a guess, Labor Day next Monday."

"Oh, oh yes of course," her cousins, the retirees, answer nearly in unison.

"I hope you can stay and visit for a while."

Both brothers intone a mutually shared murmur of "No really we don't…" and "Didn't mean to interfere…"

Emma interrupts them, "While I'd like to think that you've come to see me, you especially Brendan…"

"Yes, yes, of course," Brendan says a bit too quickly.

"I'm guessing it's the journals you'd like to see?"

The brothers stop talking immediately.

All three look at each other, one to the other.

Brendan raises his eyebrows.

"Aha!" the lovely young cousin says to her elderly heavy and heavier set relatives. "Perfect opportunity, I had wanted to go back over some of the earlier volumes myself. I think I had forgotten a bit of the history." And then she adds, "Maybe you could help me."

Emma remains standing for a longer than expected moment, and Brendan begins to wonder if everything is ok. Maybe they really should not have come over unannounced.

"There has been," Emma says cautiously, "as you may or may not know, controversy about the journals."

"Oh?"

"Within the family."

Brendan hesitates, "No, I didn't know. In fact there is a lot I don't know."

"I see," Emma answers, "Well let's get started then, shall we?"

CHAPTER 4

To Pique or Not to Pique
Friday, August 31, 2001

"W HICH IS IT?"

"Volume 7, it's dated 1866."

"Okay," Emma says, "yes, let's take a look. I had pulled that one out but hadn't gotten very far."

They re-arranged themselves so that they could all sit on the couch, Emma in the middle, journal in hand.

"We were just reading a bit when you came in," Brendan confesses, "it was sitting right there on the table."

Emma holds the journal carefully, trying to make out the squiggly cursive of the author, and says absentmindedly, "right," in a distant sounding, place-holding tone of voice.

She reads:

> *The Canadians fought valiantly, even if for the Queen. What a*
> *sorry lot from Buffalo. Of course they had history on their side.*
> *Even with the odd slaughter the tide was clearly going to turn as*
> *indeed it did in such short order.*

Emma straightens her back, takes a moment. While still holding the journal she says, "I'm not sure why it reads 'even if for the Queen.' I'm assuming this is the War of 1812."

"Oh," Eddie says, a little unpleasantly.

"Remember," Emma adds, "that the British burned Buffalo in that war, I think they burned Washington, D.C. too."

"Actually," Eddie says slowly, in a manner that makes Emma and Brendan both turn to look at him. He notes their attention and says, "December 30th, 1813. And it was before they burned Washington."

Brendan nods his head, "I'll be damned. When did you take such an interest in history? This is something new."

"Well actually old, I mean the burning thing." Eddie takes a moment and says, "This whole unpacking the family history saga, finding Paddy O'Neil's trunk at the farm, the journals themselves, it peaked my interest."

"It piqued your interest?" Brendan asks, "'piqued' with the letter 'q'?"

"Peaked, yes sir, peaked with the letter 'k.'"

"Well, good for you cousin. Maybe that explains all the trips you've made here," Emma says, lowering her voice "minus your brother," and adds, "December the 30th huh? In Buffalo."

"Happy New Year," Brendan adds.

"All but three of the buildings burned to the ground," Eddie says.

The small group considers this, until Emma says, "Those Brits can be mean bastards."

Brendan is about to second her comment when Eddie says, "It was in retaliation for the American forces burning down the town of Niagara-On-The-Lake in Ontario."

"Oh," Emma says. "I like Niagara-On-The-Lake. They do great shows there in the summer. Live theatre."

"Right," Brendan adds. "Don't they do some George Bernard Shaw there?"

"I think maybe, yes," Emma says.

There is a slight pause in the conversation, a re-shifting of priorities. Brendan says to his brother, talking past Emma who sits in between, "You come here a lot?"

While Eddie hesitates with his response, Emma says "And so can you, my friend," patting Brendan on the leg, which Brendan thinks may be a first.

Eddie says, "This is where the journals now live."

Emma adds, "And me."

Brendan has the impulse to return the favor and pat her on the leg, but her skirt is very short, and he's not exactly the touching type anyway.

"I can tell you," Eddie begins, "why Uncle John wrote 'even if for the Queen.'"

"May wonders never cease," Brendan says.

"Oh, I like that," Emma says admiringly to Brendan. "Did you just make that up?"

The two brothers look at each other across the slender expanse of their young cousin. Eddie says, "Hardly."

"It's an old saying," Brendan adds.

Emma hesitates. "I see. That's why I didn't recognize it. Something from a much earlier generation."

"Yes," Eddie says cautiously.

"You know, long before my time." She pauses, "You know, like a long time ago," she says, emphasizing 'long.'

Neither brother speaks for a moment. Brendan envisions a light cloth covering a warm loaf of bread, rising. This seems so peculiar that he momentarily forgets Emma's question until she repeats it.

"So how, Eddie, do you explain 'even if for the Queen'?"

"Ah," Eddie says, "where do I even begin?" as he settles back in the couch, which causes Brendan and Emma to lean forward and turn so that they can see him. What they see is Eddie's expression of amused thoughtfulness.

"Oh god," Brendan says, sounding pained. He stands up and moves over to the armchair that faces the couch.

"You okay?" Emma inquires.

"Fine, yes," he answers, nodding his head toward his brother, "be prepared. This may take a little time."

"Okay," Eddie says, "think about what was happening during this time."

When he sees that Emma and Brendan share the same blank look, he continues, "Did you read the passage just before these lines?"

Emma shakes her head, looks a bit embarrassed, "To tell the truth, it's been a while since I looked at the journals. I remember that the later journals get more interesting. I tried to do a kind of speed reading here and there. I wouldn't recommend that, by the way. Sorry."

Her two cousins look at each other. Eddie thinks Brendan looks relieved.

"Brendan?" Eddie asks.

"Why are you asking me?" Brendan says, "You were with me when we started reading at that same spot. So I don't have a clue but," he hesitates, "I'll tell you, the name 'Buffalo' jumps out at me. Something I can relate to."

Emma says, "There we go. 'Buffalo.'"

Eddie is not sure what Emma means and asks her, "Okay but why at first did you assume that this was the War of 1812? The writer, our uncle…"

"Great uncle," Brendan corrects.

Eddie pauses, "Our great uncle, and Emma, apparently your great-great to the fifth generation or whatever."

"Okay, I get it," Emma says, smiling.

"He was writing, on this very page, in his own hand, mind you."

"Cool," Brendan interjects.

"In the year, what, 1866."

All three take a moment to consider this.

"So that was how many years after the War of 1812?" Eddie continues.

Brendan appears to be thinking about something, and says, "53 years."

Eddie looks over at Brendan, then at Emma. "So 53 years later. That's quite a chunk of time."

"54 years," Brendan corrects, adding, "well at least 54 years if you count from the start of 1812."

No one speaks for a moment, till Emma repeats, "Buffalo."

Eddie and Brendan look at each other, and then Brendan says, "You want to say more about that?"

"Well, Buffalo, that's the answer."

"Oh," Eddie says, "that's the answer," and Brendan wonders if Eddie is being sarcastic, though he doesn't appear to be, so Brendan asks, "What's the question?"

Eddie says, "I can see we're making good headway here," as Emma snorts in reply.

"What?" Brendan asks.

Emma says, "I'm telling Eddie that the reference to Buffalo is the reason I assumed the War of 1812."

Brendan suddenly registers a look of surprise, but not about what was just said.

Eddie notices, and asks "Yes?"

"I just remembered, when we were dealing with the Canada farm, and the trunk, and hoping to get answers?" And then he stops for a moment.

Emma asks, "Answers about what?"

Brendan seems to reboot, "We were, remember, trying to discover why we knew so little about Ireland and how the family came over here and then didn't pass along stories and we wondered why so little was ever shared with us?" all voiced in upspeak.

Emma waits and asks, "Is that a question? By the way, I can partially relate, about the not hearing family stories part, except of course we had the journals from Dan Donohoe." She hesitates for a long moment remembering things she had heard, stories stretching back from a family tree that cast an ever-deepening shadow. And then all of a sudden, she brightens, blinks both eyes and says, "What a kick it was when we ran into each other. Long lost cousins."

"And," Eddie joins in, sharing her enthusiasm, "where should it happen but right in front of the ancestral farmhouse in Dunnville."

Emma smiles, "Kind of spooky, huh?" She hesitates, remembering, "I just wanted to go on a day trip, drive by the old place. I felt pulled, almost."

"Yeah," Brendan says, enjoying the memory but not wanting to lose his train of thought, "There was," he continues, "this Professor, talked on the phone, Toronto."

Eddie hears his brother bumping along into the narrative that he well understands. He decides to see if his brother can straighten out the story on his own.

Brendan takes a deep breath. His voice now lower in register, calmer. "We had some consultation calls with a Professor of history in Toronto."

"Oh, indeed." Emma remarks.

"And he told us, in speaking of Canadian history, that there was this skirmish around the time."

"What time?" Emma asks.

"1866" Eddie interrupts, nodding to his brother to continue.

"And it's not well known. Called the Finland Rebellion, or something like that."

"Finland?" Emma asks. "What's Finland got to do with it? Oh god, not another Viking invasion, I trust."

Eddie says, "Not Finland, but that's close. The name was Fenian."

"Finian's rainbow?" Emma asks.

"That was another good show," Brendan says. "Fred Astaire. You know who else was in that movie? Petula Clark," answering his own question before Eddie might.

Eddie appears surprised, "You're kidding! Not the singer Petula Clark?"

"The same."

"Who's Petula Clark?" Emma asks.

"*When you're alone and life is making you lonely you can always go,*" Brendan sings.

"*Downtown,*" Eddie joins in.

Emma looks at both the brothers. "You two have good voices!"

They nod their heads, as if they are an aged traveling act. Eddie says, "It's the Irish, don't you know."

"So what did the Professor say?" Emma asks.

Eddie sits forward a little in the couch, looking less relaxed, waiting to hear what Brendan will say.

Brendan makes a nearly inaudible sound, more like a moan.

Emma looks at Brendan. "Let me guess. You don't remember."

"Well no, of course I remember," Brendan says, "just not all the details."

"It was 1866," Eddie answers for his brother.

"During the Civil War?" Emma asks.

"Right after," Eddie says.

"Wait, no, I think," Brendan says, sounding more animated, "it was something about retaking Ireland."

Eddie joins in, "Civil War veterans invaded Canada."

Emma looks carefully at the two of them, trying to determine if they are serious, which they seem to be, but you never know with these two. "Let me get this straight. Americans, in 1866…"

"That part is solid," Eddie interrupts.

"Americans," Emma continues, "invaded Canada to retake Ireland?"

"Something like that," Brendan says.

In a low and doubtful tone of voice, Emma repeats, "Something like that. The Professor said there was some truth in this…history? This is non-fiction?"

Both brothers answer in unison, "ye-yes."

"I never heard about any of this," Emma comments.

"No," Brendan adds.

"And I was a history major at SUNY Buffalo. Well," Emma admits, "a history minor. You'd think I would have heard of this before now."

"You would, wouldn't you," Eddie adds with a touch of empathy.

Brendan takes a moment, says "Well, really, I don't think it was all that big a deal. It was just that one time. Former civil war American soldiers, probably drunk."

"Yeah," Eddie adds, "which is why maybe it wasn't taught at your college, Emma."

Emma looks down for a moment, and when she looks up at Brendan she says, "Still. That's a pretty big deal. They actually did invade?"

"Canada?" Brendan says, "Yes. For all of 3 days or something."

"Embarrassing." Emma says. She takes a deep breath and asks, "Was Paddy O'Neil part of this?"

"What?" Brendan asks. Brendan looks at his brother whose facial expression is as opaque as the couch's fabric. Brendan looks at Emma and says, "My dear brother has read ahead in the journals."

"Skimmed, would be more accurate a description," Eddie says, raising his chin in a pre-pontificating gesture.

Brendan shifts in his seat, sighs. "I have a confession," he begins.

"Another one?" Eddie asks.

"I don't know a thing about Mr. O'Neil other than that he has a trunk named after him."

"Reportedly," Eddie concludes, in the posture of an academic wanting to be scientific, factual. "In regard to the naming of the trunk, that may remain one of life's mysteries." He raises his eyebrows and lowers them again. To Emma he says, "Whether the trunk was part of this invasion, we have no documentation."

Brendan considers his response, and adds, "It would have been a tad cumbersome for such an adventure, don't you think, brother?"

"One would think that, yes," Eddie agrees.

Emma takes a deep breath. "Mother of God."

There is an extended moment of silence until Emma asks, "More coffee?"

Brendan and Eddie mumble their assent mixed with gratitude while Emma stands up. On her way to the kitchen Emma sings softly, "No cream, sugar, black," as if this were the start of a nursery rhyme. When she returns, she asks, "By the way, you never invited me over to see the trunk. Who has it now?"

Eddie says, "Brendan has it," as he prepares to remove his cup from the tray.

"You're not hiding it from me, are you?" she teases Brendan, adding, "you must have had some surprises when you opened it. Real treasures."

Brendan sips his hot coffee with care. When he puts the cup down he says, "Dad's high school textbooks, along with notebooks."

"Notebooks?" she asks with some excitement.

"His Latin translations."

"And a bunch of newspapers from the era," Eddie adds.

"Oh," Emma asks, "what era? Anything of interest in the papers."

"1915?" Brendan asks.

"More like 1917, the early 20's. Eddie says. "Some great ads for cars, laundry soap, recipes for cooking with lard."

Emma takes her turn to sip her coffee. "Exciting," she says, sounding not all that excited. "So you know, Paddy was a shopkeeper's son, his dad owned a general type store in town. They were one of the first Canadian families the Donohoes met, very helpful to the newly arrived immigrants. Their own family had come over several years earlier. He died around the turn of the century, 1900 I think. If this is his trunk, none of those things you found sound like they were his."

There is a thoughtful pause. "It's interesting," Eddie says, "somehow the Donohoes ended up with his trunk and, you're right, none of that stuff seems related to him."

Emma pauses for a moment, says "You know we're related to Paddy, by marriage. He bought some property on John Street out in the country and was a farmer for the rest of his life. Maybe that's how the trunk was inherited. He married your paternal grandmother's mother's sister, whose name was Catherine Harkens."

While Brendan seems to be glazing over, Eddie says, "Oh so he's an uncle to our paternal grandmother."

Brendan tags along and says, "By marriage."

"Exactly!" both Emma and Eddie say, as if Brendan understood perfectly.

Eddie adds, as if this would make everything perfectly clear, "Paddy is a brother-in-law to our paternal great grandmother."

Emma hesitates and says, "He married a wonderful woman who by all accounts took over the farm during periods of time when Paddy was away."

A moment is taken to digest branches of the family tree, squirrels hopping from one branch to the next.

"Okay," Brendan says, "this is all so great, but I remembered something else we found in the trunk."

Eddie and Emma fall silent until Eddie says, "Oh I know what you're going to say."

"There was this drawing," Brendan begins, "sort of 3 by 5 on a heavy card stock, all done in pencil, quite nice. But not well preserved. The pencil marks were smudged. We looked on the back and it might have said 1870 something or, you know how it is, it might have been someone's name, or a jotted down recipe."

"For lard," Eddie chimes in.

"What was the drawing, what did it look like?" Emma asks.

"The person had some artistic ability," Brendan answers, "nice looking little thing, one small sail. It was a boat."

At first Emma's face appears transfixed, and then just as quickly she squinches her forehead into an unvoiced question.

Eddie notices. He asks, "Yes?"

Brendan turns quickly to look at his brother and cousin, not wanting to miss anything, such as Emma's expression, which he had just missed.

She takes a moment, then says, "You know he traveled to Ireland. We think. I wish Uncle John could have been more transparent."

"It's suggestive, but, yes," Eddie says, while Brendan looks on, appearing dumbfounded.

Emma notices Brendan's expression and says reassuringly, "Later in Uncle John's journal."

"Okay?" Brendan says, not reassured.

"This is where there is some mention," she says.

"Yes?" Brendan says, still a hesitant goalie.

"Paddy," Eddie shoots for the net, "going to Ireland."

Emma sips her coffee and puts the cup back down on the table. "Going to Ireland like that. Not an easy trip I would assume."

Emma looks at her coffee cup in a way that Brendan thinks has a wistful, almost romantic air to it. Brendan, trying to regain some stability, spins an accompanying fantasy, "Maybe he was on a clandestine mission. Politically, you know."

The air in the room seems to stir, waffle, fold in on itself, then become silent as a clam.

After a moment, Eddie pronounces, "Patriot Games."

"Yes," Emma agrees quickly, then reconsiders, wondering if she missed Eddie's meaning.

"Patriot Games," he repeats. "1992."

"What?" Brendan and Emma say almost in unison.

"Richard Harris played the character whose name was Paddy O' Neil."

Emma looks at Eddie wide eyed, "Oh for god's sake."

Eddie hesitates, "Possibly, but probably not. Though the Lord always helps."

"The hell!" Brendan says.

"That would be more serious," Eddie says.

"I saw that movie. Or part of it. The name never occurred to me before when we were talking about the trunk," Brendan says.

"It was when you mentioned politics. The clandestine bit," Eddie says.

"The IGA," Brendan says.

"The IRA dear," Emma says, who has never called Brendan 'dear' before. It looks as if she is about to reach out and touch Brendan's leg again but decides against it at the last minute. Eddie notices.

All three settle in after this movie mini moment of discovery.

Brendan says, "Harrison Ford was in that movie."

"Wasn't it Sean Connery?" Eddie asks.

"Possibly," Emma adds, then confesses, "I'm not really a fan of that kind of action movie."

"No," Eddie says, meaning to sound understanding. Both he and Brendan enjoy the genre.

There is a prolonged moment of hesitation. Brendan thinks about reaching for his coffee cup but instead, he says, "Anyway, can you imagine any relative of ours being involved in a spy, revolutionary kind of thing?" He expects an immediate and humorous endorsement.

He watches as Emma's face seems to cloud over.

CHAPTER 5

Onward Salesmen Soldiers, Christian or Not
Tuesday, September 26, 1933

Bill steps off the sidewalk and begins to cross the street. He could do better at watching where he is going.

He carries with his left hand the leather briefcase, the latch of which moments before he had snapped closed, a quality snap. He is returning to his car, and he is leaving with the usual supply of order sheets, product promotions, and on this occasion a receipt pad that includes a surprisingly large order of Epsom Salts. Moments before they had shaken hands, a hearty handshake, beefy, warm, enough to deliver the goods.

"Donohoe."

"Yes sir," Bill had answered.

"Good Irish name eh?"

What surprised him was the word 'eh.' This wasn't Canada after all. Not anymore.

He couldn't really claim that his salesmanship had made the sale this time, as it sometimes might. The owner of the little pharmacy in town, Rafferty, made the request out of the blue.

"High school football, see, it's been a big deal here, our boys from Olean against these fellas from Bradford PA, played last Friday night. Quite the action. Sprains, ligaments, who knows what. We could use what you're selling. Good head protection though—should see those leather helmets they use, well made, solid. Ever seen one? Still, it's not our national pastime is it now? Too many collisions. No sir. Never will be, especially not with the way the Yankees have been playing. They were in Boston two days ago, heading to Philadelphia tomorrow against the Athletics. Don't know how they can travel like that, but say, you would know a thing or two about that Mr. Donohoe. Man like you, all in a hurry, hey no harm intended, I know you've got places to go, people to see."

Bill privately calls him Richard "non-stop" Rafferty. He's a good sort.

A car, Packard maybe, no, more likely a DeSoto, seems to be aiming straight for Bill though it's still a little way off. He hesitates mid-stride, decides to wave his free arm in part by way of friendly greeting, small town manners.

It's a woman driver. When she finally lifts her head, Bill can see the fashionable hat she is wearing, the small set of feathers clumped to one side, nearly discarded, as he hopes not to be. She can see him now under the brim of her hat, she seems startled, though not enough to turn the wheel. Bill waves more vigorously, with a hard-jerking motion pointing toward the side of the street that she ought to be on.

The Packard/DeSoto swings away from him, and he can see how she purses her brightly colored lips as she passes by, not so much a kiss as a pout, a blowing off of air, a comment on what almost, but didn't, happen.

One more safe crossing. He opens the door of his car, gets in, puts the briefcase on the passenger seat. When he closes the door, he has the metallic assurance of his own safe captivity. He reaches out to grip the wheel. Auburn Straight Eight, they called it, with the smaller 98 horsepower engine that came out in 1931. It was said to be the "Business Man's Coupe." He had gotten a good deal, of course. Told the fellow at the dealership to sharpen his pencil, over and over again, until the price was agreed upon. His profession, after all, sales. Thankyou Depression, here and there good deals for the taking.

He takes one hand away from the wheel, adjusts his fedora in a downward slant to the right. Double breasted blue suit, shoes always shined. He is no longer on the farm. No sir. And yet there is this damnable yearning. The quietness of the morning, the sound of doves in those Canadian woods, songs echoing between trees, maple, oak, and the tall lofty elms. He remembered the rare appearances of vehicle passing by the farmhouse out on the sandy Bird Road. Back then it would have been a horse and carriage. Almost always a wave, almost always someone known to the family. This is where they lived, he and his five brothers, four sisters, along with the two sisters who had died before the age of two. The age of two became an unspoken victory line to cross, one of the many unspokens of those years.

He was born in Canada, his father had been born in Ireland. His father emigrated for sheer survival, stories of famine and all that though he never heard any real details. Bill's older brothers began to leave home while he was still in grammar school. Their emigration was for money, fortune. The siren sound of the States. There was no question now of survival, this being the gift his parents had given them all, the ten surviving children at the turn into the Twentieth century, so full of promise, fabrication, fast moving machinery, the smoking soot of modernity.

And Bill had been one of the last to leave. He had to consider this. Last to leave. The big war had come and gone and he'd nearly been caught up in that tightly woven net of aspirations and patriotism. Canadian trooper, he would have been. It was a close shave but he had bypassed all that, did a soft shoe tap and with a twirl here and there, taken his turn at last to cross the Peace Bridge into the open if not welcoming arms, of Buffalo New York, USA.

He's American now. And while some of his brothers had started their own farms in the Finger Lakes of New York State, remaining servants to the soil, he and his younger brother Pat had said goodbye to farming life. They had bought suits, hats, shoes, clothes that made the man. And in his case, he had purchased this Auburn Straight Eight. Pat was still in a Model A.

No, this is home now. As if to emphasize the point, he turns the key in the ignition and hears the pleasantly rumbling and mildly muffled roar of the engine, not as big as the 1929 model, but big enough. A popular car for rum runners, fast, and wasn't he stopped near Hornell last year? Yes sir, summer of '32.

He'd seen the motorcycle in his rear-view mirror, a patrolman accelerating quickly from wherever he had been. At a certain point, the cycle slowed, hung back and kept a steady and equal distance. Being followed, for sure, but it went on long enough that he thought perhaps he had proven his innocence for all the steadiness of his steering, his circumspect manner of going forward. Alas. The cycle moved closer, and a large arm began to wave, not a greeting, a warning, a command to pull over to the side, yes, now, the sooner the better.

After the patrolman dismounted, he stepped forward slowly, with a bit of a cowboy's bow-legged swagger. The patrolman had to adjust his pants, showing off the dark metal grip of his gun neatly secured in its black leather holster, a pair of handcuffs among the assorted items stowed on his belt, the belt that held up his pants.

Bill lowered his window. "Officer," he intoned, with as much respect as he could muster. "What can I do for you? Fine looking bike by the way. That an Indian River or a Harley?"

From what seemed a great height, the voice responded simply, "What can you do for me?" And taking a moment, the voice slowly removed his sunglasses.

Bill hesitated, "That's...yes, that's what I asked." Bill had to make a slight adjustment in his seat to crane his head up and to the left. The patrolman was not young, probably 20 years older than Bill who would turn 36 later in the year. The patrolman was not smiling. He gave no evidence of being friendly, no quick wit, at least not at this moment.

The officer tipped his head downward, "Maybe it's what I can do for you. In trade, see." And here the patrolman invited Bill without saying so to look around at their immediate environs. Farmers' fields at the noon time dinner hour, several large barns nearby, not one other human in sight. No witnesses.

"I'd say you were doing 57 mile an hour." 'Mile', not 'miles', Bill noted. The cop had done things to keep his job at his advanced age, still riding patrol on a motorcycle. Just as likely he could be slopping hogs. His badge read 'Village Police.' He wasn't a state trooper, wasn't a county sheriff. What village? Wasn't he out of his jurisdiction? Did he have a jurisdiction? He had a gun in a holster, a swagger in his pants, and a missing front tooth.

"Oh," Bill said, not surprised by the direction of this roadside chat. "My speedometer read 49."

The patrolman looked skeptical, hoping that Mr. Business Suit wasn't some downstate New Yorker, the kind that has legal connections. "I'm thinking that you might need to take it into a shop, that speedometer of yours. I just happen to know a good repair place. Happens all the time."

"I bet."

"Auburn, huh?"

"Auburn Straight Eight…cylinders," he added for clarification.

"Yeah I can, uh, read that right on the side here." The patrolman hesitated, "you know who likes these kinds of cars?"

Bill looked straight ahead down the road, and when he turned to look upward at the patrolman, answered, "people with good taste."

The patrolman looked at him. "Oh, you're one of these funny guys, huh?"

Bill hesitated, "Not particularly."

"Not particularly what?"

"Not particularly funny."

"You got that right." And after a moment, he added, "So look it here."

"Sir."

The patrolman seemed surprised by this one word, cajoled. He actually shifted his stance, from left to right, and asked, "You wouldn't have any good quality spirits aboard, would you?"

Bill wanted to say: not good quality, no. He noticed meanwhile that his throat was getting dry. "You can take a look if you want."

The patrolman hesitated. "What I wondered was if you might have something in exchange for this here ticket I might otherwise write you."

He thought about saying: I could sing you two verses of "Danny Boy." Not everybody knows the second verse.

THAT was last summer. Bill takes a deep breath, puts his hands on the large steering wheel again and looks over at the small-town pharmacy, sees that Mr. Rafferty has come out to sweep the front sidewalk. It is a bright warm day in late September, Indian Summer, just a few colorful leaves have started to fall. Rafferty looks over in his direction but doesn't see him, doesn't expect, probably, that he would still be parked across the street. Bill is invisible, a timeless ghost forever disappearing, as everything seems to do.

He probably doesn't have to worry anymore about being stopped for his transporting whiskey not that it wasn't without its adventure, fun times. New York voted in favor of the 21st Amendment on June 27th, the ninth state to do so. The states were on a roll, starting with Michigan back in April. Roll out the barrel and all that about ending Prohibition. They would need three fourths of the 48 States to finally end this juggernaut of legislation, he might call it, that had started 13 years before. He'd read in the Geneva, NY paper the other day that Vermont had joined the band wagon September 23rd, and Colorado was expected to be next. That would make something like 23 States and counting. But then again, his travels with whiskey were across the border, Canada to the States. A different matter.

He can feel the heat from the sun, he can see the brilliance of the light, and he wants to believe that this season will remain, against all odds, unchanged. Have it stay just the way it is in this moment, he thinks, where he is parked under the leafy trees along the sidewalk, dappled light cascading onto the front hood of his car, motor still running but without forward motion. He wants to believe in the magic act of things remaining still, wants to ignore the slowly changing angle of light, late September in upstate New York, the sun holding him in this warm embrace, as if to encourage him not so much to move as to take a nap, sink more deeply into the driver's seat.

The next sales call is over by Cuba, NY, 16 miles via Haskell Rd and Co Rd 6. Big sigh. He looks over to the passenger seat, opens his briefcase and sees the pad with the schedule he has made for himself, the calls that he intends to make on this trip. He reaches for the pad, studies it a moment and starts to leaf through until he reaches Tuesday September 26th. Rudy Figenscher, owns the store in town. German. Orderly, precise, decent man. Wife died couple years back, hit by a car when she was visiting family up by Canandaigua. A little sparse with his orders, just enough to get by, Bill always trying to encourage him to add a little extra but, so far, no luck with that.

He listens to the sound of the engine humming, the promise of the acceleration to come. It is this sound that will be his companion for so many miles, over long stretches of straight and curving roads, more two lane than one lane affairs. Another salesman had told him that he'd heard of a Ford that got a radio installed and he thinks that would be grand, but then again...

He is still savoring the sunlight. He forgets to check for traffic, there is so little of it in a small town like this. It happens so quickly, so unexpectedly. He turns the wheel and begins to pull out, hears the sound of a car horn that is ever so close by, cannot imagine how something can be that loud, that close and then it hits him, not mind you, the other car with its large running board and vaulted fenders mere inches away, no it hits him that he is responsible and that the unseen can be oh so dangerous, the consequences, a day, a life, ruined by the foolishness of not paying attention to what would be his fault.

The other car stops, unharmed now but stops, and he can see that the driver considers getting out of the car, maybe to check on him to make sure he is alright. The driver does not exit but turns in his seat and Bill sees how the small back window neatly frames the image of a man raising a hand, not to help but to give him the finger. It looks as if he is mouthing "asshole!" with the exclamation mark duly noted.

Bill stays stock still, hands gripping the wheel. If he could raise his hands he would raise his shoulders as well, the sign of a shrug, an admission that accidents happen, perhaps not owning up to his own role enough, his instinct to escape, to find blame elsewhere. It's just as well then, that it takes him a couple seconds to peel his fingers away from the steering wheel, during which the other car honks aggressively, gratuitously, Bill thinks, Christ give it a break, get on with ya. The other car finally pulls away.

This time, as he is once again ready to pull forward, he composes the thought to look in his mirror, turn in his seat and look as far back to the side as he can. He thinks these words, word by word like some kind of especially slow reader, a student driver trying to please the invisible instructor in the passenger seat.

There are so many dangers we don't know about.

He is not like those solitary farmers he sees along the way, the ones that turn and wave and the ones too deeply lost in their own footsteps, next steps, boots caked in mud and manure. He is a travelling salesman, his office is his car, he is always on the go, on to the next stop, and the one after that, a life on the road, well dressed, shined shoes that step up and step down from the running board, when he is leaving, when he is arriving, the next destination.

He comforts himself with the plan to spend one night at his brother and sister's home near Rushville, especially at the end of a long work week like this one. He is on the move again, and he can see in his rear-view mirror the last few clusters of buildings that mark the outskirts of Olean. He has passed beyond the town's boundary and is once again out into wild open spaces, the sea of fields that separates such periodic settlements. After Cuba NY there will be Angelica, Hornell, Dansville.

His hands are wrapped around the large steering wheel and he shifts his weight slightly on the cushioned front bench. He can feel the powerful motor up front that drives him forward, a slight vibration shimmying up to his fingertips, the same vibration that travels the length of the heavy metal body right out to the rear bumper.

He glances out to his left, waves to a farmer who does not see him. Unseen and moving on, comfortably seated, a man in the driver's seat.

CHAPTER 6

The Weavers

Tuesday, September 26, 1933

FIGENSCHER HAD TURNED OUT to be a pretty good sales stop. Luckily Rudy did not like the salesman who had stopped by the day before, the man from Emerson Drug. Bill knew the guy, big lunk, pushing Bromo Seltzer unsuccessfully, creating an opportunity for Bill to talk up the benefits of Norwich Pharmaceuticals' big seller, Pepto Bismol.

Rudy had invited Bill to walk back with him into the small dusty back room that served as an office. Everything appeared to be fading, needing a good pick-me-up. Evidence of the passing of Mrs. Figenscher, Bill thought. Rudy had taken a seat at the small desk.

Just before he signed for the surprisingly large purchase, he turned to look up at Bill and said, "Not like the remedies we sold in the old days Mr. Donohoe."

Unlike Bill, Rudy was always very formal in his greetings. One of Bill's bosses once told him that he should address Rudy more formally as well, match the customer's usual style of speech. Bill thought this was hooey, and it seemed to him that Rudy was relieved, if anything, to have someone address him by his first name more informally, more American-like.

"The old days?" Bill asked, but he knew what Rudy was going to say. He wanted Rudy to explain this little piece of history again. Rudy seemed to enjoy doing so, forgetting that he repeated many of the same stories. Maybe it was more about the telling than what was told. The visiting trade salesmen added a new weave to the everyday quilt of the customers coming and going in the small-town drug store. New stories to hear and tell, or old ones just as well. He would see Bill every six to eight weeks when Bill made this Southern Tier trip, all the towns just above the Pennsylvania border. Hilly country. Foothills of the Alleghenies.

Twenty years before, Bill was told once again, Norwich was selling Cannabis Indica, Extract and Tincture. "You know these drugs?" Rudy asked, his voice barely masking his German origins.

Bill had once seen an old price list dated 1913. George Schulman had shown it to him. George had long since retired from Norwich. Spent his time fishing for Muskies and Pike. Retired. Not a concept known to the farming generation.

"Here," Rudy said, opening a drawer in the desk, pulling out a faded book, "Eighteenth Catalogue and Price list of Pharmaceutical Preparations and Specialities."

Bill was thinking about his next stop and the one after that, resisting the urge to look at his watch. Good move because just then Rudy looked up. Bill was standing nearby, sales bag in hand slowly shifting his stance from his left foot to his right, not wanting to appear impatient. Where he would stay tonight would depend on how far he might get. He was on a first name basis with the better small hotels, though with luck he could make it to Frances' and Joe's.

"Let me read this to you," Rudy said, looking down at the document he was holding, and then looking up at Bill again, "this is, mind you, your company's manual, Norwich."

"Ah, yes,"

"Okay," Rudy adjusted his glasses, coughed once loudly. The cough seemed to disturb dust on nearby shelves. "'Cannabis and Codeine tablets, 100 pills for $.29. To quiet the nerves', it says."

"Yes."

"Okay, where are we, yes, 'One to three pills every half hour.'" Rudy put the book down, looked up at Bill.

Bill hesitated. "You don't have any left, I don't suppose?"

"Wouldn't you just like that." He tapped the younger man on the wrist.

When Rudy stood up, Bill gave him his hearty salesman's handshake, and he felt Rudy's surprisingly strong grip in return. Rudy hung on to Bill's hand just a little longer than was expected. Someone's hand was sweating. It wasn't clear whose. Rudy was the first to let go.

The two walked out of the backroom. A couple of customers had entered the store during their conversation. Rudy had a newly hired young clerk who was dealing with the first customer up at the counter.

Bill thought about making some kind of small talk by way of exit. "You know they got John Dillinger, last Friday I think it was."

Rudy was focusing on the second customer who was wandering slowly, unattended, down one of the aisles. Rudy looked over at Bill, said, "Who?"

Bill second guessed himself, said, "Hey another time. It was good to see you again."

"The gangster?"

"The same."

Rudy was studying the customer. He said, "Good riddance," and for a moment Bill thought he was talking about the customer. The customer was a darker skinned man, unusual for these parts, most likely some passerby.

Rudy said "Where was that?"

Bill hesitated, said "Dayton, Ohio," though he wasn't sure Rudy had heard him. He added, "Arrested at the Boarding House where he had been staying."

"Good riddance," Rudy said again. "We need to feel safe." When he turned toward Bill to say goodbye, he said with some emphasis, "Safety, especially in this day and age," and for some reason, his German accent brightened, strengthened considerably.

Bill felt as if a presence had rushed into the little store and brushed him sideways, tried to knock him off balance. He stood looking at Rudy and was speechless. Not a good thing for a salesman, to feel dumb-founded.

Thankfully, Rudy was looking at the wandering customer who had stopped in front of some item in aisle two. Rudy started to walk in the man's direction. He said over his shoulder, still speaking to Bill, "Not good for business, if you don't feel safe. No sir, not good."

Rudy approached the customer and said, "Mr. Cummings, how might I help you today?"

Mr. Cummings looked up and said "Yes suh!" enthusiastically.

Bill watched Rudy's face brighten with the warmest of welcomes, it was like the sun rising in aisle two, sunshine that revealed an old wooden floor, scratched and worn along foot paths, the dependability of returning customers, the meeting of needs that can be placed in the smallest of paper sacks.

It took Rudy only a moment to help his customer, and then it appeared that he wanted to walk with Bill to the front of the store. Before reaching the door, he put a hand on Bill's arm to detain him for one last moment.

In a few of the prior visits, they had spoken briefly about the current state of affairs in Germany. After Bill had shared his personal appreciation for the new President, Mr. Roosevelt, Rudy seemed all the more eager to confide in Bill. Rudy spoke about his sense of dismay, disbelief, almost betrayal. How was it possible that a bright and shining country full of brilliant people could be so affected by one individual.

He knew Bill had to go but he wanted to share something he had just heard. As only Rudy could pronounce it, something called the Reichskulturkammer had been created in Germany at the direction of Propaganda Minister Joseph Goebbels. This was the government's Chamber of Culture, and all "creators of culture," including Film, Theatre, literature, music, radio and even the press were required to register, in order to continue to have the privilege of continuing their cultural work.

"Well," Bill said agreeably, "they are a very organized society." He was hoping to say something to bolster Rudy's spirits.

Rudy pulled a little on Bill's sleeve, and said, "Non-Aryans are excluded." He released his hand, looked at Bill and turned to go back to his office.

Bill stood still for a moment, feeling the tight grip he kept on his sales bag. Without intending to do so, he took a deep breath and slowly exhaled. The front door beckoned, its large glass panel illuminated with the light of the world beyond.

CHAPTER 7

One Good Meal Deserves Another
Wednesday, September 27, 1933

"Frank, this looks wonderful."

His older sister Frances walks toward the table with a white towel that she uses for a potholder. She is bringing the bowl of mashed potatoes for which there was initially no more room on the small table.

He had hoped to arrive last night but there was some confusion about an order when he was in Hornell, and he almost missed the stop in Dansville before closing. People in Geneva knew him and it was a cinch getting a room there for the night. He arrived at Joe and Frances' by late morning.

Frances is 49. She never married and by all accounts it looks as if she never will. There was a fellow from Toronto who had seriously wooed her for several years. Her brothers saw something in this suitor that apparently she did not, or did not care for. The brothers had an inkling that he would indeed become the owner of the prosperous trucking firm that had sprouted up and grown roots along the coastline of Lake Ontario. At first there were offices in Pickering and Whitby to the northeast of the city, before turning and heading, as he himself and his affection seemed to do, toward the southwest, branching into Brampton, Mississauga, Oakville and Burlington, Ontario, clearly headed for the Niagara Region.

Had she listened to her brothers, she would be worth serious money by now. You see his trucks all over the place, even occasionally in Buffalo. But she said no. She had her own reasons. And she was making a life serving her younger brother Joe, himself a bachelor, on the Finger Lakes farm that Joe owned. Seventy five acres of good farmland that sloped gradually downhill toward the other farms which in turn led to Canandaigua Lake. A lovely place. Big white two-story wood frame house, small front porch, large unattached barn for the cows and goats. The barn was painted white too, with green trim. Fancy. There was a hand pump in the front yard, but it was rarely used as Joe had arranged to have a small pump installed to the side of the kitchen sink. A heavy red-painted iron handle was perched right there, indoors mind you.

Bill watches as Frances sets the bowl down, then sits down herself. She moves a strand of her hair to the side, grey hair that has become unattached, wispy, dangling, like an unwanted loose thread tingling her forehead.

"There," she says, taking a moment's leave, looking at the dishes on the table, counting them, it appears, before looking at her brother who is 13 years younger, fast approaching his own middle of ages.

"Wonderful," he repeats.

"Joe should be in any minute now, had trouble with one of the heifers last night. He's been working so hard." And then as if wanting to be careful that she does not show favoritism, adds, "You need to keep up your strength, businessman like you, oh my." She turns and looks out the window. It's propped open with a little screen that is holding it up. It's been unusually warm for this time of year. "Hoo-ey," she says, looking out toward the road that passes the house. The nearest neighbor is a quarter mile to the west, on the road going toward Geneva. "I'm glad you took off your suit jacket there Billie... don't know how you can stand it in all this heat."

Bill continues eating, and finally asks, "Is this one of Joe's chickens?"

Frances sputters a stifled laugh. "Don't tell him when he comes in. You know Mr. Pearsen? Married to Evelyn Pearsen. That's Pearsen with an 'e.' They have five children, each one of them cuter than the other. Don't know what nationality that is, but they're good Catholics. He used to be in banking but said it wasn't the life for him." She hesitates. "His brother you know never made it back."

"From New York? The city?" he adds needlessly.

"France."

"Oh."

She shakes her head. "Terrible things those boys had to endure. World shouldn't be like that." She looks back toward Bill, "I will never forget how your brothers helped you miss that one, God love them."

Bill takes another bite, swallows, "The Canadian government had the wrong date on my birth certificate. Too young, they said."

"And here you are," she says triumphantly.

Before Bill can say anything more, he hears the harmonically rich voice of his brother Joe, three years his senior.

"Yes indeed, lady and gent, I am here to grace your presence. One sick cow now on the mend."

Bill twists in his seat to look back at Joe who gets the drop on him, puts a hand, a hand with big muscular fingers, on Bill's shoulder. "Don't get up," Joe says squeezing Bill's shoulder, then asks "just get in?"

Bill looks over at Frances as if for approval, "Half an hour ago?"

"Not even," Frances says, looking like she realizes she needs to stand up again, fix Joe's plate.

Joe is wearing his well-worn overalls, a light blue denim shirt underneath. He wears tortoise shell glasses that are nearly round, after the fashion of Harold Lloyd the comedian. He is several inches taller than Bill. Bill is only slightly taller than his father James who was 5'5." Everyone, except the girls, were taller than Uncle John Donohoe, his father's older brother.

Joe is good looking and knows it, but his handsomeness has done nothing to hasten any prospects of considering a marital partner, at least not yet. Bill does not wear glasses but does maintain a stylish and always neatly trimmed mustache unlike clean shaven Joe.

Joe is well read. In the front parlor he maintains a small library and it's where he keeps a copy of Einstein's book, "Relativity: The Special and The General Theory." Bill was astounded to see it there on one of his periodic visits, but he never asked his brother about it. He had no clue that his brother had such an interest in science.

Joe goes over to the sink, pumps the handle a few times without the expected gush of water. He could be a writer who had chosen to maintain the farming life, not unlike Uncle John Donohoe, with whom he seemed to have had a special relationship.

Joe keeps raising and lowering the pump handle, adding a little more effort. He mutters "Come on for Chrisake, sorry Frank, taking longer than I wanted. Probably low, you know, water in the well."

"Oh, really?" Bill says.

"Used to happen back home. Do you remember?"

"On the farm?"

Joe looks over at his younger brother, the one all duded up in his woolen pants, vest, the brother who is finally loosening his silk tie. "Did you have a different home from mine?" he asks, to which Frances seems to speed up the delivery of Joe's dinner plate.

He pumps the handle a few more times and water begins to flow, "Ah," Joe says, returning his attention to cleaning his hands of whatever should not come between himself and his hot meal. "Yes," he adds as an afterthought, stealing a quick glance in Bill's direction, and it is not clear whether he is answering his own question or simply appreciating the arrival of the cleansing waters.

Frances places the plate on the table and says "Father had to get a man from Dunnville to deepen that well one time. Cost him a fortune, apparently. I'm not sure you boys are old enough to remember that. He told mother that he would never have had to do that back home, not with all the rain that seemed to fall forever on the landlord's property. They shared the well with neighbors and that particular well, at least, was always full."

Joe is wiping his hands on the white towel that hangs near the sink, he hesitates a moment, turns to look at Frances. Bill notices and in turn looks over at his sister. She is arranging the table just so and seems to recognize that it is time to serve herself. She has the sense to know that her brothers are looking at her. She also has the sense to not look directly at them.

"Back home, don't you know," she hesitates. "He meant Ireland."

Bill had never heard this little story about father. There are times, he thinks, though he has never shared this with anyone, when a communal cloud of unknowing is briefly pierced. The energy released puts a pause on the scene, like a photograph, like the photographs he enjoys taking.

But not all such moments create pretty pictures, ones that are rosy, bright and gay.

CHAPTER 8

Your Common Cow Diseases
Wednesday, September 27, 1933

"Don't know what I'd do without you," Joe says to his sister, five minutes into the baked chicken, mashed potatoes and gravy, field peas, homemade relish, freshly baked bread, and large glass of unpasteurized milk from one of the girls in the barn.

"It's called what?" Bill asks, Bill who has uncharacteristically finished quickly before his siblings. He has his eye on the pie that lays over on the counter. Some kind of squash, she'd said, adding that she was sorry he hadn't been here when the rhubarb was in season. Oh my, she'd said, you would have liked that pie. Not too sweet, not too sour.

"It's called BRD, my boy," addressing his younger brother with a voice that wished to be more senior than the three years which separated them. There were times when Joe would speak in ways to suggest that Bill had missed critical moments of shared family life, especially in the earliest of years. In a large family the elder children gained authority in proportion to the tales they would not tell beyond innuendo, the wink of an eye, the hard slapping down of a card in a raucous game of Euchre. The youngest born inherited the remains of mystery, a view of deepening fog. Some stories about the past were merely withheld, while others were lost forever.

"Okay," Bill says, "there's the answer, BRD. By god. Could have guessed that."

Frances looks up uneasily.

"BRD," Joe repeats, assuming that Bill, Bill the salesman, is bluffing. This is the brother who, when it was his turn to leave Canada, did not pause at Buffalo nor the Finger Lakes but continued on east all the way to Great Neck, Long Island, of all places, on the far side of Manhattan. In the early 1920's, wasn't it? All hell breaking loose, Prohibition starting up, women wearing short skirts, bobbed hair styles. Joe had read recently that the country's wealth doubled in that one decade, not seeing what was about to happen. More people moved to cities than lived on a farm, KDKA from Pittsburgh went on the air, the first radio station they would receive. 'Roaring' they now call it, the roaring twenties. How differently it all looks less than a handful of years later.

"Joe?" Frances inquires. "You okay? You looked a little lost there for a moment."

"He was about to tell me more about his animal husbandry, Frank. Working himself up to it," Bill says.

Joe puts down his fork, his knife, puts both hands on the table, one on either side of the plate. He looks at his brother. "Did you ever have rhinitis?"

"Rye what?"

"Rhinitis, okay or bronchitis."

"Oh, sure, just last…"

"Pneumonia?"

"Don't you remember? I was…"

"Nine I think," Frances interjects.

Joe pauses, puts his hands back in his lap, considers taking up his knife, his hands start and then stop moving toward the table before resting again in his lap. "Lack of appetite, see."

"What?" Frances asks.

"Nasal discharge."

Bill looks at his plate, a small cluster of smudged remains slithered across the brown gravy, the glossy china beneath, a single green pea hiding behind a micro dollop of white potato.

"Purulent discharge. Then, night before last, rapid, shallow breathing."

"This is the cow we're talking about," Bill says, in part to reassure Frances who is looking quite concerned.

"Can be caused by dehorning, weather changes, anything that causes stress." Joe hesitates, pronounces the next few words authoritatively, "Bovine Respiratory Disease."

Bill acknowledges this moment of enlightenment, "QED."

"BRD," Joe corrects him.

For a moment no one says anything. Then Joe adds, "In the end stages there can be a hard cough, a honking sound."

"Oh," Bill says, "that was when I pulled in the driveway."

Frances starts to look amused but doesn't want to be.

Joe pauses a moment, "Reducing stress, that's what she wrote," he says as he picks up his knife and fork and prepares to address his plate, commencing finally.

Frances is looking at Joe, assuming he will say something more. He is chewing manfully, clearly enjoying this hot noon time dinner. She then looks over at Bill who sits back in his chair, surveying the scene.

"Reducing stress," Bill repeats, acting like nothing more needed to be said. He raises and lowers his eyebrows, a summation for the otherwise wordless who desire little conversation.

Frances and Bill wait. Joe swallows, reaches for the glass of milk, hesitates. "Careful handling and sanitary conditions, that will do it. If you're lucky."

Frances looks from one brother to the next, finally she asks Joe, "were you lucky?"

Joe looks up at his sister, a bit startled with the question. He too begins to survey the scene, looking out the window and the fields beyond, and then finally back over at the red handled pump, its heavy iron weight, bolted soundly along the ledge next to the sink.

Bill waits just long enough, "Joe," he says warmly, this being a necessary ingredient at the moment, "we're talking about the cow. Not your love life."

"Oh for god's sake!" Frances says brightly, getting up suddenly and beginning to remove Bill's plate. As she moves on toward the sink she adds "I never..." in a lighter tone.

Joe takes a large bite from the fresh bread, white bread, still dusted with flour on top and cut moments before with the bread knife that lays near at hand. "Wonderful," he says a little ambiguously, appreciatively. "Careful handling and sanitary conditions" he repeats. "Works for the ladies as well."

"Get out of here, both of you!" Frances scolds.

"You'll have to excuse him, Frank," Bill says.

"Your bread is wonderful," Joe says to his sister.

Frances is putting more dishes in the sink. "It's the same bread I always make."

"And it's always just...the best."

Frances has her hands fully immersed in the dishpan. "And you think you can just waltz away with a comment like that."

The boys, as she would call them, remain quiet for a moment until Joe asks his brother, "You want to come out and see the little heifer?"

Bill says in a quieter voice, though not quiet enough, "She stayed overnight?"

"Stop it!" Frances says.

Joe, sizing up the moment asks his sister, "Frank did you see what time it is?"

"Did I what?"

"See the time."

She lets out an exasperated sigh. "The clock is right there in the parlor. Last I looked it was half twelve."

Bill hesitates, asks his brother, "Half twelve?"

Joe straightens in his seat, assuming a greater height, command. "The way they used to tell time in Ireland."

"Still do," says the older sister moving some of the plates to the drain board.

"What is that?" Bill asks, "like 11:30?"

Bill sees his sister shake her head in disbelief, a rare practice for someone so devout.

CHAPTER 9

Row Row Row The Boat, Gently Down The Dream
Wednesday, September 27, 1933

"Where did you stay last night?" Joe asks.

They had stepped out on the front lawn after the noon time meal. Joe was packing his pipe, Bill was about to light up his cigarette. Frances hated to have them smoke in the house.

"Geneva Hotel."

"Geneva Hotel?" Joe looks at him in disbelief, holding his pipe out from his mouth in a state of suspense. "That's so close by. Why didn't you just come on over when you got back to the area?"

"It would have been too late."

"We're talking, what, 10 pm?"

"More like 8."

"Oh for god's sake."

"I do have an expense account."

"Oh, please, excuse me. I don't seem to have one of those."

"And I rarely use it as much as I might. Actually at the last minute I realized I had a lot of sales reports to complete, and I figured it would be easier to do that in my room."

"At the hotel."

"Correct, and as it turned out I did a good three hours of paperwork. I hit the sack a little after 11."

"I was long gone by then, asleep see. Peaceful out here in the country, Bill."

Joe looks out at the surrounding land. It is reminiscent of their childhood farm in Canada though the traffic here in front of the house is a bit more. Maybe four cars per hour vs. one. And across the road, no thick stand of bush, or 'woods', as he has learned to call it.

When he looks back at his younger brother, he sees that Bill is staring off in the distance at some sight unseen.

"Well then," Joe begins, his voice softer, "it would be easier to entertain company at the hotel, eh?"

Bill turns toward his brother and looks over the top of the cigarette that is perched securely between his lips. He squinches his right eye to see past rising smoke but does not bother to answer.

"I'd like to stay in one of those corner rooms, the ones that look like a turret on some old castle," Joe says. "They've got…four floors there, the hotel?"

"Six."

"Six, okay. Tallest building for miles around." Joe looks away for a second. After clearing his throat, he looks over at Bill again. "Did you ever get to see one of those corner rooms?"

It looks at first as if Bill hasn't heard him. Bill takes a long drag on his cigarette. The ash is building up. He takes a couple steps out onto the lawn to carefully tap his cigarette, and while doing so says, "I like cozy."

Joe tips his head, "Pardon?"

"The rooms along the corridor."

"Oh," Joe says, pausing a moment. "You mean you're a skin flint."

"The hell?"

"Oh, there is the expense account, having to answer to the boss."

"Ha, not the way I've been selling lately."

Joe looks at his brother, "It's been good?"

"Even in these dark economic times."

Joe could have said Amen. Instead he says, "Dark political times."

Bill looks at Joe. "Nazi's got you going again?"

Joe says, "Little brother, you're not taking this seriously. Enough.

They have a church over there, Christian mind you, called the German Evangelical Church."

"It's not a Catholic Church."

"No, but I just read that 2,000 assembled ministers voted to approve what they call the Aryan paragraph for the church bylaws, expelling any Protestant minister who had a Jewish ancestor."

"Yeah I just heard about something like that."

"It's not looking good. We're not talking about the effect of a single leader, like that guy Gerbils."

Bill looks at his brother, "You know that's not how you pronounce his name."

"I know, I just like saying it that way. Makes me picture a little rat with fat cheeks."

Bill looks away for a moment. "They do seem to have something going on about being a superior race."

"You can say that again."

Bill considers something, says "What about our Negro fellas, got their own baseball league. Can't play with the whites."

Joe looks at Bill, "That's different."

"Oh?"

"And they're damn good ball players too."

"I'm glad they have your approval," Bill answers.

Joe looks at Bill out of the corner of his eyes, decides to refocus attention but stay with sports. "The Washington Senators clinched on Thursday, you know. Beat the St Louis Browns."

Bill looks at Joe. "What do you think about football?"

"This new thing? National Football League?"

"Yeah."

"Not much."

"Yup."

"Can't see it really taking off. It's okay for college level."

"Too bad Frank isn't out here."

"To see that we can agree on something?"

They both notice that a car is approaching from the direction of Geneva. They watch silently as the car raises a cloud of dust and seems to slow before it reaches the house as if considering stopping, but then picks up speed and continues on its way. Joe waves at the last instant and the driver returns the friendly gesture.

"Know them?" Bill asks.

"Never saw them in my life." Joe looks out again at the fields beyond, says, "Remember how father would talk about the odd castle here and there?"

Bill is clearly stumped, Joe adds "In Ireland. I was thinking about the Geneva Hotel, sometimes reminds me of things father would say."

"No," Bill says, removing the cigarette and putting a finger near his mouth to chase away a loose bit of tobacco. "I didn't get to hear all those stories." He looks down at the ground a moment. "Pat and I, left out."

"Left out?"

"Of the conversation."

"Oh, well, you were younger."

"Still am."

"And, I think, we all didn't, you know…"

"No."

"We all didn't think you might always…understand. Actually…"

"Yes?"

"I think at times we were protecting you. Not just me, Jim, Kathryn… all of the older ones. Some of the stories were pretty brutal for young ears."

"Frances too I guess. Protecting me."

"Yeah, I suppose so."

Bill thinks about the life he has created for himself, is still creating. He looks up at his brother, "They know me there, at the hotel. Geneva."

"That's because I introduced you years ago, when we used to have our euchre tournaments."

"Ah."

"I still stop in at the bar every so often."

"Mmhmm."

Joe thinks about what he is going to say before he says it. "Really pretty red head there for some years."

"Lena," Bill says.

"No, Jenny."

"Oh right, Lena was a brunette."

"Blond."

Bill looks at his brother as if he is understanding something a little more clearly. After a moment he says, "Is that right?"

There is a pause as both pursue their separate smokes, ashes.

After a while Bill says, "I wish I had told Rudy about the Autobahn."

"Rudy? Someone at the hotel?"

"No, customer in Cuba, New York."

"What's with the Autobahn?"

"Mr. Hitler just had a ground-breaking ceremony over the weekend. It's going to be a system of superhighways."

Joe waves his hand, his pipe, in a gesture pointing to the country road in front of the house, "Glad that's not coming through here." He looks over at Bill, "Your customer is German? You could share the good news that Karl Fuchs, this was just this past Sunday, saw it in the Geneva paper, escaped arrest by the Nazi's during a roundup of German Communist Party members."

"Who is Karl Fuchs?"

"One of their eminent scientists."

After a moment Bill says, "I know you may not believe this but the Church, you know, won an agreement a couple weeks back with Nazi Germany, each pledging not to interfere with the other. So…"

"Yes?"

"Maybe things will turn out ok."

There is a long pause before Joe says, "Dream on."

CHAPTER 10

Das Boat

Wednesday, September 27, 1933

THEY HAD GONE OUT to the barn where Bill had actually proven to be of some help, spreading the hay.

When they come back to the house, they step into the small entryway and Joe says, "Bill, check your shoes."

Bill looks and says, "Oh, crap."

Joe shakes his head in agreement. "Yes, probably. One doesn't always know. Maybe Frank can help clean them up."

"I can do that."

"I suppose you can."

Without any discussion, both brothers take a moment to remove their shoes. In the process of doing so, Bill says while bending awkwardly and seeming to address the shiny silk sock on his left foot, "I have a story to tell you about a boat."

Joe makes no response, and Bill is uncertain whether Joe has heard him.

When they walk into the front parlor, they find Frances comfortably ensconced in one of the two stuffed armchairs. She looks up, surprised that they are back so soon. She stands and replaces a book that she has been looking at, carefully slides it back on the shelf where it fits snugly among other volumes.

"I'll leave you two," she says, looking down and noticing that both of her brothers are in their stocking feet. "Well," she says, with some hint of satisfaction, seeing that her brothers are getting along nicely this evening.

Joe and Bill wait to sit down until Frances leaves, and then they each take a seat, Joe choosing the more comfortable stuffed chair Frances had not used.

Bill says, "She always takes good care of things."

"What?"

"Your book there that she was looking at."

"Not my book."

Bill looks at his older brother. "It was the Einstein one, that book."

Joe clears his throat with great precision, deliberation. It may have been an intentional practice, something he'd read in one of his magazines, advice about health care, ways to clear phlegm before if might become a problem, leading to the direst of diseases.

"Not my book," he repeats.

"No?"

He clears some phlegm again, less this time, perhaps the technique is working. "Hers."

"Well…" says Bill, continuing to muse.

"You were going to tell me about a boat?" Joe asks.

There is among the Donohoe boys a decided tendency toward impatience, restlessness, the present moment being only as useful as to what might come from it. Next. It is the next thing that is always valued, a step lively-hurry up tempo to peruse the horizon, grab the opportunities that others might overlook. Get ahead in life.

"The boat," Bill answers, a little surprised that Joe had heard him.

If there was an unspoken tension likely to form between the brothers as they settle into their seats, it would be: this better be good.

Bill had been travelling on route 39 between Geneseo and Avon. Bold beautiful day, this was sometime back, midsummer. He had come up and around a bend when he saw it, probably one hundred feet from the road and smack in the middle of a field of tall grass, Queen Anne's lace. He slowed down but had passed by before deciding to pull over and stop.

So now what, he thought. If he were going to take a look, it might be best to leave the car here and walk back. It couldn't be all that far. Not worth taking the risk of backing up over the uneven gravel on the shoulder.

He sighed, lifted the door handle release and stepped down past the running board onto the stones and dirt. There were flies buzzing nearby in the hot sun, heard but not seen, and no shade trees in sight. He was aware of the fine crease in his wool suit pants, the shine of his expensive shoes that, already, were picking up a film of grit though he had not yet taken one more step.

It wasn't so much that he had decided at some point to start walking. No. It was more like he had relented to being pulled. He nearly gave in to the urge to lift his arms, midway to the boat, a flight of some fancy indeed. But he was a salesman, a well-dressed one, out in the middle of nowhere in particular on a hot afternoon, in a decade that would slope midstride between a fallen stock market and a dread that only few imagined, far far away it was, the independence of minds being gathered one by one into a hysterical mass of upraised salutes, goose stepping feet.

His feet meanwhile stepped over the mounds of a formerly plowed field that the tall weeds hid from the public. He had given up on protecting his shoes. He could see the boat more clearly now.

A mosquito buzzed by his right ear and he slapped at it. He continued to move slowly forward. He could see that the boat rested on several bales of hay. The hay looked old, weathered, rotting. From his vantage point he could see that one corner of the boat was tipping ever so slightly downward, as if doing its best to ride a slowly eroding wave. Here the boat remained, otherwise immovable, an altar to agricultural husbandry, a sacrifice in the offing, a scream yet to be heard or long ago spent.

He stopped in his tracks. More mosquitoes took advantage of his delay. There was no wind, just hot air steaming up, an aroma of spicy decaying weeds. When, eventually, the season's change would bring wind and snow, the suffering would lessen, the boat on its altar would be covered in a shroud of forgiveness. But this had not yet happened.

What the hell is he thinking about? —is what he thinks. He resists the urge to jump back, as if he might avoid harm.

He likes boats. He had always liked boats. And this one had otherwise all the right ingredients. It was a short rowboat, maybe 10 feet, with a 4-foot beam, one oar surviving and still in the oar lock. He had seen one like this on a trip to Maine once, he had been on a pharmaceutical sales get together in Portland.

He remembered the name: Chaisson Dory. Joe told him one time that he had a strange memory, he was always forgetting things he should remember but then he had these glimmering bubbles of recall that popped up with no effort at all.

The designs on this lovely creature were all wrong for the area, the Finger Lakes and Great Lakes. This little beauty had the rounded freeboard of a boat that worked the ocean's coast, lines that flowed down and away from the forward bow, curving sinuously until it reached the water's edge, released there, allowing the little craft to slip buoyantly forward, all the better to ride the kind of swells and currents at the edge of a vast sea.

Out of place, she was, with all her sensuous designs, in this place of contained lakes, not unbounded waters. Lake boats had sharper edges, closely defined angles, built to slap at repetitive waves of lesser magnitude. But here she was, poised, posed, against all odds: this little craft on bales of hay, in an unplowed field absent of recent history or recognizable purpose.

He remembered seeing, now and then, larger rowboats beached at the foot of High Banks on Lake Erie, not far from the Canada farm where he had grown up. He'd walk up to such a boat, wonder who owned it, and admire how the front seat connected to the bow, the hidden space underneath the seat, a magical place of hiding for a six or seven year old, a place of refuge in an imagined squall.

He was there at the beach, feet in the sand. He could practically smell the fresh air coming from Lake, and he thought at first that the yelling was from the large gulls high above, the way they would swing overhead, dive bomb fashion.

"Hey! Buddy!"

Bill raised his head, the call came from the roadside, quite a distance away. He had not yet turned around to look.

"Buddy! Hey! Fella!"

CHAPTER 11

Armed Chair

Wednesday September 27, 1933

"**J**ESUS BILL," JOE SAYS with some exasperation, "I say that prayerfully."

Bill looks at his older brother, feels the edge of the arm rest, tufted velvet. He is listening.

"You could have gotten shot!"

"Shot?

"Please, brother. Look, you're the one that left the farming life for the big city," he looks away, adding when he looks back at Bill, "and all its snares and ways."

"The hell...?"

"Yeah, well, that too."

Bill says, "Look it was just a local farm field."

"Local to who?"

"Local to whom?" Bill corrects.

Joe adjusts himself in his opposing armchair. "Think about this, for crissake. Guy in a fancy suit, driving a gangster style car, standing in the middle of someone's private property." He repeats the phrase for emphasis, "Private property."

Bill glances away. When he looks back at Joe he says, "Brother, I think even you would have stopped to take a gander. Such a beauty. Just sitting pretty right there out of harm's way, for no particular reason."

"No known reason."

"Okay, but…it's so incongruous."

Joe looks as if a cloud has passed before his face.

Bill says, "So out of place."

Joe huffs, "Look I know what…conger…ruse means."

"It got me thinking."

In a very low voice Joe says, "This is what I was afraid of."

"I do remember one story that father used to tell."

Joe does not so much look away as to look uncertain, confounded, as if too many images were being reviewed rapid fire, more than could be digested.

It is at this moment that Frances walks in, takes one look at Bill and then at Joe, and stops midstride. She has a dish towel in her hand that she begins to twist slightly.

Joe has lowered his gaze to the well-worn parlor rug, its brown and green faded weave. He says, "He told a number of stories. More to the older ones of us, as you just said, or maybe it was me that just said that."

Bill notices how Frances tightens her grip on the dish towel.

There is a brief pause after which Frances, her voice noticeably pitched upward, asks "Joe can I get you a glass of milk? It's already in the ice box."

Bill wants to say, yes thank you. His brother, still looking at the rug says, "No thanks Frank, the milk sometimes nauseates me."

Frances looks at her brothers again, purses her lips, says "Bill?"

Bill scans quickly from Joe to his sister and back to Joe, during which time Frances adds, "You're probably used to something a little stronger."

"Oh, no, that's…"

"Well, that's fine. We do live the simpler life here. Well, now, if I can get either of you anything, just let me know." Frances turns and goes back into the kitchen.

Bill could taste the milk, he was going to say yes. It would have been cold, thick, very smooth. Comforting. Not store bought. Nothing beats fresh.

Bill notices that his brother's eyes are still on the rug, and he wonders what he is seeing. Bill stretches his legs a little, tips his feet this way and that, the better to inspect his shoes. Cost him an arm and a leg but in business, appearance counts for a lot. You could walk down Park Ave and someone might think you were a millionaire, none the wiser.

When at last his brother looks up, Bill says, "Our father had this childhood friend, Paddy...Burke, I think it was."

Joe takes a breath. "Paddy Burke was in your class. You might mean O'Neil."

"Yes! Thanks, O'Neil," Bill pauses. "Oh god, Paddy Burke, I'd almost forgotten about him, was always a bit of a wurp."

"Wet blanket?"

"You got that right."

"He's still in Canada."

"Dunnville?"

"Toronto. Bit of a four flusher, he is."

Bill looks at his brother with some amazement. "How do you know that?"

"Being a four flusher?"

"Being in Toronto."

Joe hesitates, "I keep up with the folks at home." Adding, "I'm not the travelling salesman."

Bill looks at Joe, "When you say home, you mean Canada."

Joe shakes his head in agreement, "Where else?"

Bill raises an arm and lets it thump down on the arm rest, "How about the good old U.S. of A?"

Joe raises an imaginary glass, as if he had accepted Frances' offer of milk, "God bless the USA," he says, adding, "it needs all the help it can get."

"Hear hear," Bill practically shouts.

There are sounds coming from the kitchen, Frances putting away dishes, loudly.

Bill continues, "We've got the greatest President ever, we're slowly recovering in this economy."

"Says who?"

"The great man himself, the finest of all the Roosevelts."

Joe hesitates, "I'm not sure that's saying a lot."

"Say, what kind kind of a patriot are you?" And then, "You know I couldn't even tell you who the head of Canada is-- what-do-they-call-them..."

"Prime Minister."

"A tad British, wouldn't you say?"

"R.B. Bennett."

"What?"

"The current Prime Minister of Canada, R.B. Bennett."

"Well how do you like that?"

"A lot of people don't." Joe says, and noticing that Bill seems uncertain how to respond, Joe continues, "Portly bachelor, see, a millionaire. Guess where he lives?"

"Uh, whatever their White House is, I suppose."

"He stays at the Chateau Laurier Hotel in Ottawa. You've seen it in your travels?"

Bill takes a moment, "Ottawa is not part of my territory."

Joe says, "I've seen news photos, swank I tell you. You want to hear something more?"

"Do I have a choice?"

"He defeated Prime Minister William Lyon Mackenzie King in the 1930 election. King was great during the good times of the 20's but when the Depression hit, he said he would consider the problem of employment, 'consider', get it? Bennett said he would end unemployment. Bennett won big time. Remind you of anyone?"

Bill hesitates. "William Henry Harrison. No, just kidding. I was thinking of Presidents with long names." After a moment he adds, "Joe?"

"Yes my boy."

"How do you keep up? I guess politics always was more your bailiwick."
Joe smiles. "Our beloved Geneva Hotel obtains several subscriptions."
"I see."

"So, if I may continue, once Bennett got in office, he did next to nothing.
At first. He was in the Conservative Party. He believed government should
interfere as little as possible in the free enterprise system. By last year, a
quarter of the workers were jobless. Bennett created Labor camps, men
lived in bunkhouses and were paid 20 cents a day."

"Sounds like he was taking a page from FDR."

"There were so many cars towed by horses, no money for fuel, see, that
they started calling them 'Bennett buggies."

"Damn."

Neither brother speaks for a moment, till Bill concludes, "Well thank
you for my lesson in world events."

Joe nods his head. "Anytime." After a digestive pause, enough to
change the subject, Joe asks, "So what did he say?"

Bill looks at his brother, takes a breath, "Father?"

"No the guy who was, rightfully mind you, yelling at you from the
road."

CHAPTER 12

Not a Hoe
Wednesday, September 27, 1933

'Chaisson Dory,' I says to him.

'Chassis what?' he says.

'Chaisson Dory' I repeat.

He says, 'That the name of the boat?'

'No,' I says, 'it's the kind of boat. You see them on the coast, you know, Maine, New England.'

Well he looked stumped there, and by now I was walking carefully in his direction, probably 100 feet away. Had to practically yell. I could see he had something in the crook of his arm, long slender thing, with a little bit of metal on it."

"Jesus."

"I think he took a step or two back. I says to him, 'You know who owns it? That there boat?'

'Who's asking?' he says.

'It sure is a thing of beauty,' I say.

'That?' he says, looking surprised.

'Yessir.'

'Falling apart,' he says to me.

"I turned to look back at the boat for a second. When I turned back to face him, and by now I was a lot closer to where he was standing, I say 'you can still see the beauty in it. Even if a little faded.'

"He seemed to think about this for a minute. He nodded his head toward the Auburn, and he says to me, 'I see you can appreciate such things. Maybe even buy them.' And then he asks, 'That a Chrysler?'

'No sir, she's an Auburn.'

'Auburn huh?' Then he adds 'What kind of business you in, if you don't mind me asking,' and at this point he shifts the piece he was holding in his arm from one side to the next, looked like he was trying to hide it.

'Can't do rum running anymore,' I say, 'what with the laws changing.'"

Joe says, "You didn't say that!"

"I did, and then added, 'just kidding, I sell pharmceuticals.'

He has a real puzzled look on his face, he asks, 'Did you say farm suits?' Well I tell you I had to work at keeping a straight face. 'Drugs,' I said, 'to wholesale and retail stores. You know Bernie Miller in Geneseo?, by any chance?'

'Bernie?' he asks, and you could tell the name rings a bell, and now I'm telling you Joe I could see that he lightened up for the first time."

"What do you mean?"

"He shifted his feet, his legs, like the military being an ease, not at attention which is what he had been."

When Joe doesn't make a response right away, Bill adds, "You learn these things in the trade, how to read body language, you could say."

"To make a sale," Joe mutters unenthusiastically.

"Greatest country in the world," Bill says.

"So…" Joe prompts.

"So his name is Whipplestein or Weintraub or one of those kind of names."

Joe raises his eyebrows.

Bill says, "I went in for the closer, I said 'Nice Model T there. You keep it in good shape. Not ready for a Model A yet eh?'

"Got to tell you, I doubted he had the money. Sorry, but, you know, farming right now. He reminded me a little of Leslie Howard. Maybe more like Fredric March. Don't know if you get out to the Picture Palace very often. You'd have to go to Rochester to see one of those big theaters."

Joe stares at Bill.

"'The boat now belongs to my daughter,' Whipple-Wein says. 'Actually came from her husband, may he rest in peace.'

"'Oh, I'm sorry,' I say.

"He says, 'Don't be. She's better off without him. Son of a bitch.'"

Joe suddenly stands up, pushes the arm chair slightly to the side, paces a few feet back and forth. Bill watches and waits. After a moment, Joe turns to face his brother and says, "I know who you are talking about."

"What?"

"Larry Weinburg. Peach of a guy. House is out past Avon, down Telephone road a bit, after where routes 5 and 20 split, heading west, you know?"

This was not clearly a question. Bill answers nonetheless, "Not exactly sure."

"Avon. That's where he is closest to, well not him, his daughter's land is out that way. Larry lives between Stanley and Gorham, not far from our place. Met him at a Men's Retreat, Columban Fathers. Good bunch of men."

"No," Bill says, wanting to regain his hand, his telling of the story. "It was Geneseo."

"No it wasn't," Joe says. "You weren't there."

"I wasn't there," Bill says in a low voice, "no, I guess it wasn't me who was there."

"I know exactly where you were. His daughter inherited the land after her husband was shot dead. It was his boat, the husband. Won it in a card game. His name was Duke."

"Nickname?"

"Surname."

After a moment, Joe regains his seat. "I'll be damned."

Bill says, "Speaking of guns…"

"Were we?"

"Well you said the son in law was murdered."

"I said shot dead. Likely had it coming."

Bill sits back in his chair, surprised to hear Joe speak like this.

Joe looks across the room, out the window, as far as he can see. When he turns to look at his brother, he says in his resonantly deep voice, "Did you know that there are 8000 KKK members in Toronto?"

Bill inadvertently shakes his head, as if chasing away confusion, or an unwanted thought. "Where do you get this from?"

"The Globe and Mail, Toronto paper," he adds in case Bill didn't know, knowing Bill did know.

Bill pauses, "Not in Canada, the KKK," he says, as if making a plea, a prayer.

"It's more than in Mississippi or Alabama." Joe takes a careful look at his brother, "You know it's here too, maybe under the surface but I don't mind telling you, not too deep."

"Doggone."

"You remember the Klan had a fit with Al Smith's nomination, the 1924 Democratic Convention."

"Al Smith?"

"He was a Catholic, of course." Joe hesitates, "You get out to the movies, did you see 'Birth of a Nation?'"

"When was this?"

"1915."

"Joe, for crying out loud I was 18 and still back home."

"Well the deal is, that film brought out a resurgence of the Klan, and they widened the tent afterward, as they say."

"Come again?"

"The Klan."

"Yeah I got that part."

"Instead of just attacking blacks," Joe says, "they added Jews, Catholics, and immigrants. The Klansmen posed as the very definition of being an American. Religious but not Catholic and, oh yes, Caucasian."

Bill looks away for a while. When he turns back to Joe he asks, "What does this have to do with my beautiful boat?"

"Your what? Oh. He was a White Nationalist."

"Who was?"

"Duke."

"So that's why he got killed?"

Joe hesitates, "No it was over gambling debts, some guy from Rhode Island owed him money and was low on cash, but Duke owed somebody else even more."

Bill waits a moment. "Where does my boat come in?"

"It's not your boat."

"Still…"

"Who the hell knows?"

Bill considers this. Life getting out of control, uncertain, dangerous. Danger is something to avoid if at all possible. Keep yourself in the clear at all times. Watch out for the big boys and the places from which they come, they may not be who they appear to be. Appearance is all, to those who cannot see otherwise.

Bill wants to bring one more surprise to Joe. "So then I found out what your farmer friend was carrying in his arms."

Joe says, "I know all about his granddaughter. He is very proud of her."

"Beg pardon?"

"Takes lessons at the Eastman School in Rochester."

"It wasn't a rifle," Bill says quickly.

"I know," says Joe.

"It was a clarinet." Bill says, hoping to find a look of surprise on his older brother's face.

"Not a clarinet," Joe says. "He drives her up there for lessons, see, and he had been paying the rental fee. Told me he thought it was a better deal to buy a used one. Still, it's a pretty dear price to pay in this day and age. I'm surprised he could afford such an extravagance, if you don't mind me saying. He was on his way to surprise her when he saw a gangster look-alike standing in the middle of his daughter's field. It just took me a minute to piece this all together, I had forgotten when he told me. It didn't occur to me that it was you."

Bill sighs. A long exhale. "Well, don't that just beat all?"

Joe was not going to gloat. He keeps his voice even. "It wasn't a clarinet. It was an oboe."

CHAPTER 13

Gavel to Gravel

Thursday, September 28, 1933

AT HIS SISTER'S URGING, Bill had stayed the night. A simple supper last evening, and a full breakfast this morning.

He has one stop to make in Rochester, it's with the big wholesale place. Afterward he plans on driving over to Clifton Springs. He's been seeing a young school teacher over there, told Joe and Frances a little bit about her, smart as a whip, very attractive. It took Bill a couple of dates to realize that he was getting serious, as they say. He had a sense that Joe wanted to learn a little bit more about this new relationship.

Joe and Frances come out to the gravel driveway to say goodbye. Frances hands Bill a loaf of her white bread, still warm from the oven, wrapped in one of her thin cotton towels.

"How do I get this back to you?" he asks, fingering the edge of the towel.

"You don't," Joe says, "You eat it."

"I've got plenty," Frances says pointing to the towel. "You'll be back." She looks out at the road a moment and when she turns back to Bill she says, "Actually I wanted you to give this to your Jenny."

"Gwen," Bill corrects.

"Yes, well let me know if she likes it."

"I'm sure she will. She doesn't bake, I don't think."

"That's good," Frances says, seeming all the more pleased with her gift.

Bill bends over to give Frances a kiss and grazes the side of her left ear.

"My boy," Joe says in his hearty wake-up-the-world voice, "I'd shake your hand but I'm not sure it's clean."

"Ok," Frances says, preparing to go back inside. "Bill, be safe. Not everyone is as good a driver as you."

Bill thinks he hears Joe stifle a snorting sound.

"I'll leave you too out here to finish your talking," she says, giving a final wave and returning to the house, her brothers watching her the whole way, how she stops at the last minute to examine a flower struggling at the kitchen window, how she carefully opens and closes the door behind her, not looking back at either of them.

Bill's intuition turned out to be right. Joe had been wanting to talk about Gwen ever since the third or fourth time Bill had mentioned her during visits to the farm. Joe, the bachelor farmer, fancies himself the senior advisor in this apparent affair of the heart. He doesn't want Bill to get hurt. Again.

"Joe, here's the thing, I'm having feelings of wanting to protect her, provide for her."

"Oh. My."

Joe asks if he can lean against the Auburn's fender.

"Trying to add a little pizzazz to those farm overalls brother?" Bill asks. "Just don't get any cow shit on the running board."

It was much easier for the brothers to talk about sports or crop forecasts than to talk about women, seriously about women, as in an actual female companion. It would mean the termination of the bachelor title for one of them.

Joe leans back against the car, moans. "My back, see. Bent over the wrong way reaching for a pail, cows were on the move. I knew it the moment it happened."

Bill tips his head, holds up his hands close together as if holding a camera pointing at his brother. "Interesting image," he says.

"Yes?"

"Middle aged farmer on the up and up."

"Yes he is," Joe says proudly. "Someone for you to take after." A moment later he says, "So when do I get to meet the pretty lady?"

"Soon enough."

"Well don't wait too long." And then he asks, "You're what now, 34?"

Joe knows that his brother is 36. Bill answers "32, last time I noticed."

Joe looks at him. "Somebody's leading the fast life. And remind me, she's just turned 18?"

Bill looks down at his feet, rocks back and forth in his shiny leather shoes. "Twenty-three," he answers truthfully.

"Jesus, Mary and Joseph," Joe says. "I say that prayerfully, of course."

"Of course."

"For her."

After a moment Bill says, "And how about you? Next year is the big 4-0. Any prospects?"

Joe doesn't answer right away. Bill wonders if maybe he shouldn't have ventured into this territory. Not today, at least.

"Not a lot of single gals at the Geneva Hotel or in church. I might have to go up to Rochester. And the girls in the barn keep me busy." He looks at Bill and it looks to him as if Bill has something else on his mind.

Bill says, "Well, you've got time. Look at our family history. Father married when he was 36. Mother was all of 17."

"So you, for one, are right on track," Joe says.

Joe looks across the yard, follows the edge of the gravel driveway up toward the house, sees some projects that he has been putting off, a loose board under the small railing.

Bill looks toward the front steps, wonders what Joe sees there. It looks tidy as ever. He looks back at his own piece of real estate, the shiny Auburn. "You know," he begins, I was kidding with that Wein something fella..."

"Weinburg, peach of a guy."

"Yeah, Weinburg the peach, well anyway," Bill hesitates.

"You wondered why he hadn't gone up to a Model A yet, still had his faithful Model T."

Bill looks at his brother, impressed that he remembered this detail, "Yes! Thankyou."

"And? Was there something more you were going to say? About whatever?"

Joe is relieved when Bill says, "Well, speaking of cars…"

"Yes."

"It got me thinking about how the Model T actually stayed in production right up until 1927."

Joe looks at his brother, considers his words. "Some things don't need to change, they have a value worth maintaining, best left alone. No need to tinker."

Bill nods his head ambiguously. "No need to tinker eh? Did you know that Ford shut down the factory then in '27 for several months in preparation for the Model A. Pretty risky business decision I'd say. But then by two years ago, 1931, he'd sold five million of them. Rolling off the assembly line, pretty as anything."

Joe considers this. "Still a lot of good Model T's around."

"Damn Depression comes along in '29 and starts the dotsie doh and swing your partner with Chevy and Ford trading places for the most cars sold."

Joe can see that Bill is on a roll here, animated. He is going to give his brother the time and space to proceed, but not before he stands up straight, then considers his back and rearranges a new way to lean against one of the Auburn's curvaceous fenders.

"The Model T was a durable product ever since 1906, but competitors were taking over even before the Depression. Henry, they'd said, had been thinking about tinkering with the size of the engine.

"In the 20's he'd tried out an X-8 motor that had proven to be unsuccessful. The Model T always had four cylinders and he didn't think a motor should have more spark plugs than a cow has teats. That was a quote."

Joe wonders if he is witnessing his brother's life in sales, whatever may have rubbed off on him over these many sales trips, the pressure to perform, produce results, hold down the floor. He takes a moment and nods toward his brother, "Interesting, brother. And I notice you call it a product."

"What?"

"A product. The car."

"Yes, the automobile. Fellow at the wholesale company told me about the teats a few trips ago. Time waits for no man the wholesaler had said."

"I could have told you about teats," Joe says, nodding his head toward the barn, "I've handled quite a few in my time."

"Not sure it's the same kind," Bill says, adding quickly "Ford's competitors were already coming out with the bigger engines. So what does he do?"

"Who?"

"Ford. He decides to jump from four cylinders to eight, because Chevy was planning to come out with a six cylinder model."

"By the way," Joe interjects, "the Model T came out in 1908, not 1906."

Bill looks temporarily derailed. It doesn't help when Joe guesses "You're going to tell me now about the V-8 engine."

Actually, Bill was, and he finds himself dangerously close to slipping back into the position of deferring, giving up his place.

Joe says, "Which brings us up to last year, first the Model B is unveiled and then, lo and behold, Model 18 with, you guessed it, the new engine inside."

Bill says, "They call it a flathead V-8."

"Do they now?" Joe looks away for a moment. "You know the Model A was the first to use that new blue logo, you know the one, with 'Ford' written on it."

Bill knew the logo. He didn't know it started with the Model A, not that he was about to admit this.

As if on cue, the two brothers turn to look back at the kitchen door, the one through which Frances had exited. When they finally turn back,

Joe says, "Well…" but in a tone that does not sound like the beginning of a fare-thee-well. It was more like Joe was not quite ready to have his younger brother leave. He has something more to say, something with an edge of caution. Criticism would be more like it.

Bill kicks at the gravel in the driveway, loosens a couple of stones, then checks his shoes.

Joe notices, says, "Shoes look good. Nor sure though about your choice of vehicle."

"What?"

"Sends a message, it does." Joe steps away from the car, looks up and down at the shiny Auburn, forward and backward, the sloping round fenders on both flanks, the mounted and perky looking headlamps looking forward to what may come, a silver bumper seeming to show the sly grin of the devil himself.

Bill looks at Joe. "Thankyou. Yes, prestige, class."

"Rum running."

Bill skips a beat, just one, "Very little anymore. Anyways, only on the Canadian trips. For family. You should complain, after what I brought you. Canadian Rye for god's sake. Don't like the stuff myself."

Joe's voice is unusually deeply toned, reassuring, "You're more of a Crown Royal man."

Bill says, "Besides, the whole country is changing with the new sobriety laws."

Joe looks at his brother. "Sobriety is going to be lawful again?"

They hear the un-oiled squawk of the screen door at the same instant, and they both watch as Frances comes out with something steaming in her hands. She sets it down carefully on the concrete stoop, and it's not until she stands up that she notices her two brothers looking directly at her.

Bill calls out, "When did our parents marry?"

"Boys!" she laughs, half startled, not sure that her laughter quite fits the situation. "I thought you had gone already. Bill, I mean."

"Yes, yes, yes," Joe intones like narrowly descending steps, a sound both comforting and alarming with its deep undertones.

"We were just talking about mother and father," Bill tells her.

Frances considers this, shakes her head in mixed agreement. "How did that get started?"

Joe and Bill look at each other under a passing shade of understanding.

Frances spots it. "Is that really what you were talking about? And Bill, I thought you were all in a hurry to get on to Rochester."

"Oh," Bill says, "Frank, I've got time. The Auburn can move quickly when she wants to."

Joe looks over at Bill, then back to Frances, "Yes Frank, Bill is getting hot to trot."

Frances pauses before saying, "You're talking about lady friends, am I right?"

"No," Joe says.

"Oh," says Frances.

"One lady friend. With whom he is getting serious it would seem."

It isn't clear whether Frances hears Joe's comment. She says, "This here," pointing to what they now recognized as another loaf of bread resting by her feet, "is a new recipe. Not sure about it yet."

"I'm sure it will be fine," says Bill.

"Sometimes new is a good thing. But not always," Joe says. "For my part, I tend to stick with what I already know. The world is changing enough all by itself." He looks away for a moment. "And there's not a lot I can do about that."

Frances looks at the bread by her feet. "It's still hot."

"What kind?" Bill asks.

"Rye."

"Oh dear," Joe says.

"What?" Frances asks.

Joe points at his brother. "He doesn't like Rye."

Bill shakes his head, "That only applies to whiskey."

"Oh," Frances says, "Billie," the name she calls him at certain times, "you don't like whiskey?" She isn't kidding.

Joe says, "His sales are off," adding, "From his border crossing days."

Frances shakes her head, uncertain what to make of her younger brothers, though glad to see that they are getting along okay. She reaches down to touch the bread. When she stands up she says, "I'm going to leave things alone for a little while."

"Good idea," says Joe.

"It needs a little more time," she adds, and then remembering, "Billie you asked about mother's wedding. My, well you were born in '97…I think it was May 15th, 1876, a Saturday, Emmett Johnson had just passed away the day before and brother Jim wasn't born yet."

Joe glances quickly at Bill, in a low voice he says, "They didn't waste any time." In a louder voice he asks, "What was the weather like that day Frank?" and just for a moment, Frances thinks he is being serious. She looks down at the still steaming bread and says, "You know mother was all of 17 at the time."

Both brothers shake their heads in agreement, Bill says "we were just talking about that."

"Well," she says, *"De mortuis nil nisi bonum."*

"The hell, Frank?" Joe says.

"Joe!" Bill says, "Easy." And to his sister he says, "Yes. At least sometimes."

Joe looks at his two siblings. "You want to translate? Either of you?"

"'Say nothing about the dead unless it is good'," she says.

Bill says to his brother, "Dunnville High School, Latin class."

"And I've been brushing up with the help of Father Moriarty over at St Theresa's in Stanley," Frances says.

Joe thinks for a moment. "What the hell for?"

Frances looks at her brother. "For moments like this." She hesitates, looks briefly out toward the road as if she might be expecting someone to show up, and when she returns her gaze to her brothers, she sighs and repeats "De mortuis," and then without a second thought says, "Would one of you bring the bread in when you're done talking?"

Bill looks at Joe, Joe looks at Frances.

Joe says, "Not sure how much longer we'll be."

"Well," Bill says, "Actually, I wanted to get back to something."

"Oh?" Joe asks. "That's okay unless it relates to this mortuary bonus business."

Bill says, "We were talking about how father mentioned the castles he'd seen in Ireland."

"Yes?" Frances says, maintaining her perch on the steps.

"I'd never heard him talk about that."

"Oh god, here we go again," Joe says.

"What?" Frances asks.

"He's feeling left out," Joe explains.

"There are stories I never heard," Bill clarifies, adding, "apparently."

Frances takes a moment, says "It might be just as well."

Joe seems pleased with this answer.

"Well," Bill persists, "I do remember father talking about his old childhood friend, O'Hanlon, I think it was. When we were talking about the boat in the field before, it reminded me of him."

Neither Joe nor Frances showed any sign of recognition.

'What boat in the field?" Frances asks.

"I'll explain it later Frank," Joe says.

"Paddy O'Hanlon," Bill says.

"Jesus but you're good with your names," Joe says.

"Joe!" Frances says, concerned with such use of the Lord's name.

"You say you work in sales?" Joe adds.

"Burke?" Bill asks, "maybe his name was Burke," addressing the air between them, "No. We just talked about this, for some reason I can't remember his name."

"Glory be to God," Joe says.

"O'Neil!" Bill exclaims. "The name was Paddy O'Neil."

"Was it now?" Joe asks mischievously, watching his sister's reaction.

Frances collects herself. "I don't think…" she starts.

Her two brothers wait for her to continue, but it looks as if she is done speaking for the moment.

Joe says, "It's true Bill, that you haven't heard all the stories." Joe then shifts his stance and his voice, and his next words are uttered in the pontifical tone of the prior pastor Father Reardon, dead now these six years God rest his soul, his rest giving the parish a respite from sermons so often punctuated with thundering conclusions.

"I have heard stories," Joe says, "we're talking father's stories." He seems to be looking to his sister for confirmation, any kind of confirmation. It is not forthcoming. "Yes," he repeats, in a softer voice now, "many stories told to me, the result of my senior status, one would imagine."

"Hello," Bill says. "Yes, Joe, it's true that you are three years older. Three short years."

Joe says, "But it was a momentous three years. Actually the momentous times came before that."

The two brothers watch as Frances bends over to pick up the loaf of bread. She juggles the loaf briefly in her hands, too hot to touch, but she manages to find a way to carry it in the crook of her arm, fingers touching it lightly, her baby.

Joe calls out to her, "You wanted one of us to bring it in Frank."

"I did," she says, before she turns, opens the door with its complaining squawk, and goes back inside without a further word.

Bill continues to watch the door close. Shut. Finally he says, "I don't think she's very comfortable hearing about Gwen."

Joe straightens himself to his full height, turns toward Bill.

It looks to Bill as if Joe is carefully composing his thoughts. Joe says, "Rest assured, that's not the issue."

Bill waits to hear more. Joe is clearly working on something, hopefully without the Father Reardon effect. When at last his brother resumes speaking, he appears committed to what he is about to say. Bill thinks at first that Joe is trying to change the subject.

Joe begins, "What is it that inspires a Revolutionary?"

Bill looks at him blankly. He's concerned that Joe is about to launch into a meandering off-topic tale.

"Okay," Joe says, "Maybe I should ask you how much you heard from father about Paddy O'Neil. You said father did talk with you about him."

"Well, yes, a little."

"A little."

"Said he had been an important pal, especially when they first got to Canada."

Joe waits. "And?"

"And, that's about it."

Joe hesitates. "I see."

Joe is quiet for what feels like a very long time, Bill looks at his watch and says, "Look, as much as I want to hear what you have to say, I do have to keep the appointment in Rochester. Will this take long?"

Joe considers this. "Not nearly as long as it took them. And yes, I can keep this short." Joe takes a deep breath. "Uncle John, you know, was the only one that could read and write, at least at first." When Bill doesn't say anything, Joe adds "We're talking the family, when they came over."

"From Ireland."

"Well, not from New Jersey."

"Right," Bill says with a little uncertainty.

"Okay, so you know that he kept some journals." And then he adds "Some?" with emphasis, as if addressing only himself.

"Yes."

"Did you ever see them?"

"Just once. Briefly. At Dan's house. I was enroute to somewhere else and didn't have much time."

"Dan has always kept them." In a lower voice, Joe adds, "Dan, of course, was Uncle John's eldest son, and to the eldest boy goes the spoils."

"For safe keeping," Bill says.

Joe gives Bill a look that Bill will long remember, and it seems a long time as well before Joe answers simply, "very safe."

There is a pause, a shift, they will have to wind things up for now. Much more to be said but no time for it at the moment. Frances has gone inside, Bill has to get to Rochester and later to see Gwen in Clifton Springs. He fishes in his pants pocket for his keys.

Bill shifts his stance, as does Joe, a dance of pre-ignition. Bill says off handedly, "I don't know why that little boat made me think of Paddy, father's friend."

Joe nods his agreement kindly, says simply, "A story for another day."

Chapter 14

Rattling Windowpanes
Monday, October 2, 1933

"It's dated November 7, 1864."

"That's," Bill starts, "like seventy years ago." He looks at Joe. "You do like to keep current don't you." He thinks about having a cigarette, but he'd have to go outside. Frances has gotten quite firm about not having to breathe what she calls noxious air.

Following his last visit to Joe and Frances' farm, Bill did get to see Gwen in Clifton Springs, and then he travelled east and spent three nights at the Hotel Syracuse, quite the ritzy affair, not like the places he would stay in smaller towns. The postcard he sent to his sweetheart said that the hotel featured 600 rooms, each with modern bath, as well as four restaurants. He underlined the place where it said that the Persian Terrace offered dining and dancing. He hoped that in some future trip he could talk her into joining him on one of these trips.

He'd made several stops at area pharmacies and then had a particularly good day at the big wholesale firm in Syracuse where he knew a lot of the employees on a first name basis. On Sunday he allowed himself to sleep in and catch a later Mass. He then spent much of the rest of the day catching up on his correspondence including a letter to his Gwen. He found that he was missing her more and more each day. It was getting that serious.

God bless the dependable United States postal service. They wrote to each other several times a week while he was on the road, and thanks to the frequent train service, mail was delivered twice a day. He would typically let Gwen know which hotel he would be staying in two days hence. One time when he sat down for a hotel breakfast, the waiter delivered Gwen's most recent letter right next to his plate. He wrote later that this was the perfect start to his busy day.

The next trip would take him back to Canandaigua near Joe and Frances and from there he had a stop in Binghampton just north of the Pennsylvania border, not exactly a short hike. He ran into some delays once again with an order and by the time it was sorted out, he called Joe to say that he was running late. Frances took the phone and insisted that he stay the night again. She worried that he would be driving for too long in the dark otherwise.

Frances was right. By the time he arrived the sun was nearly spent for the day. They had a light supper of ham, cheese, and boiled potatoes followed by an apple pie that Frances apologized had been baked the day before. When she took it out of the icebox, she examined it carefully and declared that it would still be fresh enough.

Frances went to bed early and Joe nodded to Bill, a signal that this would be an opportunity to talk further about family history. It was actually easier to do this knowing that Frances would be in peaceful repose.

"TORONTO Globe," Joe says. "Listen to this letter they published.

> *It is well known that the Fenian organization has a network throughout the whole of Canada, and at any given time the different corps will rise en masse and deal destruction to all Protestants.*

"The hell?" Bill asks.

"Let me read on," Joe says.

> *Our hitherto peaceful country is to be devastated by similar horrors to those perpetrated by the midnight assassins in Ireland. Murder and arson will stalk through the land unless*

prompt action is taken to nip the rising spirit in the bud.

Bill takes a moment to respond. "This is Toronto you're talking about. 1864."

"The same. Could be Berlin 1933, don't you think?"

"How so?" Bill asks.

Joe hesitates, "Well, let me amend that, actually it's far different. The only similarity being civil disturbance. I was thinking of that Hitler fellow, made a Chancellor earlier this year, now stirring up more trouble. "

"Well, I wouldn't know so much about that. That's more your territory. But what was all this fuss in Toronto?"

"You know, of course about the Fenians?"

Bill has a blank look. "Is that a family? Maybe before my time."

Joe takes a long-suffering breath. "Of course it's before your time. We'll save that for later. But to cut to the chase…"

·"Yes that's good. Time is of the essence, as they say."

"To make this simple, let's see," Joe considers his next words.

"That may not be so necessary," Bill says, "I'm a quick study."

"You are eh? And when did that start? Okay, so let's just say there was this movement to free Ireland from Britain."

"Oh, I like that."

"Yes, well, these folks wanted to do it by invading Canada."

Bill looks puzzled, says nothing.

Joe picks up the dried and wrinkled pages of the paper again, "Here let me read an adjoining column, I'll paraphrase what it says--and before there was any invasion, they had this show of force, they deployed 300 armed men into the streets of the city and they rapidly seized strategic points including the few on-duty Toronto Police constables in their stations."

Joe stops, and repeats, "300 armed men, mind you. Downtown Toronto. Of course it wasn't so large back then, not like now."

Bill appears to be paying close attention. Joe says, "I'll just read what it says here.

By morning they assembled into two large companies on opposite sides of the city before dawn and started firing muskets into the air, rattling windowpanes everywhere, then they melted away as quickly as they had appeared, leaving a frightened Protestant populace who thought they might be murdered in their beds."

Bill considers this story and says, "Firing in the air isn't going to accomplish a lot."

"Some commentators say it triggered a panic that spread throughout Canada for the next couple months."

Neither of them speak for a moment and then Bill says, "I don't know why they were planning to invade Canada. Sounds like they were already there."

Joe looks at his brother, purses his lips and puts the yellowed and fragile looking paper back on the table. He considers placing it back in the large cardboard box he had hauled out when Bill arrived.

Bill watches him and says, "I will say this, you have quite a treasure trove of old newspapers there. They might be worth money to someone who would be interested."

"I bring the box out for special occasions, such as this. Frances is not all that interested. It actually seems to irritate her when I bring them out, and she doesn't need that."

Bill takes a moment. "Well, I should say then that I am honored, dear sir."

"It's nothing, really. Well, not nothing."

"Wherever did you get them from?"

Joe brightens up at this, and the memories that ensue. "You remember that old trunk, the one with the rounded top."

"It was in the bedroom back home."

"Correct. All these newspapers were there."

Bill looks a little puzzled. "That can't be right. I used that trunk in high school. It was empty. I didn't have shelves in my room so it was handy."

"You were lucky to have your own room." And then Joe adds, "It was empty because I emptied it. All but a couple of old looking drawings at the bottom. I think I left those in there. I was more interested in the news than art."

"So who did the old papers come from?"

Joe takes a moment. "I assume from the owner of the trunk."

"Oh for Chrissake. He must have had a big interest in the news."

"Political news, especially," Joe adds. "Which maybe helps explain things."

Bill remains quiet, his look full of unspoken questions, one bumping into the next in a long line of succession.

"He was, you know…" Joe begins

"Paddy,"

"…Paddy, an early chum of father's, when they first arrived from Ireland. Paddy's family had been here some years earlier."

"In Canada," Bill clarifies.

Joe wonders how much detail he should share. He feels a tug on his jacket from unseen hands as if from the dearly departed. He takes a breath, "They had a dry goods store in Dunnville. The O'Neil's," he adds, before Bill might clarify again. "Apparently they helped our family early on, destitute as they were, poor souls."

Bill remains silent, partially satisfied.

Joe adds for clarification, "The O'Neils."

"The O'Neil's were destitute?"

"Our family was, the Donohoes."

"Oh, right. I'd heard as much."

"Maybe the O'Neil's too, but not so much after they had the store in town. Dunnville."

Bill ponders something, says "Didn't he marry into the family later on--Paddy?"

"He did. And sometime after that came the big falling out. Father always felt mixed about this, but his parents, our grandparents, clearly came down on one side. Didn't want his two sons, our father and Uncle John to socialize with Paddy. But I know for a fact they did, the two boys."

"Where was I?" Bill asks.

Joe looks at him quizzically. "You weren't born yet. Neither was I."

"I mean where was I that I didn't know about all this?"

This is the old refrain that Joe tires of hearing. Still, he wants to be helpful. Though it's not yet the season, he hears the lyrics 'What is the spirit of Christmas, surely it's brotherly love.' He says, "You did know about the big falling out, right?"

Bill takes his time to answer. He knows he might sound as if he is whining. He says, with assurance, "I know that damn trunk was helpful for storing my school work. Kids nowadays don't have homework like we used to."

Joe nods his head. "Kids don't have the farm chores like we used to. Speaking of which."

"Okay," Bill says, "I'll take a pass on the gals in the barn tonight."

As Joe stands up to leave, he says "Knowing you were coming over, I spoke to Dan and borrowed a couple of the journals. Dan was a little— well we can talk about that another time." He walks over to a well stuffed bookcase and pulls out two leather volumes. As Joe returns, Bill has the sudden image of the priest at Mass, bringing over a sacred text from the side altar.

"I thought you might be interested in looking at these. This one in particular," he says.

Bill carefully receives the volume from his brother, opens to the inside page, reads, "Volume 7."

CHAPTER 15

Crossing the Bar
Monday, October 2, 1933

Bɪʟʟ ʀᴇᴀᴅᴊᴜsᴛs ʜɪᴍsᴇʟf in the chair, takes a moment to look around the parlor in the farmhouse that his brother and sister share, have shared for many years.

Across the room with its faded brown and green rug, there is an old metal lamp with a large and ornate glass globe. It rests in the middle of a small walnut table near the entryway. He can see the dining room beyond, the dishes from supper neatly put away and new white china laid out for the next day's breakfast. A large cereal bowl placed atop a china plate, arranged for three settings. His siblings at either end of the table, his own place setting between them, as always.

He had been reading from his uncle John's journal, though it was slow going at points. There were odd flourishes here and there in the cursive writing, and at one point, when he lifted his head, coming up for air, he realized that the lamp on the table used to be a kerosene lamp. Someone had modernized it, electrified it. He could see the single cord draped down behind the table, leading to the sole outlet on that side of the room. The lamp shed a much more fulsome light, he imagined, than in its former life. Little flickering allowed.

Joe had handed him volumes 7 and 18. He'd wondered whether Joe had made a mistake, the journals being out of order. He is making his way through an entry in volume 7 when he hears, at last, the sound of Joe opening the door to the outer mudroom that leads into the kitchen. The kitchen is beyond the dining room, not visible from where Bill sits. The house has a comfortable rambling assortment of rooms, large enough for a good size Catholic family, though of course his bachelor brother and spinster sister are childless. Plenty of room. Always welcome to stay.

He hears the scraping of boots, Joe probably removing them and putting on the old slippers he typically wears indoors.

"Well sir," Joe says, when he steps into the parlor.

Bill stands up, though he doesn't have to. It feels good to stretch his legs a little.

Joe motions with a hand as if he were about to say please don't get up, but he doesn't say this. Instead, he sees the journal that Bill has been reading. "Find anything interesting?" he asks his younger brother.

Bill takes his seat, "Yes, actually," he says, "there is a piece here that talks about O'Neill."

Joe makes a face that Bill does not see, he raises his eyebrows, and goes to pull up a chair so he can sit next to his brother. "Does it now?" he says with a mixture of surprise, concern.

"I wish I had looked at these journals more closely before. I didn't realize."

Joe, now sitting close-by but not enough to see the page, says "And didn't we talk about this before? I knew you'd be interested if you took the time. O'Neil eh?"

"O'Neill indeed," Bill says, putting his hand on a page to mark the spot. He looks over at his brother, "Did you know he was involved in this raid business?"

Joe leans back in his chair, takes time to consider his response. "We need to be careful here."

"Careful? That affair was over a long time ago."

Joe takes a breath. "Some things have, what's the word? Repercussions, see, for what happened. There are consequences. People have different feelings about what our history—how people can still hold grudges. Even act on them."

Bill looks at his brother with an air of impatience. "Say look here," he says, "I think maybe you have a point about fearing this Hitler fellow, though I doubt it, but take these Finergans you were reading about earlier?"

"Fenians. And it's not just about them."

Bill shakes his head dismissively. An idea comes to mind, he decides to take a new approach. He's not a pharmaceutical salesman for nothing. He can talk a good game. "I think we could take some pride in fact," he begins, and then notices that Joe is gesturing to keep his voice down, voices carry in this house. "Okay," he agrees. "So, anyway, you know O'Neill had a leadership position?"

"Leadership?" Joe considers this. "Well maybe, but he had to be quiet about it always. Given his role in it. What he needed to do."

Bill is paging toward the back of the journal quickly, and while he does so, he says, "this interest you have in keeping old newspapers didn't apparently start with you."

Joe looks at his brother, says, "Come again?"

"You didn't see some of these clippings in the back of the journal?"

"Oh."

"Uncle John apparently saved news articles like you do." At this, Bill pulls out a neatly folded square of old newspaper and carefully opens it. "I don't why he would need to be quiet about what he had done."

And now it's Bill's time to paraphrase. "Here he is charging Morgan of Morgan's raiders across a bar in the Ohio river. Morgan had, what does it say here? 2,460 men and artillery and plunder and here comes O'Neill with his cavalry, cavalry mind you, of less than 50 men. O'Neill was so savage in his attack, not quiet, do you hear me?" and again Bill sees when he looks up, that Joe is waving his hand asking Bill to lower his voice, not to wake Frances.

Bill continues in a softer voice, "So savage and sudden that 600 of Morgan's men were driven toward U.S. Navy gunboats and captured. Without supplies, Morgan surrendered several days later."

Bill sits back in his chair, looks at his brother with a sense of triumph, wondering if his brother might now surrender as well. But his brother is smiling, not looking vanquished.

After what seems like a long time to Bill, his brother leans forward and says, "How do you spell the name, one 'l' or two?"

Bill thinks his brother might be trying to pull a fast one. Nonetheless he looks down at the page of old newsprint, and says "Two."

Joe grins all the more, sits back. He says, "One too many. It makes an 'l' of a difference."

CHAPTER 16

What a Difference a Letter Makes
Monday, October 2, 1933

"WHEN IS THAT DATED?"

Bill had been so excited to find the small square of newsprint that he hadn't really paid attention to anything other than seeing the name 'O'Neill' in print. He looks down at the article and says, "Oh," and then he lets his shoulders sink.

"Yes?"

Bill reads slowly, "1863."

"That was the civil war."

"Well yeah."

"You're telling me he was in that too?"

"I'm just reading the news. Apparently so."

"Bill, it would not be all that common for a Canadian to be in the American civil war."

Bill thinks about this a minute, remembers something father had talked about. "Didn't we have a relative who signed up? The story I remember hearing was that only his boots were returned."

Joe recalls the story. "Ok, you're right on that count."

"Well how about this count?" Bill says, as he turns back, this time to Uncle John's journal itself. "Ah!" he says, "Here it is:

O'Neill must have been exhausted having made the trip so far.
And here he is getting off the barges from Buffalo across the

Niagara, so the papers report, with 600 men, some of which went north down Niagara road, but the main force went with him to Fort Erie. Things were about to unfold quickly, and our boys were not, at the first, prepared, though rumors had been spread for quite some time. After those with the green coats and other embroidery had failed to appear once or twice before, as recently as March, we had all become somewhat lax in our apprehensions. "

"When is that dated?" Joe asks.

"Let's see," Bill says, looking for some kind of date. "Must have been later in '66. But Uncle John wrote the date June 1, 1866 for the actual invasion. Look here," Bill adds, holding the journal up for Joe to see, "I'm not making this up, the name is clearly O'Neill."

"Oh brother," Joe says, in a tone of subdued lament, "this is not the same O'Neil."

"This is not the chivalrous O'Neill who in the Civil War overcame an enormous force with only 50 of his own cavalry?"

Joe says, "No, that in fact is the same O'Neill."

"Well then," Bill brightens, about to seize a rare familial victory, "I rest my case."

"Billy," Joe says, a name that only Frances uses on occasion. "Does our uncle give you O'Neill's first name in his journal?"

"Not that I have seen," Bill protests, "he only writes the last name, 'O'Neill.'"

"One 'l' or two?"

"You asked me that already," Bill says and then looks back at the journal, "Okay," he says, searching, "yes, two 'l's."

"Okay, let me look at that news article that was stuck in the journal."

Bill hands over the small square of newsprint, and notices how Joe handles it carefully, almost reverently. The fragility of words on a thin slice of decaying paper, the delicacy of remembrance, so easily lost to the ages.

"Ah, here, 'John O'Neill' it reads."

"John?" asks Bill.

"The same. The chivalrous cavalry officer in the civil war, and the fellow who was also a leader in the Fenian invasion near Buffalo."

There is a lengthy pause before Bill says, in partial defeat, "Maybe 'Paddy' is a nickname."

Joe remains silent for a while. "You'll read about the other O'Neil a little later in the journals, though Uncle John more often refers to him simply as Paddy. One 'l' by the way in his last name."

Bill looks down at the carpet, and after a time he raises his head to look at Joe. "Not chivalrous? Savage and sudden? No cavalry?"

Joe takes a considered breath. "Maybe chivalrous."

CHAPTER 17

The Fenians Are Coming, The British Are Staying
Monday, October 2, 1933

"BILL IT'S GETTING LATE." He looks at his brother who appears eager to share a new passage in the journal. "I suspect you traveling salesmen keep very different hours from those of us in the farming life."

Bill looks at watch. "Oh my lord, it's 9:40! That's half ten with a twist, or is it half 9 and then some? The way Frances tells time."

Joe suspects that his brother is being a smart aleck. He says, "Okay, one more story before I, at least, go to bed."

Bill is already turning to the page that he wanted to share. "Here he is, our Uncle John, writing about news of the day, though," he adds parenthetically while looking up at Joe, "I'm sad to say I've been informed that this is not the O'Neil I thought it was.

> *O'Neill came over from Buffalo and seized the town of Fort Erie. Adult males were rounded up and read a proclamation that the Fenians fight was with the British and not with the Canadians. Those same townspeople were sent home under some kind of house arrest, and one of the young lads said that before being dismissed, the Fenians said they were going to Quebec. They asked, can you imagine, if Canada was seven miles across, and one of the young fellows answered that it was ten miles across. I'm not so sure we should be in envy of the American schools. They are always the big shots, are they not? It is said that a young*

lad From Fort Erie, a countryman, had gotten a neighbor's horse and went on a wild ride yelling that the Fenians were coming, sure he was like that American fellow years before in Boston wasn't he. The young lad was, come to find out, a veteran in the American Civil War, served with General Grant, joined for the bonus pay and adventure. Bet they never expected to meet one of their former comrades."

Bill stops and looks over at his brother. "Hello? This young lad, a Canadian mind you, had enlisted in the American civil war? Yes?" Bill is looking for just a small bit of validation, but it is not forthcoming.

"Bill, fascinating indeed. You know I've read this all before, is there much more just now?"

Bill shakes his head ever so slightly in disbelief, sighs, "Okay, almost done, but get this next part.

The Fenians themselves were made up of a number of former Civil War Veterans from all over the States. O'Neill himself, born in County Monaghan, was the Fenian's commanding officer. There were Fenian regiments from Tennessee, Cleveland, Buffalo, Kentucky, even a New Orleans company, the Louisiana Tigers they called themselves.

The renegade sampling was made into a kind of juicy sauce, so to speak. Never was there seen such a bungling camaraderie, just ripe for the picking. The Canadians fought valiantly, even if for the Queen. What a sorry lot from Buffalo. Of course they had history on their side. Even with the odd slaughter the tide was clearly going to turn as indeed it did in such short order."

Joe waits, and when it becomes clear that Bill has stopped his reading, at least his public reading, for the night, he says, "Okay, yes, well I'm glad to see you are picking up an interest in your history."

Bill takes a moment. "Speaking of which, what is this part about, 'even if for the Queen'?"

Joe considers the question carefully. He says, "July 1, 1867." He would have preferred to use the Father Reardon voice, but not with Frances asleep.

Bill pauses for a breath, says, "Yes," as meaningfully as he can.

"You don't know what I'm talking about, do you?"

"No."

Joe looks away for a moment, and when he turns back to his brother says, "When our uncle was writing this, Canada was on the cusp of becoming Canada."

Bill just looks at Joe without speaking, so Joe adds, "The day our homeland became the Dominion of Canada. But it was still a colony mind you. Self governing."

Bill says, "Sounds complicated."

Joe hesitates, appearing deep in thought and maybe, Bill thinks, carefully considering what he might add.

Joe wants to say that Uncle John is commenting on a deep, almost unexplainable, mish-mash of feelings about loyalty. The Queen. Separation and independence, especially for the Irish Canadians, the Catholics among them. He thinks about the subsequent histories of Canada, of Ireland, the bloody after-birth, especially for the latter.

Joe is exhausted, he looks at his brother and says, "Perhaps for another time," and slowly stands up, overcoming the stiffness in his joints.

Bill stands in turn, almost at attention.

Joe asks, "Where are you off to tomorrow?"

"Binghampton, Elmira."

Joe shakes his head, acknowledging. "Be safe in your travels."

Bill says, "I'll be seeing you before I go."

"Five o'clock at the barn?"

"Seven thirty at the dining room table."

Joe hesitates on his way toward the stairway, turns and says "She'll probably make you pancakes to go with your eggs and bacon. I prefer my Wheaties."

"'Breakfast of Champions'," Bill says enthusiastically, repeating the newly coined ad and then singing the familiar radio jingle "'Have you tried Wheaties?'"

Joe looks at his brother, "Salesman eh?" and then turns and heads for the stairs.

CHAPTER 18

Journal Volume 18
Monday October 2, 1933

Bill has been reading ahead in the journal, volume 7, skimming some entries that looked too mundane. He decides to get himself a glass of milk, anticipating the cold raw flavor of the milk straight from the ice box.

He takes his glass back into the parlor and puts it carefully on the table, not too close to the two journal books, one open, one closed. When he sits down, he looks across the room once again, taking in the silence and nighttime solitude of the farmhouse.

If he were to get up and walk over to one of the front windows, he might, just barely, see the light of the distant neighbor's house. At this hour probably all would be dark over there, except the single streetlamp that stands across the street from that residence.

He recalled a story Joe had told years ago about his valiant effort to oppose such a streetlight for Frances and himself. Joe felt that the streetlight would pollute the clarity of the night. Despoil the heavens. Ruin his occasional hobby of identifying the constellations. The town eventually won, resulting in a light that dispels the darkness for a small stretch of country road out in front of the farm. Progress.

He notices that across the parlor, the solitary table lamp creates a bubble of light around itself, its brilliance dimming as it spills outward. Bill glances at the area above the lamp, sees how the darkness progressively seeps in, more and more as he looks away across the room. The darkness wins, he thinks, unless it is opposed. Which takes great effort. The can-do spirit for the right cause. He should tell Joe about this. Dark and light, each has its own advantage.

Bill is not accustomed to such moments of reflection. He is a modern man on the go. He is the first in the family, after untold generations, to leave the country life behind, receding in the rear-view mirror of the snazzy motor car parked outside in the gravel driveway.

Bill rearranges himself in the chair, glances at the journals, wonders again if Joe made an error giving him two volumes out of order. Out of order is not something the Germans do. And look where it gets them, so soon after a devastating defeat, the war he missed, Deo Gratias. He is safe, he reassures himself, no more Canadian conscription for him, and now he is an American, all that much more protected. It's unlikely that his new country will allow itself to get into another such conflict. For one thing, there wouldn't be the money for it. He has seen firsthand some of the factory closures, and the broken glass on sidewalks as he drives carefully into some of the smaller cities, signs of civil unrest.

He decides to take a look at the other journal. As he closes the cover of volume 7, he considers how simple life would be with such easy closure, cover closed, the feel of old leather, the place where he lets his fingers rest awhile, before sliding them over the edge of the binding.

And then it's time to open the next volume, time traveling some 11 years ahead into the 1870's. He notices an increased shakiness in Uncle John's handwriting, a sign of aging perhaps. What had been a bumpy road to read, is now a text full of small ditches, cross-outs, over-written smears of ink, ink instead of pencil. More progress.

He reads:

> *I decided that I should go back and recall some of the events*
> *preceding before they are lost forever to the memory that is*
> *not unlike the great Falls at Niagara. Over they go, all those*
> *events and tellings of them and they are lost forever. Perhaps a*
> *few show up downstream, taken by great currents and lodged*

against an uninviting boulder along the river's edge. My great friend would remain, so often, mysterious, inscrutable. I notice, might I digress, that my language has been changing the longer I am in this country, Canada, across such a great sea. Father never did learn to read or write, at times staying with his native tongue for added measure. I've wondered whether this showed his lingering resentment of the English, to avoid using their language. But would I dare ask him this? So too to bring up what I had heard from my dear friend P. O. He who even with me on the odd occasion, down a deserted alley in town, would only speak of the "brotherhood" in the quietest of tones. Such staying power has this drive for secrecy. On one occasion, he saw Stephens himself in the great city of New York. He told me it was a kind of reunion which I at first did not appreciate. He brought home the newspaper, a treasure to me, as he would appreciate. We had our tradition of many years from when we first arrived in '49, how he would share his old copies of the various papers. This one, lying here before me, The New York Times June 25, 1866, the copy he gave me upon his return those many years ago, the title was "Mass Meeting of Fenians." The gathering in Jones Wood in that big city. 10,000 were said to have attended to hear the great man.

Bill puts the journal on the table, once again letting his fingers rest before they slide gently off the page.

He looks at his glass of milk, half emptied, and the two journals. He surveys the simplicity of these three things and the uncluttered room beyond. When he raises his head, he observes the air itself between the lamp, the chairs, air that unites and separates, its apparent emptiness, and he decides to breathe it all in, a deeply measured breath.

Not like himself, he is. This feeling pulled as if by some unseen attraction, forgetting for the time being that he is living a modern life, with running water, electric lights, automobiles. It is 1933 after all.

He looks back at the page that he had just been reading, its awkward style, its hilly cursive meanderings. These simple marks on the page made by the very writer of the words himself, not like cheap newsprint pounded out by the thousands from a monstrously large, noisy machine.

He is that close. That close to the stories the writer wished to keep alive, choosing which few to keep.

Bill raises his head and sighs, remembering a wisp of that which will not be remembered, and how is this even possible? As if for the first time, Bill notices a small painting on the wall just off to his right. The frame is dark wood, ornate, antiquated. The picture portrays a rugged seacoast, in the far distance a large schooner with all sails flying, leaning heavily into the waves. His eyes slowly shift away from the ship, out to the frame, moving carefully over the twists and turns of its wood, carved as if to forbid exit, a frame nearly as wide as the picture mounted within. At the very edge of the frame, he hesitates. He can see it, as certainly as he feels the unexpected touch along his shoulder, his forearm. A presence.

He knows what comes next.

CHAPTER 19

A Proclamation
Tuesday, October 3, 1933

IN THE PRE-DAWN DARKNESS of the barn and under its simple string of overhead lightbulbs, Joe thinks he sees a wavering shadow. This happens to him every so often. A sudden streak of movement, a flash, enough to have him turn to look at usually nothing.

Not this time. Further movement, a presence striding toward him. He stands quickly, putting one hand on the cow he's been milking, a warm hide of stability, "Hello?" he calls out with unusual force, a deep baritone warning.

"Don't shoot!" Bill calls out jokingly.

"The hell!" Joe answers, relieved, annoyed. "Your breakfast wasn't ready on time?"

As Bill comes into the barn, he stands momentarily at the threshold by the large barn doors, his features roughly displayed in sharp contrast with the darkness of the world beyond. Before taking one more step he says, "We've been invaded."

Joe takes a deep breath, "Mother of God," he says with great intensity, "the Germans?"

"Oh," Bill says, hesitating with his next half step, his answer a humble bowing forward, an apology. "The Americans."

Joe turns toward the cow, beginning to stroke its back, tap on the animal's body with his closed fist. It takes him a considerable period of time before he stoops down to pick up the stool he'd been using, and when he stands up and looks at his brother he says, "That was the last one. To milk."

Bill comes no farther, if he had a hat, he'd be passing it from one hand to the other. As it is, he shifts as he stands from one foot to the other while Joe finishes up what appears to be a well-rehearsed routine.

"Didn't mean to startle you," Bill says. He almost adds 'old boy.'

Without saying a word, Joe turns and walks away across the floor of the barn, disappearing now in deep shadow toward the back. When he returns, Bill can see that he is holding some sort of tool, axe perhaps, or shovel. Joe approaches slowly, walking beneath one bare lightbulb to the next, a succession of light and dark islands.

Bill remains standing at the entrance, and when Joe finally reaches him, Joe hands over a long and narrow wooden box. Bill holds the box with both hands, looks down at it and then raises his head to discover that his brother's face is impossible to read, a silhouette of shadow.

Joe says simply, "It's time to go in. I want to show you something."

The two brothers start their walk back to the house, to the beacon of light they see pouring out of the kitchen window, their shoes mutually crunching the gravel of the driveway, the only sound heard until they reach the kitchen door that Joe holds open.

The light in the kitchen is almost blinding, Bill says "Where do I put this?"

"Right there on the table. Frank won't be getting up just yet so we have a little time to look at it."

Bill carefully moves the china plate and cutlery that he will be using when breakfast is served and places the box on the thick oil cloth table covering. He stands back and asks, "So what is this?"

"Open it up," Joe says.

The box has a simple latch that Bill opens. He sees inside a series of papers rolled together.

"Take the larger one," his brother says over his shoulder.

Bill takes a heavy weight tube of paper, removes it from the box and unrolls it carefully on the table. He puts one hand at the top while Joe places a hand at the bottom so that they can read it.

To the people of British America:

> *We come among you as foes of British rule in Ireland. We have taken up the sword to strike down the oppressors' rod, to deliver Ireland from the tyrant, the despoiler, the robber. We have registered our oaths upon the altar of our country in the full view of heaven and sent out our vows to the throne of Him who inspired them. Then, looking about us for an enemy, we find him here, here in your midst, where he is most vulnerable and convenient to our strength. We have no issue with the people of these Provinces, and wish to have none but the most friendly relations.*
>
> *Our weapons are for the oppressors of Ireland, our bows shall be directed only against the power of England; her privileges alone shall we invade, not yours. We do not propose to divest you of a solitary right you now enjoy. We are here neither as murderers, nor robbers, for plunder and spoliation. We are here as the Irish army of liberation, the friends of liberty against despotism, of democracy against aristocracy, of people against their oppressors. In a word, our war is with the armed powers of England, not with the people, not with these Provinces. Against England, upon land and sea, till Ireland is free.*
>
> *To Irishmen throughout these Provinces we appeal in the name of seven centuries of British inequity and Irish misery and suffering, in the names of our murdered sires, our desolate homes, our desecrated altars, our million of famine graves, our insulted name and race — to stretch forth the hand of brotherhood in the holy cause of fatherland, and smite the tyrant where we can. We conjure you, our countrymen, who from misfortune inflicted by*

the very tyranny you are serving, or from any other cause, have been forced to enter the ranks of the enemy, not to be willing instruments of your country's death or degradation.

No uniform, and surely not the blood-dyed coat of England, can emancipate you from the natural law that binds your allegiance to Ireland, to liberty, to right, to justice. To the friends of Ireland, of freedom, of humanity, of the people, we offer the olive branch of these and the honest grasp of friendship. Take it Irishmen, Frenchmen, American, take it all and trust it. We wish to meet with friends; we are prepared to meet with enemies. We shall endeavor to merit the confidence of the former, and the latter can expect from us but the leniency of a determined though generous foe and the restraints and relations imposed by civilized warfare.

T. W. Sweeney. Major General commending the armies of Ireland

Bill stands back. The paper, so used to being rolled tightly in its casket of a container, begins to re-roll itself as soon as the brothers remove their hands.

"What in the Sam Hill?" Bill asks.

Joe looks at his brother. "It wasn't the Americans who invaded."

"Come again?"

"It was," and Joe leans back over to read the bottom of the page, "the armies of Ireland."

"Yeah," Bill says sarcastically, "the commending armies of Ireland. What did they do, compliment each other all the way?"

"I think it's a misprint, should read 'commanding.'"

Bill takes a moment, looks at the page, looks at his brother who is still reading the page, "I think it's symbolic."

Joe straightens up and looks at Bill. "Oh, high toned language there, eh? Is that how they talk in New York City?"

Bill answers, "With all due respect, I think it's all a bunch of hooey."

"Watch your tongue there young man," Joe says in almost complete sincerity.

"Tommyrot."

"Definitely not that."

"Blarney."

Joe hesitates, "Now that might have an element of truth." Joe looks away, considering this conversation, notices the coffee pot over on the counter. "Coffee?" he offers.

"Please."

They move the paper enough to arrange the coffee cups that Bill gets from the cupboard. Joe pours the coffee.

They sit solemnly for a moment, the council of two, until Bill has taken his first sip of a brew that is strong enough to make him say "Wow," as he replaces his cup on the saucer.

"I know," Joe says, "it has a certain effect."

"It's strong."

"Well," Joe begins, "they were men of passion."

"I mean the coffee."

"Ah," Joe says, I made it myself."

"I can tell. When does Frances get up?"

Joe turns to look toward the stairway, and when he turns back, he grips the coffee cup tightly, a worried look on his face.

Bill considers asking his brother if he is okay but decides a little diversion might be useful instead. "I mean, really, it's an embarrassment." It works. His brother looks over at him with renewed interest.

"How's that?" Joe asks.

"Americans invading our dear land of Canada."

"Fenians invaded. And, by the way there were two schools of thought among them."

"Joe, nonetheless, the Fenians were all Americans."

"They weren't All-Americans."

"What? Yes they were, and with that can-do thing run amok."

Joe considers this, "Interesting you should say that, I thought you sales types were all for push push push, you know, take over the next guy, come hell or high water, it's all about winning, isn't it?"

Bill sits back. "We're talking about a sovereign, or almost sovereign country."

"Sovereign now," Joe says, "Statute of Westminster 1931."

"Canada, we're talking?"

"Yes."

Bill looks at his brother, "Well I'll be. Took them awhile."

"It's still not over, but they are pretty independent."

Bill looks at his brother, "Pretty independent?"

After a moment Joe says, "Canada can be quite patient, don't you know."

Bill considers this, "We could use some of that."

They hear the sound of footsteps upstairs. Joe stands abruptly and rolls up the proclamation, carefully putting it back in the long narrow box.

Bill says, "What is that anyway?"

"I'd call it a declaration."

"No, I mean the box."

"Oh. That's nothing. It's convenient. I used to keep some old tools in it. Got it in an auction down the way."

Bill takes another sip of the coffee, despite his better judgment, "Why do you keep it in the barn?"

Joe turns to face Bill, raises a finger and points upstairs.

"Frances?"

When Joe responds, it's clear that he is keeping his voice down. "She's not so happy to be reminded of this history. Being an older sister there may be things that she's heard that I don't appreciate. You know how that is. The older ones know more."

"You might think so," Bill answers, attempting and failing to get Joe's eye. Joe seems focused instead on getting the box back to the barn.

Joe pushes his chair back, lifts the box, "I shan't be but a moment."

"I'll come with you," Bill says.

When they step outside, they stop for a moment mid-way to the barn to notice the sky lightening in the east. "Going to be a good day to get some work done," Joe says.

"And to drive to Binghampton," Bill adds.

When they walk into the barn, Bill follows as Joe goes to a remote spot in the back corner. He lifts a couple of burlap sacks, moves them aside and puts the box down neatly on a ledge.

"That's some hiding place," Bill says.

After Joe moves a couple of sacks over, partially hiding the box, he stands up and says, pointing to the house, "She has threatened to get rid of all the old papers."

"Oh my god," Bill says.

"Usually it's only when she is in a snit," Joe says. "Still."

They turn to head back toward the house but Bill hesitates, puts his arm on Joe's. Joe looks at Bill and says "It's going to be okay. Everything will turnout alright," before adding, "maybe."

"No," Bill says, "I wanted to tell you before. I had this experience last night."

Joe looks surprised. "Did you go out after I went to bed?"

"No. It was about... I was sitting in the parlor. Wind and water."

Joe remains motionless, despite every intention to return to the bright lights in the kitchen, the anticipation of a larger than normal breakfast, better than what typically might be expected. Frances always cooks extra when their periodic guest remains overnight.

"What pray tell are you talking about? Wind and water."

"Our friend Paddy sailed to Ireland, didn't he?"

"Paddy?" Joe says, surprised. He looks closely at his brother, before adding, "You read that in the journal." And then, "So you know how to read between the lines."

Bill hesitates, "It wasn't always legal was it? Whatever it was he was doing?"

Joe stops, takes an involuntary step back. After a moment he says, "I suppose it depends on who you are talking to."

Without speaking, the two brothers resume their walk toward the lights of the kitchen.

"Wait," Joe says, stopping in his tracks. He reaches for his brother's elbow, a supportive gesture to slow things down. As if to no one in particular he says in a very soft voice, "No, not in the journals." Joe turns to face Bill, sighs and says, "Some stories never got recorded."

"How's that?"

They are very near the kitchen door, and they can see Frances moving about through the lace curtained windows. Joe leans very close to Bill's ear. "They were told to me."

CHAPTER 20

Paddy Aboard the W. T. Robb
Friday, June 1, 1866

J.D., THIS LETTER IN particular, my dear friend, please keep under your hat. Speaking of which, I'm picturing that threadbare tweed cap that I think you've worn since you landed on our dear country's shores. It's time for an update my friend, I think you need a bit of brim in the next hat to protect you from the fierce Ontario summer sun. I'm thinking Derby, or maybe Stetson, eh? The Mrs. won't know what to think and the cows won't complain. I am seeing a bit of the world as you know, and it has its effects.

Okay enough of the haberdashery talk. I wanted to record some events of the recent day in detail and I am entrusting this letter to you for safe keeping. I ask your indulgence for including detail that may seem excessive, but I am keenly aware that history is being made. It's my privilege to be but one witness, if not an actor in a minor role.

So here is where I begin. It was hot. That I remember for sure.

The Thirteenth Battalion, commanded by Lieutenant Colonel Alfred Booker had left Hamilton and was on its way to Dunnville. The town was all abuzz. Someone later told me that when they had left The Great Western Railway Station in Hamilton, a brass band of the British Sixteenth Regiment played "The Girl I Left Behind" among other stirring tunes, to the great cheers of the gathering assembled.

I had to be precise to be of help. I had to know the names of the armed associations. I didn't need to know the names of the music played, however. "The Girl I Left Behind" indeed. The Lieutenant Colonel, it was later reported, departed without a map, or a pencil and paper, and without his horse. The troops lacked all basic necessities, few knapsacks, no canteens, outdated rifles and only five rounds of ammunition for each of the troops.

One had to query, what were they thinking? Such pompous, glorified notions, the military itself often a haggard volunteer group led by the cream of the business and social worlds of Toronto, military action being an important social steppingstone.

Booker's top man, the British commander of the whole operation, Lieutenant Colonel George Peacocke, had only a postal map torn from an almanac, on a scale of ten miles to the inch, showing mail delivery routes but no roads or topographical features. This was later shared with me by my colleague in subterfuge, Charles Clarke, himself no stiff. He would call himself, only to me, a Frontier Constabulary undercover agent. His pedigree was one of experience rather than moneyed estate. He was a Toronto police sergeant and a British Army veteran who once told me he had seen action at a place called Kandahar during the First Afghan War. I shared with him some of my overseas travels and we got along famously, if very secretively.

In Dunnville there were reports that the Fenians had invaded Fort Erie and were marching on Port Colborne. One fellow told me that he saw refugees, wagons overloaded with household belongings heading out of the Niagara region. They said they'd heard that the Fenians were intent on destroying the Welland Canal.

As if Dunnville weren't lively enough that day (perhaps 'lively' isn't the best choice of terms, seeing as what was to come), the Thirteenth marched into the centre of town shortly before 4 pm. They had come by way of Caledonia to pick up four officers and forty-four men of the Caledonia Rifle Company. The Battalion was billeted among the homes in town and some of the soldiers were given dinner by townspeople, but not everyone got to eat. It was reported that Booker himself, as was often the case, had little trouble securing a meal for himself.

This hubbub of frenzied anticipation, a veritable brouhaha, was not long to last. It all succumbed to an order from Peacocke himself to abandon Dunnville and advance to Port Colborne by train, a one hour's journey. The order was received that same evening.

A friend later told me that with all the running about, he overheard one of my father's long-time customers say to him, "Mr. O'Neil, I'm so glad that you've kept your shop open!" You might say there was an air of panic to be sure. My father was never a quitter.

Our family's store often had business with Mr. Lachlan McCallum, the Scotsman down by the Feeder Canal. Over time as you may know he built up a small empire of stores, mills, shipyards and, perhaps most importantly, a fleet of tugs for towing rafts of grain, lumber and the like. I think it was a couple years back that he formed the Dunnville Naval Brigade, a marine rifle company. He wasn't always the most pleasant man you'd meet but you had to admire his ingenuity. His steam powered tugboat christened the W.T. Robb, would make the area locally famous. It was reported to be one of the fastest vessels on the Great Lakes and it was only a matter of time before the wily Scotsman would approach the government about outfitting the fine craft to be a fast-running gunboat.

I always loved the water as you know and looked forward to any excuse on behalf of the family store to visit the shipyard. I'd spend a little time in Port Maitland and sometimes hitch a ride out on the Lake. I particularly enjoyed seeing the lighthouse at Mohawk Island down the way. It's hard to believe that fine structure is almost 20 years old already. The Naval Brigade was made up of our local merchants, small business leaders from town, so of course I knew many of them. They thought I had an interest in joining their ranks.

I think my father had his own idea what I was about and he was not about to let any of the Donohoes know, at least not right away. He was secretly supportive of the time I spent away from the store, under the illusion that I was helping these Fenians. Later the Donohoes, as you well know, were furious under the same illusion. Such was the secret I swore to keep. An actor, eh? I was not about to aid this branch of the brotherhood that was hell bent on troubling Canada. It's Ireland I'm about, and Stephens is my man.

I would get another chance to sail that very day of high excitement. A telegram arrived with orders to set off for Port Colborne, where men of the Welland Battery would join the Dunnville Naval Brigade and we would then steam further east to the mouth of the Niagara River. It was thought that we would pursue retreating Fenians leaving Fort Erie, chase them down and deploy the Welland gunners and marines along the bank of the river.

With a wink and a nod I was allowed to board when the W.T.Robb was about to leave Dunnville that evening. While some eyebrows were raised, it was understood that permission had been granted from a senior unnamed officer. That officer, I can tell you but only you, was none other than Macdonald himself. He'd ordered secret service chief Gilbert McMicken who in turn was looking for the odd man such as myself, to infiltrate, something he'd become rather adept at doing during the American's Civil War.

I do recall that we left Port Colborne in a hurry around 4 A.M. after the Welland Battery boarded. We numbered about seventy-one soldiers, steaming at high speed as a fine mist lifted off the lake. It was a morning of calm water, a slowly dawning sky, an open horizon free of any other vessels out on the Lake.

When we reached the mouth of the river, a small white craft approached us, the first boat we had seen, and it was understood quickly that this arrival was to be expected, no alarm need be raised. I boarded swiftly and by myself, fearful at one point of losing my balance, not wanting to bring any more attention to my singular departure. I bid the lads who saw me my best wishes for their coming adventure.

There would be, that morning, no retreating Fenians.

CHAPTER 21

After Binghampton
Thursday, October 5, 1933

"J_{OE}?"

"Yes? Am I wrong? Your voice sounds tentative there Bill. Like a penitent."

"I have a confession to make."

"Bingo eh? How about that!" After a pause he adds, "And you can tell me all about your last trip and how you found Binghampton."

"On the map," Bill shoots back quickly. "Very handy and usually free at the Esso stations."

Joe had walked out to meet his brother when he heard Bill's gangster-looking car pull in the driveway. He had helped his brother bring in an expensive looking leather valise while Bill brought the bag that held his sales receipts. Frances was out at the moment and in short order the brothers settled themselves at the kitchen table while Joe poured two cups of very dark coffee.

"We also have some unfinished business from our last conversation or two," Joe adds, "But what pray tell is your confession?"

Bill looks down into the depths of the coffee, and when he looks up at Joe again, says in all seriousness, "No milk?"

Joe mutters something about Frances being better at attending to such things, goes over to the ice box and brings back the white ceramic pitcher, very cold to the touch.

As Bill pours the milk he says, "Remember when we talked about the falling out?"

Joe watches as Bill carefully places the pitcher back on the thick red and white checked oilcloth covering the table. He begins to smile, says "There've been quite a few I'd say. Which ones are you referring to?"

"Uncle John, our Father, Paddy, and our grandfather. How grandfather didn't want Paddy coming around after a while?"

Joe pauses a moment, sips his coffee, black, the way he likes it. Unadulterated. "Actually it was mostly between Uncle John and our grandfather. Grandfather wanted nothing to do with the likes of Paddy. I think, mind you this is speculation, that our grandfather was suspicious and maybe jealous of Uncle John's ability to read and write. And then there were the political issues. But, nonetheless, Uncle John was a long-time pal of Paddy as was our father. Uncle John wasn't about to stop seeing him, if only on the sly in town. He and our father both, good chums of Paddy they were, and stayed so if on the QT."

As Bill sips his coffee, Joe looks at him closely. They share an extended silence during which Joe looks quite uneasy.

Bill finally says "What?"

Joe says, "That's what I want to know. What's the confession?"

"Oh," Bill says, "It's that I didn't know about the falling out."

Joe looks even more closely at his brother. "You just said you did, and described it, the players, by god."

"No, I mean I hadn't heard about it before you told me."

"What?"

"You had said 'you know about the falling out, right?', and I acted like I did. But I didn't."

"Oh for Pete's sake." Joe sits back in his chair and says, "You've been thinking about this since your last stop here?" he looks at Bill closely, "I'd call that a case of compunction."

"I'd call it having a finely tuned conscience."

"Saints preserve us! So," Joe looks at Bill slyly, "Do you have any other confessions?"

"More than likely, but I'll leave those for Father Reardon."

"Have mercy on us all. You want them broadcast from the Confessional?"

"His voice, you mean."

Both brothers hesitate, one after the other they take a sip of coffee. It's very hot.

Bill says, "On my way here, I thought about picking up a cake for you and Frances. Nice little bakery in Geneva."

"Oh," Joe says, sounding delighted.

"But I didn't," Bill says.

After a moment Joe says, "They say it's the thought that counts." He looks down at his cup resting on the table, takes a moment to push the handle one way, then the other. "I don't agree."

Bill holds his hands open near his cup, says simply, "No cake."

"Is there anything else you don't have?"

Bill says, "Well, I don't have all day."

Joe thinks that his brother is kidding, though he is not entirely sure. This is the brother who gets to visit the big cities, sees what they have to offer for better and worse, richer and poorer.

"In that case," Joe says, "we have this other unfinished business."

"Okay," Bill voices hesitantly.

Joe takes another moment to look at his brother, finally he says, you don't remember, do you?"

"About what?"

"Our unfinished business, I just said that."

Bill raises his eyebrows, asks "Do I owe you money?"

"Jesus, Mary and Joseph."

"I know," Bill says, "you're saying that prayerfully."

"You really are the wheeler and dealer, aren't you."

Bill smiles, relieved. "I don't owe you money."

"Yes, maybe—but that's not the point."

"How much?" Bill asks, now clearly giving Joe the business.

Joe takes a sip from his cup, as much to gather his thoughts as to taste the coffee, which is less hot. He starts by saying, "It's actually not a bad thing that Frances isn't here at the moment."

"Oh? How so?"

Joe sighs. "Simply put, well, like I told you, maybe you don't remember, she doesn't have a lot of tolerance for talking about the past. Perhaps you picked up on that."

Bill thinks about this for a moment, "Not particularly," and then remembering, "oh, the bit about all your keepsake newspapers. Paddy's papers. Frances doesn't like the clutter."

Joe tilts his head, says "Paddy? Not Paddy's papers. And trust me, it's not about clutter. That would be too easy."

"You said they came from the owner of the trunk, Paddy's trunk, so Paddy's old papers."

"Ah, I see, okay."

"I'm glad someone does."

"The newspapers were from Paddy and some from Uncle John as well. And…" Joe hesitates, clearly figuring out how to proceed.

"See," Bill says jumping in, this is where I missed out on all the stories, all that you older ones knew."

Joe takes a moment, "You might not have missed as much as you think."

"What?"

"A lot of the older members of our family could be pretty tight lipped."

Bill considers this. "What is it with our family, all this hush-hush business? Happy days are here again says the President. What do we have to fear?"

"That's now," Joe says, "in the modern era." He takes time again to gather his thoughts, consider how he wants to proceed. Finally he says, "See, remember father died in 1914, so that's nineteen years ago now, and then his older brother, our dear Uncle John passed away…"

"…Just a few years after," Bill interrupts.

"1918. Here's what I want to tell you. After father died, Uncle John took me aside, he knew I enjoyed politics and reading the papers. I think his younger brother's passing triggered something he'd been putting off for a long time. Meanwhile Paddy had died, I think in 1900."

"I would have been 3 then. I don't really remember him."

Joe has a faraway look in his eyes and Bill waits for him to speak, as if waiting for Joe to come out of a trance. At last Joe says, taking on a magisterial tone, "He says to me, 'When I gave you the trunk, not everything was still there. I had taken out his papers.' I corrected him, see, and said 'No, Uncle John there's plenty of papers that were in it.' And he says to me, I'll never forget it, 'Not the newspapers. His papers, the ones he wrote."

Bill, for once, resists the urge to push for immediate clarification about whatever in hell his brother is talking about. It is as if an angel taps him on the shoulder and tells him that he should wait, this time. In just so many unspoken words. This is new information, and it's complicated. The angel adds, by way of post script, or maybe it's Bill's own fledgling consciousness, please don't say again how you were always left out of the stories.

Joe looks down at his cup of coffee, decides against picking it up. When he looks up at Bill he says, "I realize this may not make sense yet, so here's the deal, as you might say in your line of work. Sometime after Paddy died, Uncle John approached me and said that he would like to pass on Paddy's trunk to me, and that there were many old newspapers still in it that I might value. That was probably around 1905 or 6."

"I would have been 8 or 9," Bill says.

"And I was 11 or 12," Joe adds. "It was kind of a legacy thing. Paddy had given our uncle his old trunk as Paddy was facing his own end, I would guess that would be in the late 90's. They had been very close years back when the Donohoes first arrived in Canada, I think I explained before that the O'Neil's had given the best of welcomes to the poor souls, our father, Uncle John and our grandparents."

Bill takes a deep breath, decides to take a sip of his coffee, finds that it is dying a lukewarm death of its own. He tries to hear the angel's voice again but cannot, for the life of him. Nonetheless he senses that some sort of presence is not far away. He keeps his peace.

"We're talking now," Joe takes a deep breath, "coming up to 1915,

1916. Uncle John is 85 or 86, and I'm feeling a bit of remorse, see, for having already passed on the trunk to you, my studious younger brother. Something I never told him. But it wouldn't have mattered in the long run."

"But you gave me an empty trunk. Or nearly empty one," Bill says, no longer able to contain himself.

"Remember," Joe says, "we talked about this. I emptied it out for your use and I kept the newspapers for myself. I knew you wouldn't be interested in them and we all, your older siblings and myself, wanted to support you in your high school work. We knew it would help you keep your books and homework organized."

Bill tilts his head, gives a look of not understanding.

"The war, my boy, the big one. You would be coming of age. Canada had a military conscription act coming up, 1916 I think it was. Only the Canadians who had particularly close British ties were in favor of it. The French Canadians were not. You know where our family came from. We had our own history with the British." Joe pauses. "We all did whatever we could to keep you out of it."

Bill considers all this information. He recognizes a pull of closer ties to family, if not to history. The unseen, the unknown, the many acts of kindness toward one's self that were never revealed by the others. The humility in that, for both the giver and the receiver.

Bill shifts in the chair, reaches for the coffee cup, touches it and lets it stand alone on the heavy oil cloth. He asks, "What did Uncle John say about the papers he had taken out of the trunk, Paddy's papers?"

Joe takes another deep breath. It sounds to Bill like a sigh. "Paddy had written letters to Uncle John over the years, or maybe more like historical essays. Told Uncle John to never show them to anyone else. His request was to keep them in a place where they could be re-opened but only after a long time."

Bill is intrigued. "Like how long?"

"Uncle John said Paddy wanted them unread until the next century."

"Next century? The 21st?"

"Exactly."

"Jesus." Bill adds, "I say that prayerfully." After a moment he adds, "So what did Uncle John do?"

"He did what Paddy requested. Paddy was quite specific with his wishes."

After a pause, Bill says "Yes?"

"After Paddy's death, Uncle John gave the letters and essays to the University of Toronto. In care of the History department."

Bill lets that sink in for a moment.

"Took them personally on the train, quite a load he told me, one or two boxes," Joe continues. "I forget who it was he talked to there, some big wig."

Joe turns to look out the window. It's a bright sunny morning, and the fields lay flat from the harvested corn and crops of the past summer, giving him a wide and deep perspective across the distance of his land and his neighbor's. A cold front had come through, the light is brilliantly clear, with a chilly silver overtone. Joe makes a nearly inaudible murmur.

"Can't you just imagine him rattling along in the passenger compartment, the T,H, and B train edging along the western shore of Lake Ontario. Every now and then this old, distinguished farmer sneaking a view of what he considered to be the sacred holdings entrusted to him, not wanting to draw attention from his fellow passengers."

Bill waits for what feels like a long time before asking, "Do you...can you..." before deciding to be more straightforward, "I'd love to know what he shared with you. Uncle John. About Paddy."

"Yes," Joe answers and then stops speaking. Bill can see that Joe's attention has shifted to something else. Finally Joe adds, "I wanted to tell you one more thing about your uncle and yourself."

"Me?"

"Hello?" Joe says, meaning who else?

"Okay."

"Remember I said, whether you were aware of it or not, that the family was pretty focused on your future and the fact of the great war rising across the sea?"

Bill does not answer. He looks expectantly toward his brother.

"You have your uncle John to thank for the suggestion that may have been the clincher, in your case. The reason you stayed safely over here, out of harm's way. I don't think anybody ever told you this."

"Glory be to God," Bill says quietly, in a voice that sounds at least half prayerful.

"He was the one who suggested that we all lie about your age. He had strong feelings about an Irishman getting into that war."

Bill turns to look out the window, the space, the freedom of such distance across the fields. When he turns back to face Joe he says, "The T,H, and B train."

"Toronto, Hamilton and Buffalo," Joe says, as if Bill doesn't remember the name. "You remember its nickname?"

"To hell and back," Bill says, raising his cold cup of coffee in salute.

CHAPTER 22

A Miniature Salute
Thursday, October 5, 1933

"I thought I was just lucky, about the war," Bill says.

"Apparently you were right about that," Joe answers.

Bill sits back, lowers his head, staring at the place where the cup rests on the table. After a silence he says, "You know, it's funny. You think history is just a page filled with a list of events. It all precedes you and you had nothing to do with it. All done by others. Almost all at random. Starting way back."

"And then…" Joe anticipates where his brother might be going.

"And then you find out that, like it or not, you and a million others are all connected like strings."

"Yes?" Joe responds.

"Minding my own business, getting out of school, walking in the fields, bringing in the cows. Outside our little town of Dunnville," Bill hesitates. "And here I have been touched, little did I know, by Archduke Franz Ferdinand."

Joe looks at his brother, "Or untouched, in your case. That grand fellow's assassination started the great war to end all wars, so they say." After a moment he adds, "Well, how about Oliver Cromwell centuries before?"

Bill shifts in his chair, says "Daniel O'Connell."

"Now you're talking," Joe agrees. "Leave us not forget Michael Collins, dead now these past eleven years."

"Who?"

Joe gives his brother a look of disbelief. "I thought you kept up to date with the times."

Joe turns to look out the window again and when he turns to look back at Bill, he says, "Dunnville High School taught virtually nothing about the 600 years of misery that the Irish experienced at the hands of lordly kings and queens." After a moment he adds, "Resentment lingers in the air, like a slowly evaporating fog."

Bill raises his eyebrows, shakes his head affirming the sentiment, the language.

"By the way," Joe says, "George V is going to be on the new Canadian dollar next year."

"Bully for him," Bill says, and then, "If history were different, if we'd had family ties to some grand English Earl rather than being a family evicted from a hovel outside Limerick…"

"You might have seen action over there and not lived to tell the tale."

Bill smiles at his brother, "Or the Earl may have paid my way into a cushy job, uniform or no."

"Actually," Joe says, "we've learned that war is not what those first soldiers thought it was in 1914. It's not a football game with live ammunition." After a moment he adds, "The romance is gone."

There is an extended silence before Bill adds, "Maybe it was the war that ends all wars."

The two brothers remain quiet for a moment, a solemn remembrance shared, sitting at the farmhouse table. Their own miniature salute.

"It's complicated," Joe says, breaking the silence.

Bill is not sure what his brother means, and Joe can see this.

"For all the evil of violence, there is the fact of asserting one's rights."

"Yes," Bill says a bit uncertainly.

"Life, liberty and all that. Freedom from oppression."

Bill continues to watch where Joe is going with this, nonetheless, his brother's next comment feels abrupt, sudden, and he will later wonder how long Joe had been wanting to share this.

Joe, no longer looking over the top of his glasses, says, "You know, by now, that dear Paddy was a member of the Fenian organization, right?"

Bill almost answers 'sort of', but then recalls a journal passage, "Uncle John wrote somewhere that he and Paddy met quietly at times and Paddy mentioned a brotherhood."

"Well yes, though he was involved in more than one, you might say."

Bill decides to wait this moment out, see what Joe might say.

"You have to read between the lines," Joe says, "but the implication is pretty clear. Fenians. Our cousin Dan doesn't agree, by the way. He makes that very obvious. And he has been the keeper of the journals."

Bill looks at his brother, asks "Does Dan know about Toronto? Paddy's papers?"

Joe looks out the window briefly, says in a lower tone of voice, "Let's just say that he's not interested in hearing from me any more on the subject."

CHAPTER 23

St. Albany

Thursday, October 5, 1933

T HEY HAD TAKEN A BREAK. Joe had to check on one of the cows in the barn. Bill took the opportunity to stretch his legs, wander through the rambling farmhouse.

When Bill returns to the kitchen, Joe is coming in the door.

"She's doing pretty well, I'm happy to report," Joe says as he takes off his jacket and hangs it up. "He, on the other hand, was pretty shaky in his story telling."

"Uncle John, you mean, what he told you." Bill clarifies.

Joe takes a seat at the table and looks directly at Bill. A delayed glance, sustained by unspoken misgivings. Slowly, gradually, Joe's appearance unwinds, settles back into a shared moment, innocent secrecy approved.

The deep mellifluous voice asks, "By god, this conversation calls for the spirits. What do you say?"

Spirits, Bill is thinking, sudden visions, the sensation of an arm being touched lightly, no one in sight.

"You wouldn't be wanting Canadian Club, no rye, no sir. But Crown, eh? Shall we have a snort or two?"

"Keen idea!" Bill answers enthusiastically, and then with an edge of hesitation, "it's not yet 3pm."

"Correct."

"And Frances isn't here."

"Correct again." Joe considers something. "She prefers a sweet wine.

Ladies often do, I don't know whether you noticed that. Of course you're settling down now I gather, no longer on the circuit with the gals, so to speak."

As Joe stands up to fetch the whisky, Bill says, "That's quite an honor you had."

"What's that?" Joe asks reaching up to a top cupboard shelf, finding the bottle and bringing it over to the table.

"That he spoke with you personally, Uncle John. I never appreciated back then what he must have gone through, leaving Ireland, such as they did."

Joe is getting a couple of glasses for the occasion. "Of course he spoke with you too, he spoke with all of us. He was a good man, I'll tell you."

Bill hesitates, "I'm thinking about Paddy's papers, though, that he would share them with you. Personally."

Joe looks at the two empty glasses for a moment. "He didn't actually share the papers, see."

"But he did talk with you about them," Bill says, hoping this is true.

Joe raises the bottle of Crown, "He told me some stories about them, maybe some other stories too," adding "neat?"

Bill answers, "Swell indeed."

Joe remains poised with the bottle near Bill's empty glass. Bill looks up at his brother, says, "Oh, a little water, please."

"I don't have ice."

"No, that's fine."

After Joe fixes Bill's drink, he pours one for himself and sits down. A moment passes and he says, "There was this one story I'll never forget about St. Albany."

"Albany?"

"I guess, but he would pronounce it St. Albany." Joe looks at his glass of whisky, the clear amber liquid, a couple fingers high, settled in the tumbler. He reaches for it, shakes the whisky from side to side and puts the glass back down without taking a drink.

"You know at times he would sashay back into his native Irish, Gaelic, you know, without realizing it. At least I think so. I only asked him about this once, when he had done so repeatedly one evening and he seemed surprised, interrupted. I decided then and there, given his age and his world of experience, to just let it all flow.

"He spoke quickly, you might remember, sometimes letting his voice drop down to the softest of whispers, as if he were running out of air or time or energy. I wasn't sure that I always heard him correctly. 85 or 86 he was then, and by that time thin as a rail. He always was a short slender kind of fellow, you remember. Leprechaun, he once told me, what his mates used to call him. If I didn't understand something, nine times out of ten I would just keep listening. He enjoyed the talk, like it was music, needing nothing more than a single listener to complete a tune." Joe takes his first sip of the Crown, notes its brightening bite, says "Yessir."

For a moment, Bill thinks that the discussion might be ending prematurely, such is Joe's protracted delay as he stares at the glass, the whisky having settled once again in the tumbler. Bill offers "'Albany'," to jump start his brother, and it works.

Joe looks directly at Bill and says, "He looked at me straight in the eye like this, see, one time and said, 'He fought for the Confederates you know.' Well wasn't I flabbergasted. I thought he might have been speaking about Canada, the work toward confederation that was going on but he straightened me out, then and there. 'Robert E. Lee and that bunch of fellows' he says."

At this, Bill decides to take his first sip. Bracing as it is, he wishes Joe had put in less water. To the look he gives Joe, Joe responds, "Mmmhmmm. I couldn't make sense of it either. Thought our dear uncle had lost it."

"Confederacy?" Bill asks, "not *the* Confederacy?" He might as well have just heard that President Roosevelt was a closet Nazi, or dictator as some of the more conservative papers were describing the great President.

"Wait," Bill says, taking another sip, wiping his mouth with his index finger, feeling his moustache as he swipes clean the whisky that he'd almost spilled. "You're telling me that Uncle John's old friend Paddy O'Neil was not only a member of the Fenians but also a traitor in the American Civil War?"

Joe sits back, smiles, holds his glass of whisky in the manner of someone who might be toasting himself, or maybe an invisible party at the table. He shifts his tone of voice. "Of course it depends on which side you were on. I met a fellow at the Geneva hotel, salesman like yourself, speaking in a very deep accent, Georgia, I think. You know how he described the U.S. Civil War?"

"The war to keep my black slaves?"

"The War of Northern Aggression."

Both brothers shake their heads, and in turn take a good belt of their respective drinks.

"Godfrey," says Bill. After a moment he says, "Does Frances know all this?"

Joe looks at his brother with a hint of a smirk, "Not about the Civil War business, no. That's for you and me to know, and well, Dan." Joe takes a deep breath, "As far as the Canadian invasion…"

"…The Fenians."

"Yes, that gets interesting, see. Frances is old enough to have heard how our father would defend Paddy to our grandfather, who, remember, would have nothing to do with Paddy."

"Our father knew about Paddy's politics and was okay with it?"

Joe thinks about this for a minute. "Honestly, from what I know, I don't think anybody understood what Paddy was about. Just the smallest hint that he might be favoring the Fenians was enough to stop all conversation. For our grandfather, there were bad memories about secret societies in the old country. No tolerance for hearing anything more about it. No sir. Discussion ended and walk out of the room if you can't keep your peace, our father used to say about our grandfather."

"The Fenians were not exactly a secret society."

"No. But close enough. Stirring up trouble, after all you've gone through to get here, to get to Canada, from their point of view. For our grandfather, at least. Start a whole new life."

Bill considers something, "Maybe the earlier generation was ready to let go of Ireland."

Joe sits back, stares at this brother. He slowly puts a finger to his lips, quietly says, "Never breathe a word like that."

Bill senses that this time, he has stepped over a line.

Joe says very quietly, "There aren't words for it yet, it's too raw. An affair of the heart. For what was and could have been. There. Not here." After a moment he repeats, "Let go of Ireland? Hardly."

It's a relief to Bill when after a considerable pause, Joe says, "It says something about how close our father and Uncle John and Paddy were in the middle of all that was going on," adding almost inaudibly, "and was to come."

Bill is thinking about his sister and asks, "Where does Frances fit in here?"

"You know Frances. Dear Frances. For all her grand graces, things are either right or they are wrong, not much room in the middle. That became her view."

"What do you mean?"

"She worshipped him. Father." Something in Joe's tone remains unfinished.

Bill asks, "Until?"

"Until some of those arguments in the parlor. You remember them?"

Bill honestly doesn't. Joe can see this. Joe says, "Maybe you were upstairs studying." After a moment Joe adds, "Anyway, whenever Frances had a chance to read the Toronto papers, she'd be very worried, upset. She agreed with grandfather's idea of the Fenians, more than whatever father may have thought of them. For her, Fenians were threatening, they were. It wasn't pretty."

Bill looks at his brother. "Lord save us."

Joe adds, "I know you say that prayerfully."

"Where the hell was I?"

"Well if you weren't upstairs, maybe you were chasing the cows home. You were actually quite good at that."

Bill shakes his head back and forth, looks out the window, takes a good size sip and puts the glass back on the table. "Okay," he says in the voice of one wanting to back up, "so what was this about Albany? That John told you about?"

"St. Albany. The story as he told it had to do with Paddy helping the Confederates conduct a raid from Canada."

Bill stares at his brother. "Again I have to ask, you're being serious," he says, primarily to reassure himself.

"He told me that there were some Confederate soldiers who had been captured in the States and who'd escaped to good old neutral Canada, a part of the British Empire at the time, you know. From Canada they were hatching a plan to conduct a raid, divert attention away from the action in the South of the States and steal a bunch of money for the Confederate treasury.

"Uncle John got me interested in this history, hearing about all this from someone who was so closely connected to it at the time. I've done some extra reading myself. Remember it was war time in the States, Canada was a tad nervous with the big country to its south, always was, I think. You know, by the way, that the St Lawrence river was referred to as a military front during the War of 1812.

"So there they are, Canadians wondering whether the Americans might attempt another invasion like 1812 and now there are all these Union troops with battle experience. When there are wars and conflicts there are going to be spies. This is where our dear Paddy came in, I think. He could get some information about the Americans and relay this back to our government."

"What do you mean our government?" Bill asks.

"Right, sorry, the Canadian government, the soon to be born Canadian government."

"So he was a spy?" Bill ventures.

"Some kind of clandestine agent."

Bill considers this. "I'm feeling better about him. Maybe he was like a male Mata Hari."

"Hardly."

"What if he were a double agent, one for the Fenians and one for the Confederates, pretending to be one of each?" Bill pauses, blows air out slowly, shakes his head. "Makes me wonder all the more what our father thought about Paddy's shenanigans." When he sees the look on Joe's face, he adds, "Maybe that's the wrong word."

Joe looks at his glass, picks it up and takes a long drink. When he puts his glass down, he says, "Remember, Uncle John started talking with me after father had died and that was 1914."

"1914" Bill repeats, a reverent call and response.

"So this was many years later, what, we're talking 40, almost 50 years after this St Albany affair," Joe says, and after a moment adds, "Father never breathed a word about any of this to us, as you know."

Bill considers this, takes a moment to look at his drink, and decides not to pick up the glass. He looks at his brother, in a cautious tone of voice he says, "I wonder how much our father knew about Paddy?"

Joe looks at his brother, raises his shoulders, his upraised palms, the soundless gesture, who knows?

The brothers share the silence, the solemnity of regret, the vision of a dead end.

After several moments, Joe says, "If only father would have talked with us."

Bill hesitates, "Even a little, like Uncle John did with you."

Joe looks at his brother. "If only Uncle John could have shared more," he pauses, "more of the treasure trove that is locked up in Toronto."

"The history department," Bill adds.

"Right."

"Not in our lifetime," Bill says. "Maybe for our kids to know."

Joe tilts his head, looks at his brother over the top rim of his glasses, "You'll have to get married first."

"Ha, yes. Well, I might be working on that."

"Do tell." After a couple of moments, Joe says, "If you get moving on this Bill, those kids might live into the next century, God willing."

Bill considers this, raises his eyebrows, says, "So they'll get to read whatever it was Paddy wrote."

"Right."

"And if you ever have kids, Joe, same with them."

They both consider this notion, future progeny, and enjoy a momentary quiet.

After a moment Bill says, "Still, if only we had asked questions back then, when we had those dear relatives. But what did we know? We were only kids. In Canada, safe and sound."

Joe thinks about this, says "Even if we had asked, I'm not sure how they would have answered. Remember, these relatives, some of them survived the worst of the worst, the famine, the ships they called coffin ships, so called because so many died en route to Canada. Probably glad to get that all behind them." Joe pauses for a moment, "Some things didn't feel so safe back in those days. It wasn't like now in 1933, when a lot of the old struggles have settled."

Bill looks closely at Joe, reaches for his glass, takes a significant swallow. "A lot of the struggles have settled, eh? You heard about this new party over in the old sod, Fine Gael?"

Joe raises his eyebrows first, and then raises his glass to Bill. "I didn't know you were keeping up. This just happened in September. Fine Gael indeed."

"The Syracuse hotel has a subscription to the New York Times. Most of the other sales gents were reading the sports section about the Yankees, so I grabbed the part they weren't reading. You know then about the Blue Shirts."

"Indeed I do, you know their history?" Joe asks.

"A bit."

"A major party there called Fianna Fail, was re-elected earlier in the year, and a fellow you may have heard of, Eamon de Valera, dismissed a commissioner by the name of O'Duffy."

"Joe, I didn't get into this level of detail."

"Well hang on, you might find this interesting. This O'Duffy fellow goes on to form another organization that he renames the National Guard, whose roots are in the pro-Treaty side of the Irish Civil War."

"Okay, so I'm not exactly up on some of this. The Irish had a Civil War?" Bill asks.

"I'll give you the match-box summary. The whole shebang started, you might say with the Easter Uprising in 1916 that lasted all of a week or two."

"Joe, hang on, some of this I've heard about. From a fellow at a bar several years ago. In New York."

"At a bar several years ago, drinking, right?"

"Well of course, but don't let me get you off track. Interesting man, maybe a story for another day. Please go ahead."

"Well okay, so conflict persisted, which turned into Guerrilla warfare and that lasted until 1921 when an Anglo-Irish Treaty was reached. This gave Ireland a fair degree of independence but not total independence from Britain. The treaty was seen as a necessary step toward full independence and championed by leaders like Michael Collins whom you say you haven't heard of. Others in Ireland wanted nothing to do whatsoever with Britain and before you know it something like an 11 month civil war broke out between the pro and anti-treaty forces."

"And Collins went on to lead after that?"

"No, he was assassinated," Joe says.

"Well how do you like that?"

"Cut to the chase, the anti-Treaty folks lost but step by step progress was made and an Irish Free State was formed, still with some ties to Britain but far less than in the past."

"Okay, Joe, so let me back up, this O'Duffy fellow was pro-Treaty so I'm guessing he made out pretty well."

Joe looks closely at his brother, wondering exactly how to proceed. "Some say O'Duffy was a bit of a hysteric, and in his effort to protect the Irish Free State from anti-Treaty folks, he created what some call a fascist paramilitary organization, your Blue Shirts."

"Okay, well I just know that when I read in the paper about these blue shirts, it sounded creepy, in fact uncomfortably familiar if I do say so myself."

"You got it brother. O'Duffy adopted the Roman straight-arm salute, had huge rallies. Membership was limited to people who were Irish or whose parents professed the Christian faith. He liked the image of Benito Mussolini."

"And he is part of this new party Fine Gael?"

"It's first president," Joe answers.

"What is it with leaders in this decade?"

"How do you mean?"

"Well, this Hitler fellow, Mussolini, and now O'Duffy."

"Some would add FDR, but not me," Joe says.

"Nor me, and I'll drink to that."

The brothers pause, clink glasses, and take a drink.

"I'll tell you," Brendan says, putting his glass back on the table, "the Irish certainly seem to have a long history of struggle to get their freedom, first one thing and then the next."

Joe nods his head, "Brother, you realize they were dominated for 800 years by another power, and a mighty power at that. Remember that declaration piece we read, the one I keep in the barn."

"Under wraps."

"You better believe," Joe says.

Bill sits back in his chair, steadying himself after taking in so much history. After a moment he says, "Say, who do you think will be remembered after we are all long gone, Hitler, Mussolini or O'Duffy?"

"My money is on Roosevelt."

"I don't think he needs any more of your money, Joe, but god bless him, for a man of wealth he knows how to reach the average fellow."

Joe hesitates, quickly gathering his thoughts. Finally he says, "Well, the struggles aren't just in Ireland right now with Fine Gael and the like."

"Oh?"

"Cousin Dan has been kicking up his own storm, I think I told you."

Bill looks at his brother closely, concerned where Joe might be heading. "You said Dan doesn't agree that Paddy was a member of the Fenians. And you told him about the Civil War business, I gather, that you'd heard from Uncle John."

Joe considers this, "Yes, brother, indeed I did. Didn't sit well with him."

"But you didn't tell Frances about the Civil War."

"No."

After a pause, Bill asks, "Do you think Dan might have told Frances?"

Joe pauses, opens his eyes wider, looks briefly over at the ice box, the stove, the places where Frances prepares all his meals. "By god," he says, apparently not having considered this before.

Bill watches as Joe's face clouds over, the uncertainty of an approaching storm, the color of regret.

In an unusually quieter voice, Joe says, "She's been going over there more often of late. To Dan's."

Bill, the American salesman, nearly says 'too late now', but instead, disliking the semblance of an impotent moment, shifts to asking what he hopes is a brighter topic. "Albany," he says, "that's a good hike from the border. I wonder if they came down Lake Champlain."

Joe looks at his brother. Bill can almost see the complexity of wheels turning as Joe hesitates, breathes, shifts in his seat, reluctant to let go of worry so quickly. Finally Joe says, "Possibly. Uncle John didn't say." He looks away for a moment, and when he looks at Bill again he adds, "I remember him saying all this in a rush of excitement, very secretively, all but telling me not to breathe a word of it." Joe hesitates. "And I never did, for a long time." Adding, "Kind of a burden, you know."

Bill takes a moment to let this all sink in. He wonders if he should slow down with the whisky. Something in the conversation seems to be fishing for his attention, what Joe said a moment ago. The words come back to him, he asks "you said something about what was to come?"

Joe looks at Bill. "What was to come?"

"That's what I'm asking."

"What was to come," Joe repeats the words, adding "when?"

"When—next. You said, how close they were, Paddy and Uncle John, and then something more was about to come, sometime later I gather."

"Oh!," Joe answers suddenly, nodding his head, "Yes."

"Yes."

"Okay." Joe reaches for his glass, takes a very deliberate taste of the whisky, slowly raising his eyebrows before he returns the glass to its resting place.

He looks at Bill and says, "Remember when you were so fascinated about that boat in the field?"

CHAPTER 24

Into the Spirits

Thursday, October 5, 1933

J OE HAD HEARD A sudden noise coming from the barn, and he immediately thought about the cow that might be in trouble, the one he had checked on earlier. He'd excused himself abruptly, leaving the bottle of whisky at hand, encouraging Bill, he was soon to regret, to make himself comfortable.

"How's Trixie?" Bill says loudly when Joe comes back into the house sometime later.

Joe quickly assesses the situation at the table, sees that the bottle has been tipped a time or two in his absence.

"There is no Trixie," Joe says, feeling irritably sober in contrast.

"Your cow," Bill explains unnecessarily.

"Yes, I gather. And she will be okay. It took me a little longer than I had planned, my apologies."

After Joe sits down, he exchanges his worry about livestock for concern, instead, about his brother, the brother who seems younger than the one he'd left moments before.

Joe looks at his brother, seated across from him, and wonders how he might encourage a return to sobriety. He asks, "Do you know by the way how they spell it in Ireland?"

"Spell what?" Bill asks.

Joe raises his glass.

Bill tips his head back slightly, asks "The spelling for 'glass'? Or whatever they might call it over there?"

Joe shakes his glass side to side slowly. "No, brother, what's in the glass."

"Well, it probably starts with a 'w.'"

"Wrong!" Joe says with delight. "Try 'uisce beatha.'"

"That's two words."

"At least your hearing is still sound. Yes. It means "water of life," and we have the good Irish monks of the Middle Ages to thank for distilling the alcohol."

Bill takes a final sip, emptying his glass and handing it over to his brother for a refill. "I knew they had to be doing something useful. They were a bit peevish about letting women in those cloistered parts."

Joe gives his brother a shameful glare, "Father forgive us," he says, "or at least my brother. He doesn't know what he's saying." As Joe refills Bill's glass, not quite so much this time, he says "Aqua vitae."

"Okay," Bill says, accepting the whisky, noticing that Joe has forgotten the water, and deciding that he'll have it straight up this time. "Sounds like something our sister would say, studying Latin."

"Aqua vitae," Joe repeats. "It means the same thing, water of life."

Bill takes a decidedly long snort, musters his mouth and lips into action and says, slurring some of the words, "Latin, as in the Vincent Lopez orchestra, brought to you from the Palladium ballroom in New York City through the magic of your radio."

"The hell?"

"Latin music, it's all the rage."

Joe looks at his younger brother. "Maybe I shouldn't have given you another drink."

"Come on Joe," Bill says, "I know you spend a lot of time out here in the sticks but surely you've heard of the Argentine Tango, Carmen Miranda, Desi Arnaz, Xavier Cugat? Hey how about Judy Garland? You heard her sing 'La Cucaracha?'"

Joe says, "Your sister loves Desi Arnaz and Xavier Cugat."

"Oh, really? And Judy Garland?"

"She prefers the male performers."

Bill raises his eyebrows, takes another long drink, says "You don't say?" his voice echoing with a timbre of intrigue.

The two brothers remain silent for a moment till Joe says, "Speaking of good Irish Monks…"

"I'd rather not," Bill answers quickly.

Joe wonders if this is the right time to proceed, but he continues anyway, "You wanted to know about a boat."

"I did? What boat? Oh," Bill slurs a bit more, "my boat in the field, that your Jewish friend owns."

Joe takes a deep breath, says "Judas Priest." He takes a minute longer before he asks, "Are you ready to hear this?"

"Ready as ever," Bill says, taking another long drink. "What am I hearing? Okay," he catches himself, "go ahead shoot."

"Remember," Joe says, talking carefully as if to a much younger Bill, "we were talking before about Uncle John."

"Very old," Bill adds, as if sympathetically, "he was very late. Not in time. In his lifetime. His age."

"Yes, yes, Bill just listen."

"All ears."

"So you remember we talked about Paddy being a member of the Fenians. But he wasn't one of the Fenians who wanted to invade Canada."

"The hell you say!"

Joe looks at his brother who appears to be teetering a little in his seat. Despite his better judgment, Joe decides to proceed. "Lord have mercy. Let me just finish this. I don't think I explained this to you. Before. When you were better at listening."

"Proceed. By all means."

"He was with the Fenians who wanted to focus on Ireland, in Ireland."

"In Ireland," Bill repeats, as if this is the heart of the matter. "Oh," he says suddenly, "he actually went to Ireland. In a boat."

Joe looks at his brother, takes a sip of his own drink, says, "Actually, he went to Ireland in a ship."

"A ship!" Bill repeats, a bit too loudly, as if he has just made a grand discovery and will be indebted to his older brother forever.

Joe looks again at his brother, "Bill, I think we'll keep this short, you've had a long trip and you'd probably like to take a nap."

Bill drains his glass and says in a surprisingly clear if elevated voice, "The intoxicating amber of old Irish monks. I always liked Amber." It looks as if he is about to say something less circumspect but he checks himself at the last minute, appreciating the company he is keeping. When he raises his empty glass for a final salute, he says, "Just what the doctor ordered, Joe. A nap."

CHAPTER 25

Moonlight in Vermont, So Was Paddy
Sunday, February 23,1879

*T*HERE'S A REASON *I don't want to address this to you personally. Better that you should be left out of it, to avoid any difficulty. As I had mentioned before, I was fully accepted as this upstart Fenian, and there were a number of my brothers who had been doing some work supplying messages hither and yon in the American war, actually for quite some time.*

This is some time ago, before the business in Niagara in 1866. I heard about a plan to have a raid and shock the pants off the Union by stirring up trouble as far to the north as could be. A way to get some badly needed funds and possibly divert the Union troops to a place they never expected to go. There was this fellow Bennett H. Young out of Kentucky, he had the misfortune to be captured the year before in Ohio as part of Morgan's Raid. He escaped to Canada in due time and met with Confederate agents there.

I'm sure you've read that at the start of the American Civil War, Britain had declared itself neutral and so, good steward that she had been, Canada and the Maritimes were also neutral. You might already realize with all of our shared past interest in reading the news that the majority of Canadian and Maritime newspapers sympathized with the South, not because they supported slavery, but because they saw the Confederacy as a small power defying a distant, larger one. Here-here, eh? Despite this, if the Toronto paper has reported it correctly, the majority of Canadians who enlisted, fought for the Union side. Some time I will have to tell you about the scalawags they call the crimpers, ruthless American recruiters. I bet you never heard that 29 of our loyal Canadians won the Congressional Medal of Honor, the highest military honour in the United States.

Anyway, I digress. I've not had much time to put words to paper of late so excuse my excess, should it seem that way. Back to St. Albans, the little town in Vermont from which the raids took place. This fellow I mentioned, Young, recruited other escaped Confederates. The ruse was that they were all on a sporting vacation, having come from St John's. Little by little their numbers increased at the local hotel in Vermont and after something like nine days a 21 man Confederate cavalry had assembled. October 19 as best I can recall, 1864, they launched a series of robberies in three different banks in St Albans Vermont, mind you, and stole a small fortune. I won't, for reasons you might appreciate, describe my particular role, but I'll tell you that I did witness the killing of the only armed villager who was part of a group attempting to resist. I'll tell you, it tore my heart out to see this poor fellow falling to the ground that he meant to protect. I soon high tailed it out of there back across the border, giving some lame excuse. I had gathered valuable information on troop movements and future plans, at least I hope it was seen as useful, so my immediate job was done for the time being. I had also been able to tell the Canadian officials, no names here, about what they might expect regarding the threat of the Fenian movement. More and more I was swayed toward Stephens' view. The Fenians should

*concern themselves with Ireland itself. Leave Canada alone. In
this way I could agree with the great flip-flopper himself, excuse
my irreverence. Canada's 'first nationalist', as some have called
him. I've enjoyed our talk about him. Thomas D'Arcy McGee,
the poor soul, to be taken down like that. And didn't he have a
grand turnout of a funeral? Indeed.*

*Looking back, I guess I have been fortunate. Amidst all the
violence, I had rarely seen death up close, though I did see some
of the wounded at the Niagara invasion, so the St Albans affair
was my first stark, what do I call it, encounter with the grim
reaper and what man can do to man. I vowed I would from then
on work to prevent any further violence to the best of my ability.
It sickens me to recall. Enough said.*

*Sometime should we have the chance, there's a lot more I could
tell you about the effect of the American Civil War on Canada,
and it's mostly for the good, you might be surprised to hear. And
not just economically. That war formed some of the guiding
principles of the legislation which created Canada, it now seems.
It was thought that in America there had been too much power
given to the States in their Constitution and there was a move
in Canada to have a more centralized federation, oh Canada,
our dear land, the place which had been the blessed terminus
of the underground railroad. I'm quite sure you've heard that
term. Probably seen it in the Toronto papers. Definitely not the
Welland press. Anyway, lo and behold we end up with a stronger
sense of Canadian Confederation, in reaction to what was seen
as American individualism run afoul. Hopefully that enormous
land to the south will learn from its mistakes some day as must
we. Our joint futures depend on it, wouldn't you say?*

*It's probably a matter of personal vanity but I like to think that
I might have played a role like Sarah Edmonds herself, though*

in a much more minor key. Not so dramatic. You may have read of her. Behind Confederate lines she was, in her various guises.

But the big story is this—I wanted to tell you that some of us are looking to book a trip back home again, to help the cause as it should be helped—on the proper soil itself. I'm done with America for now (I do sound like McGee wouldn't you say?), and with Canada, at least for the time being. It's Ireland that calls me to herself, to be set free at last, would that I might lend a hand to that blessed outcome. It won't have, pray to the Lord, the drama of the first trip.

CHAPTER 26

It's History, It's Important, Stay Awake
Tuesday, September 4, 2001

"Y ou boys are still at it, eh?"

"Yes sir. I hope I'm not catching you at a bad time. We just had our Labor Day yesterday and I know school will be starting up for you soon. I didn't know if you have the same holiday."

"Labour Day, yesterday indeed, but with a slight difference."

"Oh?"

"Spelled with a 'u.'" While Brendan is mentally picturing the word, the Professor adds, "Also known as Fete du Travail. But that would be east of here, Quebec."

"Yes, yes," Brendan says, playing catchup which he hopes isn't too obvious.

"We're bilingual up here," the Professor says. "You probably knew that. Different from the States."

"Yes, we just have English as the only official language," Brendan says, happy to make an American contribution.

The Professor hesitates. Finally he says, "Common misunderstanding. Actually the United States doesn't have an official language."

Brendan wants to say "What?" but he stifles it. He doesn't want to sound rude. He'll let the Professor's remark remain unchallenged.

"Bill, isn't it?"

"No, Brendan, sir, or Professor."

"Oh of course, Brendan it is. And your brother is Edmund, or Eddie."

"Correct!" Brendan says, impressed. "Actually we saw each other four days ago, it was just last Friday." Brendan immediately wonders why he added this detail.

"Well that's nice, brothers keeping in touch. And I will say the timing of your call is good. We're between semesters, and I only have one small seminar running right now. The new semester starts next Monday, September 10th."

BRENDAN is glad to hear the Professor's voice again and it sounds as if the Professor is happy to hear that the Donohoes are still pursuing what he once called their 'family quest.'

This University of Toronto historian had been very helpful before, when the family originally discovered the old trunk. A mutual acquaintance had connected the Donohoes with the Professor and he had seemed, from the start, to take an unusually personal interest in what they had been discovering.

"If I'm not mistaken it was three? Or maybe two years ago, you had gotten hold of some old books."

"My Great Uncle John's journals," Brendan says enthusiastically.

"Yes?" Professor Brown asks, sounding uncertain. "But I remember you had an old trunk too with some treasures in it. Am I right about that?"

Brendan hesitates, "Oh, yes, my dad's old high school books."

"Right, right," the Professor says laughing, "from Welland?"

"Dunnville."

"Oh yes. And didn't you find some of your dad's Latin translations?"

"From his notebooks, his homework, yes."

"I remember. I thought that was rich."

While the Professor is clearly enjoying this memory, Brendan recalls the disappointment of that day's discoveries. The hope had been to find clues that would tell them stories, how their family had arrived from Ireland and settled in Canada, stories about how this had all come about,

the stories that were not passed down, and what was the deal about that…
not having stories?

What they found was a somewhat mildewed copy of "Ontario High
School English Composition," another one was "Ontario High School
Arithmetic." They also found a copy of the St Michael's Parish Almanac,
1917.

"I remember now," the Professor muses, "It was 1999, the last time we
talked. The last century."

"Yes sir."

"And here we are, still alive and able to talk about it."

Though they might be close in age, the Professor, heard but not seen,
provides a fatherly pastoral image to Brendan, probably in some way
echoing the voice of his dad and the men in his dad's generation, the way
they talked, vestiges of their fading accents. He had forgotten how he
enjoyed hearing the Professor speak, something about that husky voice
dotted with Canadian lilt and literacy.

"Remember all the Y2K business?" the Professor asks.

"Like it was yesterday."

"It practically was. At any rate, nothing happened eh? Nothing
untoward." He hesitates a moment, "Well you folks in the States did have
a lively election there last time. A bit out of the ordinary. But maybe the
new century will shine brightly on us all."

Neither of them speaks for a moment. The Professor asks, "Brendan
you had other family members with you, didn't you, when you found the
old trunk?" He then adds, "I hope I'm not being forward here."

"Oh, not at all Professor. Yes, Eddie and I have three other siblings,
Tricia, Larry and Sally, and yes they were with Eddie and myself on that
quest. We all went to Dunnville together."

"That's where your dad grew up, if I remember correctly."

"Yes!" Brendan answers excitedly. "I wish my memory was as good as
yours."

"Well," the Professor chuckles, "occupational hazard maybe eh?

History. So are they still pursuing the family information along with you and Eddie?"

Brendan hesitates just long enough for the Professor to comment, "Usually Brendan, the genealogy bug is of interest to many at first, but only a certain few get really bitten, if you get my drift."

"Indeed I do."

"It's not exactly a pandemic."

"Yes, thanks, well Eddie and I were, are, really bitten."

The Professor almost says 'that's good' but instead he says, "I think I interrupted you there, something about a Great Uncle's journals? These were separate from the contents of the trunk?", and for a moment the Professor smiles at the thought of finding treasures like old high school homework. Latin translations.

"Yes," Brendan says, "these old journals," feeling a sense of relief without really knowing why.

"Well, alright then."

Brendan takes a deep breath. "We…I…we…were hoping you could help us understand some things we've uncovered. History. The context."

After a very slight hesitation, the Canadian voice responds, "I see," hesitant, encouraging.

"Sometime after we last spoke, we re-connected with a younger cousin whose great- great something grandfather was my grandfather's brother, John Donohoe, a man we had known little, actually nothing, about."

"Interesting. Yes I think you told me something about this, but not about any journals."

"Turns out this Great Uncle was quite the writer of sorts, kept a pretty detailed record of things."

"Terrific!"

"And, best news, we now have access to them. They had been there all along, kept by my Great Uncle's side of the family."

"Bingo!" the Professor exclaims. "So let me see here, somewhere your family had a disconnect with part of the family?"

"Well," Brendan begins, feeling a little protective, "we lost contact, yes."

"Happens a lot. Sometimes it's just carelessness, nothing intentional, time passes by and we all get caught up in our lives, another generation comes along." The Professor pauses for a moment, and then says, "Or... something intriguing may have happened, eh? A little family drama?"

Brendan hesitates, "Not sure about drama, We're not exactly the dramatic type. But so anyway we've been..."

"Edmund and yourself."

"Yes and our cousin Emma, going over the journals to see what we can learn."

"Motherlode!" the Professor erupts, an historian's cheer.

"Well," Brendan says, his voice dropping.

"No?"

"Not quite. He writes a lot about farming life at that time, and then he gets, how to say it, very obtuse sounding, if that's a good word."

"That's a good word. About what? What's so obtuse?"

"Politics, I think."

"Nothing surprising there. In your country as well as ours. Politics can be pretty dull. Or..." The Professor hesitates, "Do you have any examples?"

Brendan wanted to be prepared for this call, not waste the Professor's time. He had been skimming ahead in the journals until he found something interesting enough to share. He found it in volume 18 and jotted down some of the comments. This section had jumped out at him, as if he were being guided. It was probably suggested by Emma, or Eddie.

"He mentions the name Stephens at one point," Brendan says, "A meeting in Jones Woods."

"In regard to what?" The Professor says, sounding surprisingly interested.

"Oh right, sorry. A little context here, right?" When the Professor doesn't respond, Brendan hurriedly adds, "See, my Great Uncle John was writing about his old buddy. The guy whose trunk we had found, so that fellow had been involved with some people you had told us about a couple years ago. When we last talked."

Brendan hears himself sounding disjointed, muddled. This is not the way he had hoped to sound. The Professor hasn't responded yet. Brendan wonders if he is still there, and then he hears what sounds like some papers being shuffled in the background.

As if speaking from a great distance, distracted, absent-mindedly, the Professor says, "Jones Woods is in New York City."

"Yes?"

"Staten Island, to be more exact."

"I see." Brendan is both pleased and befuddled. He is surprised to hear how definitive the Professor sounds. He also feels oddly protective. New York City is American.

Neither of them speak for a moment, till the Professor, sounding a bit more cautious says, "What was Mr.Trunk doing in New York?"

Brendan shakes his head involuntarily. He thought he'd heard the Professor ask about the New York tabloid gadfly.

"And can I ask you, what year are we talking about?" the Professor adds.

"The journal entry was written in the late 1870's but he is describing a scene in, what? 1866."

"1866," the Professor says, "big year for the Fenians."

"That's it!" Brendan practically yells, immediately apologizing.

"Whoa, that's ok Brendan. Does my heart good to hear some enthusiasm about the field of history. Better than sorry excuses for a student's paper being late." And then he asks, "Was it your relative that saw Stephens at Jones Woods? What's his name again?"

"Great Uncle, well no, just John Donohoe. No it wasn't him."

"Okay," the Professor says, sounding patient, waiting a beat.

"Oh, sorry, you want to know who was there."

"Yes, who was it that saw Stephens?"

"This Stephens fellow, that's a name you recognize?"

The Professors clears his throat, "Yes, and now again who was it who saw him?"

"His old buddy, well, my great uncle's old friend, last name was O'Neil."

Brendan hears a loud squawking noise, like an un-oiled chair being pushed back suddenly. After a moment's silence, he thinks about asking if everything is okay.

When the Professor comes back on the phone, his voice sounds a bit shaky. He says in a tone of voice that is attempting to steady itself, "You know Eddie, I'm sorry, Brendan, that this time period is uh, my special area of interest."

"Oh, yes?"

"Canadian, Irish, American relations of that time."

"Well that's a happy coincidence." Brendan feels, oddly enough, that he has regained his own composure, his ability to talk more easily. The Canadians always sound so articulate, in his experience, or maybe it's deliberate. That little bit of accent, a hint that they had remained closer to Europe. More cosmopolitan, less cowboy hick.

After what seems like a long delay, the Professor asks, "You wouldn't know which O'Neill this is, do you?"

"Which?" Brendan asks.

Brendan thinks he hears the Professor take a deep breath. In a moment the Professor says, "This was a critical moment in our history, Canada, I'm talking about, Brendan. Some feel it was a major factor in the formation of the Dominion of Canada. The perceived threat of invasion. I'm sorry, I don't think I'm being clear. The Fenian business. It's largely why I've taken a special interest in this time period."

"Yes sir."

"There was a Fenian leader named O'Neill who had been an officer in the American Civil War."

"Oh really," Brendan says with interest.

"Did you ever hear whether this friend of your great uncle had been in the Civil War?"

"Civil War," Brendan repeats. "You know, I'd always heard that there was some relation of ours, a Canadian, who had gone off to the Civil War. Story was that only his boots were sent home."

The Professor waits a moment, says "Poignant," and then, "not him."

"Oh."

Brendan wishes he could see the Professor's face. That would be a helpful guide, the Professor does sound a bit animated, almost less Canadian. His dad the salesman used to tell him that body language is important to observe. Brendan takes a breath and as silently as possible exhales while pursing his lips. "Stephens," Brendan asks, "this guy Stephens, what's the story about him?"

"Ah yes," the Professor says. "I'll try to cut to the chase here. It's a long history." In a softer tone of voice he says, "It always is."

The Professor takes a moment, Brendan guesses that he is gathering his thoughts and envisions the start of one of these new-fangled Power Point slide shows. History made orderly. Unlike its original.

"Stephens," the Professor begins and then stops. "No, let me say this. In the mid 1860's the Fenian movement more or less broke into two factions. One group was led by the traditionalist Ireland First wing led by the original founders, our man Stephens and another fellow, O'Mahony. James Stephens was the Fenian chief in Ireland.

Among the American Fenians, there was a second faction led by a man named Roberts. So there was, so to speak, a Roberts wing, and the Stephens wing. Are you with me?"

"Please."

"The main difference, if you'll forgive me, is that the Roberts folks were pushing for an attack on Canada, as a way to get Britain to free Ireland. Stephens, the Irishman, also wanted a free Ireland but felt that the fight should be on Irish soil. "He was quoted as saying, 'The temple of Irish liberty must be of Irish build, and done by Irish hands upon the land upon which it is to be consecrated.' Don't you love how they talked back then eh?"

"Well…"

"Meanwhile, back at the ranch as you Americans might say, British authorities in Ireland reacted finally to the Fenian movement by seizing the Irish People newspaper and arresting senior Irish Republican Brotherhood leaders."

"That was another group?"

"Well, in Ireland they all sort of worked together. Anyway, Stephens became a fugitive and escaped to the States. This triggered John A. Macdonald to order the secret service chief in Canada, a man named McMicken, to infiltrate undercover agents deep into Fenian groups."

"Hmm," Brendan mutters.

"John Macdonald by the way later became Canada's first Prime Minister."

"Oh, like, he became your George Washington."

Brendan thinks he hears the Professor groan. He might be wrong. Maybe he was clearing his throat again.

"There was a Fenian group in Toronto," the Professor continues, "led by a tavern keeper, Michael Murphy, who had been born in Cork, Ireland. He had become the president of the Hibernian Benevolent Society. He remained loyal to the Stephens-O'Mahony group and condemned any planned invasion of Canada. I might say, by the way, that at its height, the Fenians had up to 50,000 members in the States, many of them trained soldiers."

"Well, that is a little…intimidating."

"The Fenians in America were somewhat famous for speeches, marches, a lot of show and little action. Bluster."

"That sounds…I'm not surprised. About the bluster."

"Well yes, up until invasions did start. So what happened was that O'Mahony, but not Stephens, was getting concerned with the plans he was hearing about from the Roberts wing. He decided he would jump the gun, you might say, and he launched his own strike in April 1866."

"This was the one near Buffalo?"

"New Brunswick. The invaders came from Maine, some islands near Campobello, of later FDR fame."

"Never heard of this."

"The British and U.S. Navies quickly put an end to it. Unfortunately, Michael Murphy's Toronto Fenians, and I'm guessing not without mixed emotions, decided to join with supporters of O'Mahony. They boarded an east bound train to join in the action that was planned, but they were stopped in Cornwall. You know where Cornwall, Ontario is?"

"Thousand Islands area, north of Syracuse?"

"Close enough. And that was the end of the Toronto Fenians. When the Niagara region invasion happened later in June, Murphy was in jail. In September he broke out and fled to the States."

Brendan takes a moment to digest what he has heard. "I have a question."

"Please."

"If the Toronto Fenians were opposed to the invasion of Canada, why did they attempt to join the attack on New Brunswick?"

"Ah yes," the Professor says, his voice sounding a little lighthearted. "Because it was New Brunswick and not Upper Canada."

"Okay," Brendan says hesitantly, his response being little more than a place-holder in the conversation. He feels himself beginning to fade. If he was in class, his eyes would start to droop. The Professor clearly loves his work. Brendan tells himself to stay awake. He opens his eyes wide for his own benefit, shakes his head a little.

"A brief history."

"Please."

"Canada used to be Upper Canada and Lower Canada, think Ontario and Quebec."

"Okay."

"The Act of Union, 1840, created the Province of Canada, which was divided into two parts, Canada West and Canada East."

"So where does New Brunswick come in?"

"Came in a little later, and it used to be part of Nova Scotia. This was an area that debated whether to join the Confederation of 1867, which created Canada as such.

"Nova Scotia and New Brunswick, by the way, had taken in a lot of the Loyalists from your American Revolution. In Nova Scotia, there was a lingering fear that the big, strong neighbor to the south would just move in some day and take over."

"That was about the Fenians?"

"Way before the Fenians. And it was one of the reasons Nova Scotia finally joined the Dominion. Safety in greater numbers."

"So," Brendan concludes, "it's complicated. I mean the loyalties. Those Torontonians on their ill-fated train ride to invade New Brunswick."

"Yes, right," the Professor says, "though I wouldn't put it just that way."

Brendan remains silent.

"Too much information?" the Professor asks.

Brendan thinks You're not in Kansas anymore. He rallies to ask, "Whatever happened to the bartender?"

"Sorry?"

"What's his name, from the tavern."

"Oh, you mean Murphy. Funny you should ask. I was just looking at something about him, so I do have some detail right here in front of me."

Brendan hears what sounds like a filing cabinet being opened, closed. "Okay," the Professor starts, "A trial was set for Autumn of that year, 1866, but on September 1st, Murphy and five others escaped from jail and fled over the border. He eventually moved to Buffalo and became the proprietor of a place called the Irish Arms Hotel. Business was poor because local Fenians suspected him of spying for the British, and they avoided his business."

"Oh, poor guy."

"Poor in health as well. Died of TB, left a wife and several children. His body was brought home to Toronto for burial and funeral services were held in St Michel's Cathedral."

"Well at least he got a good send-off."

The Professor hesitates a moment, "If you believe in such things." Adding after a moment, "He was 42 years old."

Neither of them speak for an extended period of time, the silence magnified by the limiting presence of a phone call, long distance. Finally the Professor's voice asks, "I hope I have shed a little light on what you called obtuse? In your relative's journals?"

"Oh, indeed," Brendan nearly gushes. "That's a lot of information you shared."

"That little quote I gave you before, about 'the temple of Irish liberty'?"

"Yes?"

"Came from a speech by Stephens in Jones Woods. A reporter from the New York Times captured it. God bless the New York Times. Almost as good as the Globe and Mail, eh? By the way, we got off track a bit, I wanted to get back to your Great Uncle's friend, the one who had heard that speech."

"Yes," Brendan says.

"You said his name was O'Neill, correct? That's his surname. What was his given name?"

"Paddy."

Brendan hears a brief moment of silence followed by what sounds like a moan, a keening, the rising tone of a whistle.

CHAPTER 27

Your Branch of the Family
Tuesday, September 4, 2001

"Do you need to get that?" Emma asks.

Edmund sits forward on her couch, reaches over to get his cellphone.

Emma watches as cousin Eddie, as she often calls him, retrieves the phone and touches some of its buttons. "That's very cool," she says admiring the little device in his hand. "What will they think of next?"

As Eddie stares at the small screen he says, "Yeah, you should think about getting one. Handy. This here," he says looking up at Emma, "is a message from Brendan. He was going to call after he talked to our old Professor friend. I'll call him back later."

After a brief pause, Eddie adds, "After we met here last week, we found we had more questions. Things we hope to clarify."

"Toronto?"

"What?" Eddie asks.

"The message from your brother. The Professor is at the University there."

"Yeah. And he's an interesting guy. He's given us a lot of help over the past couple of years."

Emma takes a moment, says "About your famous trunk."

"Well," Eddie says, "yes, but even more, we hope, about your famous set of journals."

Emma nods her head, "Blessed be the Great to the x power Grandfather Dan, to secure those journals."

Eddie puts his phone away and asks, "How did that happen exactly anyway?" He hasn't been offered coffee yet. He noticed when he walked in that Emma had some wonderful looking donuts on the kitchen counter.

As if reading his mind, Emma stands up and says, "I haven't offered you coffee. What's the matter with me?"

Eddie answers, "Not much," in a way that seems both to please and embarrass his momentary host, whom he would have called hostess in the old days. How some things change. With the exception of coffee and donuts.

"Listen," she says, half turning around like a dancer, so slender and light on her feet, two qualities Eddie never remembers possessing, "I have some donuts too. You usually like them." She can see his response without his saying a word. "Alright then," she almost purrs, before continuing on her way into the kitchen.

When Emma returns with the coffee and the whole box, lid open, she knows that he will pick the Boston Crème which she has placed closest to the front.

She settles the donuts and coffee on the coffee table between them and takes a seat in the chair opposite the couch. She watches as he carefully picks out his favorite selection. She wonders if he knows that she re-arranged the donuts on purpose.

Eddie says, "I mean, it's curious that we never knew about the journals, our side of the family."

Eddie watches as Emma appears momentarily confused, uncertain. Her smooth forehead now suddenly wrinkled, her eyebrows lowered, dark and questioning. Lovely eyebrows indeed.

Eddie takes a bite of the donut, tastes the chocolate on top, the crème inside. He makes a small moan of delight, then puts the donut back on the plate. After a moment he says, "So the Dan Donohoe branch of the family secures the journals," as if priming a pump.

"Right. Dan was after all the oldest son of his father John. John who is your Great Uncle, brother of your Grandfather James."

"Correct."

"So of course Dan gets the journals, oldest male and all that, sexism wasn't even a word then. Maybe."

"And Dan keeps them," Eddie says emphasizing 'keeps.'

"Well…" Emma seems to be considering her response.

Eddie takes a deep breath and asks, "Of course it wasn't just the journals we never heard about," Eddie pauses, opens his eyes wide in a politely admiring way, "we also never heard about you. And your relations. A side of the family we lost touch with." Eddie continues, "Which also meant not knowing that our grandfather James had an older brother."

"Great Uncle John," Emma repeats quietly, "to you." Emma looks down at the coffee table and decides to give her hands a task. She reaches for her cup, but not of course a donut, though she does like the blueberry filled ones, with the white sugar frosting.

Emma takes a considered sip of the hot coffee, murmurs, "Mmmmmm," which Eddie takes as both an appreciation for the brew and anticipation for an agenda.

She puts her cup down delicately on a coaster that protects the shiny wood table, looks up at Eddie and says, "I mentioned when we met that there had been misgivings within the family about the journals?"

"I think you said something before…more like controversy." After a hesitation, Eddie adds in a quiet voice, "What journals?"

"Oh, right," Emma acknowledges. She looks across the room for an instant before turning to face Eddie. "Your dad is Uncle Bill, right?"

Eddie pauses, says "Yes," tentatively, surprised with how defensive and guarded he suddenly feels. Emma apparently notices.

"Cousin!" she says, "it's okay. We're all friends here. Family even. Reunited," taking a moment to add, "something we can continue to celebrate."

Eddie looks at Emma, "Okay, right. Sorry if I—"

"No, please," Emma interrupts. "I want to answer, if I can, your question about how you guys, your branch of the family, was out of the loop, so to speak."

"So to speak," Eddie repeats, dimly aware that his seniority just slipped a notch, 'you guys', she had said, a youthful American equalizer.

"And so you didn't know all the players." She adds "Uncle John, I mean," seeing the look on his face.

"I see. Okay."

"The reason I mention your dad is that I had heard, over the years, Uncle Bill and another of his brothers…Jack?"

"Probably Joe."

"Yes! That's right! Well anyway, that when they got together there were some strongly expressed points of view exchanged and, one thing led to another, Dan became increasingly uncomfortable with Uncle Bill and Uncle Joe in particular."

Eddie sits back in the couch. "I'd heard they had loud games of Euchre. Actually, come to think of it, that was only with Dad's siblings."

"Well," Emma says, "I'm told that Dan had some strongly held beliefs."

"About playing cards?"

Emma takes a deep breath, and says, "About who should be the keeper of the journals."

"Oh."

"Actually it was even more about what the Journals describe."

"What the journals describe," Eddie repeats. "Is that because of Uncle John's handwriting or something more substantial?"

Emma ignores Eddie's question for the moment and focuses on the issue of ownership. "From what I've heard, Dan's belief was that the oldest boy should be bequeathed the sole honor of protecting the journals."

"Rank, eh?"

"To say nothing of sexism as I say, even if only a historical sniff of it."

Eddie looks down at the coffee table. He is taking this all in, along with another bite of the Boston Crème. Emma, beautiful Emma, had always been quite the feminist even as a young child. And here she is, a woman of her own generation. Strong and determined. Suffers no fools.

"So my great-something Grandfather Dan," Emma continues, "felt it was his duty to be the shepherd of those many volumes."

Eddie takes a moment, realizes that his donut is rapidly diminishing in size. He asks, "And the part about what the journals describe? What? The family thought they needed some further exegesis?"

Emma jerks her head slightly in surprise, looks taken aback.

Eddie notices, says, "Something I said?"

"I thought," Emma begins, "you said Exit Jesus."

Eddie quickly grabs a napkin to cover his mouth as he coughs and nearly chokes.

"You okay?" Emma asks.

"Sorry," Eddie says, recovering, trying to wipe the remains of spilled coffee, donut and a grin off his face.

"Oh," Emma says, "Okay, I get it, I misunderstood. I must say, you and your brother have quite the vocabulary at times."

"Thank you."

"All those archaic words from long, long ago. Not how modern people, you know, 'with it people', talk." Emma is giving Eddie the business. She knows he knows it.

"'Exegesis' means like doing an interpretation," Eddie says, "often related to sacred scripture."

Emma considers this, "Well, that fits. John Donohoe's sacred words so to speak. And maybe the exit Jesus part too, which I will tell you more about."

Emma takes a sip of her coffee and considers how to continue. "You've read some of the later volumes? You took a few home with you last time didn't you?"

"Yes, and given what you say about Dan, I appreciate your style of stewardship."

Emma nearly blushes. "Well, I think being a librarian is a better model than being a museum curator."

"Just to be clear," Eddie says, "I tend to skim a lot, not get too caught in the details. Brendan is a much closer reader, takes his time."

"That may be why he hasn't returned some of the journals yet," she says smiling. "Also it was so nice to see him the other day. I hope he makes it more of a habit to visit." As an afterthought she adds, "I don't even know what kind of donuts he prefers."

"Jelly filled," Eddie answers without hesitation.

Emma looks at the blueberry filled donut on the table, untouched. For now. After a moment she muses, "Uncle Bill and Uncle Joe. I wish I had met them. You actually knew them," she says, suddenly laughing, "well of course you did, I hope you knew your own father!"

When Eddie doesn't immediately answer, Emma says "that was so long ago," adding "for me." She looks at Eddie with a new sense of admiration. "You knew a number of those aunts and uncles that I've only heard about."

Eddie reaches over for the last bite of his donut. "Yes," he says ruefully. "I'm that old."

Emma takes a moment to reposition herself, both in the chair opposite Eddie and in what she wants to say. "Your dad," she begins, "and Uncle Joe, disagreed apparently with Dan and some of the others about one character in particular, and I'm guessing you might know who that is."

Eddie thinks about his dad and Uncle Joe, some of the things he had heard. "Our Aunt Frances," he teases.

"What? Oh. Yes, there was a Frances, wasn't there. I don't remember how she fits in to any of this."

Eddie realizes that he has never really talked much about his dad with this young cousin. He tilts his head to the side for a brief instant and says, "When my dad was in his final days, he often mentioned our aunt. He called her Frank."

"Oh, that's interesting. That he called her that name."

"So, he was in a very weakened state and we weren't always sure he was still, you know, with it, mentally."

Emma is looking supportive, waiting for Eddie to say more, realizing the novelty of the moment, though thinking that this is probably the wrong word for it.

"He said several times," Eddie continues, "'Paddy is right. No shame.' I didn't have a clue what he was talking about. In fact when we found the trunk, I still didn't put two and two together. I had sort of let go of those death bed, excuse me, jumbled words."

'Two and two', of course, is a figure of speech. At the same time, names are spoken aloud, talk strikes a spark of memory as if out of pure darkness. Here comes the light, but not just yet.

Two and two. Paddy and John, Joe and Bill.

CHAPTER 28

Some Call It Hogwash

Tuesday, September 4, 2001

Emma repeats what she just heard, speaking thoughtfully, like someone observing the words as much as speaking them. "Paddy is right. No shame."

Eddie takes a moment and says, "They could get pretty loud during their card games. Sometimes you couldn't tell if they were kidding each other or not. Well, they were Irish."

Emma looks at her cousin, "Still are. May they rest in peace and maybe now in a much better place." She looks at the box of donuts, "Another?"

"Oh, please no," Eddie says, "but Brendan would love that jelly filled one I see."

Emma lowers her shoulders, "Yes, of course," she says with no enthusiasm. "I'll wrap it up when you're ready."

Eddie notices that his coffee cup is empty and that Emma hasn't noticed. A small light seems to flicker and then flash in the corner of the room and he turns to look at it but sees nothing. Most likely a reflection from somewhere else.

"You okay?" Emma asks, turning as well to see what Eddie might have seen.

"Yes, fine," Eddie says quickly and apologetically. "They had issues of course, I guess we all do."

Emma gives Eddie a look of not understanding, and Eddie feels that he has succeeded in being both abrupt and vague. "Sorry," he adds.

"You know we, you and I, may be entering some territory here that has been taboo," Emma says.

Eddie hopes that he is not blushing.

"Not for nothing, there is this history, isn't there?" Emma asks.

"Yes," Eddie says, not sure what he is agreeing to.

Emma looks at Eddie for a moment. "The way things fell out in the family. Well, you didn't even know that you had a triple or quadruple to the x power great Uncle John, right? Oh, sorry, just Great Uncle John for you, one 'great'? Closer in age. John would be your dad's uncle," she says, partially to remind herself.

There is a sense of intimacy dancing toward an uncertain edge, and Eddie thinks they both know it. It doesn't help that he can't stop admiring the lithe and graceful way Emma moves, even when just shifting in her chair. "Right," he answers, "no triple x for me."

"What?" Emma says.

"Uncle John, not triple x Great, not that distant." He almost adds 'I'm that old.'

Neither of them speak for a moment. Emma finally says, "Mind you, this is maybe hearsay, no," she corrects herself immediately, "it's many layers of hearsay."

"Yes?"

"Well, stories I heard were that John," she interrupts herself, "can I just call him that? Rather than my distant pedigree 'great great' etcetera?"

"Please yes, I know who you are talking about."

"I always heard that John didn't really say all that stuff that Joe supposedly told your dad, Bill."

Eddie looks puzzled, Emma notices. "Your dad didn't tell you any of this?" she asks.

"I don't know what this is. Dad didn't talk about Dan. He did talk about Joe but, remember, I never heard anything about John."

Emma looks at her cousin, "So no stories."

"Not from John. Not about John. There was no John."

"Interesting. No stories and so, what? Nonexistence."

They both consider this. Eddie says at last, "A bit extreme, eh what?"

Emma appears to be biting her lip. Eddie repeats her words slowly, "John didn't say what Joe told my dad." He leaves out her use of the word 'supposedly.'

"Correct."

"So what are the stories that Joe told my dad?"

"Well," Emma begins, "according to my relatives," she looks at Eddie, "sorry, they're your relatives too of course," she doesn't see any immediate reaction from her cousin so she continues, "a kind word for it might be 'hogwash.'" Still no clear reaction from Eddie, so she adds, "you know by now, that John's writings were suggestive. His journal, we're talking about. Not actually declarative. Different readers can take away what they want."

Eddie considers what he is about to say, and says, "Well, I think they are more than just a little bit suggestive." He looks at his cousin. She is, after all, from that other side of the family.

Emma notices that Eddie's cup is empty. "Hey," she says, energetically standing up as if releasing a wound-up spring, "you didn't tell me. You need more coffee. Be right back."

Eddie watches Emma leave, he breathes deeply, and a short moment later watches her return. After she places his cup on the table and another one for herself, he is relieved to hear her say, "I'm with you, cuz. All those levels of generation to my behind," she says awkwardly, "have freed me up. I think his writing is very suggestive." She hesitates, her face clouding over for an instant. "I don't want to offend you. Speak out of turn. Honor your elders and all that. Actually it's not so much what John wrote in the journal."

"No?"

"No, it's what Joe claimed that John had told him. Personally."

"Oh, well, that's…" and for one of the few times in his life, Eddie finds that he has run out of words.

After one quick breath, Emma says, "I'm afraid to tell you that hurtful things were said."

There is a hesitation, and Emma is relieved when she hears Eddie say, "Sounds like there has been enough hurt already, and we don't have to carry any of that farther than this coffee table, these donuts, this newly filled cup of coffee."

Emma looks at Eddie in a way he will long remember, very tenderly, brimming with compassion. A part of him anticipates the intimacy of her next words.

When she begins, "My forebears characterize Uncle Joe, great great…" she hears Eddie groan.

Emma hesitates, asks, "You okay cousin?"

Eddie did not intend to groan, not audibly. He takes a medium size breath, and decides it's safe to say, "We discussed this already, the title, the repetition. You can let it go, just 'Uncle' Joe is fine."

"Right, sorry. I do get caught up in measuring the 'greats.' Well, anyway, the story was that Uncle Joe, they said, could be extravagant with his speech. Dramatic. Bring attention to himself. I've seen," she says as an aside, "photos of him. He was good looking. But I heard he was something of a dandy."

"Dandy?" Eddie says, voice rising more strenuously than he intends.

Emma looks at Eddie, wondering if it is safe to continue.

"He was a farmer for god's sake," Eddie says.

Emma pauses, "Eddie are we ok?"

Eddie is surprised by his reaction.

They both hesitate. Emma suddenly starts to shake her hands vigorously as if wanting to get rid of something she might be holding. Eddie watches and starts to smile. He asks, "Do you have any sage"?

Emma looks puzzled. "For your coffee?"

"No, to burn. Ward off evil spirits. Old Native American practice."

"Ah," she says, reaching for and taking a sip of her coffee. When she replaces the cup on the table, she says reassuringly, "We're okay. We're not them."

"May they rest in peace, as you say."

Emma watches as Eddie takes another sip of coffee and appears to decide against choosing another donut. She says, "I'm afraid to say that I think your dad caught a lot of grief for talking about Joe's stories."

"Caught a lot of grief," Eddie repeats. "That part fits."

After a moment Emma says, "Amazing he never said boo about his uncle John."

"No. Not boo. Booze maybe."

Emma looks at Eddie closely, taking her time. "You serious?"

Eddie sits back, takes a deep breath. "He was a good man, good provider." He looks around the room, the neatness, the organization, the way his home never looks so tidy. "I think he swallowed a lot in other ways."

Emma nods her head. She thinks they can agree on this.

CHAPTER 29

The Kicker

Tuesday, September 4, 2001, Several Minutes Later

"No," EMMA SAYS, "NONE of this is in the journals, you're right."

Eddie pauses, frowns and looks away. When he turns back to face Emma he says, "He was in the Civil War? Paddy, you're saying, fought for the Confederacy no less?" Eddie shakes his head, "You got to be kidding."

"I know," Emma agrees, voice rising in pitch and intensity. "This is what was passed along, the kind of thing Joe told your dad. Number one it's almost laughable, so unrealistic, a Canadian fighting in the Americans' war, and number two, he could have at least invented a story that he fought for the Union's side."

"Well, wait a minute," Eddie says, "we always did hear that some Canadian relation was in that war. Only his boots returned."

Emma looks at Eddie with more than a note of caution, "And you have some proof of this?"

Eddie hesitates, "It was a story we heard. More than once. Fuzzy on the details."

Emma says "Fuzzy sounds right. Phony maybe."

Eddie senses again a stirring of defensiveness, an impulse to argue. It arises so quickly from such a deep and old place, that he is surprised. It is then that he feels something brush lightly against his right shoulder, enough that he nearly turns to look.

Emma pauses, observing her cousin.

Eddie takes a deep breath, watches a wave of irritation depart harmlessly. He decides to simply observe emotions. For now.

"Maybe," Emma begins, "you can appreciate why Dan and his group were so adamant, I guess that's the right word, to quash any rumors. There's a lot of family pride involved. They didn't want the family to be ridiculed. You know, for all the pride we see today, back then there was still this image of the Irish being an argumentative, ill-mannered and often drunken minority. Immigrants. So they were still a little, what? defensive, protective."

"Judgmental," Eddie adds. "Not what you would call kind, in particular to the Germans and Japanese."

"I can see that."

"And the Italians. Greeks."

"What?"

"Poles."

Emma looks at her cousin. She waits a moment and says, "African Americans?"

Eddie pauses, looks at his young cousin, "Father forgive us, huh? I don't think Black folks were even on the radar enough to be condemned."

Emma hesitates, "Good old days. They say." And then returning to the topic, adds, "So they didn't want Bill passing on these made-up stories. I think, sad to say, they weren't very kind to him."

"To Joe?"

Emma frowns, shakes her head. "I'm sorry, cousin. No, like I say, to your dad." After a moment she adds, "Your dad was a salesman, wasn't he?"

Eddie looks at Emma with an edge of caution. "Yes, sold pharmaceuticals. Traveling salesman. Now they would say he was a sales rep. Did well, financially at least, even in the Depression, can you imagine?" Eddie watches as Emma smiles in a way that is kind, sweet, if backlit with a shadow of sadness.

She answers, "He was the first in the family to leave the farming life, go off to the big city and all that. That kind of set him apart perhaps."

Eddie considers this, appreciates her comment. "You do know some of the history. Thankyou. Yes. He was proud of being that kind of pioneer, first one off the farm."

Eddie looks away for a moment, thinking about his dad. When he looks back at Emma he repeats, "Travelling salesman. He had one particular car early in his career that he loved. Started with the letter 'A.'"

"Oh," Emma says, "The Ford? Model A?"

"No, that wasn't it. Brendan and I talked about this not too long ago. Named after a town in New York."

"Albany?" she asks.

"No, that's okay," Eddie says, not wanting to get sidetracked.

There is a pause in their conversation while Emma considers what she is about to share and Eddie digests a rapidly departing fleet of brief memories.

"More coffee?" Emma begins.

"No more, thanks," Eddie says.

Emma takes a moment, says, "I'll tell you the real kicker."

"The kicker," Eddie repeats. He watches as Emma's face shifts from a look of concern, to sadness, and finally hope, a triduum of expression, conveyed by forehead, eyebrows and lips.

"You know that in Uncle John's journals, he talks a bit about Paddy going to Ireland."

"Yes."

"Well, Uncle John seems very, what's the word, circumspect about any of his friend's travels. You'd think this would be something to report about, other than just alluding to it. You'd think that Paddy would have told him some stories, things that John would have recorded."

"Yes?" Eddie answers with a question.

"Well," Emma says, "That always struck me as odd. And not just me."

Eddie looks at his young cousin, waiting to hear what might constitute a 'kicker.'

"You see," she starts slowly, carefully, "this lack of information in the journals, specifically about Paddy's travels, fanned the flames of some rumors that had meanwhile started."

"What?"

"And back at that time it seems the Donohoe clan went, I guess you'd say, underground, really silent. At least about certain topics."

"What topics?" Eddie says, observing a rise of unwanted irritation, "Or can't you talk about it? Family taboo and all that."

"Eddie," Emma says, putting out a hand to signal stop, "We are in the next century, it is 2001. That was then, not now."

Eddie takes a deep and considered breath. Observing emotions, he reminds himself. "Okay. What are the certain topics?"

"What I'm about to tell you."

"Okay."

Emma takes a moment, says "Mostly politics."

Eddie answers slowly, "I see," anticipating a sense of relief. The Irish and politics. Nothing new here.

"And, also," Emma says, as if imitating Eddie's slower answer, "a question of murder, a death. And the legal consequences thereto."

Eddie looks at his cousin. She is looking expectant, almost maternal.

To Emma, Eddie looks dumbfounded. Finally, and very slowly, she hears him say, "Wait...wait... ," the voice of a man rising from a grave, ever so carefully. "Nothing in the journal, there is," he speaks Yoda-like, faltering.

"No, indeed there is not," Emma says with welcome affirmation.

"Then...?"

Emma looks at her aging cousin, raises her eyebrows and says, "You might guess the source."

"Someone murdered someone in our family?" Eddie says, voice rising.

"Oh, no no no," Emma reassures him, almost calling him 'honey.'

"Sorry."

"Then who?"

Emma reaches over and touches her cousin's hand. At first he seems to welcome the contact, his hand is very warm, but then she feels a small tremor as he pulls his hand away. "Who was murdered, you're asking?"

Eddie barely moves his head to the affirmative.

"The man's name was Burl, from what I recall."

"Burl?"

"Yes, but remember, this is the story I heard passed down the line, and this was long after Grandfather to the x-power Dan Donohoe tried to put the kaibosh on the whole thing, not to talk about it. Which didn't work." After a moment she adds, "The story is that he came from Leitrim."

"Who?"

"This Burl fellow."

"Leitrim, New York?"

"And," she adds, not answering his question, "he was apparently not very popular." She is trying to avoid overloading her cousin but recognizes immediately that this tidbit is not likely to help. He already looks more confused.

Emma speaks more quickly. "Not New York, Eddie. It was Ireland."

"Ireland," Eddie repeats, as if saying so will be helpful.

"Late 1870's. At least I think so. If that helps."

Eddie is not feeling all that helped despite his cousin's good wishes. He feels a need to clear a path, clear something, make a move forward. He says, "This is from Uncle Joe then, originally."

"Well, as the story goes, Uncle Joe said that he heard this from Uncle John who heard it from Paddy himself."

"Okay," Eddie says, considering whether he might repeat this litany of lineage, just to help him remember, or at least slow things down. Instead he says, "So Paddy is the horse's mouth."

Emma suddenly recalls old photos of family farms, barnyards, specially loved horses with unidentified riders, usually men, proud and almost smiling. She doesn't want to get distracted just now. She looks closely at Eddie and says, "It was uncle Joe who told your dad, my great-something Uncle Bill."

"Who," Eddie adds, "never told Brendan or myself, his own family."

"So I've learned, since we've become re-acquainted," Emma says, "and that's probably because of the hornet's nest that got stirred up."

Eddie pauses, looks closely at Emma and asks, "And what's the hornet nest?"

Emma hesitates, returns Eddie's gaze. "Fear of prosecution."

Eddie senses that a log has just been placed across the path. Emma sees this, and says, "Paddy was said to be involved somehow."

"Paddy was in Ireland?"

"Yes, and he knew important information about the murder of Burl. And, bottom line, he high tailed it out of there."

"From Ireland."

"To back home," Emma says.

"To the States."

"To Canada," Emma says.

"Oh, right." Eddie pauses before saying, "This was a long time ago." Eddie is on overload, knows it, knows he can't take in a lot more information just now. He has the odd thought of wishing that he could feel something brush against his shoulder again, but there is no such sensation. Instead, he senses a dawning new appreciation, this previously unrevealed history. Too much to take in. Better to make the best of it.

After a long moment, Eddie says, "I kind of like it," and then, "Paddy on the Lam." He recognizes that Emma might not know what he is talking about. "That's a phrase from the 1930's," he says.

"I know," Emma says, "I watch the old movies sometimes." She looks at him, one eyebrow rising, skeptically. "I'm glad you like it. I can see what side of the family you're on."

CHAPTER 30

Just A Few Feet of Land

Friday October 13, 1933

"WELCOME BACK FROM CUBA. Is that where you get your fascination with Xavier Cougat?"

"Hello to you too Joe. You do know it's Cuba, NY."

"*Ah si!*" Joe says, "*Nueva York.*"

"And then it was up and over to the City of Lights."

Joe looks at his brother, "Commonly known as Buffalo."

"Buffalo and a number of stops over that way. So it's been a busy week since I visited your rural yet lovely establishment."

Joe is calculating the dates, "Nine days actually," adding, "hope you're not superstitious."

It takes Bill a moment to do his own calculation, "Oh, Friday the 13th."

"A scholar and possibly a gentleman," his older brother says kindly. "Fortunately we don't have Norse roots as far as I know."

When Bill gives him a blank look, Joe adds, "That's where the superstition comes from."

"I see," Bill says, still standing with his valise in hand, "but some of those Norse fellas married Irish gals when they showed up. I gather they weren't invited."

Joe looks at his brother, "I'm not sure 'married' is the right term."

Bill looks down at his hand, feels the firm grip he has around the handle. "That's right," he says, "those Norse weren't Catholic."

Joe takes a moment, "You are planning to stay, I hope. You can take a seat you know, put your bag down."

Bill goes into the parlor, puts his valise down and when he turns around says by way of summary, "Yeah it was a good trip." He hesitates and adds, "Sorry about last time."

"Sorry?"

"I had a mite too much to drink."

"Well, anyway, I'm very glad to see you. While you've been off galivanting on your trip…"

"Working," Bill intervenes.

"Right, well I've been doing a little research, newspapers, used to be in the trunk, and I wanted to show you something. It relates to where we left off."

"You're going to have to help me there."

"You remember we were going to talk about the boat."

Bill returns a blank look, says "Okay."

"I can show you a little background before we get to that story."

Bill hesitates, "Before we do that, can I just say I have spoken recently with cousin Dan. A little."

"Say no more."

"He's really upset. Wants me to stop talking. Here's a quote: 'your brother Joe is full of you know what.'"

Joe looks at Bill, and after a moment says, "He's jealous."

Bill looks at his brother. "You serious?"

"Not really but look it really doesn't matter. The truth will come out, and I can't help it if Uncle John chose me, the lucky heir to whom he would pass on family history. Actually, he didn't so much choose me as I was there, just the right age I guess. Back home. Older cousin Dan had already seen the great lights of Buffalo and crossed the border. You were in school and I was helping out at the farm, father had died, and there was our dear uncle John, sitting in his usual rocking chair, watching the stop sign, as you might say in your travels, getting very close."

Joe watches as his younger brother picks up his bag. Joe says, "You probably want to wash up. Take your usual room. I assume you'll appreciate the accommodations, though by now you know it's not the Waldorf."

Bill nods his head and as he starts to walk toward the stairs, says to Joe without turning around, "Frances in?"

"Ladies Auxiliary," Joe calls out to his brother already halfway up the steps.

"FRESHENED up?" Joe asks some moments later.

"Fresh as fresh can be," replies the brother, mustache neatly trimmed, no longer wearing his double-breasted wool suit and brightly colored tie, with silk handkerchief in the jacket pocket.

"The hell is that?" the younger brother stops and asks, seeing the small pile of pages that appear ready at any moment to turn to dust. He recognizes them as old newspapers, fragile, yellow, newsprint already badly fading. They are stacked reverently on a small table in the parlor.

"Have a seat," Joe says.

Bill pulls up the closest chair, its dark wood frame showing signs of decay, varnish peeling, though the plump needlepoint seat appears to have been recently upholstered. He points to the chair and asks "From the farm?"

"Canada? Yes," Joe answers. "Good Provincial seating."

"Ontario."

"Where else?"

"But is it safe to sit on?"

"For Chrissake will you take a load off?"

As Bill sits down he says, "Well lookey here. Did you just take these from the Geneva hotel?" and peering over the paper on top reads out loud, "June 13, 1886, The New York Times." Looking up at his brother he asks, "Anything in here about Hitler yet? I know he's got you worried."

Joe decides to ignore his brother's remarks, picks up the paper and says "I want to turn to page 10."

Bill waits for his brother to find the right page, then asks "No coffee?"
"Correct, no coffee. Here we go."

"You see," Bill says looking at the top of the page, "the price is three cents?"

"Yes, I do see that," says his brother. "Okay now, let me put this here where we can both see it, and I'll read certain sections."

The New York Times

June 13, 1886

Irish Slaves of the Soil

The Late Earl of Leitrim and his tenants

A remarkable contract which the earl's serfs signed—

an instrument of oppression and cruelty

The Earl of Leitrim, one of Ireland's most cruel and oppressive landlords, was murdered in the highway near his country seat, in Donegal, on April 2, 1878. With him were killed his clerk and his driver. He was 72 years old, but advancing years only served to harden his heart. To the poor slaves of the soil who worked his lands because there was no hope of getting bread in any other way he was merciless, and there were men in Donegal who had sworn to avenge the terrible wrongs that their helpless sisters or daughters had suffered at his hands. Near the spot where his body was found was the ruined cabin from which he had driven a starving widow, and just before his death he had declared his purpose to eject families from their little holdings"

"Sweet guy. I thought Dillinger was bad."

Joe puffs his cheeks, blows out slowly, "Makes you appreciate the time and place we came from."

Bill thinks about this a minute, says, "But the family came over in 1849, thirty years earlier."

Joe looks at his brother, impressed, "May wonders never cease, you got that year right. The thing is, the great famine didn't stop instantly and everywhere across the country."

Bill considers this. "We didn't hear stories like this from father. Or Uncle John and company."

"Do you wonder why?" Joe asks.

After a moment Bill says, "I'm sure there must have been some good landlords."

Joe looks at his brother askance, then says, "let me jump ahead in this piece. Here, read this."

The poor serf whom the lease calls a "tenant," is bound by an almost interminable list of "agreements."

"Later on," Joe interrupts, "it describes a list of crops the tenant could grow and just how and when, at his peril."

The tenant also agreed to trim the hedges and cleanse the ditches, gutters, and water courses every year; to "weed and defend the young quicks in the fences"; to carefully preserve all timber, underwoods, and saplings, and to pull up all thistles, docks, and nettles not only in his land but also on the adjoining roads. As he binds himself to preserve "all game, rabbits, wild fowl and fish exclusively for the landlord," it follows of course that he agrees "not to keep any kind of Hound, Setter, or other kind of Sporting Dog."

"The bastard," Bill mutters. "And what are young quicks?"

Joe shrugs his shoulders.

"But you're the farmer," Bill says.

"Not in 19th century British dominated Ireland, thank God."

The late Earl seems to have been moved by a desire to prevent his fortunate tenants from falling into habits of idleness and sloth.

"Don't you love how those old-time newsmen wrote back then? May newspapers and journalists forever be free," Joe says.

"It's not free, it's three cents."

They were required to draw every year a certain number of loads of coals, turf, or other fuel for his use from places not more than 12 miles distant, and also a certain number of loads of stones, timber, or other building materials "for any works at or near this Mansion house." But for this they received no wages. The Earl generously agreed to pay "the traveling expenses, if any."

"Look at this farther on," Joe says.

When the Leitrim tenant wanted new drains or a new barn there were two courses open to him, and if he took either of them he was probably sorry that he hadn't taken the other.

"It's a good thing we got out," Bill says. "I can't imagine why any folks would have stayed."

"Well, hang on, look at this bit."

When Mr. Tuke, a quiet English gentleman, was on the shores of Mulroy Bay in 1880, he wrote as follows about "a curious instance of the late Lord Leitrim's capricious treatment of tenants." : In passing by a tenant's holding, Lord L. noticed that a good new cabin had been built in place of the miserable hovel. He stopped and asked how it was he had not been consulted, and at once ordered his bailiff to pull the chimney down and partly unroof it, and the man was compelled to leave it and live in the old hovel again."

"You got to be kidding."

"I kid you not, the tenants under their leases were completely at the mercy of the landlord, as far as eviction, removal, or rents were concerned. The tenant was bound to make such repairs as the landlord shall demand, it says somewhere in here. Or, get this, to pay for them if the landlord makes them.

"There is an account in here farther on about a kindhearted country banker of Hertfordshire, and what he wrote on a journey that reminded him of scenes of the great famine 30 years earlier, in the winter of 1846-7."

The scene of Lord Leitrim's murder was passed at a spot where the road is densely wooded on one side, and a few furze bushes afford shelter on the other and a short, abruptly steep hill necessitated a car going at a walking pace.

"They didn't have cars then."

"I think that was a description of a buggy."

We visited a number of cabins, from some of which the inhabitants had been evicted by the late Lord. The present Lord had permitted the people to return and this was felt to be a great act of kindness by priest and people, but it appeared of doubtful future benefit to permit people to return to the cabins which had been unroofed and ruined by the late Lord. The rents are higher than they had been. The cabins were absolutely windowless and quite dark. One elderly woman had come back alone to her ruined homestead and out of the stones had constructed herself a hovel, in which she was living. It was doorless and windowless and the size of a pig sty. Such is the extraordinary attachment of the people for their homesteads that they are returning and patching up their miserable dwellings as best they may.

"Look at this last part."

They are like shipwrecked sailors on a plank in the ocean; deprive them of the few inches by which they hold on and you deprive them of life. Deprive an Irishman of the few feet of land by which he holds on and you deprive him of all that makes life possible.

Bill looks up from the paper that he is reading along with Joe. Joe leans back, takes off his glasses and rubs his eyes.

"What do you think?" Joe asks.

Bill starts to nod his head slowly, "I think I want a smoke."

"I'll get us some milk and meet you outside."

"Milk?"

"Couldn't be more fresh and it's loaded with all the nutrients you need."

Bill hesitates, "All the nutrients they didn't have."

Neither of them speak for a moment, they are like silent, well removed witnesses. Some crimes reach the horizon of being unspeakable.

Joe puts his glasses back on, reacquiring his more familiar appearance. "Meet you outside," he says.

CHAPTER 31

Recording More Than Sales

Friday, October 13, 1933

THEY ARE STANDING NEAR the front door. Bill takes the cigarette out of his mouth to accept the cold glass of fresh, unpasteurized milk, passing the cigarette to his left hand so that he could hold the glass with his right. It's a chilly bright afternoon and they will stay outside for as long as Bill's cigarette has any life left in it.

Without any outward signal, they toast each other with the clink of their glasses. They each take a sip and proceed to look out at the open spaces in front of the house and off to the side, as if mirror relations.

After a time Bill says, "You know, thinking about all that old history..."

"Yes?"

"Remember when we were talking about the Blueshirts and you gave me the thumbnail sketch about the Irish Civil War? I mentioned I had met this wonderful old timer several years ago, and didn't he have a lot of stories, political stories."

"Irishman?"

"Couldn't be more so, right from Ireland, had the accent. He loved to talk. We were in the bar of the Algonquin, maybe, or the Lincoln. Might have been Hotel Astor, the one with its rooftop bandstand."

"I hear some broadcasts from New York. By the magic of the wireless, not like you, in person."

"Trying to think of his name. Divan, Deloy...first name was John, that I remember."

"Divan is a couch."

"You wouldn't believe everything he had done, the people he knew."

Joe looks at his brother, takes another sip of the milk. "Was he on the up and up?"

"Had to be, or else he was quite the student of history. I remember going to the library later to check out some of the names he was dropping in the middle of his various escapades."

"This was in the bar. He was drinking. You too I assume."

Bill ignores his brother's doubt. "You should have seen that library. And the comely young librarians."

Joe looks at his brother, "Cute looking gals in the library?"

"Hey, it's New York City. Lots of pretty women working there. Got to find a way to make ends meet, especially in this day and age."

Joe is a little uncomfortable, he looks down at his feet, notices some pieces of hay sticking to his left shoe.

Bill tilts his head to see where Joe is looking. Bachelor farmer, he thinks but doesn't say.

"Oh!" Bill says suddenly, causing Joe to look up in alarm. "I remember. You ever hear of Patrick Pearse?"

"Patrick Pearse? No, sorry."

"Michael Davitt?"

"No. How do you remember these anyway?"

"I wrote down some names in my sales account book to remember them. A little space in the back. And I did some reading. Gals in the library were very helpful."

"I bet."

"Oh, here's one you might know. Parnell, Charles Stewart Parnell."

Joe's eyes widen, he shifts his stance. "You serious?"

"Yessir."

"You remember why he is so famous?"

Bill looks down at his cigarette, sees that it is approaching its fiery end. "No," he has to admit to his older brother. "I know he had something to do with what they call the Easter uprising. Wait, no, I think I have that mixed up. That was someone else. Anyway, this old timer at the bar worked with Parnell."

"Man's name again?"

"Parnell. Oh, you mean my friend. Delroy? That's close. Should have written his name down too. Maybe I did, I could check one of my old sales books."

"When was this?"

"A fair time ago. I think he passed away before the stock market crash in '29, so the late 20's. Saw his name in an obituary, must be 5 or 6 years ago. I was spending a lot more time in the city then."

"I remember that. Don't think I wasn't worried about you."

"I was fine."

"More about your eternal soul."

After a moment, Bill says, "I remember he was involved in the newspaper business."

"Who was?"

"My old friend in New York, the Irishman. I remember now, it was some kind of Irish Catholic rag. He was lamenting that it wasn't selling as well as in the days of yore, as he might say."

"God bless the free press," Joe says, "even if it does cost three cents. By the way, speaking of news, do you notice how many democracies around the world are going belly up?"

"Hope that doesn't happen to dear old Ireland. If they are a democracy. I think they are. Are they? Of course they are," Bill concludes.

Joe takes another long look at his brother, "Asks the classy travelling salesman, who does not, God love him, seem to be all that affected as many of the rest of us are by this damn Depression." Joe looks away for a moment, "And then of course we have that fellow Hitler, elected this year."

"Oh, so Germany is a democracy," Bill says, as if to make a reassuring comment.

Joe looks down at his feet, and in a low voice says, "Maybe you missed the news flash. You heard about the Reichstag Fire Decree?"

Bill looks at his brother, "I'm sorry?"

"This was last February. Basically it abolished most civil liberties, and that was followed by something called the Enabling Act. Don't ask me to tell you the title in German. Their President Hindenburg signed it, and you can guess who was behind it. Gave Hitler plenary powers. It was termed "Law to Remedy the Distress of People and Reich.""

Bill hesitates. "How the hell do you remember all that?"

Joe looks at his younger brother, "Maybe it's the irony. And God help us if we have to go over there again to deal with them."

"Well," Bill muses, "at least democracy is safe over here."

Joe raises his eyebrows, clearly questioning Bill's statement.

Bill notices, says "Hey, we have laws, a Constitution."

Joe takes a deep breath before saying, "They used to have those too."

Bill wants to lighten the conversation, "Most of the business folks I deal with think we can stay out of it. Europe is a long way away."

A disagreeable pause ensues, and before it might take on a life of its own, sending out small waves of dis-ease, Joe makes a brief shuddering sound, a snort, like one of his cows in the barn might do.

Bill looks at his brother, "You okay there Bessie?"

"What was the name of that paper?" Joe asks.

"What paper?"

"The one your old Irishman wrote for."

"Oh. Let's see. Maybe, Celtic American. No, that's not quite right. Maybe Gaelic…"

"Glamour," Joe says.

Bill sees that Joe's mood has lifted, thanks be to god, he is actually grinning if only a little. Bill says "Fashion models eh? Stars of the Picture Show. That would sell better than political tales of woe from the old sod. Hot looking dames."

"They have them," Joe says.

Bill finishes his cigarette, and holds up his empty glass of milk, to which Joe nods. Both brothers notice that the weather is changing, getting colder.

"Rain?" Bill ventures.

"More likely snow," Joe concludes.

When they walk into the farmhouse, Bill starts thinking about hot chocolate but when Joe offers coffee, he is pleased to accept. Joe goes immediately into the kitchen as Bill steps into the parlor, wandering from window to window, glad to be inside, listening all the while to the familiar sounds of china and silverware being moved, a gas stove firing up, an icebox door opening and closing. He starts to look at the small library and finally settles into a comfortable chair, not the one with the needlepoint cushion.

After several quiet minutes, Bill hollers out, "I can come get it Joe."

"On my way already," Joe says, walking in from the kitchen with two cups. "You can suit yourself with cream and sugar, right out there on the table."

When they settle at last, Bill watches as Joe takes his first careful sip.

"It's hot," Joe says.

Bill nods his appreciation for the warning, and asks, "We were going to talk about the boat."

"Yes, we were." Joe looks over at his brother, puts his cup down, and then looks down at the rug. He seems to be having trouble starting.

"Is this another Paddy story, he who tells Uncle John who tells the illustrious farmer of Canadaigua, New York?" Bill asks.

Joe looks at his brother, nods his head. "Indeed, okay get ready for this."

"Ready. Maybe."

"Remember I told you that Uncle John spoke quickly, and sometimes so quietly that I could hardly make out what he was saying. And he had that thick Limerick accent."

"He told jokes?"

Joe ignores his brother's comment. "So, I have to say, I wasn't always terribly clear if I heard him correctly."

"I remember," Bill interrupts, "that if you couldn't understand Uncle John, it was your own damn fault. Says he."

"Didn't exactly invite you to ask him to repeat what he had just said," Joe concurs. "Speaking of which, I did hear him say one time clear as a bell, 'The damnable Earl had it coming.'"

Bill raises his eyebrows, "The one we just read about."

"Correct."

"Well," Bill says, "I think Uncle John may have been right about that. And now *excusez moi*, while I put some milk in my coffee."

As Bill heads for the kitchen, Joe calls out, "That must be Quebec French there eh? Sounded more Canadian than Continental."

After Bill returns and settles himself in the chair, Joe says, "Paddy was there you know."

Bill nearly spills his coffee, he'd put too much milk in his cup. He steadies his hand and takes a good long sip to lessen the risk of a future spill. When he puts his cup down he says, "The town we just read about, Leitrim?" eyes widening, "Where the Earl was filled with daylight?"

"What?"

"You know, plugged."

Joe looks at his brother. "You're talking Edward G Robinson."

"James Cagney," Bill shoots back. "Any chance you've seen "Little Caesar"?" Bill asks.

"No."

"There's a new one, "Lady Killer.""

Joe looks at his brother. "Some of us have to work, from pre-dawn until nightfall."

"And no expense account."

Joe takes his time drinking his coffee. Finally he says, "No."

Bill is almost smirking, "There's a reason I left the farming life."

"I mean no, Paddy was not there in Leitrim, though he was close by." Joe looks at his still simmering coffee for a moment, watching the steam rise. As an afterthought he adds, "I think everything is close over there. By American standards."

Joe ventures a sip of his coffee, returns the cup to the table. "When I say he was there, I mean he was in that area, actually it was the following year, and there was still a lot of buzz in the air about the murder, you can imagine." Joe pauses for a moment. "He went for what is called a monster meeting."

Joe sees that Bill looks bewildered. Joe repeats "Monster meeting."

Bill asks, "Is this one of those Irish fairy stories, you know banshees, beings that live in a well?"

Joe looks at his brother, "Like the *daoine sidhe*?" As he thought it might, this gets his brother's attention, at least for the moment. He adds finally, "A monster meeting is a huge rally, you might say."

A momentary quiet settles over the brothers, an informal intermission.

Bill fidgets in his chair, restless and impatient. He looks up and asks, "So what's with this damn boat?"

Joe looks over at his brother, "A damn boat is it now?" When Joe sees that Bill is waiting to hear more, he adds, "Actually it was not unlike the little number you admired in the field that time. Do you remember?"

Bill looks at his brother. "No." And then all of a sudden says "Oh! The Chaisson Dory." Bill is looking a little more hopeful.

Joe says, "Well it wasn't that. But close, from his description. Maybe a little larger. Held up to six men."

Bill is watching his brother, waiting to hear what comes next.

When Joe looks at his brother, he says, "He did talk so quickly, as I say, and in such a soft voice, heavy accent and all."

Joe pauses, recalling the conversation with his uncle from nearly twenty years before. He is gathering his thoughts. Something is wrong. He starts to breathe quickly, he wants to be an honest witness to his brother, an honor to his Uncle's memory, he wants to forget what Dan has been saying about him, but his mind becomes distracted, his focus shifts to his heart, beating rapidly. He knows men who have had heart attacks, one minute they're here and suddenly.... He takes several deep breaths.

"You okay brother?" Bill asks kindly.

"Sorry, yes, sure, fine." Joe blows out a big breath. "I may be getting my stories out of order here. I want to keep them straight."

"Okay," Bill says tentatively, keeping a closer eye on his brother.

"I'm the one he chose to talk to."

A pause, Bill says "Uncle John."

"Correct."

"Alright," Joe says, shaking his head, looking like he has recovered, "Okay," he says, both to reassure himself and his brother, "So out of all his stories, there is one word I'll never forget, something he seemed to stress. He said it had to do with Paddy."

Bill hesitates, "What was the word?"

"'Escape.'"

Chapter 32

Let's Blame Parnell

Friday, October 13, 1933

"Escape?"

"It was all jumbled up, Bill. I wish I could be clearer." Joe looks out the window, sees that it has started to snow lightly. "I hope," he says absent mindedly, "that Frances drives carefully."

Bill notices the snow coming down, asks "Is she a good driver?"

Joe doesn't immediately answer, and instead he asks, "Is your beauty out there okay?"

Bill hadn't thought about his car. "I'll go out in a couple minutes to check."

"Okay," Joe says. He sees that their cups are not yet in need of a refill. With little enthusiasm he asks, "Is there anything else I can get you?"

Bill looks at his brother who has turned again to look outside. He guesses that Joe is calculating the need to get out to the barn sometime soon. Make his own escape. He waits till Joe turns to look at him, and says, "Some answers."

"Right," Joe says, momentarily adjusting his horn-rimmed glasses. "Yes," he says, "she's a good driver, when it's not snowing." He waits a moment, sees that Bill is waiting to hear more.

Joe stands up, groaning in the cadence of a moan, stretches. "You should get up too. Good for the joints. Man was not made to sit so long, even in such a beautiful piece of machinery as yours out there," he says pointing toward the driveway.

Bill is afraid that his brother is about to walk away but instead of heading into the kitchen, he walks over to a small shelf of books in the parlor. Bill watches as his brother finds and carefully retrieves a large volume. As he heads back to their chairs, he starts to look at the table of contents, apparently finds what he is looking for and exclaims, "Aha! Got you, you little rascal," as if Joe has just found an errant baby pig. Country folk research. Joe pronounces authoritatively, "Parnell and the Land League, volume 2, chapter 21."

"I see," Bill says.

Joe sits down and says, "This is from A History of Ireland and Her People, Eleanor Hull, 1931."

"I guess I can't argue with that."

"Parnell, see, the great and apparently controversial Charles Stewart himself. The man your New York City old timer mentioned."

"Ah, yes."

"Parnell, who is famous for a lot of things, was actually in Westport at a Land League meeting in 1879, the same year that our Canadian immigrant Paddy O'Neil was in Ireland as well. Parnell was calling on farmers and peasants…"

"Peasants?"

"…to show the landlords how to hold a firm grip on their homesteads and land."

"That they didn't own."

Joe doesn't skip a beat, he is paraphrasing what is on the page. "The New Fenian movement, among other political forces, was demanding establishment of proprietorship. This had been a major theme of Parnell's work in the Parliament for a long time."

"Parliament?"

"Parnell was the leader of the Irish Party, had been in the British Parliament for a few years. Home rule for Ireland was a major issue for him. They were demanding separation from England."

Bill waits a moment, says, "I guess that wasn't asking too much. In 1879."

Joe is looking for something in the book, says, "Here we go:

> *On April, 22, 1875, Charles Stewart Parnell took his seat as Member for Co. Meath, in place of John Martin, who had suddenly died. The slim and quiet young man who unobtrusively entered the House...gave no sign of the power either over Parliament or of his own party that he was destined to attain. His own maiden speech was brief and nervous, uttered in a thin, unaggressive voice and with a marked English accent, but it contained the keynote of the position he was about to take up. 'Why?', he asked, 'should Ireland be treated as a geographical fragment of England? Ireland is not a geographical fragment. She is a nation."*

"Whoa," Bill says. "But you said English accent?"

"Ready for another shocker?"

"Go on."

"He was a Protestant."

"Mother of God!"

"In fact a Protestant landlord himself, living on his property at Avondale in Co. Wicklow. That's in Ireland."

"I figured." Bill hesitates, "So, that had to be something different. You wouldn't think a fellow like that would care for such a cause."

"Indeed not. His family was part of the Anglo-Irish gentry. It was said that this gave him some respectability in Parliament."

After a moment Bill says quietly, almost more to himself than to his brother, "I wonder what made him act so differently given that heritage."

Joe doesn't hesitate, "His mother."

"What?"

"She was American and held very anti-British views. His parents separated and his father died when he, Parnell, was in his teens. He inherited the estate from his father."

Bill takes a moment to digest all this, and finally says, "So I want to switch back to our dear Paddy for a moment."

"Yes," Joe says reassuringly.

"Paddy goes over there for this Monster Meeting."

"Yes. The first one ever. In Claremorris, County Mayo."

"How far is it from Claremorris to Westport?"

Joe looks at his brother as if Bill had just asked permission to milk one of the cows.

Bill notices his brother's expression. "You said that Parnell was in Westport the same year, for that what's-its-name-meeting."

"Land League meeting."

Joe tips his head backward suddenly, "Oh, ok." Joe smiles at his brother. "You're wondering whether our Paddy ever met Mr. Parnell in the flesh?"

"You got me."

Joe leans back in his chair, looks outside and sees that the snow has stopped, leaving a light coating of pure white on all the world outside. When he turns back to his brother he says, "Thirty-five."

"Miles?"

"Kilometers."

"How do you know all this? Never mind," he says.

"Uncle John gave me some details, and I jotted down the odd note here and there to help me remember. I've always been good about numbers. Have to be in farming."

Bill looks at his brother with a new appreciation for his apparent knowledge of Irish affairs.

As if reading his mind, Joe says, "Also, I had to fill in some gaps in what Uncle John told me. During the winter, things get quieter around here. I like to read, visit the Geneva library." He pauses for a moment. "The fine librarians on staff are a tad more matronly than in your big city experience."

Bill smiles, says, "I'm so sorry."

"But by god are they a whiz at directing you in the right direction."

"I suppose that's important too."

"One of them recommended this particular book here. I ordered it but didn't tell Frances what it cost."

Bill shakes his head, affirming what his brother is saying. He adds, "And you were the lucky recipient of whatever it was that Uncle John shared with you and you alone, you lucky devil. That must have whet your appetite for learning more of the history, I'd say."

"You'd be right about that brother."

Joe looks out the window again, though it looks as if he is seeing something other than the renewed brilliance of the world outside. When he turns back to his brother he says, "And now it's me that has a confession to make."

Bill looks at his brother, waiting to see what this might be about.

"I realize as I am bringing up some of these details, that I have led you astray a bit. I know this sounds a little disjointed. I've actually been wanting to talk about this with you for quite some time. Somebody who would listen." Joe looks away for a moment. When he turns back to his brother he says, "I too have wondered whether our Paddy met Parnell in Westport that year. In fact, he did meet Parnell."

Bill becomes aware of the fact that his mouth has opened. He closes his mouth and strokes his mustache, as if this had been an intentional movement.

"And, sorry, I'm not sure if it was in Westport. Where he did meet Parnell though was in the States, the following year, 1880. Paddy did some traveling after he returned from Ireland and apparently he was still doing some work for the movement."

Bill hesitates, but before he can formulate his question, Joe says, "The brotherhood. Freedom in the homeland."

"Canada?"

"The other homeland."

Bill sits back in his seat, trying to take this all in. He shakes his head. After a lengthy silence, he asks slowly, "What does the meeting…"

"Monster meeting."

"…Yes, have to do with this issue about escape? You said Uncle John stressed that word when talking about Paddy."

Joe looks uncomfortable, he looks down at his shoes, and when he lifts his head to look at his brother, he answers in his deep baritone voice, "Absolutely nothing."

Bill looks at his brother in disbelief, his voice rises, "And then it turns out he did meet Parnell, but that was a year later, and in the States?"

Joe answers slowly, "He may have met him in Ireland too, we just don't know." He hopes to be reassuring, the voice of reason, a calming sense of distance.

His brother does not look one bit calmer, so Joe adds, "Sometime I'll have to tell you about all the boycotting that went on over there. Captain Charles Boycott, land agent. Next time you're in the big city library, get one of your young ladies to look that up. It should be easy. But at any rate, I digress."

There is a lengthy silence.

"Yes, you do," the younger brother intones slowly.

"You'd like to hear about the boat too."

Bill says nothing, leans forward.

After a moment, Joe says, "You know you said it was quite an honor that Uncle John shared some secrets with me. A kind of gift. One I didn't ask for."

Bill is listening closely.

"It's also kind of a curse, his telling me things that Paddy told him not to share, things that are largely waiting for Toronto."

"Toronto?"

"The papers that will be opened to the public at the University."

"Oh."

"Next century."

"Great," Bill answers sarcastically.

"I was so excited to be able to share this with you. I figured you'd be more receptive than our dear cousin Dan."

"Okay."

"So relieved, you might say, that I tripped over my own words, memories."

Bill looks at his brother, nods his head, a hint of compassion.

Joe clears his throat, loudly. "I think when you mentioned that your old timer at the bar knew Parnell and had worked with him, well frankly, that threw me for a loop. So I guess I could blame Parnell for my getting a little excited, and then confused. God knows I wouldn't be the first. Parnell, I mean, with the people of his time, creating some confusion, controversy... okay, never mind."

Joe looks away, and when he faces his brother he says, "Now let me put the record straight, first things first."

"Okay."

"Paddy had made an earlier trip to Ireland." Joe looks away for a moment, "That must have been something, travelling overseas that long ago."

"When?"

"1865."

"1865?"

"'It was by sail, my boy,'" Uncle John told me in his thick accent. He was so excited to tell me. I think it was an adventure for him to talk about it. He was returning home to Ireland by proxy, seeing himself in Paddy's shoes, a legitimate traveler with decent accommodations. Not," Joe stops and shakes his head, "like some poor beggar cast away, as we've been told."

Joe sees that his brother may not be following him. "The famine, the horror," he says, "the stories we've heard from father. 1849." When he sees that his brother is struggling to follow him, he adds simply, "When our family came over. We talked about this. Probably in the kind of ship the history books call a coffin ship."

For a moment Bill doesn't say anything. Finally he says, "I never heard a lot of these details."

Joe looks at his brother, says, "That's right. I'd forgotten. They wanted to protect the youngest, I think," adding after a moment, "you might be better off not knowing."

Bill looks out the window and sees that the snow is starting up again, covering up the world outside in every which way, trees, grass, his car parked in the driveway. The snow blankets everything with the lightest touch.

After a moment Bill says quietly, "Not knowing," repeating his brother's words, adding "better off."

Joe watches his brother, this younger brother who continues to look out at the fields around the house, fields that go on and on like an endless sea. He doesn't want to interrupt whatever his train of thought might be at the moment. He thinks it will be helpful when he can share what he was about to say a moment earlier.

Bill will probably appreciate this. When Uncle John had spoken about Paddy's trip in 1865, Joe had not appreciated the history, the story he was hearing. Such a quiet voice, virtually whispering as if someone in the farmhouse down the road could mistakenly overhear him. It was a drama he urgently needed to share with someone, too long kept imprisoned in his failing body, arthritic hands that could no longer hold a pen.

Uncle John had sworn an oath to Paddy to remain silent, but it had become too difficult to remain faithful. And what harm was in it, after all these years? When John spoke at last with Joe, he had been living alone, aside from the occasional kindnesses of more distant relatives and friends. So many of Paddy's old comrades had passed away. Surely Paddy was no longer in danger of betrayal. John's own end was fast approaching.

Bill continues to look mesmerized by the land, the call of wide-open spaces, the light blanket of snow. Joe wonders if had personally inherited Uncle John's need to share secrets at last, the terrible pressure of keeping quiet for so long.

Joe will share this story with Bill: Stephens, the great man himself, formerly the author and editor-in-chief of the Irish People newspaper, was considered one of the principal leaders of the Fenians in Ireland. In 1865 he was arrested in Dublin and put in jail. It would take a fellow named John Devoy and several others to help pull off a successful escape, aided and abetted by a Canadian adventurer.

CHAPTER 33

Let's Blame Parnell Part Two
Friday, October 13, 1933

JOE WAITS, WATCHES HIS brother who has turned once again to look out the window, he seems to be staring at the lightly falling snow. He wonders what Bill makes of what he has just heard, the story of James Stephens' rescue and Paddy's part in it, such as it was, told in deliberately abbreviated fashion. It was Joe's hope to test the waters a bit, hopefully maintain Bill's interest while satisfying his curiosity, and lessen, dear god, his brother's complaint of feeling left out.

After an extended silence, Bill's first two comments are not what Joe anticipates.

"Frances is still at her ladies auxiliary thing. Those gals can talk." And, as Bill turns slowly away from the window, "Isn't it a little early to have snow? For Chrissakes it's only mid-October."

Joe looks at his brother, answers "Yes," adding unhelpfully, "It happens."

After a brief moment, Bill says in a soft-spoken voice, "So I see."

Joe watches as Bill raises his eyebrows, then lifts his index finger to feel his mustache, followed by opening and then closing his mouth. Finally, Bill says slowly, "So, wait a minute, you're telling me that Paddy O'Neil, our Paddy, was involved in a daring escape way back in 1865, in Dublin?"

"Yes indeed. Well, outside of Dublin, a suburb I guess you'd say."

"Of a famous Fenian named Stephens?"

"Yes."

"When were you going to tell me this?"

Joe looks at his brother, says simply, "Now."

"Now?"

"I just did."

Bill looks away for a moment, and when he turns back to his brother he says, "You're a man of mystery Mr. Donohoe. Who knows what other stories remain untold?"

Joe nods his head and begins to smile. "So you're ready to hear some more?"

Bill looks at his brother and says with more than an edge of sarcasm, "Hello?"

Joe takes a moment to gather his thoughts. "Pleased to hear it. Now look, what I just told you was a truncated, shall we say, summary of the story uncle John told me."

Bill looks at his brother, "Truncated, is it?" He takes a moment to look away and when he turns back, he says "Say that would be a swell idea some day!"

"What would?"

"To publish stories, novels, anything really, in a shortened fashion. They could call it Trunk books or trunk notes."

"'Trunk'? Like Paddy's trunk?"

Bill considers this, says "No, wrong image. Image is everything. What is a very small piece of luggage?"

Joe decides to play along, thinks for a moment, "How about briefcase?"

"Bingo! Get your briefs here, eh? Say we could make a mint!"

Joe looks at his brother. "I'm not sure you've hit on the right image. In these parts your customers will be picturing long johns."

Bill shakes his head, "Okay farmer Joe. Well, you and your farm set can read all those pages, the novels, the stories. You have your long winter evenings, with time to spare. But the rest of us are on the go in this fast-paced life."

"You and your fast-paced life," Joe says.

"Hey fella, you got to make a buck. Somebody's going to invent something like that. Just you wait. Reading Briefs, yessir."

Joe sighs, appreciating all the more the fact that he stayed on the farm for all its demands, maintenance, uncertainties, whims of weather. The rewards of breathing clean air, appreciating the peacefulness in the country, being more or less one's own boss. Less, as of late. Also, sister Frances' home cooked meals and freshly made bread.

Joe looks at his brother, hoping he hasn't lost him already, fast paced indeed.

Bill catches the signal, says "Go ahead, shoot."

"And now the rest of the story," Joe says, but sees that Bill is not about to wait.

"Paddy rescues this old guy," Bill begins immediately, "who is supposedly famous, Paddy doesn't tell anyone but his good friend our Uncle John, who after many years and at a very advanced age tells the young and highly impressionable Joseph Donohoe. A story with god knows how many mistakes in the telling."

Joe shakes his head, "I guess this is one of your 'Briefs.' I must say it leaves something to be desired. Or not. The fellow rescued was not old, by the way."

Joe looks down for a moment and when he looks up again he says, "Yes it certainly is possible that information got jumbled, you know how it is, you're riding along in the tractor out in the field, along the way baling wire gets loose, a bit of hay falls out here and there by the wayside." He checks to see his brother's response. His brother is, surprisingly, all ears.

"It's what," Joe continues, "1916 or thereabouts when our dear Uncle John anoints me with his whispery, brogue-heavy set of broken promises to Paddy, information Paddy wanted to keep mum. I'm 22, dealing with the loss of father still, taking care of mother, barely thinking about having a life of my own otherwise."

Bill hears Joe's recollection as if for the first time, nods his head more in appreciation than agreement. He quickly interjects, "I hope to god there is a boat in the middle of all this."

Joe looks away, looking as if he needs to be careful about proceeding. In a quieter voice Bill asks, "This is the story about an escape?"

Joe turns back to face his brother, nods his head, "The right one," he answers apologetically.

Before Joe might have a chance to continue, Bill suddenly shouts "Stephens!"

Joe, startled, looks at his brother, saying cautiously, "Yes, Stephens, that's who I mentioned."

"Stephens!" Bill shouts again.

Joe takes a breath, says, "Okay, there's something I'm not getting here."

"We read something before about Stephens, earlier in Uncle John's journal, remember?"

Joe looks puzzled. "Uncle John's journal? Uncle John wrote a lot, god knows, but not…I'm not remembering anything he wrote about Stephens."

"Volume 18 if memory serves."

"I should say, my young fellow, how do you remember that?"

"Jones Woods, that's what he talked about. New York City. It got my attention. You know, New York City. Full of bright fellows and beautiful dames."

Joe looks at his brother with concern, "In the library."

"In the library and everywhere else. Hey brother, you've got to get out of Geneva and the Finger Lakes sometime."

Joe squinches his eyebrows together, "Alright, Jones Woods rings a bell. A very little bell."

"Uncle John described it as a kind of reunion Paddy had with Stephens."

"What year was this?"

"18 something or other. Later than 1865."

"I see. I find your exactitude suspicious if not alarming."

"That's a compliment, right?"

"Reunion, eh? So there's a bit of evidence that Paddy met Stephens at an earlier date."

"Well, hello, good Godfrey!" Bill exclaims, "Of course that means he met him before." Bill notices that Joe looks a tad befuddled, and says by way of clarification, "Look, the grand rescue, escape, whatever the hell it was that you haven't finished talking about, that took place in 1865."

"Yes," Joe answers.

"And the meeting in Jones Woods in New York was later, so that meeting in the Woods was at least their second meeting. A reunion, see? I rest my case."

Bill takes a moment while his brother digests this information and studies Bill's face.

Bill continues, "Unless you are making this up about our dear Paddy. Rescuing some Irish upstart." He looks closely at Joe. "You aren't making this up, are you?"

Joe frowns, looks down and away before looking back at Bill, "You've talked some more with Dan?"

"Regretfully, yes. Although not for much longer."

Something shifts within the closeted atmosphere of the farmhouse.

Bill looks out the window again and notices that the snow has stopped. His car is lightly coated but it looks as if the snow is already beginning to melt. He says, as a kind of afterthought, "No Frances yet."

Joe says, "She usually takes her time getting back. But it could be anytime now."

Bill says simply, "Cigarette."

THE air is very cold outside, Joe sports a long scarf, thickly woven of blue and green plaid, but he leaves his coat inside unlike Bill who wears his finely tailored camel hair overcoat.

Joe takes a couple steps away from the front door so that he can check up and down the road, anticipating his sister's imminent return.

Bill appears to be silently focused on his cigarette and whatever thoughts may be flying up and around its wisps of smoke, billowing, thick and thin, disappearing into the otherwise clearing skies of the Finger Lakes countryside.

After a time, Joe says "Well," noticing that his brother appears unaware how dangerously close the glowing red tip of the cigarette is approaching a mustachioed upper lip. The cigarette remains stubbornly perched in a mouth that otherwise remains closed shut.

At the last possible instant Bill utters, "Damn," and quickly swings the remains of the cigarette out of his mouth and away in one steady motion. The glowing embers of tobacco sail ten feet out into the snow-covered yard and are immediately extinguished in an inch of white fluff. "Jesus Christ," Bill says, and Joe knows that this is no prayerful anointing of the front lawn.

Joe is thinking how his salesman brother is usually careful, circumspect. When it comes to lighted cigarettes, he would always, assiduously in fact, have a pre-planned ashtray nearby.

As Joe waits, Bill begins to rock back and forth on his feet before saying, "I know you are getting tired of hearing this, but I am forever amazed how much I don't know about our family's history." Adding, "A daring rescue indeed."

"No one knows," Joe replies quickly. "That is, for the longest time no one knew."

Bill looks at his brother, "And then you told Dan."

Joe looks out toward the street, sees that Frances is still nowhere in sight, in fact sees no cars in sight. After a moment he says, "Among others."

"Jesus, Mary, and Joseph."

Joe looks sharply at Bill.

"I say that prayerfully of course," Bill adds.

After a long while Joe says, "I was intending to tell you this earlier. But," and now Joe seems to stand up straighter, finding a plausible line of argument, "Dan is Uncle John's oldest son. And he has always been the keeper of Uncle John's journals."

Joe looks at Bill, continues, "Speaking of which, like I say, it was not exactly a simple blessing that I was in the right place at the right time for Uncle John to start sharing stories, stories that were not written in the journal. May you never have a family elder entrust such things to you."

Bill steps back, twists his head to look at Joe sideways and says, "Too late."

"What? Oh, yeah, ok. Well join the club."

Bill looks down at the ground for a moment, and when he raises his head, says to Joe, "You'd think that, once Paddy had passed, if Uncle John just couldn't keep quiet about his friend, he would have at least said something to his wife, or maybe his oldest son."

Joe looks at Bill for a moment, and says, "In fact that's exactly what he did. But it was years earlier before he got around to telling me."

"What?"

"Which is part of why Dan was so upset, learning that his father had started to speak with someone outside the immediate family."

Bill doesn't say anything for a moment, and then says slowly, "Uncle John had spoken with his wife and oldest son already—"

Bill remains silent, while Joe studies his face. Joe finally says, "And what, you might ask, was their reaction when Uncle John shared Paddy's stories with them?" Without waiting further, Joe answers, "They wanted him to keep quiet, honor Paddy's request for secrecy. Frankly, I think they were afraid."

Bill looks out over the lawn, out past the road and the fields beyond. When he turns back to face his brother, he asks, "Afraid of what?"

"Paddy was not the simple farmer he appeared to be. He, they feared, had risked the family's safety by doing his political jig steps all over the place, spying here, spying there, and Canada was still closely tied with the Crown." After a moment he adds, "Add the Crown was not exactly Ireland's best friend."

Bill hesitates, "But that was Paddy's doings, not Uncle John's."

"Too close for comfort. Dan told me his mother didn't want to hear anything about it, and when his father turned to himself as the oldest son, Dan sided with his mother, told his father just so. Quite strongly, I gather. I don't think Uncle John got very far with how much he told. And then he went quiet. Until some years later when he turned to his handsome nephew who is standing here before you."

"Mother of God!" Bill says.

"So then yours truly begins to blab sometime later, well, you can begin to see how Dan might have felt."

Bill turns once again to look at the fields. Uncluttered distance, as far as the eye can see. He remains silent for several minutes, until in a far-away tone of voice, one that sounds diminished in such a wide-open space, he says "Last week I was with one of my customers." He turns back to face Joe, speaking more clearly, "Did I ever mention Rudi Figenscher to you?"

Joe looks at Bill, "No, but it's a fine Irish name."

"Yeah, well anyway, he mentioned that a relative of mine had been there and told him not to believe everything I might say about politics."

Joe says, "By god Bill, I don't know the man."

"Rudi is German, see, and is feeling very threatened about this Nazi business."

"Well, Like I say…"

"It was Dan. Not a place he normally visits but I must have said something once to him about Rudi and he remembered and introduced himself."

Joe considers this. "He was probably just being friendly," and after a moment adds, "He wouldn't share any of our history. Rest assured. It's the last thing he'd do."

Bill looks at his brother, "But that's my territory, my business relationship, he has no business meddling in my livelihood."

"Of course."

"And you know the kinds of things he's said about the Paddy stories."

"That's family."

"Yes, and what he has said specifically about you and the Paddy stories."

"Well, that's family too."

"Right, but how do I know whether he might start to include me. You know, in the kind of things he says, sorry, about you."

"Well, see, maybe Frances is right. Maybe I should never have started to pass along what I'd heard."

Bill hesitates, considers this, says, "Well swell, it's a no-win, in that event the whole thing goes underground, until my future kids, if I ever have any, have to learn about it from some whoop de doo Toronto fella." After a brief moment he adds, "That is, if I don't tell them first."

"Bill?"

"Yes?"

"It's already water over the dam, in terms of what Dan is saying about you, but only to the family, mind you. Sorry to be the one to tell you that."

Bill stops and stares at his brother, the colorful scarf around his neck, the horn-rimmed glasses, the absence of a coat, the exhalations of words disappearing in the cold air, Joe's breath made briefly visible. Bill raises his voice, "Well doesn't that just gum up the works!"

"Bill, ok, slow down. Look I've already decided."

"What?"

"No more of Paddy's stories for Dan and the others. Only for you, if you don't mind."

"Mind? I've been wanting to know more about the family my whole life." After a moment Bill adds, "Sorry Joe, I just get steamed sometime."

Joe looks at his brother sympathetically, "I know, family can do that to you sometimes. We're in the same boat." Joe immediately regrets his choice of words and watches his brother for any reaction. Seeing none, he adds, "It seems that we need to be careful now. It's not worth the family getting more riled up. And I, we, need to honor Paddy's request."

Bill mutters, looks for another cigarette and decides against one.

"Patience, brother," Joe says, "remember, the truth will be known."

A car appears coming over the slight rise from Geneva.

Joe's scarf is getting loose, he takes one end and flings it successfully over his shoulder.

As they watch the car on its final approach, Bill says, "The boat."

"Yes," Joe says.

"It's about time," Bill says.

Joe looks at his brother with the hint of a smirk. "Well yes, but more precisely it's about the passing of time," and with an air of pontification, "one might say, history itself."

Bill looks closely at his brother, continues to look even as he decides at last to pull out his pack of cigarettes. He deftly smacks the tightly knit group so that he can pull out his next smoke. He holds the cigarette now between his thumb and forefinger, a move he had seen in a recent war movie, a German Colonel, the world's only World War. As he brings the unlit cigarette up to his mouth, he lowers his head while still watching his brother and says slowly, "And now you will tell me about this boat. Hopefully, no bum steer this time."

"What?"

"Last time you got your story mixed up."

Joe hesitates, finally says, "About the boat, I may have exaggerated some things just a tad, its place in the story." Seeing a change in his brother's expression, he adds, "I really wanted to gain your interest. I know how much you admire boats."

There is a long delay, during which Bill strikes a match, bends his head toward the small flame, cigarette in mouth. Ignition. A deep breath.

When Bill looks up toward his brother, the first wave of grey smoke rises, temporarily hiding his face.

Another moment passes. Bill says, "Joe, you should remain in the farming trade." And after a final thoughtful hesitation, "Don't try your hand at sales."

CHAPTER 34

The Fire Maiden

Friday, October 13, 1933

"OH, THERE SHE IS," Joe says, taking his scarf that had become loose and throwing one end over and around his neck again, tightening the noose.

The brothers watch as Frances drives the final distance down the road in front of the house, slows down to approach the farm's driveway, nearly comes to a dead stop out on the road as she approaches the driveway, and finally with an abundance of caution turns the wheel, causing the gravel to sound like bacon starting to cook on the iron skillet.

"By god she's ready for the race track," Bill says.

"Bit of a handicap, but gets over the finish line."

The brothers leave the front stoop where they had been standing and come out to greet the car. Frances pulls up, methodically looks at the dashboard, appears to rehearse the motions needed to turn off the engine, and then does so, to her delight, a sense of accomplishment.

Before opening the door, Frances reaches for a paper sack on the front seat, and then while carefully balancing the sack, begins to stiffly extricate herself. She opens the door, steps down to the running board and then down to the gravel driveway. Once free of the machine, she turns and gives the door a good metallic closing.

"Whoeee," she says, lightheartedly, "not as young as I used to be."

"Need help?" Joe asks.

"All set." She holds the paper sack out in front as if to demonstrate the slightness of the burden, "Preserves from Geraldine, you know her, married to that nice fellow Barney, not Catholic but a good man, hardworking, and their daughter, oh you should see her Joe, cute as a button, how fast she's grown. Geraldine's parents live over in Gorham out a ways, you might remember them Bill, often went to Mass as St Teresa's."

As the three of them begin the slow walk toward the side door of the house, Frances says, "Goodness Joe where is your coat? All you're wearing out here is that scarf? Look at your brother, he's got that wonderful warm looking affair. Bill always wears the nicest things."

"Well," Bill starts to say but before he can say another word Frances says, "So what have you two been up to?" at which point Joe kicks Bill's ankle, discreetly, and hard.

JOE told Frances that he needed Bill's help in the barn. Bill had changed into one of Joe's old coats that he used for milking and other chores. The sleeves were too long for Bill but he wore the role of being the younger and shorter brother without complaint. A city slicker disguised as an erstwhile farmer's helper.

It is surprisingly warm in the barn, and the air is thick with the presence of well cared-for farm animals and fresh hay. Joe points to two bales of hay on the floor along the wall, he holds out his arm, "Please," he says, inviting his brother to take a seat, "be my guest." Bill notices that they are just out of sight of the farmhouse, should Frances be looking their way.

"Okay," Joe begins in his familiar baritone voice, though a little more pronounced than usual. "Back to our regularly scheduled program. I want to pick up where we left off." He could be broadcasting from the well-known Famous Door on 52nd Street in the big city. Count Basie and his Orchestra about to begin.

"Where were we?" Joe continues, "Here we go, our Paddy was part of what was a large contingent of Irish patriots the day of Mr. Stephens rescue."

"How large?"

"Thousands. This isn't well known. They quickly captured some of the ring leaders, but others, including Stephens himself, avoided capture for several months. And then of course the great majority of those who had volunteered were never identified nor touched. The authorities had no idea how many were available to help if help had been needed. So, all those extras got away, slipped away in the night, and a rainy one it was. And our Paddy was, thanks be to God, one of them.

"Pretty ingenious, Stephens escape. Used a wax mold of a key and then helped him get up and over the prison walls with a rope, all planned out, they knew the routine of the guards making rounds."

"Inside job."

"You better believe."

"Did Paddy help with the rope or the fake key or…"

"Paddy," Joe cuts in, "was part of a diversion plan, a bit of fakery, sleight of hand you might say, using a boat."

"A boat! Oh Mother of God!" Bill exclaims with relief.

"He and his comrades were to rendezvous a little farther down the coast, south of Dublin, and make like they were about to receive the famous gentleman and whisk him away. Confuse whatever spies might be about to report on what was happening. Only, what was happening was a tremendous down pour, wind and rain, darkness all about. And it wasn't only the British authorities who would get confused if they had any inkling at all about what was happening."

"What do you mean?"

"Well the team that was assigned with the boat was all at the ready but they were missing one of their trusted lads."

Bill looks at his brother, shifts his weight and feels a few pointed ends of the hay bale poking through, right leg, upper thigh. He readjusts himself again, considers what Joe is telling him and says after a moment, "Oh… no." as his eyes widen.

"Here's the bottom line (he almost says 'kid'). He missed the boat, see."

At first Bill is silent, and then Joe hears his brother utter, "Oh my god."

And then, "did he even make it to the right place, you know, where the boat was?"

"Yes, and apparently got quite the ribbing. But all in good humor because, by that time, word was received that the plot had succeeded, Stephens was out and safely in place wherever he was to be hidden, also part of the plan. Paddy's co-conspirators told him there was no shame in it for him to miss the boat like he did, heavy rain and all. Uncle John said that Paddy repeated this part of the story a number of times."

"What part?"

"That the lads told him there was no shame in it, failing his assignment like he did." After a moment Joe adds, "I wonder though if Paddy didn't feel a wee bit guilty after all."

Bill looks away for a moment, and when he turns back to Joe, says "And that's the grand story about the boat? And what about his escape?"

"Stephens?"

"No Paddy's."

"Oh. Paddy didn't have to escape. He took his time, Uncle John told me. Went to France for awhile."

"Wait, what?"

"Here's the thing. Let me back up. I knew you were interested in boats. I wasn't so sure about your interest in history. I thought the boat part of it would be a good way to get your attention. Ever since you talked about that fellow's boat in the field. You remember? On one of your business trips, we talked about this."

Bill looks away for a moment. "But damn, Joe, this boat story of yours is…" and just for a moment Bill senses a resurrecting flicker of hope. He looks at his brother carefully, "Is there more to it?"

"The story of Stephens rescue?"

"No, the boat. Missed. That's it? End of story?"

"No, no, far from it." And then Joe hesitates.

"Yes?" Bill prompts.

"Stephens was in hiding for several months before he was finally captured, and then he…"

"No, I don't mean about Stephens. I mean is that it, as far as the boat?"

And now it is Joe who looks carefully at his brother, sitting there draped in an oversized work coat, part of the collar ripped. "Bill," he intones, "the boat is not the most interesting part of the story."

Bill looks away, in a low voice he mutters, "Not for you maybe." After a moment he asks, "Do you even know what kind it was?"

Joe looks puzzled, asks "What was?"

"The boat!"

"Oh," Joe says, sitting back on his bale of hay, looking over toward the cows. "I know Uncle John told me, wait a minute."

"I've been waiting quite a while."

Joe recalls a memory, "Uncle John was really something. I wish you could have heard him tell these stories. Whispering so that no one would hear, mind you, as I've said, talking fast in that heavy brogue, nearly out of breath.

"Looking back on it, I think he felt a little guilty for not keeping his promise to Paddy, you know, to stay silent. He was committing some kind of sin in his mind. But I'm sure he had faith that Paddy would forgive him after they met again."

"Met again?"

"Heaven."

"Oh, right."

"They were that close, had been for years."

Bill watches his brother, sees that he is still looking at the cows but doubts that it's cows he's seeing. He gives Joe another moment before saying, more quietly now, "Boat?"

Joe looks back at Bill, "Yes."

Bill waits. "Did it have a name?"

"Oh, I wouldn't know that."

"No, again I mean what kind of boat it was? Like a skiff, or dinghy or something like that?"

"Oh, yes, okay, he told me. I think he said something like 'Slacker.'"

"You sure about this?"

"Yes. Wait a minute. Holly? Is there a type of boat called a Holly? No I think it was called a Jolly."

Bill looks at his brother closely. "How do you remember all this?"

"Well, I'm not doing so well naming the boat."

"No, but otherwise. I mean, you have a lot of detail for all that he told you in a rush and that was like, what, 1917 or whatever and now it's 1933." Bill hesitates a moment. As if for review, he says "All this that you're telling me, what you heard from Uncle John."

"Correct."

"Who heard it directly from the horse's mouth."

"Paddy."

Bill looks away for a moment. "Did Paddy record all this in the material he took to Toronto?"

"Uncle John took it to Toronto."

"Right."

"On the train."

"Riding on the 'To Hell and Back'," Bill says.

"Yes," Joe says, delighted, "you remember I told you. Toronto, Hamilton and Buffalo." Joe looks over toward the stalls again, "As far as how much Paddy recorded, we won't know for quite some time, but I gather it was quite a bit, one or two full boxes as I mentioned before. Next century, getting closer all the time, only 67 years from now."

Bill calculates the time, "I'd be 103 years old when the papers are opened. And I'm younger than you."

"You might have a chance," Joe says, in a tone of wistful optimism.

Both brothers look away for a time until Bill asks "Back to the story?"

"Sure."

"Stephens escape or Paddy's?" Joe asks again.

"Paddy's, but he didn't escape, you say."

"No, not as such." Joe clears his throat, forcefully. "He still had to be careful. Paddy, we're talking about. He'd been quite involved in undercover shenanigans before, well, that's putting it mildly. I made the mistake of telling Dan at one point that Paddy had actually consulted with the Land League people over there in his later trip."

"Ireland, we're talking. He was a consultant?"

"In a manner of speaking yes. A landowner from the new world of Ontario, Canada. He could talk about how differently land ownership was handled over here. Not encumbered with the old ways of the Brits. Think about it. This was a time when Canada was way ahead of dear old Britain-ruled Ireland."

"Well doesn't that beat all. But why Paddy?"

Joe looks at Bill a moment. "Think about it. He was a known commodity to the Brotherhood."

"The Fenians."

"Indeed. And all the more reason he needed to play his cards close to his chest. Not get any government folks on either side of the ocean looking too closely at his past."

"Dan was not happy with this story."

"Maybe you can see why now. But. Speaking of Paddy's earlier affairs…"

"Affairs?"

Joe looks at his brother quietly for a moment, and finally says "Let's go back from 1879 to Stephens escape again, 1865. Do you remember 1866?"

"No. I wasn't born."

"Smart guy. What was the big event of 1866?"

Bill thinks about this for a moment, ventures "Lincoln was shot."

"That was the year before. Which led by the way to Andrew Johnson being elected in 1866 and he was a real stinker, you may remember."

Bill hesitates, "No, I don't. You're the one who reads history."

"After the Civil War and all that struggle, would you believe Congress overwhelmingly passes the Civil Rights Act of 1866, the first federal legislation to protect the rights of African-Americans, and, ready? President Andrew Johnson vetoes the bill. Fortunately Congress is able to override the veto."

Joe looks away for a moment, caught up in his recall of that era. Quietly he adds, "May we never have to put up with a leader like that again. Imagine having the leadership of Lincoln followed by Andrew Johnson. The great one is followed by such an embarrassment."

Joe takes so long staring in the direction of the cows nearby, that Bill begins to wonder if one of them has taken sick.

Finally Joe shakes his head, says "Where was I?"

Bill says, "Sitting on this bale of hay. You're still there."

"Sorry, oh, I left off with Paddy in France. What happened in 1866 was the American, sorry, Fenian invasion of Canada, up and over the border they came from Buffalo to Fort Erie, Ontario."

Bill is nodding his head, Joe hopes Bill remembers this history.

"We know that border well," Bill says, émigré that he and his siblings are. "Good race track there, Fort Erie. Won forty dollars once. Exchange rate not too bad at the time."

Joe was hoping for a bit more enthusiasm about the history. Bill looks distracted. In a quiet voice Bill says, "Charlie Fitzpatrick and I did some of our transactions there, during the Prohibition."

Joe looks at his brother. "Which is thankfully over."

"You can say that again."

"I'm talking about the risks that you took. Don't think we weren't worried sick."

"Good old C.F." Bill says, with some reverie. "I was afraid at one point that I would get old Charlie in the Hoosegow."

Joe gives his brother a blank look.

"Jail," Bill says, "and it would have been my fault."

Joe waits a moment, remembering his worries about Bill and his pal Charlie Fitzpatrick. He wants to get back on track, finally he says simply, "France."

"Right, Yes. Gay Paree."

"Well, maybe. We don't really know, but I wouldn't be surprised if Paddy was doing some groundwork over there for what was going to happen the next year see, part of his Fenian Brotherhood work. 1866. This part is a bit murky."

"This part?" Bill asks.

"Either he didn't tell his old friend John Donohoe much about France or his old friend maybe felt it was too sensitive to tell me?" Joe says, an open question. "At any rate Uncle John didn't tell me."

"Saints be praised," Bill says and after a moment adds, "I bet I know why he didn't talk about France."

Joe looks leans back on the bale of hay, arches his eyebrows and gives his brother a cautious look of skepticism. Finally he says, "Okay, I'll bite."

Bill smiles and says simply "Gay Paree."

"Yes Bill," Joe says patiently.

"You did say 'affairs' before. And clandestine might be about more than politics, if you know what I'm saying, especially in Gay Paree."

Joe sighs, not wanting to lose Bill's attention. He shifts his weight on the hay, and suddenly the idea comes to him.

"You know Bill, I don't know if you knew this, but years later when Paddy took his second trip, we're talking now 1879 again, he traveled on one of the earliest steamships, one that still had sails as well."

It worked. Bill is listening.

"And one of the fellows he met up with was someone who took part in the Stephens rescue with him years before, man's name was John Devoy."

He really has Bill's attention now. Bill's eyes are wide and shining.

"Who did you say?" Bill asks.

Joe is tempted to tease his brother, ask if he isn't more interested in learning the name of that grand steamship. He doesn't ask, finally, because he can't remember, though it did seem to be a fitting name related to Ireland. Instead, Joe looks at his brother and repeats "John Devoy."

"Oh my god!" Bill shouts. "Short little man? Involved in the newspaper business?"

Joe sits back on the bale of hay, "I wouldn't know," he answers, surprised. "You've heard of him?"

232 DRIVING THE AUBURN

"Heard of him?" Bill practically shouts, "I met him! New York City library. Well not in the library. In the bars there, he called them pubs. Would talk your ear off. I told you about him."

Joe leans forward. "I don't remember," he says at first and then "I remember you talked about your lady friends, wait, yes there was a fellow who talked a lot, you called him Divan or something, you couldn't remember his name, yes."

"For heaven's sake! John Devoy, quite the character. He knew Paddy?"

"Knew him? Apparently they were in cahoots as liberators," Joe says.

"That fits. He had a lot of stories. Knew everybody."

"Did he ever talk about Paddy?"

Bill considers this. "Well if he did, he didn't mention him by name, of course I never knew there might be a connection," adding, "He did talk about Parnell whom he knew well." Bill looks away, "I don't remember hearing the name Paddy O'Neil."

Joe considers this. "I'm not surprised. Uncle John said that Paddy would always be on the alert that one of his past lives, you might say, would surface. There might be hell to pay. A man like Devoy would know that."

The two brothers take a moment to digest their discovery. After a moment, Joe slaps his hand on his brother's leg, says "You had yourself a very close encounter there. Directly back with the history makers themselves."

Bill considers this, "In that bar in New York. If only I'd known."

Joe nods his head in agreement. After a moment he says, "You asked me earlier how I remember all these bits of information, the stories I heard from Uncle John."

"Yes."

"I took notes."

"You took notes?"

"How else could I remember?"

Bill hesitates, "Well, Godfrey, where are they?" Bill starts to look around the barn, "Are they in that tube with the old proclamation you showed me?"

"I did show you that didn't I," Joe says, pleased.

"Yes, so…"

"In my room, safe from the reaches of the older sister, she who seems to be the opposite of me regarding an interest in the past. She threatened…" Joe begins, now asking a question, "did I ever tell you this?"

"Threaten what?"

"To burn all the old newspapers. And maybe whatever else she might find of the same ilk. Imagine. No sir. So I keep my notes in safe hiding."

"Yikes," Bill says.

"You can say that again."

Joe gives his brother a look that seems full of unspoken words, Bill shifts his weight on the bale of hay, waits for his brother to speak and finally asks "What?"

"I did one time write down an observation that I thought was particularly important to remember, something Paddy had told Uncle John. When I read through his journal, I didn't see any reference to that particular topic. I'm tempted to get over to Dan's one day and when no one is looking slip the note into the last volume. Nobody looks at those old books anymore. It will be safe there."

Bill looks at his brother. "Safe from what…oh the fire maiden?"

"Ha," Joe answers, "No, safe from stirring up any more controversy. Yessir, that could be my little contribution to history eh?"

Bill cocks his head, "Well…" indicating that Joe may have made a wise move after all. "Don't let this go to your head," he adds.

Joe returns Bill's gaze, "What, fear of Frances?"

Bill begins to smile. "What I mean is, that I am about to give you a compliment."

"May the saints be praised!"

"You do a good job with your history taking, keeping track of all this ancient stuff. If it weren't for you…"

"…The family might get along better," Joe interrupts, looking away briefly. When he turns to face his brother again, he sees that Bill is looking directly into his eyes, deeply, seriously. The intimacy is unnerving, intense.

Joe shakes his head involuntarily, trying to disconnect, and he succeeds, looks away. He takes a breath, and when he looks at his brother again, Bill's look has softened. "By god what is it with you?"

Bill takes a moment, he answers, "You know, like what you said about Paddy, I don't think there is any shame for you either."

"How's that?"

"For you to share the stories you've heard. And so, okay, we're going to honor Paddy's request. We'll hush up. But. In the event that either one of us should someday have kids…"

"You sure you want to open that can of worms?"

"What? About having children?" Bill asks.

"No, I thought you were about to say, that we could then tell our children."

"Well you're right, I was," Bill says.

"Brother, after what we've been through, I'd say that what those children don't know won't hurt them."

CHAPTER 35

The Nina, the Pinta and the Santa Maria
Tuesday, September 4, 2001

WHEN EDDIE FINALLY RETURNS his brother's call, before he can get a word in edgewise, Brendan says excitedly, "Brother, do I ever have news for you!"

"Well now," Eddie says, "same here. I just had a very interesting visit with our young cousin earlier today. I'll bring you up to date."

"Okay," Brendan says, taking a deep breath. "Why don't you go first. Maybe it will dovetail with some things I've just learned. From the professor," he adds.

"Yeah, I thought that might be why you were calling."

"Go ahead," Brendan says.

"Are you sitting down?" Eddie asks.

Brendan hesitates, pulls the phone and its cord over to the kitchen table and pulls back the chair. "I am now."

"Good. So here's the thing. I learned why there was a cut-off with Emma's side of the family."

"Oh."

"Including why we never heard about having an Uncle John, our grandfather's older brother." When Brendan doesn't respond, Eddie continues, "I can give you the play by play as Emma told me the story or just jump to the summary."

"I was raised on Cliff notes in high school. Give me the quick summary," Brendan says.

Eddie hesitates, clears his throat, and doesn't speak for a moment.

"You okay there partner?" Brendan asks.

"Yes thanks. Did you know by the way that Cliff notes originated in Canada?"

Brendan pauses, "Doesn't sound like I am getting the short summary."

"In just a moment," Eddie says. "They were Canadian study guides, called Coles Notes."

Brendan answers "With that information and the proper bus fare, I'd be able to take the bus. But I hate taking buses." He pauses a moment, "I do have some pretty interesting info to share on my end, so if we can get on with your news, that would be lovely. The brief summary first, please."

"Okay," Eddie says, taking a very deep breath. "Here goes. Uncle John didn't say all that stuff that Joe told our dad. Our dad was criticized for believing what Joe shared. Hogwash, is what the family at large called it. And Paddy was in the Civil War. Fought on the side of the Confederacy. Oh, also that Uncle Joe said that Paddy O'Neil had a secret stash of letters that no one has ever seen but Uncle Joe would always refuse to say where they were kept. That's my quick summary."

After a split-second delay, Brendan says "Wow!" He takes a moment to gather his thoughts. "But I have to ask, all what stuff Uncle John didn't say supposedly? Whatever Uncle Joe told dad...who knows?"

Eddie has the sense to pause, and when Brendan speaks again, there is a new and more somber tone in his voice. "Dad being criticized. I wonder if that's partly why he, you know, didn't say much."

"Yeah, well I can fill you in," Eddie says.

Eddie pauses, "Maybe things are on the mend now. Meeting Emma, learning the history."

"A little late for dad."

Eddie hesitates, "Speaking of Emma, let me tell you more about what she shared."

"Okay."

"The rumors she'd heard growing up, more from distant cousins I gather, were that either Uncle John was wildly fabricating the supposed exploits of Paddy O'Neil, or that Uncle Joe was doing so, or both. I guess Dan told Uncle Joe to stop spreading these stories and he did, but dad, maybe being on the road a lot and all that, wouldn't stop talking about them until sometime later."

"Good for him," Brendan says. "The truth shall make you free."

"If it was the truth. There wasn't, as you know, anything in Uncle John's journals that clearly prove or disprove the stories that were told about Paddy," Eddie says.

"What stories about Paddy?"

"It's all innuendo. Paddy was involved in some kind of secretive brotherhood or so Uncle John hinted. He said that Paddy was involved in something shady during a trip to Ireland. And then there was something about trouble at the Welland Canal. Not in that order. Not in any order."

"Interesting," says Brendan, whose voice now sounds considerably brighter, reassured.

"Do you remember," Eddie begins, "the time that you joked about Paddy being some kind of secret revolutionary? Emma and I didn't say anything at the time."

Brendan hesitates, "No, not really."

Eddie, who has been working on observing his emotions better since his recent talks with Emma, notes a small bubble of disappointment, irritation. "Well, anyway," he says, "neither of us said a word when you made your comments."

"Neither of us?" Brendan asks.

"Emma and myself," Eddie answers. When Brendan doesn't respond, Eddie adds, "I had a sense then that Emma knew some things she was not yet telling us. She and I had spoken a little but not in any real depth at that time. But now I know what some of that was."

"Okay," Brendan says, not sounding as surprised to learn the new information as Eddie had hoped.

"One of the stories," Eddie begins, "I guess the biggest one, she called it 'the kicker' is that Paddy was somehow involved in a matter of violence."

"Hmmm," Brendan starts, "more like a murder, wouldn't you say "Watson?"

Eddie pauses. He wants to be Holmes, not Watson. "You heard something about this from your Professor?"

Brendan takes a moment, "Now it's my turn to ask if you are sitting down?"

Eddie pulls needlessly on the long phone cord that reaches his recliner chair. He doesn't know why, but he wants to stall for time. He sighs, a bit too loudly, he imagines. "Yes, but I have to tell you one more thing, another possible tall tale."

"Yes?"

"Uncle Joe said that Paddy had been writing a good bit, some were private letters to Uncle John, and others were more like essays. None of this is in the journals. Can I tell you something about that?"

"Please."

"Okay I know this is a little off the track, but this intrigue whether Paddy had actually written letters, it makes me think about the mysterious third letter of Fatima, revealed in 1960. You know, where the Blessed Mother appeared to those three little children. I know that's weird," Eddie adds.

"The Nina, the Pinta and the Santa Maria." Brendan says.

"What?"

"What's weird, brother, Fatima or how you made that association?" Brendan asks.

"I get this mixed up with the visions at Medjugorge, 1981," Eddie says.

"Boy are you Catholic. Okay, I can give your soul some rest. Many of the Faithful get those two places mixed up, and it's not a sin."

"Well, that's certainly consoling," Eddie says, "no geographical desecration, eh?"

"No," Brendan answers, "But that would apply to Sarajavo."

"Isn't Sarajavo the place where the Archduke was assassinated? It started World War I."

Brendan pauses, "Well you're more the student of history than I am. I was thinking that Sarajavo was the place where the Winter Olympics were held, 1984."

"And then the war in Bosnia started, 1992," Eddie concludes, as air seems to escape through the telephone receiver.

Neither of the brothers speak for a minute.

"Brother," Eddie says, "I think we went off on a tangent there."

Brendan takes a breath, "What do you mean 'we', Kemosabe?"

"Ha!" Eddie guffaws, "Excellent, if you're Tonto, I get to be the Lone Stranger."

Brendan takes a deep breath which slides into a sigh. "Going back to Fatima—"

"Yes, lovely, we should someday."

"I think I can put your wandering mind to rest."

"About Fatima?"

"About Paddy's private letters and papers."

"Oh, indeed," Eddie says, taking a moment to adjust his grip on the handset, wiggling the cord like a jumping rope for no apparent reason, "Paddy's private papers," he echoes.

"They exist."

CHAPTER 36

And Then It All Gets Buried
Tuesday, September 4, 2001

"HE PRACTICALLY DROPPED THE phone, the Professor," Brendan says. "Then he tells me in so many words, that it's almost creepy, my calling just when I did. He didn't say 'mystical', but it was that sort of thing. The timing."

"A coincidence?" Eddie offers.

"Way more than that. He had just opened up the letters and papers for the first time, and then I called. That's when he realized that Paddy O'Neil was part of our family. He Hadn't gotten that far yet in the documents. It was all a gift to the University of Toronto, not to be opened until this century."

"Paddy's papers, you're talking. He gave them to the University?"

Brendan hesitates. "Yes, and he is certain of their authenticity, don't ask me how. History professors must have their ways."

"And they just got around to looking at this stuff?" Eddie asks.

"Not to be opened till this century," Brendan repeats. "And give the university a break, it's only 2001. Y2K thankfully was a bust." Brendan is quiet for a moment, "Speaking of which, we should count our lucky stars. They almost lost the whole kit and caboodle. They were discovered back in the stacks of some archives. I guess a graduate student stumbled on it. Made his day."

"The student or the professor?" Eddie asks.

Brendan answers, "Yes."

Brendan pulls out some notes he had kept, turns a page over. "The Professor, maybe you remember, is a specialist in the history of the Canadian Confederation, and that time period."

"When?" Eddie asks.

"Roughly around the time of our Civil War and a little after," Brendan says. "Do you remember that he talked about the Fenian movement?"

"Yes, the Canadian, Irish, invasion, or something."

"Well guess who was a prominent, or I should say, at least a secretively prominent member of the movement?" Brendan asks.

"The Professor confirmed this? You're talking our great great uncle by marriage."

"Okay, that's too complicated," Brendan says.

"He married our great grandmother's sister. He married into the Flanagans," Eddie clarifies.

"Let me cut to the chase. Paddy O'Neil himself. One 'l' by the way, so I learned."

"Voila," Eddie says.

"And he wasn't exactly fighting on the side of the Confederacy in the American Civil War."

"No?" Eddie asks, sounding almost disappointed.

"He was more like a spy. He joined them only to learn about the strength of the Union forces, in the event the Americans might threaten the homeland."

"The homeland," Eddie repeats slowly, needing time to take this all in.

"Canada."

Eddie takes a moment. "So he was a spy, but not really a Fenian, because the Fenians were going to invade Canada."

"No he really was a member of the Fenians, just not that branch."

Eddie pauses, asks "Why can't history be easier?"

"He was with the group called the Stephens camp." Brendan checks his notes, "They wanted the fight for the liberation of Ireland to take place on the old sod itself, none of this business of trying to invade Canada as a way to put pressure on Britain."

Eddie takes another moment to absorb what he is hearing. He looks down at the dangling phone cord and asks, "So is there anything about his traveling to Ireland?"

"Ah," his brother responds, "it's interesting. Yes, there was a letter about planning a trip, this was in the later 1870's."

There is a pause in the conversation. Eddie has a sense that Brendan has more to add, finally he asks "And...?

"And there is a reference that suggests he took an earlier trip."

There is a lengthy pause in the brothers' conversation, during which time they both stand up, unbeknown to each other until first one, then the other, makes a groaning sound in the middle of a stretch. Eddie arches his back, Brendan bends his left leg, grasping for his ankle before pulling it upwards.

"You okay?"

"Yes," Brendan answers. "You?"

Resuming his seat, Eddie answers, "I've been better, but, yes."

Brendan takes his seat and asks, "You said that there was 'a kicker' issue, when you talked with Emma?"

"Ah, yes."

"'Matter of violence'" is how you phrased it," Brendan says.

Eddie hesitates before saying, "I don't want to be Watson."

"What?"

"Never mind," Eddie says. "Yes, matter of violence is what I said, or Emma did, trying to soft pedal what she was about to tell me."

"Hmmm," Brendan murmurs suspiciously like a famous detective. "Well," he says, now speaking more like an officer in charge, "It was indeed a murder."

"Murder," Eddie repeats. "So you do know something about this great 'kicker' episode. Man's name was Burl."

Brendan can't help himself, after a brief hesitation he says, "Not Burl Ives, I hope."

Eddie pauses before saying, "Oh, ok. No, Burl Ives, god bless his soul, was not yet born."

"Thank the Lord for small blessings," Brendan says, before adding, "actually the murder victim was called Earl."

"Earl Ives, Burl's uncle?"

Brendan pauses again, "I'm glad to hear that you weren't too offended by what Emma had to say. All the things she'd heard from her side of the family. Going back many years."

"Ouch," Eddie says without thinking.

"Amen brother," Brendan adds reassuringly. "The Professor says they have a lot of material to examine. This business about the Earl was something Paddy wrote related to land reform. The first of Paddy's papers by the way are dated in the late 1870's."

"Interesting. I wonder why those years."

Brendan considers this. "Well, they were the ones on top. Apriori, I guess you'd say, that part is quite simple."

"I'm not sure that's the proper use of the phrase." Eddie hesitates, asks, "Do you mean the first or the most recent?"

"Yes. The first ones that he looked at are the most recent." Brendan waits for Eddie to respond, but not hearing anything, he adds, "At any rate, apparently it's quite a collection."

"Mmmm."

"He is, I'm telling you brother, especially eager to read some of Paddy's earlier papers, closer to the years of the 1860's, that being his specialty area."

There is another extended pause, made all the more striking by their mutual silence, the difference between a phone call and sitting together, face to face.

Brendan asks, "You still there?"

"All these stories Uncle Joe told, passing along what Uncle John had told him," Eddie begins, "and the harm that came when part of the family wouldn't believe them."

"When," Brendan adds, "from Emma's point of view, her non-believers thought they were the ones preventing harm. To stop what they thought were lies, made up stories."

A moment passes, "And then dad gets hurt. For continuing to speak."

"Until he stops speaking," Brendan says, "to spare the rest of us any similar grief from that side of the family."

"And then it's all buried," Eddie concludes.

Brendan takes a moment, "At a pretty steep price."

Eddie hesitates and says, "Family members disappear from view."

"Our view," Brendan adds.

The brothers remain silent for an extended moment until Eddie says, "There is some irony here."

Brendan waits to hear what his brother has to say.

Eddie says, "You say that Paddy actually wanted his stories to remain hidden until revealed to later generations. He had a complicated political history. There's always the danger of repercussions. For himself."

Brendan considers this, adds "And maybe for the family as well. Maybe he knew that opening this treasure too soon could become a curse, put the family at risk."

"Right. But the truth wouldn't be suppressed."

Brendan considers this, says, "The truth shall make you free!"

Eddie, the older brother, hesitates and says, "If only."

The brothers fall silent until Brendan says, "You know what?"

"What?"

"I think we may have finally cracked this case!"

For the life of him, Eddie tries very hard not to answer, 'By Jove!' Instead, he says "Do you think we are walking up to our own Fatima moment?"

Brendan hesitates, "You mean…?

"The apparition of truth, finally to be revealed."

CHAPTER 37

Out of the Shadows
Tuesday, August 26, 1879

I'M AWARE OF THIS little bit of freedom come our way, so that I can call you by name, John, in a letter from your traveling friend. So much water over the dam, eh? Times change.

I'm reminded of the times we would get away back home, just to talk, all the while watchful. My favorite walks were on the beach, below the cliffs at High Banks. No one was in sight then, do you remember? The only witnesses were the swooping gulls, and the ever-changing waves on the Lake. Devoy, you know, says that he was always on the look out when he went back to Ireland, fugitive that he was, watching for a shadow. I guess he is a fair one to imitate.

Ah, Mohawk Island. We always called it Gull Island. Its beckoning light standing but two miles from the shore. There is something so compelling about its loveliness, its isolation. It must take a special kind of man to live out there as a keeper of the light. Such memories about the place, a place of rescue when it came to your own dear life. No tempest in a teacup, that storm. Lake Erie, the Great Inland Sea. But forgive me, you may not be wanting to be reminded of that.

Here's the point I wish to address: I'm hoping to write a more detailed account of that which I have witnessed, of the activities in which I have been privileged to take part. As I put pen to paper, I am thinking of those who are not yet born, how I might yet reach them. Some magic in this wouldn't you say? So if it turns out that there is no life in the hereafter (god forbid) these words might yet live on, and I in them. Is that too grand a thing to think of myself? The thing is, in those future days, I need have no fear of who will read my words. Speaking of which I am indebted to you for receiving and keeping these occasional commentaries to date in safe keeping.

We shall discuss at a future time, a remedy for you to secure such correspondence, in fact well beyond our lifetimes. That is why I am writing to you from Toronto, having just had a meeting with some officials at the University here. Will explain later. Otherwise, I still need to be careful to whom I am talking, especially in Dunnville, so please continue to keep all these words in your deepest confidence. There are those who remember, among other events, how I tagged along on the boat ride as those American Fenians elsewhere were heading for Niagara. How I disappeared for days after.

You my dear friend, are the exception to my need for vigilance, especially in these times and I am eternally grateful. It is a relief for me to have such a release, and I hope I am not unduly burdening you with secrecy in the meantime.

I had to tell someone. All the divided loyalties, Fenian but not that kind of Fenian. A pro-Canadian Fenian, against my homeland being invaded just as I feel the same about Ireland being invaded all these centuries and now still by Her Majesty's aging hand. And now it is changing, clearly. She is losing her grip. Put myself in a pickle eh? But the course of history is on our side.

Speaking of history (by the way you should visit the campus here, most impressive) can you believe it is already three years since we were reading about the defeat out in the American west, Colonel George Custer. And my prior voyage is already 14 years in the past. Some feel, don't you know, that the Fenian uprisings of that time were all for nought. Nay sayers. While I want to thank the Americans for their support in '67 when the skirmishes began at last in Ireland, somebody surely made a mess of it with late arriving arms and comrades.

I think the current Land League effort can be seen as a child of that earlier call for freedom. History is like that. Not always so obvious, the connection of one thing to the next, even if the following generations don't realize what they are doing and why.

On to more pleasant things! Glad to be back on solid ground but what a difference now in travel on the high seas! New York to Cobh in Ireland on board a ship that they call an ocean liner, imagine. So unlike the vessel I boarded for the drama of '65. Even more, apologies again for not wishing to upset you, how it differed from what you told me about your "coffin ship" of '49, when you first came to our dear Canada.

I don't think we talked about the SS Celtic, part of the White Star Line built in Belfast. No timber for a ship this time, she was all iron, steamship powered with four enormous sails now used as auxiliary power, destined to move forward on a journey regardless of the winds aloft, capable of making speeds of 17 miles per hour day and night. 437 feet long, with a beam of nearly 41 feet, no paddle wheeler, she is a single screw steamer, 'SS' you see? And I was one of the 1000 3rd class passengers with suitable quarters, occasionally seeing one of the 166 better-heeled first-class passengers going up or down the stairs. Butter upon bacon, I'm telling you. Apologies for being so long winded with the details, but you know I have always felt a kinship to such sea craft.

I know we talked a little about the purpose of my trip, all above board I assure you. At least, my part. Nothing that might cause the local constabulary to raise their eyebrows in my direction this time. Not at me personally. This Land League organization is quite the movement. Their goal simply put is to have farmers own the land they work on. Reduce the vast tracts of landlordism, and you know who many of those landlords are, of course.

I have to tell you, the imagination of 15,000 to 20,000 tenant farmers, can you picture it, was so stirred that they began to have a series of rallies called Monster Meetings and wasn't I fortunate to attend one of the very first, in Irishtown near Claremorris.

I cut out an article from the Connaught Telegraph, dated 26 April, 1879, to give you a quick jist of what I saw. Here is what some of it says, I'll paraphrase:

Since the days of O'Connell a larger public demonstration has not been witnessed than that of Sunday last. About 1 o'clock the monster procession started from Claremorris, headed by several thousand men on foot, the men of each district wearing a laurel leaf or green ribbon in hat or coat to distinguish the several contingents. A monster contingent of tenant farmers on horseback drew up in front of Hughes's hotel showing discipline and order that a cavalry regiment might feel proud of. They were led on in sections, each having a Marshall who kept his troops well in hand, They wore green and gold sashes, two deep, occupying an Irish mile of the road. This was followed by a train of at least 500 vehicles from neighboring towns. On passing through, the sight was truly imposing, the endless train directing its course to Irishtown, a neat little hamlet on the boundaries of Mayo, Roscommon and Galway.

Very grand indeed. By god I think the people over there are finally pulling themselves out of their centuries' old slump.

I need to wind up this note if I have any chance of getting it mailed out tonight, which I am anxious to do. As much as I say I find myself breathing easier these days, I still find myself looking over my shoulder. My mind pictures the odd figure who might suddenly duck into an alley or stand behind a light pole for his concealment.

I say this especially because I left out something that I'll tell you more about when we meet in person. I'll say this much, that on my journey to our original homeland, I was joined by an old comrade in arms. He whom I have already named and about whom, much will be written by the historians in the years to come, I can assure you.

CHAPTER 38

A Canadian Fenian
Tuesday, September 4, 2001

W ELL, THAT WAS INTERESTING.

The Professor looks out the window, not seeing the grey skies of Toronto, nor the students walking along the sidewalks of the campus far below. He is seeing Paddy's sailing ship, the SS Celtic. As much as he has been an expert on 19th century politics and all things Fenian, he had never really investigated the world of ships on the high seas, the question of the steam engine revolution, how it melded with the technology of tall masts, billowing sails.

When Brendan Donohoe told him about his Canadian relative who had met Stephens in New York and noted that it was not the first time they had met, he almost shouted out loud, like some kind of American. He did everything he could to keep his cool, not let on to Brendan what he hoped, what he fantasized.

For some time among his fellow historians there had been speculation that a particular Canadian, as yet unnamed, had been involved in the Fenian Brotherhood at a very high level. Stories however were elusive and often contradictory. Was this individual actually Canadian, or an American posing as a Canadian? Either way, such a muddle, grist for academic debate. What was clear was the underlying passion for freedom, to wit: the liberation of Ireland.

America had achieved its independence. Canada was on its own course, not completely separated from the Crown. Scholars of this period in history, all ten of them to be truthful, noted that it was only faculty from Canadian universities who had written papers about the existence of 'CF', the Canadian Fenian.

Rumors festered or flowered in the University community for years, depending on one's point of view. All would agree however that if such a person existed, they were exemplars of both the secretive Brotherhood and the emerging Canadian persona in this regard: being cautiously undemonstrative. Until now.

Scholars from the West of Canada, of course it had to be from the west, had suggested that CF might ultimately be revealed as a ghost, an illusion--a character, they said, created by the projection of complicated needs. Someone who might sow seeds of understanding along the rough furrows of mixed political soil from such places as the United Kingdom, Ireland, and the States. Canada's version of Johnny Appleseed. Oh Canada!

And then, of course, Brendan would have to say that his relative's name, this fellow who had met Stephens after his escape *and who had met him before*, was named none other than Paddy. Paddy, for god's sake.

A cloud of doubt arises. 'Paddy', couldn't that easily be a common nickname, or even a ruse, a mask? He hoped it wasn't a virtual 'John Doe.' The Professor takes a breath, remembers that this Paddy is a member of a known family.

He looks again at the yellowed pages that he has begun to read, the many yet to come. His fingertips don't actually feel the dryness of the paper though he imagines what brittle must feel like. He looks at his hands and sees the blue latex gloves covering them, stretched tight, one size too small. What he feels is rubberized plasticity, the distance of millimeters, the price he pays to protect this moment and the unimagined moments of future researchers. What does Paddy say about himself? He looks over the letter again, ah, a 'pro-Canadian Fenian.' He names himself.

Paddy's letter to his friend John Donohoe had been resting in a very dingy single corrugated cardboard box, received and filed by University staff and seemingly undisturbed in the stacks since...when? Maybe early in the 20th century. He will have to speak again with the Donohoes now that the treasure is being unearthed. From what he can tell, the family has a minimal understanding about their relative's place in history. Potentially. That would make sense if indeed our Paddy was the secretive revolutionary figure he might turn out to be. Mum's the word, eh?

He looks back at the letter again, sees where it reads 'joined by an old comrade in arms.' He might not know much about the advent of steamships but he sure as hell knows about the illustrious John Devoy. He takes a moment to remind himself that there may not be more than twenty people on campus who would recognize the name let alone call him illustrious. He can at least count on his students. Or so he hopes.

Just in the past month he had given a class this question on a surprise quiz: 'What Irish Catholic newspaper published in the United States was, along with the "Irish Nation," owned by John Devoy? Hint: it was also a weekly publication of Sinn Féin, among the foremost Irish ethnic newspapers until the Great Depression when its readership declined?'

One student answered 'Arsenal or possibly Manchester United.' He put a smiley face next to these English football team names. He could at least give the student credit for being a smart-ass.

Most of the students answered correctly that it was the "Gaelic American," and on his desk, somewhere, he has an issue where Devoy wrote extensively about another patriot, Michael Davitt. Devoy had used his publication to write a series of articles to look back on the Land Wars of the late 1870's, and something that he had just read in Paddy's letter to John Donohoe rang a bell. The monster meeting in Claremorris and the business of hiding in plain sight.

The Professor puts his hands on his large wooden desk, preparing to stand. He sees again the overlapping fortune of material laid out before his eyes, the academic articles and books that leave no clear view of the desk underneath. Hap-hazard, his secretary calls it, to which he always replies, that he can put his hands on whatever he needs at a moment's notice. He had momentarily forgotten however, that the Devoy articles were over in the left corner of the desk, partially hidden under a stack of unread student papers that he will, finally, get around to grading.

Amidst the wealth of research material spread throughout his office and overflowing his shelves, this is almost too easy to retrieve, as if someone knew he'd be looking for it. He partially stands so that he can lean over and retrieve the issue of the Gaelic American, dated 1906. He forgets, a moment too late, that such a reach is not good for his aging back, and he knows that he will pay for such a simple move in the next few hours.

He resumes his seat, material in hand, looks for a certain article, turns a few pages and says aloud to the empty office, "Here we go."

CHAPTER 39

Hiding in Plain Sight
Tuesday, September 4, 2001

THIS IS ONE OF THE LINES from Devoy that he remembers reading in the "Gaelic American":

'I landed in Waterford on 1 April 1879 (making an April Fool of the British Government)...'

Professor Brown knows the back story only too well. He had intended to focus on John Devoy for his doctoral thesis but he was encouraged to focus instead on the much more well-known "uncrowned kind of Ireland," Charles Stewart Parnell. It was all part of a gambit at the time to satisfy political tension within the history department. So much for academic freedom.

Devoy had been arrested in February 1866 for, among other things, helping the Fenian leader Stephens to escape from jail in Dublin. He was tried for treason and sentenced to fifteen years penal servitude. He had been a troublesome prisoner, successfully organizing prison strikes, and he was released after five years on condition that he leave Ireland and never return.

Professor Brown puts the newspaper back on the desk. He is feeling a sudden restlessness, something brewing that he is not yet able to articulate. He had recently written some notes for a class and he wants to refresh his memory. He stands up and goes over to a large bookcase where he keeps his files and quickly finds notes that he had taken for a recent lecture.

Luckily they were typed this time rather than hand-written and he reads:

'Once free, Mr. Devoy sailed for America with Jeremiah O'Donovan Rossa and three other pardoned men, who became known as the Cuba Five, named after the ship that carried them into New York harbor where they received a rapturous welcome, including blazing torches and booming cannons. On the 28th of January 1871, the New York "Irish People" recorded that the released prisoners were praised by a local dignitary for their devotion to Ireland.'

No mention of a Paddy anywhere, he muses to himself.

When he looks back at his desk, he sees the rumpled looking box of Paddy O'Neil's manuscripts sitting on a nearby table, just waiting for him like a chest full of Inca gold. He returns his notes to the bookshelf, walks back to the desk, sits down and picks up the "Gaelic American" once again. He is looking for a particular passage similar to what O'Neil had written, the business of avoiding attention.

Devoy was remembered as a small and intense man, intellectually brilliant. When he had snuck back into the country, he was risking imprisonment, and he would have certainly remembered the experience of being held in solitary confinement before his release. As he made his way across Ireland, he was ever on the alert for police, for detectives he called 'peelers.' He was determined to get to Claremorris and Irishtown for one of the large gatherings called monster meetings. The Professor remembered that this was the heyday of the Land Wars, and Devoy had been instrumental in the movement referred to as the New Departure.

It's complicated, he remembers telling his students, and he can remember seeing heads tip sideways in the lecture hall, eyes all but going blank, as he attempted to describe what Devoy and others were working toward. It was no simple thing to bring about cooperation among differing factions, all of whom wanted a free Ireland. One goal was clear and that was to work toward ownership of the land by the farmers who worked the land. Several students would suddenly blink at this, raise their heads upright again. Yes, this made sense.

Devoy had gotten tired, Fenian though he was, sworn to secrecy by its Oath, by the way the Fenian movement was devolving in factionalism. So here he is at the age of 37, back in Ireland illegally, working in ways that Great Britain would not appreciate. Now a newly arrived New Yorker with maybe a hint of New York attitude, by god he would get to the meeting, the likes of which he had been hearing about.

Ah, here are the comments Devoy wrote in the "Gaelic American":

> *Davitt told me he thought it would be dangerous for me to go to Claremorris, on account of the crowd, the extra police, the reporters and the public men who would be there. Some of them might recognize me...I told him frankly that I wanted to feel the pulse of the Mayo men...and that I wished to see one land meeting before returning to America....Arrived at Claremorris I saw two tall strapping 'Peelers' standing in a sort of yard outside the station and a group of young fellows stood near them, as if watching for somebody.*

> *It was not my habit to have friends wait for me at a railroad station and recognize me in the presence of the police, and none of them had ever done it before, so I did not expect that anyone would be waiting for me. I was walking past the young men when one of them stepped up to me and within three feet of the policemen asked me: "Are you Misther Doyle?" That was the name I was to take in Claremorris, so I promptly said "No."*

> *As I knew the 'Peelers' had heard and I saw they were looking at me, I walked right up to them and said: "Would you be kind enough to tell me which is the best hotel in this town?" "Well", answered one of the constabulary-men, "there's two, and they're both about the same. If there's any choice between them it's in favour of the one next the barrack. We'll be going down in a minute and if you wait we'll show it to you." I thanked them, waited and walked into Claremorris in the company of the two policemen.*

I knew, from experience while 'on my keeping' in 1865-6, that my action had disarmed the suspicion aroused by the imprudence of my friends and would cause the latter to give me a wide berth during the evening, which was what I wanted. I wore a suit of Irish tweed and carried a frieze overcoat on my arm, my accent was home-made and there was nothing about me to suggest the returned Irish American. But I had to do something to account for my arrival there on a Saturday evening on the eve of a land meeting: so I told the policemen confidentially that I was a correspondent of the "Times," sent to report the meeting. I felt sure from their manner that they did not like me any the better for this announcement, as they looked like farmers' sons, but they were very polite during the rest of my intercourse with them, and quietly gave me the names of the speakers the next day. And I must say they seemed to like the speeches very well.

On arriving at the hotel door I asked the policemen to take a drink, and they told me the sergeant was very watchful, but they would slip in the back way, as there was a common yard for the hotel and the barrack. They each took a half glass of whiskey and the same for their 'morning' the next day. This consorting with the hated 'Peelers' had its proper effect on those who saw it.

A group of young fellows standing in front of the hotel, as I watched the crowds marching in on Sunday morning, were evidently discussing me, and one of them, looking defiantly at me over his shoulder said: "ah, sure we don't care if all Scotland Yard was here." That young man was 'onto' me and was bound to let me know it.

Professor Brown puts the newspaper back on his desk, leans back in the chair, looks up at the ceiling. What he sees are the words Paddy O'Neil had written. Paddy had been at the Claremorris meeting and, hello, had written 'comrade in arms.' He was talking about John Devoy, 'he whom

I have already named.' 'On my journey I was joined,' Paddy had written. They traveled over together? They met up at some later point? Curious that Devoy never makes any reference to Paddy or someone like him.

He checks his watch. He'd like to give a quick call to the Donohoe family, Eva, was it? Erin? The family that manages those journals. He can see through his office window that the early evening sky is bright, he has a seminar but not for another hour.

But first things first. He goes over to the table, slips on another pair of blue latex gloves, carefully opens the cardboard flaps and begins to look at the next document in the box.

He stops suddenly, stands up straight, and takes a moment to read what is written in large cursive script, words that flow at the top of the page from one side to the other.

Chapter 40

Late For Class

Tuesday, September 4, 2001

I̲T̲ ̲D̲I̲D̲N̲'̲T̲ ̲T̲A̲K̲E̲ ̲H̲I̲M̲ long to read the newest document. Professor Brown sits back in his chair, looks up at the ceiling and takes a deep breath. He feels like a kid in a candy store, all these riches, including the call he had just completed with the Donohoe woman whose married name he could not remember, first name Emma .

Emma's voice was simply lovely. Luscious even, resonant and warm, once he explained who he was and the purpose for the call.

The only disappointment was a minor one for now. Emma had not been able recognize the names he had mentioned, but then again, it was a very quick call, due to his own time constraints. She said that she'd be seeing her cousins soon, so perhaps there would be more data that he could verify with them, information from their Great Uncle John's journals.

At the risk of seeming pushy, he suggested a meeting with her cousins and herself sooner rather than later. He didn't explain his rationale for scheduling. The new semester was starting Monday September 10th, and the Department was just now learning about Paddy's gift to the University.

One small consolation in the call with Emma was that she was able to clarify this reference in Paddy's letter to John:

> *It must take a special kind of man to live out there as a keeper of the light. Such memories about the place, a place of rescue when it came to your own dear life. No tempest in a teacup, that storm.*

Lake Erie, the Great Inland Sea. But forgive me, you may not be
wanting to be reminded of that.

Emma said that there had been some drama about John Donohoe nearly
drowning, sailing out of Port Colborne, happened near Mohawk Island,
what the locals call Gull Island. A story for another time, and time was
very short, with a seminar class coming up.

He looks down again at the paper he had just read before his call to
Emma. He holds it carefully in his glove covered hands, a sacrament of
preserved and precious life, living knowledge. The exceptional moment
and privilege of being the first to read this primary source material, such a
gift. He inhales, he inhabits, the air and the spirit of an earlier era, one that
he knows so well.

He will give it a careful second reading.

Across the top of the page, in very large letters written in cursive, dark
ink that was beginning to fade, becoming a shadow of words once boldly
stated, in Paddy's own hand:

MEETING THE GREAT MAN

I had met up with Devoy again a little after he left the train
station in Claremorris. I had been well prepared to watch my
goings on, and I could see at one point that some awkward fellow
approached him too soon and nearly caused him to be taken in
by the police. I knew the risks he was taking and I in turn had
no interest in local officials nosing into my background. Well, in
due course, we were able to meet and spend some time together.
He it was, who prepared the way for me to meet others who had
risen, since my earlier days, in the organization.

After much too short a time, (he said he was often "on the jump"
during this visit back home), Devoy slipped away yet again, but
not before telling me to come and see him in New York, Lord
willing, some time. I remember that he had some fanciful ideas
of starting a newspaper. He envisioned a journal devoted to the

*cause of Irish independence. I can remember his voice now,
it would include "Irish literature and the interests of the Irish
race."*

*I remember watching him walk away after we bid our farewells,
so discreetly I might add. I said to myself there goes a huge
figure in Irish history, that short little fellow in his later 30's,
who could have been mistaken for a school master rather than
a master of all things political. I saw that a policeman would
be crossing his path down the side street and as it happened,
Devoy just tipped his hat as calmly as ever at the officer. I had
hesitated a bit too long watching this and I nearly aroused the
suspicion of a couple of young uniformed lads across the street
from where I stood. I made a gesture as if I were just getting my
bearings, which was true, and any suspicion they may have had
soon melted away, just like my patriot friend had done moments
before.*

*Devoy had given me the particulars where I could meet Mr.
Parnell and with sweaty palms, I entered Morrison's Hotel soon
after. I'm still with some reverence recalling how I met the great
man himself, seeing him sitting in a large armchair, reading the
paper, which he lowered enough so that he could look my way. As
in many other things, he was coolly prepared for my approach.*

*I simply said good afternoon, "Yes, I should hope so," he
returned in his high-toned upper-class accent, a voice that
immediately set him apart, a person of high standing, not from
here. To my surprise he offered me a section of the newspaper
he was reading and nodded in the direction of a comfortable
looking chair close by.*

*He was either putting on a feint to appear as casual as possible,
or, in fact, he was just that relaxed. At any rate, it was the exact
opposite of my own internal state, and I noticed, as did he, that*

my hands were shaking when he handed me the paper. I could see that he had passed along an article dealing with the agenda of the Land Reform meeting.

He had his own retinue of supporters sitting and standing nearby, some of whom I knew. If you didn't know better, you might think that these gentlemen were unrelated to the fellow who had handed me a section of his newspaper. The monster meeting had brought in an unusually large number of visitors and this certainly helped dilute any strangeness or surprise to see unfamiliar faces in this small town. His face, however, was anything but unfamiliar to anyone current with the press, readers of the "Freemens Journal" and the like.

After a moment during which I read and reread the same opening paragraph several times, the voice hidden behind his section of the paper said, "Canada still tied up with the Queen I gather." A simple statement, an implied question, a humorous jab, oh so droll? Before I knew what I was saying I responded "Rather," in that slightly exaggerated way of the English, emphasizing the second syllable. I was embarrassed that he might think I was making fun or trying to emulate his upbringing.

His response was to lower the paper, look directly in my eyes, and say something that I will treasure forever. "We will not," he began slowly and pointedly, "forget your history of service Mr. O'Neil on behalf of this nation, which will, one day, be free."

Professor Brown looks away from the paper in his hand, takes a deep breath. And then remembers the Tuesday seminar. He checks his watch. It will take him 15 minutes to leave his office, go down the stairs, cross the courtyard over to the building where his students will be waiting. He likes to get there early, look over his notes and gather his thoughts, but today with 7 minutes to go until the start of the class, he races out the door and as he bounds down the stairs, sings in a muffled voice, "Canadian Fenian, Canadian Fenian, Canadian Fenian…"

When he finally reaches the classroom, he sees his students' faces expressing variously looks of regret and expectation. This is when he realizes that his notes are still in the office.

CHAPTER 41

The Known Before the Unknown
Tuesday, September 4, 2001

THE SEMINAR HAD BEEN a disaster, but he was practiced at fumbling his way through something when his mind was elsewhere. It had been, however, the first time that a student would inquire, quite seriously, whether he was feeling okay.

"What? Yes. But thank you Miss Pruitt."

After a moment, the attractive young woman from Saskatchewan—was it?—repeated, "Are you sure, sir?" at which point he paused, took a mindful breath, noticed her look of genuine concern, and nodded to the affirmative without saying another word, at least on that subject.

HE is beside himself, caught in a quantum moment, as one of his scientific friends might call it, the way an object can be in two separate places at the same time.

There are answers he hopes to find, definite answers, at last. But is he ignoring, as a colleague might advise him, small warnings, lingering doubts? Shadows waver in the evening light, the venetian blinds of his office remain open.

This could make his career, after all.

Professor Brown sighs, he knows the background only too well. He is one of the better informed historians in all the Provinces to understand the story of James Stephens, his role in the rise and fall of the Fenian movement.

He recalls that there are a small handful of Faculty out in British Columbia that have taken exception to some of his work. The Fenian history, hell the history of Ireland itself is full of strongly held contradictions here and there. No matter. His wish, right at this moment, is to add a significant character to the narrative of Stephens' arrest and subsequent escape. If he can, he will add a Canadian flourish, someone who operated at the highest levels of the Fenian Brotherhood.

Years ago he had discovered one of his favourite near-contemporary works of history from that era, and when he looks over at his bookshelf, he sees it resting there, waiting, waving at him, asking to be re-opened.

He stands up, retrieves the book and returns to his desk, moaning slightly as he settles into his plush black executive chair. Faux leather. He looks once again at the cover, a faded yellow, printed in the unmistakable manner of 19th century speech, the kind that he holds so dear.

He hesitates for a moment, looks up at the table holding the cardboard box full of Paddy O'Neil's work. A sigh, a sigh launches him into the task of reviewing the known before reaching further into the unknown. He will be the careful scholar now, the professor who remembers to bring his lecture notes to the seminar room, the eager faces before him. He opens the book in his hand.

James Stephens

Chief Organizer of the Irish Republic
Embracing An Account of the Origin and Progress Of the
Fenian Brother Hood
Semi-Autobiographical Sketch of James Stephens with the story
of his arrest and imprisonment;
also his escape from the British Authorities 1866

Professor Brown opens the book with the care and attention of a not-young son reaching over to touch the hand of an elderly father. Paddy will have to wait for now. In the meantime he wonders if the familiar text at hand might offer clues about a Canadian adventurer.

He begins reading:

SEIZURE OF "THE IRISH PEOPLE" OFFICE.

Knowing James Stephens to be identified with "The Irish People" newspaper, on the night of the 15th of September the office of that paper was seized by the police, and its types and presses taken possession of by the government officials.

The Professor pages ahead, looking for highlights, letting his eyes rest here and there, like a fisherman watching the surface of a very still lake for signs of movement beneath the water, just out of view.

The events immediately following the seizure of The Irish People office are of such recent date as not to require repetition here. How hundreds of brave and loyal Irishmen were seized and thrown into prison on suspicion of being Fenians ; how Americans in Ireland were also suspected, arrested, and ordered to leave the country ; how some of these patriotic men were brought to trial, and how nobly and defiantly they bore themselves ; and how they were sentenced to years of penal servitude, are matters well known to the public.

On the day following the seizure of The Irish People office — the 16th of September — a reward of £200 was offered for the arrest of Mr. Stephens. As days and weeks rolled on, and he still remained at large, this reward was increased publicly to £2,300 ; while privately it was known that whoever should produce in court the arch-conspirator, would receive from the Government and individuals an incredible amount. Yet while the ingenuity of the British Government was taxed to the uttermost to secure his arrest ; while detectives were following every trail, and spies lurking in every corner — that gentleman remained quietly at his own residence in the suburbs of Dublin, pursuing his usual avocations.

He remembers the story better than the Bible passages he was made to memorize years ago. For seven years Stephens had been a conspirator in Ireland, typically living in Dublin yet he was largely unknown to any policeman. And here he is now, his newspaper seized and many of his cronies taken, and he remains at large for another two months. When he was finally discovered and taken into custody, his wife asked permission to visit him in prison. To which Stephens replied, and here the Professor looks ahead in the book,

He replied : " You cannot visit me in prison without asking permission of British officials, and I do not think it becoming in one so near to me as you are to ask favors of British dogs. You must not do it — I forbid it."

The Professor jumps ahead, and sees another place where Stephens is quoted.

" I have employed no lawyer, nor have I put in any plea in this case, neither do I intend to do so. By so doing, I should be recognising British law in Ireland. Now, I conscientiously and deliberately repudiate the rightful existence of British law in Ireland, and I scorn and defy any punishment it can inflict on me." The greatest excitement prevailed in the court-room in consequence of this defiant speech, and every man present felt that, in consequence, Mr. Stephens' doom was surely sealed. A few moments sufficed to conclude the examination, and the accused was remanded to prison for a further hearing. This occurred on Saturday ; on the following Tuesday he was again arraigned, and then formally committed to Richmond Prison to await his trial before a Special Commission which had already been ordered to convene.

The Professor reads on:

The excitement in Fenian circles, in consequence of the arrest and imprisonment, was most intense, and schemes for his rescue, some of which contemplated the destruction of the prison, were discussed far and wide. These plans were all put

aside by the bold and skillful man to whom Mr. Stephens had entrusted the direction of affairs during his incarceration. This man was Colonel Thomas J. Kelly, formerly a staff-officer in the army of the Cumberland, who won his laurels and his promotion upon the battlefields of West Virginia, Kentucky, and Tennessee. In April, 1865, Colonel Kelly, who, while still in the American army, had tendered his services for active work in Ireland, and who was then a tried and trusted Fenian, joined Mr. Stephens in Dublin, and during the few months succeeding his arrival, had displayed so much skill and ability as to win not only the confidence of his beloved chief, but the respect and good opinion of all the leading revolutionary spirits of the time. Colonel Kelly had resolved, from the moment that Mr. Stephens was seized, that he should never be brought to trial, and he took measures to enforce that resolve, as will be seen.

The details of the escape of Mr. Stephens from Richmond Prison, and the names of the persons who assisted therein, cannot be given to the public in full until the Irish Republic shall be recognised among the nations of the earth, and those prisons, which have proved the tombs of so many noble patriots, have become portions of its possessions. It is a fact, however, that those who assisted in the escape were so completely masters of the situation, that for days they laughed to scorn all idea of their beloved chief being brought to trial. Indeed, the fact that he was to escape, and that the well-laid plans to secure his release would be put into effect on a certain night, was well known to the organization throughout the whole of Ireland, and had even been communicated to Colonel O'Mahony, in America ; yet so perfect was the organization, and so devoted its members, that not a whisper of such purpose ever reached the ears of British officials. Sufficient details of this escape, however, can be given here without incriminating those who assisted therein, and who are yet residents of their native land, to clear up somewhat the mystery which has surrounded this transaction, and which will, at least, have the merit of being truthful.

"Aha!," the Professor says aloud. He's thinking about where Paddy O'Neil might fit in with this documented history. He suddenly thinks about the recent series, the British children's books "Where's Wally?" or as they're known in North America "Where's Waldo?"

All arrangements having been made to the satisfaction of the Colonel, he, on the morning of the 24th of November, together with a few other bold spirits, repaired to the prison. It was a cold night ; the rain fell in torrents, and the wind howled dismally through the almost deserted streets, as these few men hastened from different directions to the appointed rendezvous. The first thing to be done was to post sentinels at some distance from the prison, to guard all the approaches, to give the alarm if the movement was discovered, and to bring reinforcements to the scene if necessary.

The Professor reads ahead, recalling how the ingenious plot involved making a copy of the cell key, knowing when the prison guards were making rounds, and then using a rope ladder to scale a 20 foot high prison wall. He skips ahead:

The rope-ladder was drawn up and lowered on the other side, and in another moment the three men had reached the prison-garden. Crossing this hastily, they approached another stone wall nearly as high as the one just scaled. The rope-ladder was once more brought into requisition, the top of the wall speedily gained, and at two o'clock and thirty-five minutes by the prison-clock, Mr. Stephens looked out upon the streets of Dublin. His friends outside were watching for him, and as they saw his form on the top of the wall, these devoted individuals closed in together, bending their backs for him to drop upon.

Lightly he sprang down, landing safely and uninjured upon their shoulders, and he, for whose capture the British Government had made such prodigious efforts, stood upon his native soil once more a free man. His friends who had unlocked the door of his cell, having removed all traces of their flight, and having taken slight measures to mislead the authorities as to their mode of exit, hastily followed the example of their leader. 'No sooner had they landed than they immediately fled in different directions. Colonel Kelly and one other alone remaining with Mr. Stephens. The three walked rapidly for a few squares, when the third person was sent away ; a few moments more and Mr. Stephens entered the house of a watching friend, and Colonel Kelly passed on to his lodgings. Both were drenched to the skin, splashed with mud, and their clothes bore evidence of the rough work they had encountered in scaling the prison- walls.

Ah, here, Paddy was no doubt part of this:

Six persons in different parts of the city and its suburbs had been led to expect Mr. Stephens that night ; all six kept their houses open awaiting his arrival, and had made every preparation to receive him. Colonel Kelly had anticipated every emergency which could arise, and had one mode of escape failed, another was open to him. Even had he been captured in the undertaking, his chief would still have escaped, and would have found his friends awaiting his arrival. The whole affair was most successfully managed, not one person about the prison being aware that the conspirator's cell was empty until four o'clock the following morning,

Eight thousand men, in Dublin, on a god-awful stormy night! Paddy is in here somewhere.

With the exception of one night, Mr. Stephens did not sleep outside the limits of the city of Dublin from the time of his escape from prison until the 13th of March following, at which time he left Ireland for Paris on his way to America.

Professor Brown sighs again, looks up at the office window, and sees that it is pitch black outside. All is in darkness except where streetlights stand watch.

It is time to shift from the well-known to the unknown. He turns to look at the box full of Paddy O'Neil's papers. He has been given this gift, original material that no one has heretofore seen, including his colleagues in British Columbia.

It's getting late, but he cannot take his eyes off the nearby table. He sits still momentarily and almost immediately recognizes two distinct sensations. The first is that the disheveled cardboard box seems to be calling him, like hidden spirits inside an Irish well, banshees whooshing about inside, threatening to be unleashed once the flaps are further loosened.

The second sensation is a tidal wave of exhaustion, sudden immobility to move his limbs, twiddle a single finger. His eyes seemed fixed, as if he doesn't have the minimal energy to glance elsewhere, frozen still like a grey cemetery statue made of stone. He begins to worry that his breathing is labored, everything seems labored.

He knows what he has to do. It is only one thing. It is the only thing.

Chapter 42

Missing the Boat

Tuesday, September 4, 2001

He has to stand up. Up it is. Up and away. Push. Toward the box, retrieve it, bring it back to his desk. Put on the vinyl disposable gloves again. Open the cardboard flaps.

Once back at his desk, he blows out a goodly amount of air, a man on a mountain expedition, one who just crossed over the very worn rope bridge.

He has been so focused on this quest, years of searching for his Canadian Fenian. Academic conferences had garnered gibes, and his exploratory papers were politely dismissed as demonstrating a matinee of imagination.

He stands at the ready, hands trembling, and reaches into the top of the box again, carefully removing the top pieces he has already seen: 1879, the letter to John Donohoe, then commentary about the Land War, comments on the murder of the Earl in 1878, visit to Claremorris, meeting the great man. Here is the 1879 piece that describes Paddy's involvement in the St Albans raid during the American Civil war years earlier.

Paddy's documents appear to be neatly organized chronologically, beginning with these papers at the top. He will be going further back in time the more he digs down, carefully sorting the material at hand. He is an archaeologist sifting through brittle pieces of paper, his version of whisking dirt from ancient bones, artifacts buried for ages until the moment that a soft tipped brush touches a hard edge, returns what had lain in the dark to the light of day.

Page by page, he dives downward, quickly passes over many items. He knows where he is headed. He makes mental notes along the way, Hansel and Gretel leaving their breadcrumbs, a path by which to return even if to lesser discoveries. Every document is written in the present tense. He is sifting through a literal time machine, everything is present.

Here are Paddy's comments about the whaling ship Catalpa, 1875, the secretive rescue of patriots from Australia. More details he will need to revisit, how the journalist John J. Breslin who had assisted Stephens escape a few years earlier, (yes!) agreed to join the American group Clan na Gael that supported the Irish Republican Brotherhood and take part in the voyage.

Several documents further down, getting closer, Paddy writes about the famous Canadian Thomas D'arcy McGee, his surprising re-election after rejecting Fenianism in 1867 and the shock of his assassination. Looks like...he was fond of McGee, if only his name. Complicated, he thinks, mixed sympathies. Onward.

Ah here, Jones Wood, 25 June 1866, Paddy describes the second meeting with Stephens at the Mass Meeting of Fenians in New York.

Professor Brown is aware that his hands are beginning to sweat. It might be the vinyl gloves, though he suspects something different. Here is something about the Fort Erie attack, Paddy sailing along on a small boat, the W.T. Robb.

Close to the bottom of the box, bingo!

November 1865 Somewhere outside of Dublin

"I thought at first you were going to be a Yank joining the cause. Your accent, see, though it was a little different," says he. "No sir," says I, "You're looking at a Canadian." The fellow of whom I speak is none other than American Colonel Thomas J. Kelly, one bright fellow I'll tell you. He tendered his services this past April, and being a tried and trusted Fenian, won the confidence of our beloved chief Mr. Stephens.

We would talk, when there was a quiet moment during the

preparations, about the Fenian movement and his thoughts of a possible coming invasion of our Canadian homeland. He had heard about me, he was that well informed, so he could talk the ins and outs of what such an attack by a largely American contingent would mean. He knew that he had my confidence as well. It was a high compliment to hear "I can trust you, O'Neil, because as they say, actions speak louder than words." And the actions, not all of which can nor need to be recorded, were surprisingly well known by him. In turn, I knew I could trust him with what was being planned.

I can speak a little, Deo Gratias, about what has just occurred in the past couple of weeks.

There were four or five possible safe houses, so they termed them, once James Stephens had been delivered from that god-awful prison, Richman, I think it is called.

My role was to join a group of lads meant to sew confusion, we finally learned, to be down at the shore with our little boat as if we were the ones to carry him off to safety. Oh and it was some kind of stormy night, I will tell you.

We were split up for awhile so as not to bring suspicion and we had a rendezvous point where we were to gather, one of the lads knew a gent that had the required vessel and for a time earlier we were under the impression that we actually would be the ones to help Mr. Stephens get off the dear island. That boat, once I saw it, would have had a time of it, trying to cross the Irish Sea especially on a night like we had.

Late in the day of final preparation, in the pouring rain and the wind howling like anything, I met my mate who was to give me the exact meeting place and time for the intended launch. We were on a dark city corner. In the excitement and hustle and wind and rain I could swear that my contact said I should go down to the port of Dublin where the river Liffey joins the sea. Besides, that would have been lovely because it was quite close by, you see. As if it wasn't bad enough that the rain and the wind wouldn't let up their howling, it turned out that my mate, my contact, was from county Meath. Have you ever heard the accent from Meath, god help us, all mumble and rumble the words are rising and falling and what I know now is that he actually said to go to Dun Laoghaire, or more precisely to a place a bit further, Dalkey, a small village south of that grand port. Go forthwith. By jiggidy jig.

Once I realized my mistake, I did everything I could to get to the proper place. Fortunately Dun Laoghaire is not more than 10 or so miles south of Dublin, but then the fun was trying to find Dalkey. The Irish, God Bless them, don't seem to believe in proper signage, maybe it's a security thing to give the Queen's men a bit more trouble. Well, they are good at not giving clear directions, in fact they excel in it. I'm afraid I was met along the roadside with a good bit of suspicion, especially being out along the road at that time of night and in those conditions and with my mixed accent. Here and there I was invited in for a wee nip but my heart was racing to undo the gaffe I had made and my need to make good the adventure.

Oh the teasing I was met with at my final destination, and by then they were surprisingly in good humour, no doubt with the aid of liquid Spirits if not the Holy Spirit himself, because I quickly learned about the successful outcome of the escape plan now completed, the details of which I will with all propriety not comment upon further. To tell the truth, the details of which I never knew, other than my little part, as fouled up as it was. The boat, all things considered, was a thing of beauty actually and I pictured myself in such a craft on our good Lake Erie, heading out from Port Maitland. I asked after it, and a few of my waterlogged mates said it was called a Smack and others said it was too small for a Smack and they called it a Jolly. Well, jolly we were, and there was no threat of a raised hand smack coming in my direction I can assure you. All good fellows, yet embarrassed I was, by my own misadventure.

I did, that night, have the great fortune of meeting a man who would know all there was to know about our leader's escape, in fact he arrived a bit later than I but in his case, by his own proper design. He brought along all the details of what had occurred that evening to the best of his knowledge. Sure I had heard his name on more than a few occasions but to meet him in the flesh, even the cold and drowning flesh of that night was a real honour. He it is who has been at the heart of much transatlantic communication, and brilliant leadership. I will exclude his name here for reasons one might understand but the frosting on the cake was to discover that he is none other than a fellow countryman and from St Catherines, Ontario, would you believe. He it was who said to me, after I shared all my apologies, "there's no shame in it."

Professor Brown gently lowers the sheet of paper to the desk for a safe and dry landing. He looks up and out the window again into the dark of the night. Among other heightened sensations, he feels his heart sinking. He has arrived at last, into an uncertain harbor.

CHAPTER 43

Making The Call

Tuesday, September 4, 2001

At the end of Brendan and Eddie's phone conversation, they agreed on the next step. This time they would call her first. They would not walk in unannounced. They had enough other surprises to share with the young and lovely descendant of the Dan Donohoe clan. Neither of them were eager to call the house but Brendan was ready with a quarter in his hand.

Eddie called 'tails', and Brendan breathed a sigh of relief.

"Did you tell her we had new information?" Brendan asks later that day.

"Indeed," Eddie answers, "and she said she did as well."

"Really," Brendan mutters, with more than a note of skepticism. "Probably more unpleasantness, shall we say, about dad."

"Actually, I didn't get that sense. I think it may be something new."

"New, as in good, for once?"

"New, as in, well, new. Actually, she asked if we could meet tomorrow, maybe in the late morning?"

"Tomorrow? So soon. Tomorrow is Wednesday."

"Yes, and the day after is Thursday if I'm not mistaken."

"Well," Brendan begins, "Okay, I guess we have a date. Her house?"

"Of course. She has an opening in her schedule so she'll be home, late morning. She seemed really pleased to hear from me."

Brendan pauses for a moment, "She always does," and then adds "we should bring something."

Eddie takes a breath, answers in the voice of one of his British caricatures, "Yes, I do so enjoy the odd donut or two. Boston Crème, if you would. And you're a jelly man if memory serves."

Brendan pauses for a well-deserved long-suffering moment, "Yes."

"Do you know the Muffin Man?"

Brendan hesitates. "Are you asking about the nursery rhyme?"

"No, it's the name of a new bakery I discovered, not too far from her house."

Brendan hesitates, "So you're proposing—?"

"A ride would be very nice. A little pick me up."

"Yes, of course."

"Escort, if you will."

Brendan holds the receiver without saying anything at first. Finally he says, "You need protection? Company?"

"The Ford," Eddie says, "with its ever-so-secure seat belts."

"That's what we might need tomorrow."

"Sorry?" Eddie asks, his voice rising.

"At Emma's. Seatbelts."

Chapter 44

Exorcism
Wednesday, September 5, 2001

"HEY FELLAS," EMMA CALLS out, as she holds open the front door. She graciously accepts a box of donuts that is still warm to the touch and invites her cousins to settle in the living room while she goes to the kitchen to put on the coffee.

When Emma returns, she notices that Brendan is mentally surveying the room from his seat on the large couch. He is sitting a bit upright at the far end, as if needing to balance Edmund, bless his heart, who looks deeply settled, stretching out his legs.

Brendan looks up at Emma, and says "Lovely as always," without adding that he appreciates seeing the unusual small clutter of magazines and mail on the side table. Not so perfect nor, he doesn't want to admit, intimidating.

"It'll be a minute," she says, taking a seat in the comfortable-looking chair opposite the couch, tugging her short skirt modestly toward her knees. The chair is covered with a vanilla crème colored upholstery, accompanied by a brightly colored throw pillow tucked neatly to the side, allowing just enough room for Emma's slender frame to slide in.

"So Brendan," she says after a moment, "you were able to get an update from your brother after he and I met?"

For an embarrassingly short elderly moment, Brendan wonders what she is asking, before he says quickly, "Oh yes, yes, and well, we think we can bring you up to date with new information that I was able to share with Eddie."

Eddie is watching his brother's apparent discomfort which he finds puzzling. He reaches for the first Boston Crème that he sees in the box, wishes that his brother might find eating to be as calming as he himself does.

Emma sits up straight, as if suddenly aware of her posture, wanting to be erect. "Yes," she says enthusiastically, "Eddie told me you have some new information. I'm so glad that we can move forward, you know, with the family saga."

Both brothers look at each other from their opposite ends of the large couch.

"I know," Emma continues sympathetically, "it must be difficult to hear certain things about your family."

"Now." Says Eddie.

"What? Oh right, yes, now. Finally. It should not have taken so long. To get the word to you."

"And to you," Brendan says.

"Oh," Emma says, surprised. "No, see Brendan I've heard these stories for a long time." She stops and looks from one brother to the other. "Okay," she says, "you have new information, so I don't want to get ahead of myself here."

Eddie can practically see the wheels turning as he waits for Emma to continue. A hint of a smile crosses her young face.

Finally she says, "You got to admit, it would be kind of kind of cool if we had a distant relative who had gotten into some kind of, shenanigans, for lack of a better word, maybe something more dire, and to have to high tail it out of Ireland, 'on the lam' as you might say."

After a moment she appears to regret saying what she just said, and her face darkens. "What's tragic of course is the storytelling that went on, the effect it had on family relations."

Brendan adds quietly, "The way that stories were denied, twisted."

Emma gives Brendan a look of uncertainty. She responds, "Once again, I'm sorry to be the one to share how the information affected others, your dad in particular."

Eddie finishes his first donut, leans back into the couch. He appears to be considering what has been said, biding his time.

After an extended and uneasy moment, Emma says, "There was never anything in Great Uncle John's journal to confirm these passed-along stories about Paddy. I know. I read them all. Again. Lately. Well, some hints that Paddy and he talked on the QT. But then again that might have been about women, who knows?"

Eddie brightens and says, "In the Donohoe family?"

Emma seems to relax a little, shifts slightly in her seat. "Well," she says, "you are from a much earlier generation. There may be some things you know that I don't. In fact, that's why you're here, right?"

"Thank you," Brendan says.

"Thank you for which part?" Eddie asks his brother, "hopefully not the part about being from an ancient generation."

The two brothers exchange glances again. Emma notices. She hopes that Eddie accurately shared with Brendan the information she had discussed, how the stories from Great Great Whatever Uncle Joe were thought to be made up. Not true. Destructive lies.

"I mean," she starts to say, "you have to admit, some of these stories seem to be pretty far-fetched."

"Such as?" Brendan asks.

"Well," she says, her voice rising in pitch, "that you have a relative who was, what, some kind of revolutionary, a member of a clandestine group. Crazy huh? Paddy, the man that you always knew to be a simple farmer, in Dunnville Ontario for Chrissakes." Emma hesitates, exhales. "Sorry. Didn't mean to get so worked up. Not sure where that came from."

Eddie leans in, "Do you have any sage?"

Emma looks confused.

"He's kidding," Brendan says. "Sage, see."

It's clear that Emma is not seeing at first, then she says, "Oh, Eddie you've asked me that before."

"Wards off any left-over negative energy," Brendan explains unnecessarily.

"Or evil spirits," Eddie adds.

"Ah," Emma says, taking a deep breath. "Yes. Interesting spice. But not better than turmeric. I love turmeric."

"Yes, splendid!" Eddie nearly shouts, immediately wishing he hadn't.

The three family members take a moment to settle, take a time out.

"But seriously," Emma starts up, "I understand how some of your relatives were affected by the stories Joe told. Paddy caught up in something that might be dangerous, or nefarious."

"Oh, I like that word," Eddie comments.

Brendan pauses, clarifies "'some of your relatives.' Some of our relatives."

Emma looks at Brendan and nods.

"'Nefarious', I've got to use that one," Eddie says, the voice of an afterthought. "The root word there is nefas, in Latin it means sin."

Brendan looks at Emma, says, "Let's ignore him for the moment. Unless you have another word with which to dazzle him. In which case, keep it handy for when you might need it."

Emma takes a moment to look thoughtfully at Brendan and finally asks him, "Your brother shared with you the story that Paddy was supposedly a spy for the Confederate Army? In the Civil War," she adds, as if Brendan might need to know which American war this was.

Brendan returns her thoughtful look and hesitates before answering. Eddie notices and freezes, his hand halfway toward the box of donuts.

Brendan clears his throat. "Paddy was actually a spy for the Union Army, except he was actually a spy for the Fenian movement."

Eddie looks back and forth at his brother and his cousin before adding, "Actually he was a spy for the Canadian government."

"And," Brendan adds, "to clarify, he was a spy for the Fenian movement that would fight for freedom in Ireland exclusively on Irish soil. He wasn't supporting the Fenians who invaded Canada."

Emma sits back in her seat, crosses her right leg over her left leg, then reverses covering her left leg over her right leg, followed by once again pulling down her short skirt.

At last, eyes wide open, she speaks with a voice that is surprisingly low and growling, a sound that could expel the dark energy of prior generations. Forcefully. She says, "What the hell!?"

Eddie sits back in the couch. A single word comes to mind: exorcism.

A time-out is taken. Emma goes out to the kitchen to get the coffee. When she returns, she is gratefully received along with the coffee that she pours without spilling a drop.

As she takes her seat once again, Brendan decides to pace his newsbreaks. After a moment, seeing that she has regained her composure, and seeing his brother look for but apparently decide to forego another donut, he says "And along the way, there was a bit of violence."

"Oh my god," Emma says, raising her hand but not quite covering her mouth. She recalls the name, "Burl someone."

"Earl," Eddie chimes in. "He was the Earl of Leitrim."

Emma's raises her eyebrows, while she lowers her hand to her lap.

"And Paddy wasn't there," Brendan adds somewhat disjointedly, "so it would be a challenge to consider him involved with the murder when he shows up at the scene one year later. Actually he didn't show up at that scene but somewhere else in Ireland. So," Brendan says as if heroically about to rest his case, righting an old and presumed wrong, "he wasn't implicated in any way when the Earl got plugged."

"What?" Emma asks.

"Shot," Eddie interprets.

"Shot dead," Brendan adds, realizing that he is enjoying this more than he probably should.

Eddie looks at his brother in an unusually disciplined way, before turning to Emma who, he notices, has just taken a very deep breath. Acting as the senior family member present, he says with what he hopes is an overtone of soothing confidence, "It is truly remarkable that Paddy was able to travel to Ireland," in a moment adding, "this simple farmer from Dunnville Ontario," repeating her words.

Emma shakes her head in agreement and at long last says simply, "Yes."

A short silence ensues before Emma says, "You know, to be honest I don't think I ever heard that Uncle Joe claimed that Paddy had killed anyone."

"Good," Eddie says.

"It was more that he was involved in something dangerous, something he had to run from." She pauses, considers how to proceed. "The stories just got so complicated, innuendo flying everywhere. I mean the history is complicated too."

"Indeed," Eddie adds.

No one says a word for a moment until Emma says, sounding distressed, "Oh my god, I'm so sorry."

"For what?" Eddie asks.

Emma looks at her cousins, "I don't know. I just felt this wave—it took me a moment, how family felt the need to shut down Joe's, and Bill's, stories. Stop spreading them. Quash them. Paddy having to high tail it out of Ireland and all the rest."

The brothers exchange looks, Emma notices again. Finally she says, "Okay, what else?"

Eddie begins, "Actually you're correct on one count."

Emma looks at Eddie, her face says, *please continue.*

Eddie takes a deep breath. "Okay right. The one count is that there was some truth in the need to shut down the stories, as you say." Eddie pauses. "Actually it was probably what Paddy would have wanted. Otherwise, why else would he have his stories sealed until the present day? So," Eddie continues, looking from his brother to his cousin, "here we are in the new century and they are just getting a first look at the letters and notes as we speak."

Emma hesitates, "What letters and notes?"

"Oh dear! Emma I'm—we have to apologize. We're jumping all over the place here," Brendan says. They probably should have gotten their game plan together before coming over. This isn't some kind of 12 step Intervention, though that doesn't sound like an accurate description either.

"So as you know, Brendan had this recent consultation with our friend the history professor in Toronto…" Eddie begins but it is absolutely clear that Emma is not about to let him say one more word, not one more word, because she is saying, actually she is shouting repeatedly, "Oh! Oh! Oh! Oh my gosh! I forgot, I forgot to tell you, I forgot to tell you!"

"What?" Brendan says more loudly than he intends.

"I got a call from your Professor, Professor Green, just yesterday, yesterday was Tuesday right? He was in a hurry, had a class or something so he didn't have time to talk. He said he remembered that one of you had told him that I had inherited Uncle John's journals, and he wanted to ask me a quick question, before he had to run off. He says to say hi to the two of you by the way."

"Brown," Brendan corrects, "Professor Brown."

Eddie leans toward his niece, waves a hand as if to silence his younger brother for the moment. "What was the quick question?" he asks, omitting 'dear' at the last second.

"Yes," she answers. "He wondered whether a particular name ever appeared anywhere in the journals."

"Okay," Eddie says, waiting, ready if needed to wave a hand again at his brother.

"It was," Emma begins, "wait, I wrote it down. No I remember, had we ever heard of a fellow named Devoy."

CHAPTER 45

Thank You Nokia

Thursday, September 6, 2001

"Well, yes, it is all rather remarkable, these papers written by your ancestor," Professor Brown answers, his voice coming from the little speaker resting on the top of Emma's coffee table. "By the way, thanks to all of you for getting back in touch so soon, I think I did tell Emma it would be best to speak again sooner rather than later. The new semester up here begins this coming Monday the 10th and for me at least, it's like a whole new world starts up again."

Emma nods her head, which she realizes the Professor cannot see. She sits in her comfortable armchair, Eddie and Brendan have captured opposite sides of the sofa, their usual places.

When they first arrived, Emma brought out her new phone and placed it carefully in the middle of the coffee table. She wished later that she could have taken a picture of her cousins' faces when they first saw it laying there.

"What is that, pray tell?" Brendan asked, staring at the small object that was flipped open, revealing what looked like a miniature keyboard. Brendan did not yet own a cellphone, but he had recently splurged on a longer spiral cord for his faithful landline. He could now wander as far as 17 feet away before feeling the tug on the end of the line.

"Welcome to the 21st century brother," Eddie said. "It's a cellphone. They call them smartphones now."

"I know what a cellphone is, I've seen yours, but I'd never seen one like this."

Eddie took a minute after asking permission to pick up the phone and lifted it as if it were an exquisite piece of jewelry. "Nice," he said, "Ah, a Nokia also, but I don't have this model."

"I took your recommendation, Eddie, to buy the new phone," Emma said, "I thought it would be good to have for this gathering."

After Eddie finished admiring her phone and replaced it at nearly the exact same spot on the table, Emma said, "Nokia 9210, just came out earlier this year. The model name is the Communicator. Has a color screen."

"Come on!" Eddie gushed, "very nice."

"It can send and receive fax messages."

"Get out!" Eddie said.

"And for our purposes today, it has a speakerphone option."

"Oh Lord," Brendan said, as if intoning a prayer.

At that very moment the phone rang, Emma pushed a button and they were off to the races.

Emma notices, a couple of minutes into the call, that when her cousins speak, more or less taking turns, they sound like they are shouting. They are animated, energized, gesturing with hands, nodding heads, leaning forward and back on the couch, as if the Professor can see them.

Though each had individually spoken with the Professor before, there had been no formal introductions during this call. The Donohoe brothers had jumped in the pool with both feet, splashing around like little kids.

It takes a moment for Emma to realize this.

"You folks," the Professor says, "certainly seem to be excited, and it's grand being able to share this treasure with the family members themselves. I dare say, the more we know about Mr. O'Neil, the more many of us here in Canada will come to see him as playing an important place in our history. He played many roles. And he pulled it off. Kept them all hidden from public view quite effectively. If you're interested, I'll keep you informed as scholarship about him continues. Keep you in the loop, eh? Is that a phrase you use in the States?"

"Yes, yes," Brendan says loudly, seeing Emma wave her arms, he knows she means tone it down.

"Can you all hear me okay?" the Professor asks.

"Perfectly," Emma answers. "My cousins are also excited about using my new speaker phone."

"Speaker phone eh? Well isn't that very (he almost says 'American') lovely. What kind if I may inquire, the brand?"

"Oh, it's a Nokia 9210."

"The Communicator," Eddie jumps in.

There is a slight hesitation, the Professor asks "That's the model name?"

"Affirmative," Eddie says, feeling just for a moment like a ham radio operator.

"Yes. So. Well, I have a Blackberry I'm quite fond of, Canadian firm you know."

Brendan is feeling lost, vision of blueberries coming to mind.

After a brief awkward moment of silence, the Professor continues. "Well, as I say, we have started to look at your relative's papers, and what a thoughtful gift that was, quite prescient of Mr. O'Neil eh? All those years ago. He had awareness of his times and the importance of recording some of the information, for the sake of the future, for history. Does my soul proud and we in the Department are very grateful to him."

"Yes, well thank you," Brendan replies, not quite sure if this is the proper response.

"We began," the Professor says, not missing a beat, "with the documents that were found at the top of the box. Those were dated 1879."

"Goodness," Emma says, "1879."

After a slight hesitation the Professor's voice asks, "It's Emma isn't it?"

"Yes, Professor."

"Well its good to hear your lovely voice again. Sorry that we had so little time to talk before. Did you tell the boys that we had spoken earlier?"

Brendan mouths *the boys*?

"Yes sir, and of course they are right here with me now." For a moment

Emma wonders why she had to say this, the obvious, and she also notices how Eddie is smiling at her.

"Well," the Professor continues, "of course 1879 was one of those momentous times in Irish history, and in Mr. Parnell's career as well. You know about Parnell do you"?

"Yes indeed Professor," Brendan answers.

"Is that Eddie?"

"No, this is Brendan," feeling suddenly younger than his years and strangely diminished.

"Of course, of course, pardon my manners. To say nothing of my hearing. Not getting any younger eh? I truly enjoyed our earlier chat on the phone, before we really had a chance to look at these papers." A pause. "And hello to you too there Eddie."

"Yes hi," Eddie answers.

"You know," the Professor says, "I feel, so to speak, like we are family together now, as I have gotten to know you. Could you please," he asks quite formally, "call me Martin from this point on?"

"Certainly sir, Martin," Brendan begins.

The Professor chuckles. "Oh my dear American friends, just Martin. Though Sir Martin does have a nice ring to it."

"Good enough Martin," Emma says, in a voice that is congenial, soothing. Not male.

"Right. Well as I say, so we can think about this, Paddy, you know, and I hope you don't mind me calling him Paddy." There is a brief burst of agreeable murmur and the Professor continues without missing a beat. "Paddy meets Charles Stewart Parnell during an auspicious time there in Claremorris, Ireland, and what we know now from history is that the following week, he would be going to the town of Westport."

"Paddy?" one of the brothers asks.

"No, Mr. Parnell, and it would be his first speech in support of the Land Movement. I don't know whether you had heard about the Land Movement. Not necessary for our purposes at the moment."

"I'm knocked out," Eddie begins.

"Oh I hope that certainly isn't the case," Martin teases.

"I mean we have read a bit about Paddy in our uncle's journals, but it was all very obscure," Eddie continues.

"For good reason," Martin says, "your uncle could be trusted to keep the secrets."

All three look at each other, their faces awash with a gumbo of guilt, embarrassment, and shame. The trinity of secrets betrayed.

"Can you still hear me?" Martin's voice asks over the tiny speaker.

Brendan jumps in quickly, "Yes sir, loud and clear and by the way you know we have his trunk."

Martin's response is delayed, "But that wasn't very revealing was it?"

Eddie answers, "Not unless you appreciate getting a bargain for woolen underwear. Oh also if you enjoy cooking with lard."

They all hear Martin chuckle. There is a collective pause before Brendan, hoping to refocus the discussion, says, "But to learn that he actually went over there to Ireland and met Charles Parnell himself and Parnell met him too, well... of course he met him too," his voice shifts from excitement to a faltering, flummoxed hesitation.

"It wasn't just a vacation," Emma says by way of rescue.

Martin is silent for a moment, and then says, "No, in fact it wasn't just a vacation."

"So Martin," Brendan says, "I have read that this was getting close to the time of Parnell's downfall. He had a long-term affair with a married woman."

"Would you believe," Martin says.

Brendan is not certain whether Martin is being facetious. He continues "And it wasn't exactly a secret, and here he is being championed as this uncrowned king."

Eddie looks at his brother, wondering how and when his brother learned this history.

"Which may have gone to his head a bit," Martin says. "Power can blind one to one's actions, and I don't mean to be offensive but that is something you've had to deal with in the States, with your last President."

"Oh," Eddie says, "yes, regrettably, and damn the torpedoes regarding all the good he had done up until then." Eddie knows this didn't come out right.

Martin hesitates, "Are you referring to Mr. Clinton or Mr. Parnell?"

Eddie hesitates, his voice rising in uncertain upspeak "Both?"

"Yes," Martin says, "I would agree with you there."

There is a brief shared silence, until Emma asks, "Martin you asked whether in our Uncle John's journal, we had seen any references to a fellow named Devoy."

"Yes, yes, yes," Martin responds.

"And, of course, the answer, as I had shared with you, is unfortunately no, although we can comb through those pages again to see if we missed something." Emma looks up from the speaker phone and notices that cousin Eddie looks suddenly pale, uncomfortable. She says to Eddie, "You okay cousin?"

Eddie murmurs his embarrassed reassurance.

Martin asks, "Everything okay there? May have been rude of me to bring up President Clinton."

Eddie speaks up, "No sorry, I…something rang a bell when the name, Devoy, came up just now. Sorry. Strange. Emma mentioned the name yesterday but just now, hearing it again…delayed reaction or something."

Martin considers teasing Eddie for being so apologetic, as if this betrays Canadian roots. He thinks the better of it and stays silent, except to add, "Well, maybe just let it be there, and maybe a memory or whatever may come to mind of its own. Don't push it." The voice of a reassuring grandfather.

"Thanks Martin," Eddie says.

"Well, I don't want to use up all your time on this call, I know we can speak again as more of the papers are examined but there is something I want to ask you, the Donohoes, about."

"Of course," Emma says, in a tone that sounds to Brendan not exactly like purring, but close. Reassuring as only she can be.

"I have to confess that I moved quickly through the subsequent documents in your relative's papers, they were all ordered chronologically, and I was wanting to get to the bottom of something, no pun, see, the bottom of the box, okay not important. There had been a remark Parnell made about Paddy and how Paddy's past assistance to one of the early and important Fenian leaders was noted by him, Mr. Parnell, and would not be forgotten."

Martin knows that he could have said this more elegantly, he also knows where he is heading, the question he wants to ask the Donohoes.

"Wow!" Brendan says. "Parnell said that, himself! To our Paddy. We're famous!"

As if on cue, Emma and Eddie look over at Brendan, tilt their heads to the side, like a pet dog questioning what is going on. Brendan notices, adds, "Well maybe not us, but Paddy, for sure. Wow."

"I can join you in your 'wow' Eddie, or Brendan is it? Yes. Your relative plays, played, a significant if not well-known role in this history eh? And we're just learning about this, as I say."

Emma and Eddie are nodding their silent agreement, there is a pause in the conversation until Emma says, "Martin, I'm afraid that there is, was, a bit of a downside about our relative's adventures."

"Oh?" Martin remarks.

"Kind of a long story. The pressure of keeping secrets. Our Uncle John…"

"…The author of your treasured journal there," Martin interrupts, wishing immediately he hadn't. He is anxious to move forward with his own agenda, he realizes.

"Yes," Emma says, "exactly. He didn't completely succeed in keeping Paddy's secrets. Secret," she adds.

"Oh I see," Martin says sympathetically but with an edge of caution.

"He only spoke to family though, no one else."

"Okay," Martin says, more relieved than he wants to let on.

"And it created conflict within the Donohoe family. There were allegations," Emma continues, "and denials, rumors had been spread about what Uncle John was sharing."

"That led to a separation between certain members of the family for a time," Eddie adds.

"That is now in the process of repair," Brendan finishes.

Professor Brown smiles, one family member answering after another. Neat little hat trick, is what he thinks, and almost says out loud, but then remembers that these American Donohoes may not be hockey fans.

"Yes," Martin says, "yes, well good for all of you, or y'all as you might say."

Emma says politely, hoping to be a little lighthearted "No sir, that's not how we'd say it. We'd say 'you guys.'"

Brendan looks at his brother, squinches his eyebrows, not understanding. Eddie whispers, "Language."

Martin is speaking, he is saying "Well, trust me, I know how stories can go underground in a family. Brendan, I think you and I talked about this briefly earlier when we spoke. The word 'disconnect' comes to mind. We're all human. It comes at a price, people get hurt, often unintentionally. And the unspoken words have a way of inflating everything out of control." After a short moment he adds, "I'm a historian, after all."

Eddie likes what he is hearing. He thinks Martin sounds more like a family therapist than a social scientist. Soothing, he is.

"And I'd have to agree with you," Brendan continues, "People do get hurt."

After a moment Emma says, quite pointedly, "And then repairs are made, just as you say Brendan."

"Well," Martin says, "sounds like things are working out for...you guys." He takes a moment to consider how to phrase his next question. This is the big one. He hopes his timing is right. 'Rumors had been spread' he just heard them say, within the Donohoe family. He takes a deep breath. He wants the family to be comfortable, he hopes they will be transparent, forthcoming, as open-minded as possible.

Even so, the response he gets, is not one he expected.

"I wanted to ask you," he begins hesitantly, "whether with all the rumors…stories excuse me…shared in your family, whether you ever heard about 'C.F.'"?

CHAPTER 46

See If?

Thursday, September 6, 2001

M ARTIN WAITS TILL THE commotion settles down. Someone in the family was choking, it sounded like, and coughing loudly. He can tell that the other family members were jumping in, doing what they could do.

"Sorry Professor, Martin," Emma's voice speaks. "Little disturbance here, but I think we're okay now."

"It was Eddie again," Brendan says.

"I see, everything okay now?"

After a moment another voice attempts to speak, "Yes," Eddie croaks, clearly not 100 percent recovered, "Apologies here. Little bit of water helps. Or something stronger," he quips, "for later perhaps."

"Ah yes," Martin answers, relieved. "Something I said? Again?"

"You sure you're okay?" Martin overhears Emma ask her cousin.

"He's okay," Brendan answers Emma.

"Woooof," Eddie says. "Don't know what got into me," and then asks, "did you say 'see if'?"

"No, I didn't say that," Brendan answers.

"I think he's asking Martin," Emma says.

Martin clears his throat, he leans into his phone as if this would help, "I'm so sorry if I upset you Eddie, or anyone. I was asking about 'C.F'"

"See if?" Eddie asks again.

"Eddie," his brother interrupts, "the Professor, Martin, is saying 'C.F', the letters. You know, like ABCD et cetera."

"Yes," Martin answers, "that's correct, Brendan."

Eddie clears his throat and remains silent for several moments.

"Hello?" Martin's voice asks over the small speaker on the coffee table.

"We're here," Martin. "We're okay, just giving Eddie a moment to come up for air," Emma says.

"Or come up with something," his brother quips.

"Okay, okay," Eddie begins, "again I'm embarrassed."

"We know," Brendan says, noticing immediately the way Emma gives him a look. Not one of her more pleasant ones.

"Like an old dream I'd forgotten, strange...does that make sense?" Eddie says looking at Emma and Brendan.

"Perfect sense," Brendan says, hoping to be helpful, and actually starting to be concerned. "I rarely remember any dreams I've had. But that's just me."

Eddie seems to be remembering more, his eyes widen, and Brendan sees in his brother's eyes something that makes him sit up.

Emma notices as well.

"So these letters, C and F," Martin begins again carefully, "that stirred, or reminded you," he falters, not wanting to lead the witness. "Well, I don't want to push you in any way."

"Actually," Eddie begins, "this goes back to my dad."

Emma and Brendan both lean forward, as does Martin in his Toronto office. Martin also grips the armrest of his office chair, lightly.

"Before he passed. We had a number of conversations. It wasn't always easy."

"I remember that," Brendan says. "It was dementia, wasn't it?"

"I don't know, some kind of memory problems. But not all the time."

"You were good at it, talking with him." Brendan says.

Eddie looks at his brother, surprised, "Well, thank you."

"This is my great-to-the-x-power-something Uncle Bill, right?" Emma asks, mainly to explain the relationship for Martin's benefit.

"In more ways than one," Eddie answers, adding for clarification, "good man."

There is a pause in the conversation. Lovely as it sounds to Martin's ears, he hopes it won't stop here. "So you had conversations with your dad," he prompts.

"Right," answers Eddie, back on track. "And during those times when he was having more confusion, he would repeat 'See if', at least I think that was what he was saying. It always seemed to be a part of a longer story. As in 'see if this hadn't happened, see if Joe was telling the truth, et cetera."

"He said that?" Emma asks. "That's his brother Joe, right? We heard a lot of stories about him, of course," she says, in part for Martin's benefit.

Eddie pauses, "I'm just giving an example, I don't know that he said those precise words. Man this is weird. I haven't thought about this in a long time. There were a lot of stories about Joe and himself. He would actually get quite animated at times. The nursing staff weren't always so happy."

Emma and Brendan are absorbing this new information and for a moment again, no one is speaking.

"Then you also had this, well, response when I mentioned the name Devoy," Martin's voice interjects.

"Right, John Devoy," Eddie answers. "Who knows? Maybe dad talked about him. He talked about a lot of people I'd never heard of. Mostly they were old business associates, customers, former priests. He had some hilarious stories about some of the priests he'd known, I mean genuinely funny."

Eddie takes a deep breath, appears to be relaxing. "Dyed in the wool those Irish Catholics." Eddie glances away for a moment. "One name I do remember was Stephens but I'm quite sure that was always in reference to the church he would sometimes attend in Rochester."

"St. Stephens," Brendan adds.

"The one and only," Eddie says.

"Wait a minute," Emma jumps in, "wasn't that an Episcopal church?"

"Still is," Eddie says.

"Quite the brouhaha about that one," Brendan says.

"Sorry folks," Martin puts in, "there is an issue here about an Anglican church? I'm sorry, my mind goes to history, see. The relationship of the English and Irish and the role that denominations played. Well, I may be getting a bit academic here, professional hazard. But, Stephens, you're quite certain that refers to a specific church, not an individual person?" Martin finds himself fumbling, "When your dad would speak of it, that is, the name 'Stephens'?"

"Hang on," Eddie says quite forcefully, and for a moment Martin thinks he may have said something offensive. "Light bulbs here, folks. He would say 'See if cannot be named' over and over again, 'see if cannot be named.' It made no sense to me. Oh, here's another one, 'no shame', as in 'there's no shame in it.' Go figure. Here come the nursing staff and that would be the end of it till another time."

Emma sits up suddenly, and the brothers take notice. She looks directly at Eddie and says, "You know you've spoken about this before."

"I have?" asks Martin.

"No, sorry Martin, I'm addressing Eddie here. Eddie has used this phrase before."

"What…?" the hell, is what Brendan wants to say.

"Actually the phrase was 'Paddy is right, there's no shame' or something close to that," Emma says.

"Well," Martin's voice says, in a new, deeply sonorous tone, "I see." Martin takes a moment and says, "You'll appreciate hearing this. I can help you out with that bit of the mystery, eh? In one of the documents, Paddy explicitly recounts that the lads forgave him for his missing the boat, and uses that very phrase. He makes it clear that he is going to forgive himself as well."

"Oh that's terrific!" Emma exclaims. "May we all rest in peace, so to speak."

"Glad I can help, and even more so that your relative is helping to add to our understanding of Canadian history."

After a hesitation, Emma says, "Are we being helpful to you, I mean in what you are piecing together?"

"Wait a minute," Brendan protests, sounding younger than he wishes to sound. "Missing what boat?"

"Yes, yes," Martin says soothingly. "A little background here eh?"

BRENDAN recalls later how the phone call seemed to shift after that point. It felt as if they were attending a graduate seminar, and given Martin's passion for the subject, quite a compelling one. Martin waxed quite eloquently, in Eddie's words, about his quest to identify this character, the Canadian Fenian, 'C.F.' for short.

Brendan is driving Eddie home from the gathering and Eddie appears to be feeling remarkably improved, in fact better than he had in a long time. By the time they left Emma's, the sun had already set, and it was a particularly dark night.

"All we had were Uncle John's vague references to Paddy's travel. And then the rumor mill blew up with stories that Joe supposedly told," Eddie says.

Brendan considers this, adds, "And no information about Stephens escape. Uncle John apparently kept pretty quiet about that first trip to Ireland."

After a moment Eddie looks over at his brother. "How do we know that Uncle John kept quiet?"

"How do you mean?"

"Could have been Joe that kept quiet."

Brendan nods his head, keeping his eyes on the road. "We don't really know," he says by way of summation, "all that Joe might have known let alone shared with Dad."

"Stephens escape could have been the big fish story," Eddie says.

"The one that got away." Brendan says.

After a moment Eddie muses, "Stephens was the big fish."

"And he did get away," Brendan concludes.

The brothers ride along quietly for a time, both of them looking down the road as far as the headlights can see.

"I must say," Eddie says, "that I was impressed with your apparent knowledge about Mr. Parnell."

"Uncrowned king, man."

"I didn't know you had so much interest in some of that history."

Brendan looks over at his brother, "I think in some small ways you've had a positive effect on me."

Eddie's eyes widen, not sure he knows what to say.

"I've picked up some of your enthusiasm for the olden times."

"I see."

"And the business of Parnell's affair is pretty interesting."

"Well," Eddie says, hoping not to sound too dismissive, "there is that."

This stretch of the highway remains unremarkable, headlights provide the only assurance of moving forward.

After a moment Brendan says, "Martin was wondering whether our dear old Paddy might have been the Canadian Fenian."

After a moment, Eddie says quietly, "Whoever heard of the Canadian Fenian anyway?"

Brendan glances over at Eddie before turning his eyes back to the road ahead. "Eddie, it's a Canadian thing."

Eddie considers this, "Actually it sounds more like an academic thing. But what do I know?"

Brendan looks briefly at his brother again and decides not to take the bait.

"Yeah, yeah," Eddie muses over his own comment. Then in a stronger voice, "I must say I was glad when Emma finally came out and asked him, point blank, you know, whether he thought Paddy fit the bill. I thought he was playing footsie a bit with us." As an afterthought he adds, "I think he might have been a little unnerved with her directness."

Brendan considers this, nodding his head as a stop sign approaches. "Well I think Martin was being polite. Canadian you know. And maybe he was being indirect for research purposes. Emma, god bless her, can be a straight shooter if she wants to be. Annie Oakley and all that." Brendan pulls up to the stop, looks both ways, starts up again, "And what did he say, that he had in fact considered Paddy as a prime suspect, but now he has some new information? He's changed his opinion?"

"Something like that. He didn't sound all that sure."

"Or maybe he was being careful with us," Brendan says.

"Careful? How's that?"

"Well," Brendan answers, "we are directly related to the famous Paddy O'Neil ourselves."

"By marriage. He married our…"

"That's okay," Brendan jumps in, adding, "Revolutionary, spy, liberator!"

Eddie hesitates, and in a perfect imitation of an old-time radio host adds, "All the while appearing as a mild-mannered farmer in the little town of Dunnville, Ontario."

Brendan is nodding his head in agreement, though Eddie might not notice. When Brendan looks over at his brother again, Eddie looks to be a million miles away. Brendan almost asks him 'penny for your thoughts'? Instead, Brendan says, "That was neat though, hearing what Paddy had actually written, you know, his role in Stephens escape. All this history we never had a clue about."

After a long moment Eddie turns toward his brother, asks "What?"

"Paddy's papers, the ones toward the bottom of the box. His description of taking part in   Stephens rescue."

Eddie considers this for a moment before saying, "You mean how our relative missed the boat?"

Brendan hesitates, says "Remember, it was a decoy operation meant to throw the Brits off. Confuse things."

Eddie steals a glance at his brother, "Okay, our family is quite good at that, confusing things." After a moment, Eddie says "I wish Dad could have talked to us about what Paddy did. The rescue escapade."

Brendan hesitates, his hands on the wheel, eyes looking forward, nodding this way and that, like an undecided bobblehead doll. "Well," he says finally, "I think Dad was protecting us. Paddy's wishes after all were that all this information should be kept quiet till now. We don't really know how much Dad knew. But we know he'd heard at least part of the story."

Eddie looks over, "How so?"

Brendan looks briefly at his brother, "What Dad said to you, 'Paddy is right, no shame.'"

"Ah, yes."

Brendan waits, wonders if Eddie will say more. He is just about to nudge his brother more on this point when Eddie adds, "My memory seems to work in fits and starts." Eddie sighs, says "Age, you know. Now I remember, now I don't."

Brendan considers this, says "I can relate."

"I thought you might."

A moment passes, a car races by and Brendan instinctively looks in his rearview mirror half expecting to see police in pursuit. There is no other traffic and all Brendan sees are the streetlights disappearing behind him, one after the other.

They are getting closer to Eddie's house though they still have a ways to go. The road surface is uneven here, and Brendan becomes mesmerized by the series of small thumps his tires make, the slight vibrations. When he looks into his rearview mirror again, all he sees are the streetlights departing, vanishing sentinels of light.

Memories stir, he is a kid riding a passenger train from Buffalo to Clifton Springs, he is fascinated by the telephone poles passing by, the way the wires seem to rise and fall with such regularity, the illusion of the wires and poles moving and not himself, looking out the large glass window. Every now and then he catches his own reflection, a small boy craning his head to look out into the growing darkness of night.

"Eddie," Brendan calls out, "what was the name of that train we took to visit relatives?"

Eddie looks at his brother for a long moment, and asks "How did you get there?"

"On the train."

"Never mind. It was The New York Central."

"No that wasn't it."

"Okay," Eddie says, elongating the word, with a slight uplift at the end of the second vowel. "Can we get back to Paddy?"

"Please."

"I was thinking that whatever stories dad had heard, it was all by word of mouth from Uncle Joe who heard it from Great Uncle John who heard it from...."

"Yes, yes," Brendan says.

"So really, we are the first ones to hear about the rescue story directly from Paddy himself, thanks to his writing."

Brendan steals another glance at his passenger. "In the modern era," he says dryly.

JUST before Brendan reaches Eddie's house, Eddie says, "You know the way that Martin described his academic work? Wanting for years to discover the identity of this CF fellow?"

"Yes?"

"It made me think that this is like a Canadian version of Loch Ness."

"That's a monster," Brendan says. "CF would be a legendary hero," adding, "if you're in favor of Irish independence."

"Ah, that I am matey," Eddie says in a voice less convincing than that of his old time radio host. This time Eddie's tone sounds neither British nor Irish for all its flat nasal expression, the sound of Western New York, his true home. "I'm referring more to Loch Ness as a mythical being. Even," and here Eddie reverts to his habit of putting on the dog, "the repository of a collective projection, the hopes and wishes of the people."

"Isn't that what a myth is?"

"Well then, I rest my case."

When they reach Eddie's house, Brendan pulls into the driveway, stops the car but leaves the engine running. He watches as Eddie struggles to undo his seat belt, which takes a moment.

"Free at last, free at last," Eddie says, which his brother understands to be an irreverent reference to the great Martin Luther King Jr.

After Eddie ambles up to the side door of his house, he turns to wave. It's not necessary, but Brendan always waits until his brother has successfully unlocked the door, reminiscent of years past when he would drive a babysitter home, make sure she got in safely.

As Brendan begins to back out, he is pleased that Eddie seemed to make a full recovery from whatever it was that had set him off. Strange. The way certain memories can be locked away but lose none of their incendiary—maybe that's too strong a word—energy. Sleeping all that time as it were, kept in reserve.

What kind of effort does it take to keep oneself unaware of something so deeply known?

And then it hits him! "Lehigh Valley" he shouts out to no one. "The Lehigh Valley Railroad." He turns hoping to see his brother for one last moment, but the light over the side door is off. His brother is securely inside.

Shortly after, as Brendan approaches his own house, the thought occurs to him: Emma never told us the first name. Emma asked if we had heard the name Devoy. But Eddie called him John Devoy. Like he knew him.

He must have that wrong, he tells himself as he pulls in his own driveway. Martin probably said the full name and Eddie was just repeating it. That must be it.

When the call ends, Martin Brown goes over to his liquor cabinet and pours himself a strong drink. Kentucky Bourbon, in honor of his American friends.

'See if cannot be named', Eddie had said. Eddie is repeating what he had heard from his father, Bill Donohoe. Bill may have learned this from his brother Joe many years before. If so, Joe was passing on what he heard from his elderly uncle John Donohoe, who had learned this directly from Paddy O'Neil. But then there is this historical knot to unfurl, the issue of much debate among his colleagues: at what point did the phrase 'Canadian Fenian' or 'C.F.' come into use? When did it take on the meaning it has for some historians? More specifically, would Bill Donohoe have understood the meaning of those initials?

It was clear that, according to Eddie, his dad was trying to share something important. And then there is this: Paddy's papers noted the presence of another Canadian at the time of Stephens release, apparently a highly placed fellow, someone whose name he could not risk revealing at that time. Another candidate for the title. Did he ever reveal the name to his pal John Donohoe? And if so, did John reveal the name to his 20-something year old nephew Joe Donohoe?

Martin Brown swivels in his office chair, to the left and then to the right, slowly, all the while keeping his eyes on the cardboard box full of Paddy's work. The Donohoes had explained a bit more about the family dispute, how Joe Donohoe claimed he had a special audience with his Uncle John Donohoe who had entrusted him with private information he had gained directly from Paddy. Line of transmission, direct links to the past, but each linkage has the risk of data loss, inaccuracy.

He looks away for a moment and when he looks back at the box, he finds himself wondering whether Paddy wrote anything further after 1879. Why stop then? He recalls that Paddy went on to live another twenty or so years. Parnell meanwhile would have a successful fund-raising tour of the United States in 1880 and go on to live till 1891. The sole box in the possession of the History Department was discovered almost by accident back in the stacks. Perhaps he should marshal some of his graduate students to take another hard look.

In the meantime, he has this treasure trove to sort through, and he knows he will have to keep his passion in check, not let it color his objectivity. What has he told his students over the years? Get accurate information, check your sources, respect the science of history.

Oh the siren call of academic glory, to be the one who could finally identify the Canadian Fenian. If he gets this wrong, he can hear the ridicule from his colleagues in British Columbia. When did you sail off course, brother? Were you swayed on a new heading by the power, the romance of that 437-foot iron steamship, all four enormous sails billowing on your journey to recognition?

Forget British Columbia. A Dunnville, Ontario farmer is aboard that ship, his second trip, heading for a rendezvous with his now famous patriots of an earlier rebellion.

Martin takes a sip of the bourbon, feels its liquid warmth, smooth, sliding, like the ship he envisions, canvas aloft, steam engines below, plowing through the waves to Ireland, sailing its way into history.

CHAPTER 47

A Wake
Saturday, September 8, 2001

THEY HAD GATHERED FOR an early meal, it would be an opportunity to 'process', as Emma called it, the phone call with Martin. Brendan had suggested the diner where he and Eddie meet at times for breakfast. This would be for a dinner, different part of the large plastic menu, featuring early bird specials.

When Emma walked in, the two brothers waved in her direction from their accustomed booth, front corner window looking out on South Avenue. The place was new for her, and as she looked around, she noticed that most of the patrons had the look of being regulars.

Brendan had been sitting opposite his brother and when Emma appeared, he stood up and stepped out of the booth, a gesture both to welcome her with a bit of gallantry and to subsequently join Eddie on his side of the booth.

Emma had actually batted her eyelashes, saying, "My my, well, how lovely to see the two of you again. Such gentlemen." She could tell they loved this.

"Seems like just yesterday," Eddie said, "that you graced us with your loveliness."

"Actually, it was the day before yesterday," Brendan said.

The waitress was very prompt, organized, and gave them some time to place their orders. They thanked her and after she left, Eddie said "I could never do that."

"Do what?" his brother asked.

"Keep track of everything and move so quickly."

Brendan turned to Emma and said, "For once, he's not joking."

Emma smiles and looks briefly around the restaurant once again, saying in a quiet voice, "I think I lowered the average age to maybe the late 40's. You guys come here often?"

Eddie shrugs his shoulders, Brendan answers, "Often enough."

"Speaking of the late 40's," Eddie says, "Some of the best bands were still playing, war was over, we were on top of the world."

"What?" Emma asks.

"Don't listen to him sister," Brendan says, a poor imitation of gangster speech.

Emma frowns slightly, briefly.

"Humphrey Bogart," Eddie explains. "My brother loves the old movies."

Emma nods her head. "I'd say more like Edward G. Robinson."

Her cousins turn to look at each other, raise their eyebrows one after the other.

"Watch out for this one," Eddie tells his brother.

"Too late," Brendan answers.

THEY have been waiting a little while for their food to arrive and it appears that the kitchen doesn't work as quickly as the wait staff. Emma is fiddling with her glass of water, turning the glass slowly, the condensation makes the glass slippery, water drips onto the Formica tabletop.

Eddie leans forward, looks at his two relatives. "You know, dad told me one time that Uncle Joe was really a history buff."

"History buff? He was a farmer his whole life," Brendan responds.

"And it was a great farm," Eddie says.

"I remember."

"Okay," Emma interjects, "I have to say again I'm jealous of you too. You actually were with and touched these family members from yesteryear. The ones I have only heard about."

Eddie sits back in the booth, "I'm not sure about touched. Okay, you're right, we did. Big hugs sometimes. Aunt Frances was famous for that."

"And for her homemade bread," Brendan adds.

"Nice," Emma says.

"Being an esteemed senior comes at a price," Eddie says.

Emma is taking her cousin seriously. Brendan knows what's coming.

"Arthritis for example," Eddie says.

After a moment, Brendan asks Emma, "Were you as surprised as we were to hear about that big escape? Stephens, the famous Fenian?"

Emma looks at both of her cousins, says, "Yes. And no."

Eddie looks at Emma and says, "I was afraid you'd say something like that."

Emma hesitates, while Brendan intervenes saying, "You'll have to forgive my brother. Most of us do."

Emma relaxes, gathers her thoughts and says, "Here's the thing, I'm from that side of the family, you remember, that has its own history of mixing up the whole stew. A little innuendo here, a touch of exasperation there. A lot to take in and then make sure you stir the pot well."

"I'm getting hungry," Eddie says.

"Or make sure you stir the plot well," Brendan says.

"Yes, yes," Emma agrees. She appears to be considering something. "Bits and pieces make some sense now, all the talk about escape. But specifically about Mr. Stephens?" she asks. "No," she answers. "Makes me want to read some of that history, now that we know we have a famous relative involved."

Eddie pauses a moment before saying, "Of course, 'famous' is relative."

On her way to somewhere else, the waitress stops by the table, does a quick assessment of the two older men and the attractive younger woman, speculates daughter? Co-worker? something else? and without missing a beat, clearly a seasoned professional herself, says "It'll be right up," before turning and taking off, likely not hearing the 'thankyous' following in her brisk wake.

Emma stops rotating the glass of water and gently pushes the glass to the side. She is anticipating the plate not yet delivered, Caesar salad with a very light dressing.

Eddie's order was liver and bacon, surprising his dinner guests. "Haven't had it in years."

When Brendan ordered eggs, bacon, hash browns, and pancakes, he added, "Hold the toast."

Eddie looks in the direction of the departed waitress, and when he turns to look at his brother, he says, "You know that order you made? It's dinner time, not breakfast."

"Breakfast is available all the time," Brendan answers confidently. "And did you notice I said no toast this time?"

Eddie is not about to answer.

"Well," Brendan answers his own question. "I for one think it's a step, quite slimming. Over time I'll lose a couple pounds."

Eddie looks at his brother in disbelief. "Except your time is running out."

Emma shakes her head, she straightens her back, takes a deep breath and lets it go. She has always been one who needs to focus, be productive. Take short rest stops only. She thinks about bringing the glass of water back to where it was. She thinks about saying, 'I don't think I've ever eaten dinner this early', but instead she says, "The farm, this is where Uncle Joe lived."

"And his sister Frances," Eddie says.

"Oh, right, interesting. Neither married, nor divorced?"

"God forbid," Brendan answers quickly, "the divorced part."

Emma nods her head, like a visitor from the future studying archaic customs. "And it was where again?"

"Lake to Lake road," Eddie answers.

"Canadaigua. Well, outside of Canandaigua, maybe ten miles from the lake itself?" Brendan adds uncertainly.

"I love the Finger Lakes," Emma answers. She raises her hand, conducting an image only she can see, "Those softly rising and falling hills, the wineries." After a moment she adds, "Well, yes, of course you know that grandfather Dan…"

"Dad's cousin," Brendan interjects, "as we have come to learn, whose father was the infamous Great Uncle John Donohoe."

"Infamous?" Emma asks, interrupting her own train of thought.

"Okay, famous, at least to us, finally." Brendan concedes.

"Thank you," Emma answers. "I was about to say that Dan's farm was in that area too."

"Indeed cousin you are right," Eddie says. "A number of the siblings and cousins in fact all lived within several miles of each other. They'd all come over from Canada and in time settled near each other."

Brendan looks at Emma, says, "Circling the wagons, one might say, one big agrarian compound."

"You might," Eddie says, "though most people would not say 'agrarian.'"

Emma looks down at the table for a moment, when she looks up at her cousins she says, "Living so close to each other and to think that they would have a falling out."

"You can say that again." Brendan almost says 'sister' once more, but not in the manner of a gangster this time. Brendan looks across the restaurant toward the kitchen, but that may not be what he is seeing. When he turns back to Emma he says, "It's almost hard now to remember that until recently we didn't know anything about John Donohoe being in the family. Didn't know he existed."

Eddie looks briefly at his brother, then directly at Emma, "Didn't know you existed either."

Emma is nodding her head. "But, curiously I knew you existed. Well, maybe not you but your whole branch of the family, Grandfather John's younger brother James, your Grandfather, and some of his offspring.

Eddie is nodding. "Curious word, 'offspring.'"

Brendan looks at his brother, "Maybe more apt for some of us than others."

"But Emma you're right," Eddie says, "your folks had John's journal and at least knew some of the history."

Emma looks at Eddie, then at Brendan, "And you had the relatives who were told, basically, to cut the crap. Stop telling stories."

Brendan looks at Eddie as if to confer, but Eddie is looking at his placemat, the napkin holding his knife and fork. Brendan turns toward Emma and says, "The stories," he begins, clearing his throat for a moment, "that we now know to be true."

Eddie looks up and then briefly over at Brendan. To Emma he says "It was only Uncle Joe and Dad who were told to stop talking."

Emma is nodding her head as Brendan adds, "And Dad complied, so it would seem."

Eddie nods his head, says "We just don't remember hearing anything about our grandfather's brother."

"John Donohoe," Emma clarifies.

"And since the journals were written by John, nothing was said about his journals either," Eddie adds.

"Ergo, bye bye a lot of family history," Brendan says. "Which has been driving me crazy."

Eddie says to Emma, one confidant to another, "Trust me, it has." Turning to his brother he says, "'Ergo'?"

Emma takes a moment, says "it is true, isn't it, that Paddy wished to keep his information quiet?"

"Well," Brendan answers, "yes according to John who went ahead and told Joe."

"Here we go," Eddie says.

Brendan hopes that he and his brother aren't coming across like some kind of tag team wrestling match. In a quieter tone of voice he ventures to say, "I'd like to think that Dan might have said something like, 'Okay, Joe, Bill, please keep this under your hat, honor Paddy's wishes. Come on, let's play Euchre for god's sake and get this behind us.'"

Emma considers this. "Interesting. 'Honoring Paddy's wishes' you say. That assumes that Dan had already heard about Paddy's wishes from his father John. Or did he? If his cousin, your uncle Joe, was the first one from whom he heard these stories about Paddy, that would have been more of a shocker I would think. But, you know, either way the stories about Paddy may have spooked the family. I mean hearing that good old Paddy was a double agent at times? The authorities in Canada, the States and Great Britain would have wanted to have a talk with him."

"A talk," Brendan says facetiously. "You know," he begins thoughtfully, "I don't know why but I'm picturing that John did try to talk with his immediate family, wife, kids, but maybe was shut down, they didn't want to hear it, for the reason you just said Emma. So when the stories surfaced later, and now spoken by Joe, a cousin, who knows what they might have thought?"

"You mean, like the cat's out of the bag?" Emma asks. She sits back for a moment, adding, "You know maybe we're being too dramatic about this."

"Too dramatic?" Brendan protests.

"Brother," Eddie says calmly, "Hello? Dramatic? If the shoe fits..."

"I don't like those shoes," Brendan says.

"Let's listen to our dear cousin." After a brief pause Eddie says, "Emma?"

"How about this angle," Emma begins, "maybe hearing about all this history whether from John and later from Joe, or even just from Joe, it served as a reminder of the pioneer family, John himself, and your grandfather James, those who crossed the mighty waters in the first place. They were missing them. They didn't want to face the grief, the loss again."

Eddie nods his head knowingly, "Dan, you mean, his side of the family?"

"Well," Emma begins, "yes, and your side too, don't you think? They all shared a lot of history behind them. They were one family coming over, my great-something grandparent was your grandparent's brother, and they were just kids I think at the time, traveling with their parents about whom, as you know, we know next to zilch."

There is a hesitation, Eddie says, "Oh I like that. Well, I don't like that."

Brendan looks at Emma, "He might be referring to the word 'zilch', while also saying he's bereft as well that we don't know much about our great grandparents."

Eddie looks at Brendan, "'Bereft' is it?" After a moment, he adds, "You know it really is interesting how quickly information is lost going back another generation or two."

"And I think," Emma begins quite seriously, "there are specific reasons why we have so little information about those pioneer parents. They were in charge of bringing over the children, namely your grandfather James and his brother John. Think about what they must have endured, how the British treated them for years, the Penal laws. The Famine."

"Mmm," Eddie responds, "Yes. Pain and suffering. That would be enough to silence the living and bury their precious stories. Not easily resurrected. There's a name for this now isn't there Brendan?

It is Emma who answers, "PTSD."

"Ah yes," Eddie says, "Post traumatic soup du jour." When he sees the faces of his cousin and brother, he adds quickly, "Okay, sorry. Sometimes I make light of something that I shouldn't."

Brendan works hard to avoid saying 'You think?' Instead he says, "You know, what they experienced had to shape their character in ways we will never appreciate. They were tough, with so much resilience. They must have had a deep well of support to draw on."

Eddie pauses, and says, "The rosary."

Brendan checks quickly to see if his brother is being serious, and then lets out a long sigh. To Emma he says, "He's not kidding."

Emma nods her head, says "Ah, the Faith, the power of religion," in the voice of one who is more a student of the social sciences, sympathetic but objective.

"And they had each other," Brendan adds.

The trio share a brief moment of silence. Emma takes a deep breath and says, "When Joe started talking, something happened."

"You better believe," Brendan says, wishing he had chosen a different word.

"For whatever reasons, the stories he told morphed into something kind of…"

"Twisted?" Brendan offers.

Eddie says, "Well only if you think that Paddy was involved in a murder a year after the poor man's passing."

"And in a different location to boot," Brendan adds.

Emma smiles, says "It's kind of like that game kids play on a bus, you pass along a secret phrase to the person next to you and each person passes the secret along, so by the time you get to the end..."

"Yes," Eddie concludes.

They remain quiet for a moment. Brendan looks at Emma and then his brother and says, "So what do we know about Paddy now? Ta da! Toronto is the answer. Thankfully he documented at least some of his adventures and sent them for safe keeping."

"Hopefully he wasn't just making stuff up," Eddie says.

"No, not at all, not according to our friend Martin."

"Who sounds like a very dear man." Emma adds.

"He apparently has corroborating sources that seem to dovetail with what he is reading in Paddy's accounts."

"Interesting," Emma says.

Eddie leans back in the booth, "And Emma," he begins--

"Yes?"

"You know if it weren't for running into you a year ago, we'd still be in the dark."

"Hear hear," Brendan chimes in. "And you, glory be to God, also happened to have John's journals."

Emma smiles, says "Thanks. But I've often felt we have others to thank."

"Beside the Professor?" Eddie asks.

Emma is pointing with one finger toward the ceiling and Eddie almost turns to look up before saying, "Oh, oh, ancestors? Still meddling with us? First of all they bring us into this world and then they won't stop making contact."

"They had, have," she corrects herself, "a lot of energy."

Brendan leans forward, "I don't think meddling is the right word. Think about it. We're on this quest to get some answers to our family history, we almost run out of gas figuratively speaking, we're standing right there in the road in front of the Dunnville farm, and as if out of nowhere along comes this young cousin, who happens to have an interest in the family history. She's from a branch of the family we have lost contact with, and she is the one who has our Uncle John's journals."

"Well, when you put it that way," Eddie says.

"Small miracles?" Emma asks.

Eddie looks at his brother and cousin. He enjoys their interest in the mystical even if he can't buy it completely himself. His thoughts are going every which way while his stomach anticipates dinner. There is a mixed aroma wafting its way from the grill. "This talk," he begins, "with Martin and all, it's jogged my memory."

"Yes?" Emma says, adding "again?" smiling pleasantly.

"We noticed," Brendan says kindly, "and you seem to have recovered nicely."

Eddie takes a moment to look at his brother. His words take Brendan by surprise. "I don't think he harbored resentment toward the family. Dad, I'm saying. He didn't have time for it. On the road all the time, selling, making new contacts. He was really good at what he did. And he loved all the driving, the freedom of it, I think."

"Oh," Emma begins, "that's nice."

"Well, yes, thanks but it's just the way he was. Provider for the family, the man's role, his era and all that."

Brendan lowers his voice, says, "Maybe he was just getting away from them all." Brendan shifts his weight on the diner's bench seat, turns to his brother and asks, "You don't think he was resentful? I for one would like to hear more about this jogged memory business of yours."

Eddie sits back in the booth, takes a moment, says simply "No," convincingly.

"No what?" Brendan asks.

"No, I don't think he was resentful, at least not for long. He didn't hold onto it." Eddie takes a moment, says, "Maybe 'jog my memory' is not the right way to put it.

"Okay," Brendan says, waiting.

"Let's call it, seeing things in a different light. The light is changing for me, I guess."

"How lovely," Emma says. "Light is really important, makes all the difference. I mean I know you're not referring to…" her words trail off as she looks up at the ceiling, the overarching florescent brightness in the diner that seems to remove all shadows.

"Well," Brendan begins, suddenly aware of how hungry he feels, "how come we never heard about Dan and that side of the family? Sorry Emma, your side of the family."

"I think," Eddie answers slowly, "he probably did talk about Dan."

"What?"

"We just didn't listen. We were kids, not all that interested."

"Wait a minute," Brendan protests.

"Brendan, who did we hear about? Who did we see?"

Brendan considers this, "Well, all our aunts and uncles, whom we knew."

"His immediate siblings. Who are numerous. And did we always relish these periodic visits?"

Brendan hesitates. "Okay, some more than others. But still, why so little connection with Emma's branch of the family?"

Emma leans forward, "You know, as you're talking, I know there were older cousins who did talk about you guys, no, not you guys, but your dad and mom. Isn't your mother Aunt Gwen?"

Both of her older cousins raise their eyebrows, and it's Eddie who answers, almost pounces, "Yes!"

"They did have picnics on holidays, that kind of thing," Emma says. Looking away for a moment, she adds "You know, I inherited a couple of picture albums, I should find them sometime."

Brendan wants to ignore an invitation that he is not yet ready to accept. He is used to the absence of stories about family, almost comfortable with the fact that information had been withheld, or so he thought. There had been all these missing gaps of knowledge. It was so easy over time, without even realizing it, to turn such gaps into solid bricks of resentment, one by one, to build walls, to cement one's position.

Did dad experience this? This resentment? he wonders. Told to be quiet. A younger member of the family, don't listen to Joe's stories.

In his father's lifetime, his father had gotten the strength, the courage to leave his homeland of Canada, to walk away from the farming life, start a career on the road, show himself to the world in grand style, become an American salesman dressed to the nines.

Something heavy settles, and he finally sees what it is: grief, loss. He can't count the number of times he wanted to reach out and ask one of his many questions. Questions he didn't have until he was much older himself, and then it was too late.

Brendan sighs and is surprised by the sensation of breathing in the sandy, gritty, sensation of the sea, the aroma of air flowing over the waves of Lake Erie. He is once again standing on the cliff at High Banks, looking out at the lonely light house on Gull Island, its stone walls once vital to life and limb, now abandoned, as if a castle in Ireland, fallen ruins that evoke memory, arising from the depths of the waters: longing.

There it is. Brendan takes a deep breath. Disbelief, regret, he can no longer ask Dad his questions. He stretches out his arm and opens the palm of his hand, nearly hitting Emma's water glass, his hand reads: stop.

"What?" Eddie asks, alarmed.

"He's gone, Eddie."

"Who?"

"Dad. And Joe. And Frances. The lot of them."

Emma glances quickly at Eddie, sees that Eddie is nodding his agreement.

"For so long," Brendan says, "we knew so little about our history, about a whole large branch of the family for god's sake."

Emma remains silent. Eddie continues to nod his agreement, affirmation, but more slowly now. Finally Eddie says simply, "Yes," and then remains silent.

Emma shifts slightly in her seat, looks at her two elderly cousins. She remains silent as well. It is the most important thing to do, to do nothing. As simple as breathing. As necessary. She recognizes what this is, here in the diner. A wake.

CHAPTER 48

Stan Musial at the Last Supper
Saturday, September 9, 2001

AT JUST THE RIGHT TIME, after a sufficient pause, Eddie says, "Maybe we're playing catch-up now, brother." He takes a moment and adds, "And let's remember this, back then all those beloved family members were busy with their own lives, as were we." Looking carefully at both his brother and his young cousin, "There was a time when there was no TV, no cell phones that make conference calls. A second world war came and went, and then Korea, the Cold War."

Emma looks at her cousins, relieved, smiles and says "Wow, this is like a history lesson told in the first person by its survivors," adding "I remember Vietnam," her voice rises in upspeak, as if heading for a question mark.

Brendan says in a low voice, "Survivors."

"Sorry," Emma says.

"I think I felt younger when I walked in here this afternoon," Brendan says smiling. "It wasn't that long ago."

"So brother," Eddie says, "meanwhile back at the ranch as they used to say in our cowboy movies—"

"Cowboy movies? Westerns, you mean," Emma says.

"Cowboys and Indians, good guys and bad guys," Brendan explains.

"Oh god help us," Emma says.

"There were a lot of relatives," Eddie continues, "and the older ones among them, I remember now, used to get together as Emma says, so it's partly a matter of timing, but also by the time we came along, think about it, what were we interested in?"

Brendan considers his brother's question, answers "Stan Musial."

Emma looks back and forth at her cousins, "Who?"

Both Eddie and Brendan sit back in the booth, Brendan sighs deeply, Eddie says, "I rest my case."

"Liver and bacon?" says the voice of the waitress who seems to tower above them. She is a fast walker and she can see that she has surprised them all, even after such a long wait.

THE three relatives enjoy this moment of delight and wonder: the food appears suddenly and is placed right in front of them. Menu anticipations are quietly compared with the presenting reality, the surprises of color, aroma. No disappointments this time, a diner that is famous for large portions, even with Emma's salad. Ah America.

"Oh my," Emma says as she looks down at the large plate overflowing with a variety of mixed greens. "It's bountiful. Fulsome," adding, "No dessert tonight."

"The desserts are great. I'll be making room for the flan, myself." Eddie says, surveying his liver and bacon, not yet sure what to cut into first.

"*Bon appetit*," Brendan announces.

"*Et toi aussi*," Emma responds melodiously.

"*Slainte!*" Eddie offers in vigorous Irish.

A few minutes pass by, sounds of cutlery touching china, murmurs of delight.

By the time Eddie has nearly cleaned his plate, Brendan is just approaching his pancakes which he kept in strategic reserve until he had eaten his eggs, bacon and hash browns. "They make the scrambled eggs just right," he says, "not every place does that. Lots of butter is part of the answer. And cooking slowly."

"Yes?" asks Emma, interested in Brendan's comment. She has not yet reached the halfway mark with her salad and is eating even more slowly now than when she first began. "I taste a little Worcester sauce, and a hint of Dijon mustard," she says pointing at the salad with her fork. "Very nice."

The shared satisfaction in the meal raises everyone's spirits. Food helps. After a short period of silence, Emma says simply "No TV."

Eddie and Brendan look up from their plates, faces showing curiosity, non-understanding. Brendan starts to look around for the TV that he knows the diner has never had.

"What?" Eddie asks.

"They didn't have TV back then. The older relatives."

"Oh."

"You know," she adds for extra emphasis, "there have been studies that people sat on front porches more often, communicated face to face with people passing by. It was all in person."

Brendan says as an aside. "If you were lucky enough to have a front porch."

"How's that?" Eddie asks Emma.

"Life before and after the arrival of TV. Speaking of which, I mentioned I have these old photos, and they had a lot of outdoor picnics at one or another's farm. Kids weren't playing video games, people weren't talking on phones."

"Yes?" Eddie says, not quite sure where his young cousin is going.

"And I bet in some of these photo albums, I'll find your relatives and mine eating together, out in someone's backyard, on a home-made table or two, corn on the cob, watermelon." Emma smiles, feels energized by her own words. "They'll be laughing, looking embarrassed, self-conscious in the moment, knowing that they are captured in that photo. Laundry hanging on the line, the edge of a barn in view at the side of the picture. Bright sunshine. Like they never had a care in the world."

Brendan holds off on his next bite of syrup drenched pancake, says "Wow," appreciatively at such a recital.

"They rarely went out to eat. That would have been too expensive," Eddie says. He self-consciously looks at his now empty plate, looks around at the other diners in the restaurant. With a slowly exhaling breath he utters, "Yeah."

"But," Brendan begins, "Lovely and all that, still, there were some harsh times."

"Of course," Emma says, "the Depression, but that was just before your time, I think?"

"Yes," Brendan says, thinking that he is momentarily younger in his cousin's eyes, "But I mean, I don't want to be a downer here..."

"Praise the Lord," Eddie proclaims, and to Emma, "I think he is seeing the light too."

Emma leans back, says "No, you're right Brendan, I'm sure it wasn't all lovey dovey all the time, in fact we know that."

"Boys will be boys," Eddie adds.

"And girls will be girls," Emma answers. "And families can spit fire at each other at times."

The three family members sit quietly for a moment. The waitress stands over by the cash register, notices that her customers have nearly finished eating, but something tells her to give them a little more time.

Emma looks briefly at Brendan, reaches for her glass of water, takes a slow sip before replacing the glass carefully. "They didn't make a show of putting out whatever fires there were. They didn't talk like we do, maybe."

Brendan hesitates, says "Now."

Eddie sits back, then looks at his brother and cousin. He takes another moment and says, "You know there can be a natural kind of attrition, folks see less and less of each other, what might have been shared, spoken about, goes by the wayside."

Brendan asks, "Did you say 'contrition'?"

"No Brendan, attrition. The act or acts of attrition." Eddie purses his lips, looks around the diner for a moment, says "Relationships take work, continual work, effort. There is no auto-pilot."

"So there is no Attrition Booth?" Brendan asks.

To Emma, Eddie says, "He's referring of course to the Sacrament of

Confession, and I might add that it sounds like it may have been awhile since his last."

Emma looks at her cousins, first one, then the other. She decides to play it straight. "Fellas," she says, seeing that she has their attention, "this is a big Catholic family after all, or was. Right?"

"Big, yes," Eddie answers.

"Catholic, check," Brendan says, "or maybe checkered."

Emma hesitates, and says "There were more and more cousins over time, right? After a while you choose to talk to certain family members more than others."

"After a while," Brendan adds, "there are too many around the table at Thanksgiving. The children's table gets moved to a different room, and then kids grow up to be teenagers who want to skip out early, smoke cigarettes, do whatever teenagers do and then—"

"Okay thank you brother, we get it," Eddie says.

Brendan persists, "And then there is more and more technology, travel is improved, it's easier for everyone to get away."

"Well," Emma begins, "Somebody once said that changes in life happen so steadily, so consistently over time, that we all keep readjusting to a new normal as if nothing has changed, as if it has always been this way."

"We don't see the change that's underway," Eddie adds, "parts of life, including certain relationships go under the radar. Which they also didn't have. Radar," he adds, as if it were necessary.

"Right," Emma continues, "and at some point we wake up to see the results, and we're surprised as in 'how did this ever happen'?"

Eddie takes a moment, says "Of course sometimes the change happens suddenly, like Pearl Harbor, and all hell breaks loose."

"Or an asteroid comes out of nowhere, hits, and eons of dinosaurs go poof," Brendan says.

Eddie shakes his head in agreement, at which point the waitress whom they do not yet see, starts walking in their direction, bill in hand.

"But usually it's subtle," Emma says, "the way life comes at us, unannounced, and we get distracted."

"Oh let me count the myriad ways one becomes distracted," Brendan says, the voice of wise disgruntlement.

Eddie looks at his brother. "Yes, we've noticed that about you. And speaking of Myriad, she was a nice gal. I miss her."

Emma raises her eyebrows, looks at Brendan.

Brendan shakes his head, and in a tone conveying both reassurance and disappointment, confides, "Don't let this trouble you. He never actually met Myriad."

Eddie hesitates for a moment, and adds quietly, "That would explain some things."

EDDIE did have the Flan. When the waitress asked if she could get them anything else, he answered, "Of course you can," meaning this good naturedly.

The waitress responded that Darlene was taking over at the end of her shift and would help them with whatever else they might need. She added that it had been a pleasure to serve them. Her voice sounded too tired to express any excessive enthusiasm.

Brendan thought about saying that it was a pleasure being served, but he decided to keep his mouth shut. He did tell her that they appreciated the time they had spent at her table, adding "We'll certainly tip in a commensurate way."

She gave him, he thought, a curious look before she walked away, coffee in hand which she did not offer.

Hardly a moment passed before Emma suggested that they re-group at her house. "We can have coffee there," she said, adding "there's something I found that I'd like to show you."

Chapter 49

The Photo Albums
Saturday, September 8, 2001

"**J**IM NOT HERE?" BRENDAN inquires, as Emma greets them at the front door. He had noticed that there was only the one car in the driveway.

Emma steps backward into the entryway and says, "Well what a welcome surprise. Haven't seen you in ages."

Emma places her hand on Eddie's elbow, a guiding gesture, and explains "The husband is working days this week, and then back to nights next week."

"On a Saturday, even," Eddie remarks.

"Some of us have to work," Emma says, as they walk into the living room. "I'll be right out with the coffee."

"Thank you, Madam," Eddie says playfully.

After the coffee has been delivered, Emma disappears for a moment and returns just as Eddie is adding the sugar and cream, while Brendan tentatively sips his coffee, black. And hot.

"Well, what have we here?" Eddie asks, seeing the two large photo albums Emma has retrieved.

"Part of my inheritance. When we were talking earlier, I had the thought we might take a look at a couple of these."

"How did you get to inherit them?" Brendan asks.

"Nobody else wanted them." Emma says in a voice that is preoccupied by positioning the first album in such a way that her cousins can easily see it.

Brendan is both enthused to see the photos and privately dismayed by Emma's remark. Not all family members share his interest, he realizes. There goes history, memories fade like black and white photos left too long in the light. Hopefully Emma's pictures have been safely preserved. He takes a deep breath, opens his eyes wide and proclaims, "No time like the present."

Emma looks over at Brendan and says, "Well, yes, I'm so glad we can look at these together."

Eddie has already begun to look at some of the pictures, only a few of them faded. Eddie mutters, "There is no time but the present."

It's not long before there are "oohs" and "aahs." They take their time looking at the first album, a slowing-down process that inevitably and pleasurably raises questions, comments, hesitations, recognizes uncertainties, and finally becomes the background for storytelling. Incidents are resurrected in the air above the coffee table, some well-known, some brand new.

"Oh there's the farm, right?" Emma exclaims, as her cousins come in close, hunching over and touching the edge of the page with careful attention.

"There she be," says Brendan, "Uncle Joe's and Aunt Frances' place."

"And that's your dad?" Emma asks. "And mom?"

The photo shows four people, in their 30's and up. They are standing near the front door of the farmhouse, close to the edge of a driveway that leads back to a near-by barn. A bright sunny day, clearly a scene in winter light, deeply angled slanting shadows that are so temporary, the time of year when darkness arrives early.

"Yes by god," Eddie says, a little surprised with his own comment, but no matter. "So good to see the old place. I would say it was just before the war. That's a '38 Plymouth isn't it?"

Brendan comes in for an even closer look. "I think that was the Ford."

"No, Dad didn't have a Ford till after the war."

"Oldsmobile maybe?"

"It looks brand new," Emma says.

"Could be the '41 Olds," Eddie says. "They stopped making them in early '42 til the war ended."

"Look at this one," Emma says. "Your mother was a looker. And Frances wasn't so bad herself." After a moment she adds, "They do look cold, no coats, and Frances is holding your mother's hands, maybe to keep warm."

Her cousins murmur their joint assent, something a little brighter than a grunt.

A moment passes. Brendan says, "I wonder who took the picture?"

Emma shifts her position, she had been looking over the top of the album from her seat opposite the couch. She stands now and comes over to her seated cousins who part their ways to let her slide in between. "Well," she starts as she settles in, "I have a story to tell you about the time these pictures were taken, there's a few more we'll see later. To answer your question, I know Great Great Grandfather had a camera. He loved to take pictures."

Brendan turns to look at Emma, asks "Dan?"

THEY are well into photo album number two when Eddie, first, and then Brendan call for a bathroom break. As they're ready to re-start, Emma says, "Did you know there was a fire at the farm one time?"

"What? No," says Eddie.

"Much damage?" Brendan asks.

"Apparently not. Kind of miraculous. Just lost a lot of old newspapers, mostly Joe's, some of his personal papers. He could be kind of a hoarder apparently, at least according to Aunt Frances. As the story goes, she wasn't sorry to see them go. Called them dust collectors, and I gather she was pretty tidy."

Without thinking, Eddie looks up and briefly surveys the room, every object seeming to be in its appointed place.

They continue to look at the photo album, slowly, lovingly, all the old images passing by, page by page. Brendan says "I guess they were lucky, I mean the house, the barn, it all survived."

The threesome remain quiet, focused on the photos. Brendan sits back and asks, "You said some of Joe's papers were burned. Do we know what those were?"

Emma hesitates, "No. Maybe they were receipts, bills, maybe something else. I guess we'll never know."

Another several moments pass quietly while they turn a page in the photo book. Eddie asks Emma, "Do you think she burned them on purpose?"

"Frances?" Emma answers, sounding surprised, almost offended. "Well the story I always heard was that there had been a thunderstorm. She was deathly afraid of them. She lit some holy candles nearby."

The two brothers look at each other.

Eddie says, "Holy Mother of God."

"You can say that again," Brendan says.

"Holy Mother of God," Eddie repeats.

Emma sits back, taking a break from the many photos, too many of them turning into mysteries now, here and there a guess at identification by her older cousins.

"I suppose," she says, "we don't know what we don't know."

Brendan looks at his cousin, "Somehow that almost sounds profound," adding "well, speaking of Joe's notes, they're down the drain now."

"More like up in smoke," his brother adds.

The trio share a moment of respectful silence. "You know," Emma begins, "I guess it's up to us to cherish and preserve what we can. We start where we are in the moment and go forward. Sometime or other let's put names and dates on the back of the photos we recognize."

"'Sometime'," Brendan says, "can be a dangerous word."

Emma nods in agreement.

After a moment, Eddie leans backward, stretching his shoulders. "Good old Uncle Joe. You know, Dad told me one time, if you run into Joe, don't ever ask him about boats."

"What?"

"Boats."

"What did that mean?"

"Well, this was later on, dad was already in the nursing home, and

Uncle Joe had passed several years before then. I didn't want to get into it at the time. He had good and bad days with his memory. I have read that folks who get easily confused, only get more upset when you try to correct them or question too much."

Eddie looks away for a moment. "I can really see him now, Dad, during one of those visits. You know it wasn't unusual for him to talk as if he expected to see Joe walk in the door at any minute."

Eddie suddenly sits up straight, says "Whoa!"

"What?" Brendan asks.

Eddie has a look that Emma later calls 'sheepish.'

"There was one time when he said "Dan will be coming over."

And now it's Emma who sits up straight. She says "Grandfather!" adding "Great Great," quickly.

Brendan is nodding his head, he asks, "Did you know who he was referring to?"

"Dan," Eddie repeats.

"Yes I know, you said that," Brendan says.

"Eddie," Emma intervenes, "Brendan is asking if you knew who Dan was, when your dad made that comment. You had said before that you didn't know about Dan back then."

"We didn't know about our Great Uncle John."

"Okay," Emma says quietly.

Eddie hesitates, "Did I recognize the name? Not as such."

"Not as such?" Brendan repeats.

"There were a lot of names he talked about. It didn't have much meaning then. Now it does. Hello Dan. Now it means something, it means a lot. Sorry."

Brendan looks at his brother. "No need to apologize." A moment passes. "But I guess Dad wasn't the only one with memory issues."

Eddie raises his eyebrows and shoulders, tips his head, a gesture acknowledging bewildered agreement.

"I will say this," Brendan begins, "You got to see Dad more than any of us toward the end. I never told you, but I really admired how you visited so regularly. I'm sure it wasn't always so pleasant."

"Not always pleasant," Eddie agrees, "but when all is said and done, well worth it."

"Anyway, I often wished I could have been there more like you were."

"Well," Eddie answers, "You were still working full time. I had begun my semi-retirement."

"Sweet," Emma says. "I can't wait till Jim and I can retire."

"Hmmmm," Brendan intones, non-committaly.

Something shifts as the three relatives sit quietly for a moment. Emma thinks about offering more coffee but decides against it.

Eddie breaks the silence. "That's when he would say 'there's no shame, Paddy was right.'"

"Your dad," Emma clarifies.

"Yes, and now that I recall, that's when he would also say 'see if' something or other."

"When," Emma prompts, "he would mention Dan coming over?"

"Yes."

"'See if can never be named' is what you had told us before," Brendan says.

"Yes! Right, thank you," Eddie answers.

"So," Emma starts, raising her question to the room, "something about my great great grandfather Dan coming to visit your dad would raise this…suspicion, concern?"

As Brendan and Emma watch Eddie's face, they both see the far-away look in his eyes.

Brendan asks, "Okay brother, out with it."

Eddie nods, says "He used to talk quite a bit about some escapades with an old pal Charlie something, Fitzsimmons or whatever." He then stops, as if this were the whole of the revelation.

Brendan and Emma look at each other. Brendan asks Emma, "Do you think there might be more?"

"Oh, sorry," Eddie says. "You know, you've heard this before, he was involved in some shenanigans at the border."

"What?" Emma says, alarmed.

"During Prohibition, yes," Brendan answers.

"No," Emma answers.

"It's possible," Eddie says, "Just theorizing here, that Dan would not have been too happy about his cousin being involved."

Emma sits back, "What was my great-something Uncle Bill doing? Rum running?"

"No," Eddie says.

"Well," Emma begins, thank the lord."

"It was whiskey," Brendan says. "Good stuff. Couldn't get it in the States."

"Could make a decent little profit if he wanted to," Eddie adds.

"He sold it?" Emma asks, her voice rising.

"No, no" Brendan reassures her, "Strictly personal use. No harm done. Personal in a broad sense."

"He had a fake floorboard in one of those cars at the time. An Auburn I think," Eddie says.

"Yes!" Brendan agrees, "I do remember hearing that."

Eddie rocks back and forth ever so slightly, he is looking down at the coffee table. "There's more?" Brendan asks him.

Eddie looks up, says, "How the hell could I have forgotten?"

"Well," Brendan says, "we knew about the Auburn."

What Brendan sees on Eddie's face is a look he had never seen before. Thoughts race by: his brother is ill, his brother is about to cry. Brendan leans forward, concerned. Emma notices. "It's okay," Brendan says, hoping to comfort his brother.

Eddie takes a deep breath. "Yes, thanks," he says, "look, one thing leads to another, a memory pops up, and here's another one right behind it."

Emma hesitates, asks "So there's more?"

Eddie looks at the coffee table, answers "Two things. This Charlie fellow was a good pal to Dad. He would refer to him as a close chum. He felt some responsibility for him, didn't want him to get in trouble, at least, that's the sense I got."

Eddie stops talking and Emma finally says, "And the second thing?"

Eddie looks directly at his cousin. "Please don't take this the wrong way."

"Okay," she says, almost but not quite like a question.

"Your Grandfather Dan was apparently very strait laced. A by-the-rules kind of guy."

Emma's face is brightening.

"You wouldn't want to cross him apparently," Eddie continues. "He'd let you know about it in no uncertain terms. So like what I said before, he would not have been happy to hear about Dad's border crossing."

Both Eddie and Brendan look at Emma and to their surprise, she starts to smile. "Fits what I've heard." Adding "God rest his soul."

A reflective moment passes for all three. Emma sits up suddenly, which clearly gets her cousins' attention. "Boys," she says, addressing them in a way she has never done before, a Bonnie to the elder Clydes. "You did say the friend was Charlie F something or other, maybe Flanagan?"

"No not Flanagan," Brendan says. "We're related to Flanagans."

"Yes I know that," Emma says, "that was a test," she teases. Emma hesitates a moment, smiling all the more. "Here's the thing, your dad did not want to rat on his buddy."

"What?" Brendan says.

"Ah, I get it my dear. Lovely," Eddie says.

"Hello?" Brendan says to the two of them.

"The initials, brother," Eddie says. "'C.F.'"

Brendan pauses, then adds, "Cannot be named."

CHAPTER 50

The 'F' Word
Saturday, September 8, 2001

"WELL I'LL BE DARNED," Brendan says. "So, that's the shame bit too?"

Eddie says, "I don't think so."

"Oh, how do you figure?" Brendan asks.

Emma stands up, waves a hand as if to say, don't notice me, but decides to say, "I'm just remembering something else I wanted to show you. I'll be right back. Please continue."

As Emma leaves the room, Eddie watches her, and then says in a quieter voice, "I think the shame had to do with the family brouhaha. The stories he heard from Joe."

"'Paddy is right, 'there's no shame in it'," Brendan says.

"You got it brother."

"What did I miss?" Emma asks, re-entering the room as quickly as she had exited.

"Here's what I think," Eddie says without missing a beat, "I think that dad felt he had nothing to be ashamed of in the way he got caught up in Joe's stories. Which were Paddy stories."

"Oh," Emma says, resuming her seat opposite the couch, holding one of Uncle John's journals in her hand. "Interesting. Hmmm." Emma nods her head, and while she remains silent, she has the look of someone who has more to say.

"Emma?" Brendan asks his young cousin.

"Okay, well," she starts with a little difficulty, "I don't think your dad need be ashamed either, but…"

"Yes?"

"Paddy didn't want his stories told yet."

"True."

"It was," and here she holds up the copy of the journal she has in hand, "Grandfather John Donohoe, may he rest in peace as well, who couldn't keep them secret."

"But not in his journals, he didn't betray his pal Paddy in writing," Eddie says.

The three relatives mull over their private thoughts, until Brendan says, "I still don't get it."

"What?" Eddie asks.

"If dad was saying 'I don't need to be ashamed for listening to Joe and sharing what I heard'—"

"Okay, please continue."

"What is this 'Paddy is right' part?"

"Yes, I see," Eddie says, speaking as an older confidant.

Emma says, "Me too, I want to hear your explanation."

Eddie looks at the two expectant relatives, "He, dad, is adding himself by way of extension, to what Paddy said of his own failed exploit."

"'To what Paddy said of his own failed exploit'" Brendan repeats his brother's words slowly. "Ah, this is a little window showing what Paddy felt about himself that night."

"For missing the boat," Emma adds.

"For not getting to the boat on time," Eddie clarifies.

"It was a dark and stormy night—" Brendan says smiling.

"Okay, okay," Eddie says. "But speaking of Martin, we're going to have to call him."

"Yes!" Emma answers with enthusiasm.

"Yes?" Brendan answers with a question.

"His quest to solve the mystery," Eddie explains.

"Oh!" Brendan says, his eyes widening.

"Charlie Fitzgibbons, or whatever his last name was," Emma says.

They all pause for a moment, and Eddie says, as if they need to hear a summary, "Dad wasn't saying 'see if'".

"Yes!" Emma says.

"And the letters 'C' and 'F' do not refer to Canadian Fenian," Eddie concludes, deciding not to say 'I rest my case.'

Brendan hesitates, "Oh our dear Professor. The way we left things, he may not realize that dad was likely referring to his partner in stealth, Charlie Fitz-Babylonian who dad consorted with."

"Yes, well," Eddie concurs. That's a bit rich."

"It was an 'F' word."

"Brendan, we are in mixed company here."

Emma ignores her cousins, and in the spirit of rising above, she raises the journal in her hand. The effect is immediate. Her cousins stare at the dark leather-bound volume. It is as if she is holding the sacred weight of history itself, its unraveling holiness, a sacrament elevated.

CHAPTER 51

A Memory for Dates
Saturday, September 8, 2001

A SLIP OF PAPER REMOVED from the back of John Donohoe's journal:

To whom it may concern. On this occasion when at last we can celebrate the independent Republic of Ireland, let it be known that such freedom was achieved by the hard work of many, and that a multitude of Canadians can proudly be included among them. From the earliest days and through the Easter Rising and beyond, countless souls lent a hand, and never was there a single Canadian recognized above others, but rather all contributed, typically without fanfare or recognition. It was not for themselves that they sought glory, but rather for the land that they helped to set free, lo these many centuries later.

May such total and complete independence one day be enjoyed in their own native land.

J.D.   April 18, 1949

"Okay, I give," Brendan says, shortly after Emma finishes reading from the small piece of paper.

"May I see it?" Eddie asks.

"Certainly," Emma says, handing over the single page to Eddie.

Brendan slides over on the couch toward Eddie so that he can take a look as well. Brendan says, "Looks like it was written on a sheet of stationery, 5 by 7, folded neatly in half, very clear creases, before it was slipped into the journal."

Eddie turns toward his brother to say, "Elementary, and well observed indeed."

"So here's the thing," Emma begins, "when Martin asked about certain names and whether we had heard any of them before, I thought I would do a quick look at the journals. As luck would have it, I started with the final volume and here was this piece of paper stuck in the back. I had never noticed it before and I knew you'd be interested."

"Interested?" Brendan says, raising his voice, stating the obvious.

"Very interesting indeed," Eddie says, carefully putting the paper down on the coffee table, next to the journal. "Who is this 'J.D.'? That can't bloody well be John Donohoe. Not in 1949."

"And I don't get this 'celebrate the independent Republic of Ireland,'" Brendan adds. "I thought Ireland got its independence with the famous Easter Rising, World War I era, wasn't it?"

"Sort of," Emma answers, "but that was only the start of things, or actually was one of the starts, a famous one. And speaking of bloody, a very bloody one."

"Do you think the writer was Joe?" Eddie asks, "Joe Donohoe, J.D.?"

Emma raises her shoulders, lifts the palm of her hands, "Not sure, but as far as Brendan's question, I can shed some further light on that."

"Hallelujah," Brendan says, "and may I say again what a pleasure it is to have someone from the younger generation take an interest in this history. Gives one hope."

Emma nods toward Brendan but before she can speak Eddie interrupts, "Oh it was 1921, wasn't it?"

"What was?" Brendan asks.

"When Ireland became an independent country," Eddie answers.

"Hang on a second fellas," Emma says as she gets up and goes over to a small desk in the corner of the living room. She finds what she is looking for and brings back a sheet of paper with some notes written on it. As she takes her seat again she says, "I was anticipating you might have some questions like this so I did a bit of research. Let me see," she says, consulting her notes.

"A scholar we have here," Brendan says not too quietly to his brother, who nods his head in approval.

"Okay," Emma says, "1921, actually 1922 when all was said and done, there was an Anglo-Irish Treaty and Ireland was given Dominion status."

"The hell?" Brendan says.

"And the 'Irish Free State' was formed," she concludes.

"That's better," Eddie says.

"And that's it then?" Brendan asks his young cousin.

"In 1937 a new constitution was adopted, and the name was changed to simply 'Ireland' and there was now a President of Ireland."

"We need to have a toast," Brendan says.

"However," Emma continues, "the King of England still functioned as executive authority."

"No toast," Brendan mutters.

Eddie sits back, says, "Not exactly copasetic, not groovy, as we used to say."

Emma shakes her head, smiles at her older cousins.

"Why couldn't they do a slam dunk act of becoming independent like Canada did, or the States?" Brendan asks.

Eddie looks at his brother, takes a moment, "You don't know much about Canadian history, I gather."

Brendan looks at his brother, "I know a lot about Fenians. Now. Sort of."

"And," Emma joins in, "the American War of Independence and what followed wasn't exactly a *fait accompli* either, as I have come to learn."

Eddie smiles at his cousin while Brendan says, "What is that? Some kind of pastry?"

Eddie looks at Emma, "He's kidding."

"Sure I am," Brendan says, "I took Latin and Greek in high school. Who takes Latin and Greek in high school? But I do love pastries."

"And then finally," Emma says, getting her cousins back on track, "there was the Republic of Ireland Act, 1948. Which was finalized," and here she looks back at her notes, "April 18, 1949. And guess what day that was?"

Eddie looks at Emma, answers "The same day that J.D. wrote that note you found in the journal."

"Well, yes," Emma answered, "but I was going for something else."

"A Tuesday," Brendan answers quickly.

"No it was a Monday," Emma answers.

"Oh well," Brendan says, "I was only off by one day."

"And what was special about that?" Emma continues.

"They didn't have to go to Church. It wasn't a Sunday," Brendan says.

"Would you stop?" Eddie asks.

"Eddie," Emma says, "no worries. I know I'm in good company here. We all love history."

Brendan nods his head, asks, "So what was special about that day? A Monday?"

Emma looks at her cousins, "It was an Easter Monday, and the 33rd anniversary of the beginning of the Easter Rising."

"Ouuuu," both brothers intone appreciatively.

"They don't seem to forget certain dates over there," Eddie says with some solemnity.

"So now they were a totally independent Republic of Ireland," Brendan says.

"Yes," Emma responds.

"Like the States," Brendan says, adding "like Canada, maybe," as he looks at his older brother for confirmation, "totally independent, having nothing to do whatsoever with Britain."

Eddie and Emma exchange glances. Eddie says, "Look at that last line again, in what I assume is a note Uncle Joe wrote: *May such total and complete independence one day be enjoyed in their own native land.*"

The three relatives remain thoughtfully quiet until Eddie says, "'their own native land' refers to Canada."

Brendan looks first at Eddie, and then Emma. In a quieter voice he says, "They're not quite all the way there yet. Not completely themselves."

"Well…" Emma intones, sounding uncertain.

After a short hesitation, Eddie adds, "Canada is complicated."

Brendan sighs, "That must be why I love Canada so much."

Chapter 52

The Lap and Thicket
Saturday, September 8, 2001

THEY HAD TAKEN A short break, Emma decided finally to make a new pot of coffee, "Decaf this time" she reassured them. When they returned to their places, Emma surprised them by bringing out a plate of pastries.

"Oh my god in heaven," Brendan exclaims.

"Here's you're a *fait accompli*, Eddie says, "in real life."

"*Tres cool*," Brendan answers.

"I figured we could use a little extra celebratory sustenance," Emma says, "even after Eddie's Flan. It's a new bakery I found near-by, the family is from Quebec. I thought you'd appreciate shall I say, the connection and the confection. Canada," she adds, in case it wasn't obvious.

"*Oui, mon ami!*" Brendan says.

The pastries are such a pure delight that even Emma indulges, carefully removing one from the box.

After a short time Emma murmurs, "Oh my, I love the thin layers, crumbly, sweet, this one has a hint of almond I think," and then dabbing at her mouth with a napkin she adds, "There's another album and a few particular photos I want you to see."

Emma reaches over for the journal, "I need to return this to its resting place," she says as she stands up.

"Speaking of your wonderful find there Emma," Eddie says, "I guess we can conclude that there was no single Canadian Fenian after all."

"Ah, perhaps," Emma says, hesitating before she steps out of the room.

Brendan leans toward his brother and in a lowered voice says, "I'm sure there were married ones however."

When Emma walks back into the room, she is holding the new photo album and she asks "Did I miss something?"

Emma sits down immediately and with focused determination starts to turn several pages.

"In all honesty," Brendan says, "I don't think so."

"Aha!" Emma says, looking up at her cousins. She pauses to take a breath. "I'm sorry, you said something."

"Yes," Brendan says. "I mean no, nothing."

"Oh, well then, I do have something."

"Wait," Brendan says abruptly, "before we move on."

"Yes?" His brother answers.

"We were talking about Joe Donohoe, our Uncle Joe, he with the horn-rimmed glasses and certain *savior faire*.

"Oh nice," Emma murmurs.

"Don't encourage him," Eddie says.

"Anyway, I'm going to assume with my brother that Joe, J.D., wrote that rather patriotic piece you discovered Emma, in the journal."

As neither his brother nor cousin offer a response, he goes on. "And I think there may be bad news, but there is also good news."

Emma and Eddie hesitate for a moment till Eddie asks, "Okay brother, what's the bad news?"

"Well," Brendan begins, "if Uncle Joe wrote that nice little piece, it makes me wonder what else he may have written."

"I see," Eddie answers, "the question of whether there was important second hand documentation lost in the Grand Flame."

"Grand Flame?" Emma asks, adding "second hand?"

Brendan explains, "Eddie is being dramatic, he means I think the question of whether Aunt Frances destroyed Joe's papers, which may have included notes he kept about his conversations with John. Aunt Frances in the role of the fire maiden."

"She didn't set the fire," Emma protests, "it was an act of God," adding "so I was always told." She hesitates, "Fire maiden indeed! Where in the world did you get such a name?"

Everyone takes a breath, and then Eddie asks, "And what's the good news?"

In Brendan's finest American accent he says, "I think it may stand as Joe's Piece of Resistance."

It takes a moment for Eddie to translate, "*piece de resistance.*"

"Oh Lord," Emma says emphatically.

"Emma," Brendan says kindly, "I apologize for my linguistic humor."

"Such as it is," Eddie says quietly.

"Joe," Brendan continues "is making a small, concise comment on the irresistible value of liberty and sacrifice, humbly performed for a greater cause than one's self."

Eddie and Emma exchange glances, Emma murmurs "Lovely. If it is Joe who wrote the note."

"And" Eddie adds, "if it is Joe, he made his grand statement for all the world to see, hidden in the back pages of the final volume of John Donohoe's journal."

Emma considers this. "The spirit of that note would have lessened certain arguments, claims of fake information, political debate."

All three family members consider this. Emma adds, "For now, we can take this under our own advisement."

They remain quiet, thoughtful, until Emma blurts out "Oh god!"

"What is it?" Eddie asks, alarmed.

Emma looks at her cousins, "I'm beginning to talk like you guys do."

"Oh really," Eddie says, "is that such a bad thing?"

Brendan looks at Emma, says, "You have our deepest regrets Madame. Mine, at least."

Emma sighs politely, and asks, "Are we ready to go on?" She can tell by their expressions that they are not sure what she means, so she quickly opens the new photo album, turning it so that they can have a good view.

The book is chock full of photos, five or six attached in no particular pattern on each page, many slightly askew. Emma remains in her chair looking over the top of the page as her cousins, seated on the couch, lean forward for a closer view.

"Right," Eddie exclaims, "this is at the house."

"Where you grew up, yes?" Emma says.

"Yes," Eddie says, "I'm surprised you know that."

"Oh," Brendan says, "there's the garage. The driveway had two narrow strips of concrete, grass in the middle. Dad's garden out back."

"The patch of raspberries Mom loved," Eddie adds.

"I hated picking those berries," Brendan says.

"Speaking of mom, look how young she looks. I'm not sure who that person is she is talking to, one of the women. It looks like—a picnic?" Eddie wonders aloud.

Emma carefully turns the page.

"Definitely picnic," Brendan says, seeing more pictures of the same event, "two picnic tables lined up together. Dad, you know, made one of them. A weekend job when he got home, off the road. Probably read about it in Popular Mechanics."

"Lot of people there," Eddie says, before he adds "for god's sake!" and leans back.

Brendan looks over at his brother, then up at Emma who is smiling.

"Yes?" Emma says.

"Damnation," Eddie says.

"You were maybe 5 or 6? It's hard to tell. And so you see whose lap you are sitting on?" Emma asks.

Brendan leans in to look at a very young Eddie sitting with an older gentleman. The man is wearing suit pants, a white shirt and tie, no jacket. Picnic attire of the time. Brendan's eye wanders farther back in the picture toward the blur of raspberries and sees— "That's me!"

"No that's your brother," Emma jumps in, "sitting with my Grandfather Dan, your dad's cousin."

"Oh wow, yeah, Brendan says, I recognized Eddie but," and here he points toward the raspberry bushes, "that's me."

Eddie and Emma both lean in to look. Eddie says, "You sure? You look like an overgrown raspberry." Eddie leans in a little more, "Or a thorny thicket. Say that fits."

"Trust me," Brendan says, "certain memories remain sharp, no pun intended."

Emma looks closely as well, trying to identify Brendan, finally she says, "Well okay," not very convincingly.

"Well, saints preserve us," Eddie says, "maybe in more ways than one. There I am sitting in Dan's lap, happy as a pig in a poke, and look at your grandfather. He looks really happy. Contented."

"He loved kids by all accounts," Emma says. "And have we not learned about shame?"

"What?" Brendan asks.

"Oh, right," Eddie says, "No shame, there's no shame in it. Let the past be where it is. In the past."

"Ah!" Brendan says.

Eddie moves on to other photos. "There is Uncle Joe, God bless him. Look how they dressed up to travel. And Frances, drinking something."

"Probably lemonade, they always had lemonade."

"Freshly squeezed," Eddie adds, "and with something a little extra for the adults."

"I don't remember that," Brendan says.

"You were younger," Eddie says, turning a page.

Brendan sighs, "Always am."

They are looking at more gatherings, some appear to be at different locations.

"This is your Aunt Kathryn's place not far, of course, from Joe and Frances."

"I loved her farmhouse," Brendan says. "One room rambling after another, great place to run around as a kid, inside and out."

And now it's Emma who sighs, "I never got to see those farms. Before my time."

They find another set of photos. "Oh these are like the earlier ones, when we talked about the cars," Brendan says. "I think you might be right Eddie, about the Oldsmobile. Just before the war."

A different season, not picnic weather, and a small group of people. A scene outdoors in early winter light, late afternoon at Joe and Frances' farm. In one of the pictures, Joe and Bill stand in front of the large open barn doors and it looks like they've just turned around to face the camera. Behind them, framed by the rest of the barn, an immense gap of utter darkness leads within to what one can only imagine. Bales of hay, Joe's herd of cows, tools of the trade. Nothing made visible.

The two brothers strike a clearly dramatic pose, Bill with his arms folded and Joe, a little taller, with one hand resting on Bill's shoulder. Joe's free hand is pointing upward toward the sky with a raised index finger.

"What the hell?" Brendan comments.

"They could be goofballs," Eddie responds.

"You know, when this was taken, we may have been at war." Brendan says.

Eddie turns toward Emma, "World War II."

"Yeah, I got that," Emma answers.

"Joe was into politics, history, up on the news. I can imagine him saying," and here Eddie shifts into one of his alternate voices, this time a deeply sonorous one, "We will defeat those Nazi bastards, Bill."

"What about the Japanese?" Brendan asks.

In the same bass voice, "Yeah those fellows too, my boy."

Emma hesitates, looks up from the photo album, "It's true what they say about the apple not falling far from the tree."

After a moment Brendan asks, "So was it Dan who took these pictures?"

"These ones, yes. I'm sure of it. He loved his camera. But there is also a story that goes along with this, as I was going to tell you. These were some of his last pictures."

"Yes?" Brendan asks.

"It wasn't long after this, early in the war, maybe that same winter. He was driving over to see your dad and mom, they lived in Clifton Springs then."

"You're right." Eddie confirms.

"He was a notoriously bad driver. Going way too fast, hit a patch of black ice. You know Stephens street in the village?"

"Yes!" both brothers answer.

"Hit a tree there, I was told. It was instant, they say."

"Oh my god," Brendan says.

"That kind of loss takes a toll," she adds.

"So that was practically in front of the house or close by. They lived on that street," Brendan says.

"Oh, ok, I didn't know that," Emma says.

"Whoa," Brendan says. "Mom and Dad could have been home then, at the time of the accident."

They remain silent for a moment.

"You wonder," Brendan says, "how something like that affects a family." He looks away for a moment, across the coffee table, past Emma's chair, to the farthest wall, as if hoping to penetrate whatever might lay beyond.

Eddie sits up, looks at his young cousin and says, "You know, I really appreciate Emma what you're showing us here. These pictures, there I was sitting on your grandfather's lap. Not a care in the world, so to speak."

Brendan initially bites his tongue, but decides to say it, "That's because you weren't the one stuck in the raspberry bush."

Maybe it's the dinner and desserts, memories of the past, photos of loved ones lost and recollected; there is a fullness in the air, a sense of time blessed and slowing, savoring its own moment. They all sit back.

"Oh my," Emma intones slowly, the prayer of arrival into their present.

"Yes," Brendan says, knowing for once that nothing more need be said.

"Amen," Eddie adds.

It actually takes a concerted act of will to rouse one's self, an awareness that life goes on, energy needs to be gathered and acted upon, simple things like searching for car keys, finding the proper words to anticipate farewell.

Standing up is a start.

"Thank you so much, Emma," Brendan says. "So whatever it was that happened with the Donohoes, it didn't stop them from gathering and... what?" he hesitates looking for the right expression.

"Being family?" Emma offers.

"Right on," Eddie says.

Brendan points to his brother while looking at Emma, "Old hippie talk."

Emma hesitates a moment and summarizes, "It's been quite a week."

"Indeed," Eddie says.

"I was realizing," Emma says, "that we actually got together three days in a row this week, Wednesday, Thursday and today."

Her cousins nod in agreement. For an extended moment they stand still, at attention.

Eddie at last says, in a quiet voice, "Maybe they just need us to remember them for who they were."

"Oh," Emma begins to say sympathetically but Eddie cuts her off.

"No," he says. "let me rephrase that. They don't need any such thing. They're fine. It's us who need to remember. Keep them with us, keep the connection alive."

Brendan looks at his brother with admiration, watches as Emma reaches out for Eddie's hand and holds it, ever so briefly, before letting go.

"They're fine," Brendan repeats his brother's words. "The grief is our grief, not theirs."

They all take what feels like one collective breath.

Emma's gaze goes down to the coffee table, the glance of a woman thinking about cleaning up.

"Well," Emma says, looking at her cousins, "I think we should follow up pretty soon with our Professor. Explain what we know about Uncle Bill's Prohibition partner."

"And maybe," Brendan says, "Martin will have more information about our soon-to-be famous relative? It does, after all, reflect well on our heritage, wouldn't you say?"

Emma and Eddie share a look.

Brendan says, "Okay, we need to give the history department time to catalog what they have. We only heard a small sampling of Paddy's papers.

Who knows, maybe they will find some other scintillating information."

"Ooooh," Emma says playfully, enjoying the moment, the promise of revelations to come.

"Meanwhile," Eddie says, "we could get together again in a week or so and make another call to Toronto?"

"Sounds good to me," Brendan says.

Emma assumes they will gather at her home, use the speaker phone. She takes a moment, looks at her cousins, "I've got a lot going on this week but maybe by the weekend, after the dust settles."

CHAPTER 53

That Ocean is Too Big
Saturday, December 5, 1941

I<small>T'S A CHILLY, BRIGHT SUNNY</small> day. At this time in mid-afternoon shadows become deeply angled, slanting in sharp contrast. Brilliant white light etches against the deepest dark, reminding everyone, as if a reminder were needed, that even at this early hour, the night will soon be falling.

Snow had been forecast but fortunately had not yet appeared, and Bill and Gwen will be needing to get back to Clifton Springs. The roads should be good before dark so it might only be an hour's drive after all. They are standing near the front door of the farm, close to the edge of the driveway that leads back to a near-by barn.

Frances' dinner was excellent and she was pleased that the meal had gone so well, though the roast was cooked a bit more than she had wanted. Dan could be fussy, but praise the Lord he wasn't on this occasion. Gwen's presence probably had something to do with that, and she appreciated having female companionship. Billy had done very well with picking this young woman. If only her Joe could be so lucky.

The kitchen and dining room were very warm, and someone suggested that they go outside for a bit of fresh air. The first step onto the small porch was enough to take one's breath away.

The drop in temperature is bracing, and while the men amble off the porch and onto the yard, Frances raises her chin and looks up into the cloudless sky, certain that she can smell the snow that is coming.

"Oh my!" Frances says.

Joe turns around, bumps Dan with his elbow and says, "Yessir that will wake you up, eh? Almost as good as Canadian air," his voice exuberant and hearty in equal proportions.

Gwen and Frances remain on the porch while the men meander slowly in the direction of the barn. Gwen watches her husband depart, raises her shoulders and begins to rub her hands together for warmth. Frances notices and puts her warm and well worked hands around Gwen's. Gwen turns and smiles, says "Okay I guess that's enough fresh air for now."

"We'll let them be," Frances says, gesturing with her head toward her brothers and cousin who are halfway to the barn.

"Please," Gwen says, stepping back and letting her sister-in-law, many years her senior, return first to the warmth inside.

As they are approaching the large and wide-open barn door, Dan says to Bill, "Your vehicle out there a company car Bill? I parked right behind you when I pulled in."

"No sir, cash on the barrel head, from hard earned wages."

"'38 Plymouth I think?"

"Wha-ho-ho" Joe chortles brightly, having insider knowledge.

"'41 Olds," Bill answers.

"This year's car!" Dan says. "I think I'm in the wrong business. Boy I'd like to take her out for a spin sometime, that must be some swell ride."

Joe hesitates, looks over at Dan and says, "I think Bill would like to keep his car for another few months."

The threesome walk slowly up to the barn doors, the barn's interior as dark as if it were already night.

"You know Joe," Dan kids his cousin, "you might want to invest in a little illumination, electric lights see, they're all the rage now. The girls inside would love it."

In a quiet voice Bill adds, "He's talking about the cows, Joe."

Joe stops just a few feet from the open doors and his relatives match his step, full stop. "You know my boy," he says addressing his younger brother, "it's fortunate that you were able to purchase that Olds when you did. Times are changing, those Germans are doing a real number on the Brits and I wouldn't be surprised to see us join the fight soon."

"Or get dragged into it, like it or not," Dan says.

"Oh, I don't know," Bill says. "At least the Japanese are staying put. That ocean is too big," he hesitates, adding as an afterthought, "maybe on both sides of the country." Bill folds his arms together, wishing that he had brought out his warm overcoat.

"Well, at any rate," Joe says, as he surveys the distance they just traveled from the house, "I don't think Uncle Sam and Detroit will be sending Oldmobiles like yours to fight the Germans any time soon."

"Maybe Plymouths," Dan says, adding "Just a minute, let me get my camera out of my coat here. I think I've got enough film left. There is something about that gaping dark barn door."

Joe lets Dan fiddle with his camera and get ready to take the snap. He says, "Dan, the barn doors aren't dark."

"Okay," Dan answers, nearly ready, "I know, it's what's inside."

"And your photo will see that?"

Something captures Joe's attention, he turns and looks up at the sky. After a moment, he puts one hand on Bill's shoulder and raises his free arm, pointing straight up with his finger. "Well lookee here," he says, as Bill follow his gaze. "I don't think it's going to snow after all. You boys should have no trouble getting home tonight."

All He Has To Do
Tuesday, September 26, 1933

BILL ROUNDS THE CORNER heading out of town, he sees the hardware store off on his left. The owner is setting out some of his wares, a shovel so new that it shines, a handsome looking rake with a tag on the handle, a bushel basket full of items for sale.

The visit with Rafferty had gone well, he'd sold more than he thought he might. The next stop will be over at Rudi's but he will make as many calls today as he can. He reminds himself out loud to no listening passenger, "Things will probably turn out for the best." And wasn't it his father who would say '90% of the things you worry about never come true.' He would always make the slightest pause, before adding in his native accent, 'but the other 10% can kill you.'

This was from a man, after all, who had escaped the Famine, who arrived in Canada in what they called a 'coffin ship,' so many of them perished enroute, typhoid, stories of bodies wrapped in canvas, dropped into the forgiving waves. Father and his family survived it all so that we could have our lives in the new land.

Bill shifts his weight on the leather upholstered seat. In the event, he thinks, that plans with Gwen and myself work out and we have children, I will need to tell them what their ancestors went through. How they need to chin up, by god, keep the faith, no matter what might befall one in life. Others have done it before you. And now it will be your turn.

The golden light of September fills the whole scene before him. In a moment he will reach the edge of town, and he knows what he will see. Small farm after small farm, still succeeding despite the dire warnings from Washington. Barns and fields, cows mildly interested in his passing by, chickens in front of the farmhouse, not interested. The farmer's children strewn about, older ones helping, younger ones at play.

He is a graduate of this pastoral life. He fully appreciates it, and truth be told feels a tug of mourning for leaving it, but saying farewell was all in the cards. Nothing of value comes without regret, even sorrow. It's his chance now to create a new life, and he honors his forebears by the very act of moving forward, even on this road now at the edge of town, the road that becomes suddenly an uneven ribbon of macadam. Push on. Things will get better.

He puts both hands on the large steering wheel, pushes himself back into the cushioned driver's seat. He has a ways to go. His brother will question how this can be called work, riding in an automobile like this, having the time of his life.

Until he reaches his destination, this is all he has to do. Drive.

HISTORICAL SOURCES

1. Bothwell, Robert, The Penguin History of Canada. Toronto: Penguin Group, 2006

2. Devoy, John, Michael Davitt: From the "Gaelic American". Dublin: University College Dublin Press, 2008

3. Flatley, P.J., Ireland and The Land League: Key to the Irish Question. Boston: D. O'Loughlin and Company, 1881

4. (No Author) James Stephens, Chief Organizer of the Irish Republic. New York: Carleton, 1866

5. Hanson, David J. Ph.D., Repeal of Prohibition: End of the Dream that was National Prohibition. http://www.alcoholproblemsandsolutions. org/repeal-of-prohibition/

6. "Irish Slaves of the Soil". New York Times: June 13, 1886

7. "Mass Meeting of the Fenians". New York Times: June 25, 1866

8. Nazi Germany. https://en.wikipedia.org/wiki/Nazi_Germany

9. White Star Line. https://en.wikipedia.org/wiki/White_Star_Line

10. What Happened in 1933 Including Pop Culture. HTTP://www. thepeoplehistory.com/1933.html

11. Vronsky, Peter. Ridgeway: The American Fenian Invasion and the 1866 Battle That Made Canada. Toronto: Penguin Group, 2011

AUTHOR'S NOTE

In Ireland, long simmering anger against the British government came to a head in 1848. In this year a group of revolutionaries known as Young Ireland launched an uprising against the government. It was a failure.

Two of the members of Young Ireland were James Stephens and John O'Mahony. In 1853, after exile in Paris, O'Mahony went to America, and in 1856 Stephens went back to Ireland. In 1858 Stephens formed a secret society that became known as the Irish Republican Brotherhood. Its aim was Independence for Ireland.

The movement referred to as the Fenians encompasses a series of Irish Republican organizations, spanning Ireland and America dedicated to the pursuit of Irish independence from Britain, by force if necessary. The Fenians' stated aim was an Irish democratic Republic. The title Fenian was taken from an Irish legend about an invincible army called the Fianna that constantly defended the beautiful, evergreen isle of Eireann, against foreign invaders.

In November 1863, the Fenian Brotherhood published the Irish People newspaper in Dublin. It had a dual purpose: it was an organ for propaganda and a collector of revenue for the cause. The Kilkenny rebel, James Stephens was the author and editor-in-chief of that publication.

The Irish People and its authors enjoyed almost two years without any interference from any source. Then suddenly on September 15, 1865 at 9 o'clock in the evening a large force of police burst into the publishing house and seized all books, papers, letters, and manuscripts. The lot was bagged and carted to Dublin Castle. Meanwhile, the police swooped in on all parts of Dublin to arrest the Fenian Leaders.

In 1865, when many Fenians were arrested, James Stephens, founder of the Irish Republican Brotherhood (IRB), appointed John Devoy to be Chief Organizer of Fenians in the British Army in Ireland. His duty was to enlist Irish soldiers in the British Army into the IRB. In November 1865 John Devoy orchestrated Stephens' escape from Richmond Prison in Dublin.

In February 1866 an IRB Council of War called for an immediate uprising, but Stephens refused, to Devoy's annoyance, as Devoy calculated the Fenian force in the British Army to number 80,000. Devoy was arrested in February 1866 and interned in Mountjoy Gaol, then tried for treason and sentenced to fifteen years penal servitude.

In January 1871, he was released and exiled to the United States. He received an address of welcome from the House of Representatives. Devoy became a journalist for the New York Herald and was active in Clan na Gael. Under Devoy's leadership, Clan na Gael became the central Irish republican organization in the United States. In 1877, he aligned the organization with the Irish Republican Brotherhood in Ireland.

Devoy dedicated over 60 years of his life to the cause of Irish independence and was one of the few people to have played a role in the Fenian Rising of 1867, the Easter Rising of 1916 and the Irish War of Independence of 1919–1921. He owned and edited the The Gaelic American, a New York weekly newspaper, from 1903 to 1928. His description of a close encounter with British authorities, found in chapter 39, comes from that newspaper. Devoy's writing in the Gaelic American about another Irish patriot, Michael Davitt, was reprinted in Classics of Irish History Series by University College Dublin, see the Historical Sources page.

The story of James Stephens's escape as described in Chapter 41 comes directly from a book published in that same year 1866, by Carleton publishers, as noted in the Historical Sources. The book is available online via The Internet Archive: https://archive.org/stream/jamesstephenschi00newy/jamesstephenschi00newy_djvu.txt

In a similar vein, it is fascinating to delve into the archives of the New

York Times and read original reporting from the 19th century online. It feels as if you have entered a time machine, being in the presence of the past. Such was my experience with "Mass Meeting of the Fenians", 1866, and "Irish Slaves of the Soil" 1886.

Finally, the Auburn was an amazing car. In the 1930's my father drove a model called the Straight Eight.

Made in the USA
Monee, IL
26 April 2023

32456978R00203